OUTSTANDING PRAISE FOR J. H. TRUMBLE
AND *DON'T LET ME GO*

"J. H. Trumble's *Don't Let Me Go* is a sexy, vibrant, and heartfelt debut that captures the drama, heartache, joy, and all-around craziness of being young and in love."
—Martin Wilson, award-winning author of
What They Always Tell Us

"*Don't Let Me Go* is a charming story about a boy who, although courageous, is no better than he needs to be—until he needs to be better. Trumble's love for the characters is evident on every page, and it's contagious."
—Robin Reardon, author of *A Secret Edge*

"Trumble's debut is a deeply moving and in-depth look at the perils and anxieties of being gay in high school. . . . Layered with the gritty everyday details of teen existence, the book provides a convincingly clear window into the many perils and sometimes scant pleasures of life in high school while never feeling overly grim; it will be appreciated by adults and teens alike."
—*Publishers Weekly,* starred

"This is a book I could go on and on about. I loved it that much. It's a stellar debut."
—GuysLitWire

"Highly engaging . . . A relevant message coupled with a charming teen romance makes this debut novel a true champion."
—*Edge*

"This is an excellent coming-out/first love novel, giving a realistic look at the feelings as well as concerns that come along with each . . . Can't give it less than five stars out of five."
—Bob Lind, *Echo Magazine*

"This high-school-set story richly and smartly captures the thrilling highs and the devastating lows of a first love between two young men who deal with far more than the typical dramas in an average teenager's life."

—*Instinct Magazine*

"Poignant." —*Next Magazine*

"A great book for teens and adults alike." —*Washington Blade*

"Trumble excels at putting the reader inside the mind of a gay young man living in a largely unaccepting community. The emotion brought to this work is its strength and will leave readers pondering the reality of life as a queer teen . . . A wonderful first book."

—*VOYA*

Where You Are

Books by J. H. Trumble

Don't Let Me Go

Where You Are

Published by Kensington Publishing Corporation

Where You Are

J. H. Trumble

KENSINGTON BOOKS
www.kensingtonbooks.com

KENSINGTON BOOKS are published by

Kensington Publishing Corp.
119 West 40th Street
New York, NY 10018

All Kensington titles, imprints, and distributed lines are available at special quantity discounts for bulk purchases for sales promotion, premiums, fund-raising, educational or institutional use.

Special book excerpts or customized printings can also be created to fit specific needs. For details, write or phone the office of the Kensington Special Sales Manager: Kensington Publishing Corp., 119 West 40th Street, New York, NY 10018. Attn. Special Sales Department. Phone: 1-800-221-2647.

Kensington and the K logo Reg. U.S. Pat. & TM Off.

ISBN-13: 978-0-7582-7716-9
ISBN-10: 0-7582-7716-4

First Kensington Trade Paperback Printing: January 2013
10 9 8 7 6 5 4 3 2 1

Printed in the United States of America

*For Steve, who adored his own children,
but didn't get to see them grow up*

ACKNOWLEDGMENTS
HUDSON AREA LIBRARY

From those early days when I was finding my way through this story to the final days of production, there were many who contributed to bringing this story to print. A heartfelt thank you to all of them:

My friend Brent Taylor (who squealed over my idea); my agent, Stephen Fraser; and my editor, Peter Senftleben—their enthusiasm for these characters and their brilliant suggestions made this story so much better than it might have been otherwise. And all those at Kensington Publishing who lent their talents to this work.

My sister-in-law, Dr. Teresa Guerrero, who's always generous with her medical expertise and rarely raises an eyebrow at my offbeat questions.

Don Stirman, who answered my legal questions, provided me with some interesting plot details, and shared his own story of falling in love with one of his students while never crossing that line. (He and Marie have been happily married for . . . well, a long time.)

My colleagues: Nancy Smith for giving her time and talent to excising my excess verbiage; Holly Walsh and Shelley Racca, whose classroom-management skills and dedication to their students inspired many elements in this story; Aimee Felio and Antoinette Sherman for their painstaking proofreading; and Sue Cox, my steadfast friend and head cheerleader.

The librarians of LM_NET who responded to my query and suggested *Robert the Rose Horse,* and thus led me to one of my favorite scenes.

And finally, my kids, Danny and Anna, whose pride in my accomplishments means more to me than anyone else's. You are my world.

They say, write what you know. And while, as writers do, I have drawn liberally from my own experiences to bring these characters to life, this novel is in no way a memoir.

Chapter 1

Andrew

You still here?
I'm giving a makeup test.
Crap! Stop by when you're done.

I close Jen's e-mail and check the time in the corner of my computer screen—ten minutes—then glance up at Robert Westfall again. He's resting his cheek on his fist now and absently doodling in the margins of his test. My heart breaks for him, and I find myself wondering what's showing at the cinema in his head. Memories of hanging out with his dad—maybe playing catch in the backyard, learning to swim at a neighborhood pool, pushing a lawnmower for the first time. Or maybe it's the moment he got the news yesterday, an endless loop of shock, terror, sadness. Or is it some future flick about life without a father?

I pick up my red pen again and straighten the stack of tests in front of me, but I don't grade any of them. I just watch him.

I knew something was going on. It was just a feeling, this sense that he was off balance and couldn't quite get his feet under him. And now as I watch him struggle with a calculus test that he'd methodically tear up any other day, I'm struck with the desire to reach out to him; I'm just not sure how.

It's funny really. I'm not usually this intuitive. While I'd like to believe that I'm in sync with my students, that I know when they're having a bad day or when their hormones are raging and they've chosen to indulge their impulses instead of doing their homework or studying, I'm not.

My freshman Algebra kids are so squirrely that all my energy goes into maintaining order and keeping those classes moving forward. My senior AP Calculus students, on the other hand, have a laser focus on that end-of-course exam. I challenge them academically; they challenge me. If anybody's having a bad day in that class, I guess they keep it to themselves.

But with Robert, I knew. He still turned in his homework. He paid attention. He even answered questions when I asked them. But he's been quieter. More introspective, I think. Just not himself.

He rubs at his eye with the heel of his hand and attempts to focus on the problems again, but he looks perplexed, as if I've written the test in hieroglyphics and he just can't quite translate the problems.

Yesterday, his absence, that empty desk in the front row, pricked at my conscience. I thought about calling to make sure he was okay. I even retrieved his phone number. But I didn't call. Kids are absent—they get sick, they oversleep, they skip. The motivation to make that phone call seemed pretty thin. But Robert's not one of those kids. His absence was noteworthy and it bothered me more than it probably should have.

I turn back to my computer and scroll through the day's e-mail—notices of meetings scheduled and meetings canceled, an it's-still-not-too-late-to-sign-up invitation to Saturday night's school Christmas party (No, thank you.), a few eleventh-hour pleas from parents for extra-credit work, and a reminder that grades are due at three o'clock Friday afternoon. The *high priority* makes Ms. Lincoln's e-mail easy to spot.

To: **Fabiola Cortez, Bob Benson, Annet Nguyen, Richard Gorman, Susan Weatherford, Andrew McNelis, Bette Flowers**
From: **Lynn Lincoln**
Subject: **Robert Westfall**

Teachers—
As you may already know, Robert Westfall's father has been battling brain cancer for the past ten years. Yesterday the family received some devastating news. Mr. Westfall's illness is terminal. According to Mrs. Westfall, the doctors estimate that Robert's father may have only three to four weeks. Understandably, this is a difficult time for the family. It is likely that Robert's attendance may become intermittent during the next few months. Please be flexible in your expectations and offer him whatever accommodations are necessary to get him through this time. If you see that he is struggling emotionally, or if you have any concerns at all, please contact me. Thank you as always for all you do for our students.

Lynn Lincoln
Twelfth Grade Counselor

Poor kid. I check the time again. Fifteen minutes now. I push back my chair and get up. It's my day to pick up Kiki, and I have a feeling that I could sit here with Robert for another fifteen hours, and he'd still be doodling in the margins.

In fact, he's so caught up in his head that he doesn't notice me approach or say his name. When I place my hand on his shoulder, he jumps.

"Sorry. I didn't mean to startle you."

His eyes fall on the test in front of him and he seems surprised that he's only addressed a couple of the questions. "Oh, shit," he mutters. Then immediately follows that with an apology for his language.

"It's okay." I pull a desk up close to his and sit. "A rough day yesterday?"

"Yeah. Pretty rough," he says quietly.

"Anything I can do?"

He looks up at me, and his eyes seem to search mine like he's measuring the sincerity of my question. Suddenly I have a feeling the one thing this kid needs is the one thing I can't give him—a hug or maybe a friend he can really talk to.

"No," he says, palming the back of his neck. "But thanks."

"You look tired." *Depressed* is what I'm really thinking. When he doesn't respond, I decide to make one of those accommodations Ms. Lincoln spoke of. "You know, you don't have to take this test," I say, reaching for it. "I'm not worried about your mastery of this unit. You've mastered it. I can just double your last—"

"No. I can take the test," he says, flattening his hand on the paper to hold it in place. I notice he's not wearing a class ring.

"Okay. But, you know, I have a daughter. She's going to be pretty upset if I don't pick her up from her day care before dark."

He drops his head and then, suddenly agitated, runs his hand over his short blond hair a few times, then sighs heavily. "I'm sorry, Mr. Mac." He grips his pencil and punches down the lead a few clicks. "I'll have it done in a few minutes."

A few minutes? I don't think so. Not even for Robert. "It's okay." I give him what I hope is a reassuring smile. "I have some time. How about I walk you through the test? Maybe that will help you focus."

I don't wait for him to answer. I collect a pencil and a few sheets of printer paper from my desk and sit back down. On the blank paper, I quickly review the first section, then wait while he works through the set of problems. I guess something about me sitting there with him chases away the distractions—he's quick and he's precise, making his marks with his distinct handwriting, which is tiny but highly legible.

When he's finished, he twists his head up to me.

"Nicely done," I say, smiling. It feels good when he smiles back.

I place a big check mark over the section, and we move on to the next. While Robert is working, I find myself studying his face—the straight line of his nose, the freckle at the base of his neatly trimmed sideburn, the stray blond hairs on his jaw that he missed shaving this morning—and I can't help wishing that I'd known him when I was in high school.

Aside from the fact that he's a stellar student and a nice-looking kid, here's what I know about Robert:

1. He's a member of the band guard. The only male member in fact. I might not have known this—I don't attend football games. No time with school and grad classes in the fall, and Kiki—but it seems to be an endless source of amusement for Jennifer.

2. He has a boyfriend. Nicholas Taylor—Nic—cheerleader, ditzy blond, ghetto queen, Whore-Hay. All the kids call him that. Jorge, Whore-Hay. It's the year-round, fluorescent-lamp-enhanced tan, I think. I honestly don't get what Robert sees in Nic. The kid's a pretentious, over-the-top, party boy. Not his type at all.

3. Robert is one hell of a brave kid. (See numbers 1 and 2.) I'd never have had the courage to be 100 percent O-U-T in high school. And he's not just Out; he's got that quiet confidence that draws other kids to him. I don't know if he knows it, but he does a lot to bring skeptics into the fold on our campus. You just can't not like him or respect him.

And right now, I can't not look at him.

When he finishes the set, he looks up at me, and I drop my eyes to the test and make a quick assessment of his answers.

Another big check mark and we move on. The next set is a little more challenging. I force myself to focus on this work. A couple of times he missteps, but a quick *uh-uh* from me makes him stop, re-think, erase, then move forward on the right track.

The last section is the trickiest, and I get a kick out of watching him wrestle with the problems. He looks at me a couple of times, but I just raise my brows and shrug. He takes that as a challenge. I don't help him on this section, so when he missteps, he finds himself in a tangle and has to back up. I'm proud of him when he finishes the last problem and slides the test across his desk to mine.

"I knew you could do it."

"You did, huh?"

I check that section, then close the test and scrawl a big *100* across the top before I look back at him. "Yeah, I did."

We enjoy a moment of what I think is mutual admiration, and then I clap him on the shoulder and take the test with me back to my desk.

Robert stands, stretches, then grabs his letter jacket off the back of the desk chair as I enter his grade in the computer. I'd like to close out my grade book, but I have some Algebra kids who are under water and need a lifeline, which I will attempt to provide over the next couple of days before grades are due.

As he leans down to zip up his backpack, I take a quick inventory of the letters on his jacket—academics, band, guard, choir. They should give letters for courage too.

He grabs his backpack by the strap and shoulders it, but seems reluctant to leave.

"I'm really sorry about your dad. How are you holding up?" I ask, coming around the desk. I lean against it and slide my hands in my pockets.

He chews on his bottom lip a moment, then says, "I don't even know how to answer that, Mr. Mac."

How do I respond to that? I hate this. They don't train us for this kind of stuff. There are things I want to convey to him: *I'm here for you if you need to talk. I know what it's like to lose someone.* But all that sticks in my throat, because the truth is, I'm a teacher—not a friend, not a counselor. And I don't know what it's like to lose someone; my own parents are safe and sound in Oklahoma. I've not lost a single person in my life, not permanently at least. Besides, does he even want my sympathy? Kids can be so hard to read.

Jennifer Went makes my indecision moot when she chooses that moment to stick her head in the door.

"Oh. You're done," she says.

"Yeah," I say as she steps into the room. Robert mumbles a thank you, hitches up his backpack, and slips past her and out the door.

"They're making them big these days, aren't they?" she says, sticking her head back out the door to watch him go. "Mmm-mmm. He's a hottie."

"You're not going all Mary Kay Letourneau on me, are you?"

"I don't know. I might be willing to spend a few years in prison for a few minutes in heaven with that one—"

"Arrgghh. Kidding, right?"

"—even if he is a little light on his feet," she finishes, then laughs.

I ignore the slur.

"So, how about I buy you a Frappuccino?" she asks brightly.

I already know that *buy you a Frappuccino* is just code for *read my next chapter.* Jennifer fancies herself a romance author. Her college roommate put herself through school writing erotica. Jen sees no reason she can't get herself out of school writing romance.

I suspect she fancies me as well. I mean, what could be more attractive than a twenty-four-year-old, divorced high school teacher with a two-year-old, a student-loan debt that rivals the GNP of any number of small nations, an efficiency apartment, and a six-year-old Civic with a crack in the windshield?

"I've got Kiki," I say.

"Aaaah. Bring her too."

"So? What do you think?" Jennifer asks. "Juicy, huh?"

Kiki is sitting on her knees and eating a yogurt parfait. I wrinkle my nose at her and she wrinkles hers back. I stack the pages neatly together and hand them across the table to Jen.

"I think you'd better change the names and maybe a few other details, or someone's going to sue your ass one day."

She laughs. "Ah, they're just placeholders. Once I get the story down, I'll run a global search and change all the names."

"So, is that stuff true? I mean, aren't both Philip and Liz married . . . with children?"

"That's really sweet, Drew. You actually believe in that stuff, huh?" She flicks a bit of ice at me with her straw. "You know, if you'd ever come out of your classroom, you might learn all kinds of things. Like, for instance, that those two leave for lunch together every day. *Every* day. Different doors, different cars, but they follow each other out of the parking lot. Like that isn't obvious.

"And then last week, I went into Philip's office to ask him to show me how to use Audacity. He was on the phone. So he says, 'Gotta go. I'll see you later. Love you.' All that crap. So then he opens Audacity on his screen, and he's showing me stuff, and a few seconds later this e-mail pops up in the corner from Liz. I'd have to be blind not to see it. And stupid not to add up two and two.

"Trust me; they're doing it. And everybody knows it."

I wonder if Philip Moore has any idea whatsoever that his colleagues are talking about him behind his back, that his little subterfuge is not nearly as covert as he thinks it is. He's one of two technology liaisons on our campus, the go-to guy for everything software related, from converting YouTube video files to getting our contacts groups to show up in Outlook. Everybody knows him. It's his job to respond to technology crises or last-minute queries about how to incorporate some little gizmo into a lesson.

But even I've heard rumors that Liz Masters seems to have more crises and queries than most. Not that I care. What they do is their business.

"So is this how you get your jollies?" I ask. "Speculating about what those two are doing in the backseat during their thirty-minute, duty-free lunch every day?"

"It's twenty-seven minutes now, and hey, a girl's gotta get it somewhere," she says coyly.

I laugh lightly and pretend I don't notice the subtle suggestion.

She throws a quick glance at Kiki. "So," she says, "are you going to the Christmas party Saturday?"

"Nope."

"Come on. Why not?"

"Why would I want to spend my Saturday night with a bunch of people I hardly know? Besides, last year it was mostly couples. Awkward, you know. And borrrring."

"You could go with me."

Don't think so. "I have Kiki anyway this weekend. I'm taking her to see Santa on Saturday, and then we're going to eat graham crackers and watch *The Lion King* again, right, baby girl?"

Kiki holds out her spoon, and I take a bite and wink at her.

"And then when she falls asleep, I'm going to write my plans for the next nine weeks."

"Wow, your social life kind of takes my breath away."

I wish it took mine away.

Chapter 2

Robert

I turn my cell phone back on as I cross the parking lot. It vibrates immediately. Five new texts. All from Nic. I thumb through them as I walk.

I'm standing by your car. Hurry up.

Answer your phone.

OMG. Where are you? I don't have all day!!!

WAITING!

I'm done. Leeeeaving.

I note the time stamps and estimate he waited a whole ten minutes. I reply, although I don't know why I bother:

Had to make up test. Have group tonight.

He responds immediately. *You could have told me that sooner.*

I might have if I could have gotten past his posse of cheerleaders. Besides, we had no plans to meet after school. We never have any plans to meet after school. We rarely have any plans to meet anywhere. Sometimes I think Nic is my boyfriend in name only, when it's convenient, when he needs some arm candy. Not that I consider myself arm candy, but I think he does the way he clings to me and parades me around on the rare occasion when we do go somewhere together.

Sorry. Text you later.

He doesn't respond. I have about an hour before I have to be at Ms. Momin's for my music therapy group—we're playing "Jingle Bells" today—but I don't have the emotional energy to deal with Nic right now anyway. And I damn sure don't want to go home.

So I climb in the car, put my phone on silent, then tilt my seat back and close my eyes.

I allow myself to drift back to the classroom, to those gray eyes with the dark rings around the corneas, and that snug sweater over a striped, collared shirt, and the chest hair at the base of his throat that always shows no matter what he's wearing.

I wonder if Mr. McNelis could smell it on me—the want to. Freshman year, in health (the sex ed unit, not the oh-my-god-that-feels-good unit as Coach Gideon liked to remind us, ha, ha), we learned that humans, like animals, give off a scent when they want to mate. I'm not saying I want to mate with Mr. McNelis, but I'm not saying I don't want to either.

I'm pretty sure I don't want to mate with Nic. Not that I haven't tried once or twice. Nine months of dating and I haven't touched him. In fact, the last time I tried, he followed his *No* with a *That's nasty.* I'd be lying if I said that hadn't hurt my feelings. I haven't tried again. I do sometimes wonder why I tried at all. Yes, he's cute. And, yes, he can be very sweet when he wants to be. But I don't know him any better today than I did nine months ago, and he doesn't know me. And I don't think either of us really cares one way or the other.

On the other hand, I wouldn't mind touching Drew McNelis. In fact, I'm indulging myself and imagining what that would be like when a sharp rap on the top of my car startles me. I turn the key and roll down the window. Luke Chesser sticks his head in.

"Hey, bro, no sleeping in the parking lot. People are going to start thinking you like it here."

"Maybe I do."

"Yeah, well . . ." He shivers. "It's cold out here. Unlock the door."

I do and he climbs in the passenger seat, slamming the door behind him. I roll the window back up.

"I'm really sorry about your dad, man. Anything I can do?"

"You want to make out?"

He grins, then laughs.

He knows I'm kidding. Luke and I have a history, but mostly a platonic one.

"You want the wrath of Curtis to fall on your head?" he jokes. "He's the jealous type, you know."

"I do know."

I study my good friend. Luke is the head drum major and my former pseudo-boyfriend. Long story. Curtis is a junior at Sam Houston State University. They're crazy about each other, and I'm crazy with envy. He settles back in the seat, grabs the cuffs of his hoodie, and folds his arms tightly across his chest to warm up, then puts his feet up on the dash and rolls his head to me.

"So what's going on with you and Nic?" he asks.

"Have I ever thanked you for fixing me up with Whore-Hay?"

"No, I don't believe you have."

"Then I won't."

He laughs. "That good, huh? Well, I never told you this, but remember when I set you two up? It wasn't *exactly* the way I told you."

"Exactly what way *was* it?"

"I told him you liked him and he should ask you out. He said—wait." He sits up and takes on a prissy air, then says, " 'I don't ask boys out; boys ask me out.' "

His Nic impression is so spot-on, I can't help but laugh.

"Listen," he says, "you should come up to Sam with me one weekend. Curtis has friends. Who knows, you might like one of them."

"What's it like dating an older guy?" I can't resist asking.

This slow grin inches its way across his face, and he flicks his eyebrows at me.

"That's just cruel," I say.

He props his feet back on the dash and breathes a dreamy sigh. "So, um, what's it like with Nic?"

"I wouldn't know."

"Really? Ha, ha. You know, one day you're going to consider that a blessing."

I already do. Reluctantly, I check the time on my phone. "I got to get going. I have my music therapy group in fifteen minutes."

"You still don't have all your service hours?" Luke asks, surprised.

"I just need a couple more."

He takes a deep breath and lets it out loudly. I do the same and he smiles. "You call me if you want to talk. Okay? Don't worry about Curtis. I've got him wrapped around my little finger." He winks and gets out.

"You sure you're up to this?" Ms. Momin asks as she closes the front door behind me. She's the facilitator of the group, an elementary school music teacher who does music therapy with special-needs kids on the side.

"Yeah. Of course."

I wasn't so sure about working with these kids when Ms. Lincoln first suggested it. I'd completed most of my sixty hours of community service—a graduation requirement—last summer working at the animal shelter, but Ms. Lincoln thought some diversity would look better on my college applications and hooked me up with Ms. Momin's group. I'm glad she did. It's the highlight of my week now.

From the foyer I see Patrick wrestling an ornery chair toward the living room. It tips. He steps back and utters a frustrated "Bah" as the chair falls over on the tile floor.

"Patrick," I call out.

When he sees me, a big goofy grin takes over his face. He lumbers over and gives me an awkward hug.

"Hey, man. Thanks for starting to set up the chairs. You want some help?"

He bears down and concentrates hard before exploding with a big "Bah."

"All right. Let's do it."

I right the chair and help him maneuver it into the other room, careful not to get ahead of him and pull the chair from his hands. When we position it, he steps back and throws his bent arms out to the side. "Bah."

"Good job, man."

"Ya. Ya."

Patrick makes me smile. He's fourteen and tall and lanky, with a sprinkling of acne on his forehead. But despite his physical challenges, which play out in exaggerated smiles and frowns and spastic movements, I think he is quite handsome. One in a million in fact, or perhaps one in seven hundred thousand to be more exact— the odds of being struck by lightning in any given year. He was only nine. Sucks to stand out sometimes.

By the time Sophie and Jo-Jo arrive, the chairs are set. Ms. Momin helps me settle everyone, then straps Jo-Jo into his chair so he won't slide to the floor, and takes up her usual position behind them all.

I look at their faces, and I'm really glad I came.

"Who's excited about Christmas?" I ask.

Patrick jumps up from his chair and spazzes a moment, then drops back in his seat. Sophie is staring off at something or nothing over my shoulder. Jo-Jo, the smallest in the group, is laughing. It's an uncontrollable kind of laugh, but I find it infectious. Jo-Jo is the least physically capable of the three. In addition to some physical challenges I don't fully understand, Ms. Momin says that, like Sophie, he has some form of autism. He laughs a lot, at nothing, and sometimes he whimpers, and sometimes he breaks down and cries. But he's laughing right now, and that's good.

"Me too, Jo-Jo. Soooo, I have a surprise for you guys. We're going to learn a new song today. 'Jingle Bells.' "

There're a couple of beats of silence, and then Jo-Jo's face contorts and he starts this snuffling crying.

"It's okay, Jo-Jo. Let's just try it. I think you'll like it."

Patrick looks like someone just farted. Sophie's expression remains blank. Ms. Momin grins at me, then tries to comfort Jo-Jo.

"I'll play it first."

I'm hoping once they recognize the Christmas song their attitudes will improve. So far, we've only played "Mary Had a Little Lamb." "Jingle Bells" requires only two additional notes. I mean, after three months I think we're ready for a new song. And frankly, they aren't really playing the notes anyway, so learning a new song is no big deal.

Despite their obvious displeasure, I place the recorder in my mouth and play "Jingle Bells"—chorus only.

With each note, Jo-Jo grows more distressed and is soon wailing.

And Patrick looks downright angry. He's agitated and throwing his arms around and drops his recorder. Then suddenly he leaps up and tries to cover my mouth with his hand. His fine motor skills are rather deficient and he misses my mouth altogether, but succeeds in smacking me in the eye and knocking my contact off center.

"Bah."

"Patrick!" Ms. Momin darts out from behind Jo-Jo and grabs his flailing arms and settles him back in his chair.

"Are you okay, Robert?"

I think I may have a corneal abrasion, but otherwise, I'm okay. I excuse myself and go to the bathroom to reset my contact. When I return, Patrick is sulking. I take my seat.

Ms. Momin smiles down at me and shrugs. "They don't much like change," she says.

Got that. I survey my charges. "All right, guys. I have a great idea. How about we play 'Mary Had a Little Lamb'?"

Patrick beams. It takes him a couple of tries, but he finally manages to get his mouthpiece in his mouth and grins with self-satisfaction.

Ms. Momin helps Sophie. Jo-Jo is gripping his recorder and sniffling and rocking back and forth. I lift his arms so the mouthpiece fits in his mouth. It's like moving a toy robot. His arms will stay exactly where I put them until one of us moves them again.

"On three. Ready?" I smile to myself. Ready enough. "One. Two. Three."

The racket that comes from the recorders sounds nothing like "Mary Had a Little Lamb." It doesn't matter. I ratchet up my own volume so they hear the tune and believe in their own performance.

We play the song maybe a dozen times, and I congratulate them after each one. And after each one, Patrick stands and spazzes because he's happy, the kind of happy that is so pure and simple it breaks your heart, the kind of happy I don't think I've ever known, or at least can remember. Sophie still stares off into the distance, but she played. I could hear her play, and that's something of a triumph in itself. Jo-Jo is laughing now. It's truly one of the sweetest sounds I've ever heard, and I can't help but smile back at him.

Sometimes it's hard to say good-bye when the session ends. Today, it's especially so.

I step in it when I get home, although I'm not exactly sure what *it* is. At first it looks like apple juice pooled in the grout grooves between the kitchen floor tiles, but it could just as easily be pee. I don't really want to know. I pull some paper towels from the roll as I scan the rest of the kitchen—a soggy waffle with one bite out of it crowning a pile of dishes in the sink, a carton of milk warming on the kitchen counter next to an open jar of peanut butter with a knife sticking out of it, the refrigerator door standing open.

I close the refrigerator door, and I'm just about to wipe up the floor when Noah darts through the living room toward me. "Wobert!" he squeaks in a voice I know means he's a little freaked out. "Aunt Whitney needs help." He grabs my hand and tugs me toward my parents' bedroom. I drop the paper towels on the counter, and with a feeling of dread, follow Noah.

Franny, who at twelve is the oldest of my cousins, presses herself white-faced against the wall as we pass her in the hallway, and I fear what new horror awaits me. At the foot of the bed, the huddled twins—Matthew and Mark—look up at me with tear-filled but hopeful eyes.

"Robert, is that you?" Aunt Whitney calls from the bathroom.

There's something about a crisis in a bathroom that screams, *You don't want to be a part of this*. As it turns out, it's not as bad as I feared. Dad is sitting on the shower floor and leaning against a plastic chair seat, his forehead cradled in the crook of his arm, his eyes closed. A towel is draped across his lap.

"Where have you been?" Aunt Whitney demands.

"You okay, Dad?"

"He slipped off his shower chair," my aunt says, stepping into the stall with Dad and gripping him around his bare shoulders. "Get this chair out, then I need you to help me lift him."

"Where's Mom?"

She rounds on me with a suddenness that makes me flinch. "I don't know where your mom is. But she's damn sure not here where she's supposed to be. Your dad's been on this shower floor for twenty minutes."

I seethe at the unfairness in her words as I brace myself against the far shower wall and lift the chair over her head and Dad's. She has no right to dump on Mom. Mom's the one who has taken care of Dad all these years—drove him everywhere he wanted to go when the seizures robbed him of his ability to drive, sat with him during endless rounds of doctors' visits and MRIs, filled his prescriptions. She's the one who supported the family because he couldn't, who paid the bills and took care of the house and me because he wouldn't. She's been the glue holding this family together, but not once have I heard any of them thank her or defend her. It's like she's the hired help.

"Where have you been?" Dad repeats in a pained voice.

And sometimes I feel like the bastard son. I set the chair in a corner, out of the way. I can tell from the pinched look on his face that his head is really hurting.

"I had to make up a test and then I had my group."

He scoffs. And the implication of that small exhalation is like a knife in my gut. I wrap my arms around him in a bear hug and heave him to his feet. He's nearly two hundred pounds of dead weight. He's weak, but once I get him upright, he manages to support himself just a little on his one good leg. Aunt Whitney takes one side and I take the other, and together we half drag him back to the bedroom.

I'm keenly aware that his towel is not traveling with us, and I'm angry all over again—this time at Aunt Whitney for not protecting his privacy, at Aunt Olivia for dumping her four kids here and disappearing, and at Dad for not dying with more dignity.

I'm not being fair. I know that.

"Where's Aunt Olivia?" I ask as we settle Dad down on the bed. Aunt Whitney lifts his legs onto the mattress.

"She's on call. She had to run to the hospital. One of her tonsillectomy patients blew out his scabs and had to go back into surgery."

"If she's on call, why didn't she just leave her kids home with Uncle Thomas?"

"You know what," she says, snapping her head up. "Your aunt Olivia and I are giving up our evenings to take care of your dad because you and your mom are just too busy with your own lives to do what's right. So I don't want to hear about it. Okay?"

I'm speechless.

The four-year-olds have jumped up on the other side of the bed and are giggling, while Franny leans against the footboard, intently studying anatomy.

Dad groans and shifts.

Aunt Whitney finally shoos the kids away and pulls the sheet up. "Hand me that oxygen tube," she says.

I want to defend myself and my mom, I want to walk away, I want to pretend like this isn't my life. But I don't do any of those things. I hand her the tubing and she gently slips it over Dad's ears and positions the prongs in his nostrils.

Dad squeezes his forehead with his one good hand. His hair has grown back only sparsely since his last chemo treatment, and he no longer wears a beanie to cover the scars and indentations on his scalp. His face is bloated from the steroids, and the oxygen tube presses into his flesh. He used to be handsome, I guess—six-two, solidly built, sandy blond hair a shade darker than my own, a wide mouth that showed beautifully straightened teeth that I rarely got to see unless he was laughing with one of his sisters.

I find it hard to look at him now.

Aunt Whitney gropes around under the mattress for a key that she uses to open the gray metal box on the bedside table—Dad's home pharmacy. She shakes out a couple of morphine tablets, then helps Dad sit up. He takes the pills with a shaky hand and tosses them both in his mouth. She hands him a glass of water. When he's settled again, she locks the box and picks up a small spiral notebook on the table.

"I brought your dad something," she says to me like she didn't just cut my balls off. She hands me the notebook. "I thought he could use this to record his thoughts for you while he still can, give you something you can hold on to, share with you his favorite memories of being your dad, his hopes for your future. Things like that." She brushes her fingers across his forehead.

I shift my focus to Dad and see tears glistening in his eyes.

I should be moved. I should feel something. It scares me that I don't.

He says something, but his voice is raspy and I don't catch his words.

"What's that, Dad?"

He opens his eyes and fixes them on me with a look of exasperation. "I need you to clean the fish tank," he says with some effort.

Aunt Whitney smiles down at him, indulgently, I think, then turns her smile to me. "He's been worrying all day about those fish. He wants you to check the water's pH and replace the filter."

The thirty-gallon tank is Dad's therapy. He set it up in their bedroom ten years ago, a couple of months after his diagnosis. Aunt Whitney says it gives him a sense of control. I say it gives him just one more way to avoid interacting with us.

"Do you need anything else?" I ask.

"Just take care of the goddamn fish," he growls in a whispered voice. He squeezes his eyes shut like he's fighting the reverberation of his words in his brain. Fighting that same reverberation in my soul, I turn to go.

"And don't forget to vacuum the gravel and do a water exchange." I look back at this stranger for a moment, then I go.

In the garage I have to move aside the lopsided, five-foot Scotch pine to get to the siphon tubing hanging on a rack on the wall. The tree has been soaking in a bucket of water for over a week now and the garage smells like a pine forest. It's unlike Mom not to have the tree up and decorated the weekend after Thanksgiving, but this year is unlike any other. I finger the needles and focus on breathing for a few moments. It doesn't feel like Christmas to me. It feels like some kind of purgatory.

I take a deep breath and remove the tubing along with the deep bucket hanging next to it. There was a time when I really liked cleaning the fish tank. It was one of the few things I ever did with my dad, but when it became all too clear that the only reason Dad let me help was because he could no longer do it by himself, the fun evaporated like the water in the tank. I was just a necessary evil, like the cane or the scooter or the wheelchair.

He despised every one of those crutches. The tumor started on the right side of his brain, in the motor cortex, and even though the doctors removed it, the damage was done. The seizures that affected his left side were pretty well controlled for a long time, but then the breakthroughs became more frequent and the weakness on his left side more prominent. Despite the radiation and the chemo, it was clear he was losing the battle. Eventually he was forced to use a cane to maintain his balance. The second surgery to zap the tumor also zapped the brain tissue that controlled those muscles, and what little use he'd retained of his left arm and leg was suddenly gone. He had to trade in his cane for a power scooter, something I knew he found humiliating. Then the cancer spread, and the scooter was replaced with a wheelchair.

I drop one end of the tubing into the tank. When I get the water flowing into the bucket, I drag the larger end across the gravel to vacuum up all the debris. I know what I'm doing, but I still feel Dad watching me. And I can't help wondering whose future he is more anxious about—mine or the fish's.

He never wanted me after all. That's a hell of a thing for a kid to find out. Maybe it's because I'm an only child that I know things I shouldn't.

Like the fact that my dad wouldn't have married my mom if she hadn't been pregnant with me, and he did that only because my grandmother went all Catholic on him.

Like the fact that when Mom got pregnant again eight years ago, Dad asked if she was sure the baby was even his. Like the fact that she miscarried my baby sister in a hospital room during one of my dad's many admissions, this time for pneumonia; she was almost five months pregnant.

Like the fact that Dad took his metal box of narcotics into the closet one night almost a year ago, and Mom didn't try to stop him.

I don't want to know these things, but I do.

I hang the siphon tubing back on its hook in the garage and return with a garden hose. An adapter is already attached to the bathroom sink.

I think Dad is asleep, or at least drugged to the gills, until he croaks, "Don't forget to condition the water."

Like I could.

I'm just wiping off the hood and the outside of the tank when I hear the garage door go up. I store the chemicals in the cabinet below and flip off the light under the hood.

"Leave the light on," Aunt Whitney says.

My mistake. Dad doesn't like the dark. It's too much like being dead, I guess. He quit sleeping at night years ago, instead staying up and messing around on his computer until the sun came up, and then going to bed and leaving Mom to get me off to school or whatever. I turn the light back on.

In the kitchen, Mom is clearing the right side of the sink of soggy waffles and dirty dishes. She glances up at me, then runs her forearm across her brow and sighs heavily. "I swear those children were raised by wolves." I smile as she shuts off the water and dries her hands. She pulls the knife out of the peanut butter jar and shakes her head. I screw the lid on as she drops the knife into the sink and opens the dishwasher.

"Sorry, Mom," I say, helping her unload the dishes. "I would have cleaned up for you, but Dad wanted me to clean the fish tank."

She stops and looks at me for a moment, then musses my hair. "How was your day? Did the kids like 'Jingle Bells'?" She withdraws her hand and looks a little guilty for touching me. It's an echo from my touch-me-not days in junior high. I regret now making that stand.

Did the kids like "Jingle Bells"? Her question actually makes me laugh, just a little. " 'Jingle Bells' was a total bust," I tell her, "but otherwise it was okay. I stayed after school and made up my calculus test. I made a one hundred, sort of."

"Sort of?"

"Yeah. Mr. McNelis helped me through it."

She smiles and hands me the silverware basket. "Since when do you need help with a calculus test?"

I don't respond, but I can feel her watching me as I sort everything into the plastic tray in the drawer. She takes the basket from me and hugs it to her chest. "I'm so sorry you have to go through all this."

"It's okay, Mom. I'm sorry the rug rats keep trashing the house."

She smiles.

"Where did you go?"

"The families we adopted picked up their holiday bags today. I was going to miss it, but they were shorthanded and since your aunt Whitney was here—is that pee on the floor?"

"Apple juice," I say, grabbing the earlier abandoned paper towels. "At least I hope it's apple juice."

Mom sighs and rubs her eyes. "What else happened while I was gone?"

You don't want to know.

Later, I haul the Scotch pine and the boxes of decorations into the house, and as we decorate the tree together, I fill her in anyway.

I can't sleep. Even though the volume is fairly low, I can still hear the TV in my parents' room. And then there's another noise, like Dad is fumbling around for something on his bedside table. It's always this way. I don't know how Mom gets any sleep.

It's been two days since Dad had his last MRI, since his neurologist confirmed what we all suspected—the cancer is out of control. Dad pushed for more chemo, more radiation, bone-rattling, anything. When the doctor told him no, he'd gotten irate, and when Mom tried to calm him down, he'd turned on her. She called me at school, and Ms. Lincoln sent me home early. Aunt Whitney and Aunt Olivia were already here, crying with Dad in his room, assuring him they would take care of him. And Mom, she was furiously cleaning the baseboards in the kitchen.

He's going to die at home. It's what he wants. A hospice nurse is coming tomorrow. Aunt Whitney says they'll do whatever they have to to keep him comfortable until the end.

I wonder if there's a hospice for the family.

A *goddammit* sets my heart pounding. The clock reads two AM. I lie still and listen and piece together what happened.

Mom, yelling: "Why didn't you wake me up?"

Dad, crying: "I'm sorry."

Mom, more calmly: "Just stop. I'll get it. I'll *get* it. Why didn't you ask for help?"

Dad: Incoherent.

Mom: "Oh, for God's sake. *Please*. Just *lie* down. I'll—"

Dad: *"Leave me the fuck alone!"*

Mom: Nothing.

I hear the hallway closet door open, then close, the kitchen faucet turn on, then shut off. A few minutes later the steam cleaner is roaring in their room. And then I get it—Dad has knocked over his urinal again.

When it shuts off, I get up. "I'll put it away, Mom," I tell her, taking the steam cleaner from her in the hallway. "Go back to bed."

She's on the verge of tears as she bends over to wrap the power cord around the hooks. "It's okay, baby. I'm already up. You've got school tomorrow. Try to get some sleep, okay?"

I let her take the steam cleaner back from me. "I'm sorry," I say.

She smiles wanly and shoos me back to my room.

I don't sleep a lot, but I do sleep. In the morning it's not my alarm that wakes me; it's Dad clanging this infernal bell Aunt Olivia gave him to summon us when he needs something. Aunt Whitney took his power scooter away weeks ago; yesterday she put his wheelchair in the garage so he won't attempt to use it alone. I don't really understand why they're trying to protect him anymore. A concussion seems like a pretty attractive alternative at this point. He's used the bell only a couple of times, but I have a feeling that's just changed.

When he's still clanging it a minute later, I get up and pad into the room to see what he needs. The running shower explains why Mom didn't heed his call.

The carpet is wet under my feet, and I'm suddenly reminded of last night. "What do you need, Dad?"

He pinches his face up when he speaks. "I need you to help me with the urinal."

At least he asked, but I don't want to do this. I really don't.

He unsuccessfully tries to untangle himself from the sheet, and eventually I have to help him. With his good hand, he grips the side rail that Mom had me install a year ago, but he doesn't have the strength to pull himself up. I grab his other arm at the elbow and help him into a sitting position. When he's stable, I swing his legs around to the side of the bed. He's nude under the sheet, his skin an odd color, slack, bruised, his useless left leg thinner than the other by half and completely lacking in definition. I support him, then avert my eyes as he releases the rail and positions the urinal. It takes a while for him to get started.

When he's done, he hands the plastic container to me. He's got the handle, so I'm forced to take it by the main body before I can make the switch. It's warm, and the instant aversion I feel makes my skin crawl. He reaches for a tissue to catch the drip, then hands me that too. I help him back into bed, then dump the foaming urine and the tissue in my bathroom toilet, resisting the urge to gag.

I'm not remotely cut out for this kind of intimacy with my dad.

So when Mom hands me an external catheter as I'm getting ready to head out half an hour later and asks me to roll it on Dad's shriveled penis, I just can't. Apparently Dad made a pity call to Aunt Whitney in the middle of the night and told her what happened, so she stopped by on her way to the clinic, before I woke up, and dropped off the catheter.

"Can't the hospice nurse do this?"

"No, she can't. She's not even going to be here until this afternoon."

"Mom, please don't ask me to do this." I hold it back out to her.

She looks at me with a mixture of anger, frustration, and sympathy, then snatches the plastic bag out of my hand and rips it open. Tubing and something that looks like a condom with a funnel on one end spill onto the kitchen floor.

"I can't do this anymore, Robert," she says through clenched teeth. She kicks the catheter out into the dining room with her bare foot, then kicks it again into the living room, then again into the hallway.

"Mom." I get out in front of her and pick up the catheter and coil the tubing. I'm pretty sure it's no longer sterile, but I don't think anybody much cares anymore. I hold it out to her. "I can't do this either, Mom."

She wipes her eyes on her robe, and I hate myself that I can't do more to help her. She snatches the catheter from my hand and fires off a string of curses. I wince at the onslaught. Then she composes herself and heads to her room. I grab my backpack and get the hell out of there.

Chapter 3

Andrew

My freshman Algebra kids surge into the room Thursday morning on a tide of whining.

"Are we doing anything today?"

"Can we just have a free period?"

"I don't know why we have to come to school these last two days. We don't do anything anyway."

God, two more days—two more days—two more days.

It's this way right before every long holiday. We intentionally schedule final due dates and tests a few days before a break or the end of a grading period so we have a couple of days for makeups or redos or whatever concessions we have to make to get those sixty-niners—those kids right on the border—over the hump. And there's no point starting something new with a two-week break coming up.

And with boring regularity, some smart aleck argues that we should cancel those last two days. I remind this current smart aleck that no matter what day we end on before a break, there will always be a last two days.

I don't think they really grasp that logic though.

Anyway, the best we teachers can hope for is to keep the kids contained until we can dismiss at two thirty on that last day (in this case, Friday).

"Yeah, yeah, yeah," I say over their grumbling. As they settle in, I turn on my projector and a collective groan rises in the room.

"What?" I say, clicking Play on my tablet screen. "You're going to love this movie."

Stephen Newman picks up the DVD case as he passes by my computer cart in the front of the room. "*Stand and Deliver*?" He rolls his eyes and tosses it back on the cart.

"Why so cynical, Stephen? How do you know you're not going to like it? You haven't even seen it yet."

"I saw it in Spanish last year. Lame."

"Yeah, Mr. McNelis," Kristyn Murrow says. "That movie's like a million years old."

"It was released in 1988," I say in its defense.

"We weren't even born. Can't we watch *Scream Three*?"

"No. And don't get on my nerves, or I will get on yours. And, Stephen, don't get too comfortable. You won't be watching the movie anyway, pal."

He looks at me in disbelief.

I motion him to my desk. He sneers, and for a moment, I think he's going to refuse, but then he slouches over.

I hold out his last test. "You didn't do any test corrections yesterday. As I recall, you chose to use that time to entertain Kristyn. Yet, despite your fascinating performance, she managed to complete *her* corrections."

"So? I didn't want to do them."

"You don't do them, you fail the nine weeks, and that leaves you very, very borderline for the semester. Your choice, but you fail, you won't be participating in athletics when we come back from the break."

I open my hand and let his test drop to my desk, then turn my attention to the attendance screen on my computer.

After a moment, he snatches it up and makes his way over the kids stretched out on the floor to the hallway, intentionally nudging a few with his foot and sending up a chorus of *hey*s.

"Let me know if you need some help," I call after him. I can't help smiling to myself. God bless coaches and their policies.

I open an e-mail from Jen. *Showing a movie?*

"Stand and Deliver," I reply. *You?*

So you're the one who rented it. All I could get was "Shrek the Third."

Oh. I'm sure that has a strong correlation to our math standards.

Yes, in fact. Mathematical logic in sentences. Pinocchio and Prince Charming. Hold on.

A few minutes later she e-mails me a scene from the movie, a scene where Prince Charming pushes Pinocchio to tell him where Shrek is and Pinocchio answers with a bunch of rhetorical mumbo-jumbo: *I'm possibly more or less not definitely rejecting the idea that in no way with any amount of uncertainty that I undeniably . . .*

I chuckle at the exchange. Now that I read it, I remember it well. It's a stretch, but I concede the point.

Is that your kid sitting in the hallway? she writes. *He's looking in my door window and mouthing something to one of my girls.*

I sigh. *I'll get him.*

I step over the kids and open my door, catching him red-handed.

"Stephen, what the L-M-N-O-P are you doing? Can I assume you've finished your test corrections already?"

"I'm working on them."

"Looks to me like you're working on something else entirely. Look through the window again. Go ahead."

He looks suspicious but does what I say.

"You see Ms. Went over there at her desk? If I get another e-mail from her or anyone else in this building telling me your face has been anywhere other than hanging over that test, you will spend your last day sitting next to me. You will be teacher's pet for the day, my friend. Me and you." I give him my brightest smile.

Apparently the thought of sitting with me is so humiliating that he actually sits his butt back on the floor and finishes his test corrections.

I congratulate myself on winning another round.

* * *

The whining continues through fourth period. It's a relief to get to fifth and my calculus kids, and a real pleasure to see my sixth-period AP Calculus class.

I'm especially pleased to see that Robert is more himself today. He gives me a shy smile when he enters the room, and I give him one back.

Robert

I half expect Mr. McNelis to show us *Stand and Deliver* the last two days before Christmas break. It's this movie, a true story, about a California teacher who takes a bunch of low-achieving Latino kids in an equally low-performing high school and turns them into calculus superstars. I've already seen it four times—twice in eighth grade (Spanish I and Algebra), once in ninth grade (Spanish II), and once in tenth grade (with my testing group during state testing week). It's actually the perfect movie for Calculus because it's, well, about calculus, or cal-CUL-lus, as Lou Diamond Phillips calls it in the movie. But there's no movie. Instead, he passes out pages of math puzzles.

Some of them are pretty challenging and they take my mind off the long Christmas holiday coming up. Others are easy, like this one:

> *A teacher writes the Roman numeral IX on the board and asks students how to make it into 6 by adding a single line, without lifting the dry erase marker.*

I copy the IX, then add an S in front of it: *SIX*.
The next question involves matches.

> *Sixteen matches are arranged in the five-square pattern below. Reduce the number of squares to four by moving only two matches. You cannot remove any matches or leave any loose ends.*

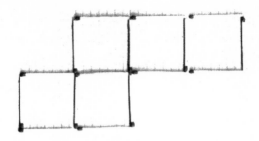

I study the figure a moment, then look up and see that Mr. McNelis has returned to his desk. He's kicked back in his chair, his ankles crossed on his desk, and he's looking at his phone. I let my eyes trail along his gray corduroys to his feet. He's wearing loafers, these two-tone brown and gray leather things with a slot for a penny on top and a rubber outsole. I'm trying to guess his shoe size when he lifts his eyes and catches me.

I quickly return to the puzzle, but I'm thinking about all the things I like about Mr. McNelis, besides the shoes.

For one thing, he cusses in class. He doesn't use real cuss words—you can't do that in public school if you want to keep your job. Instead he says stuff like, *What the L-M-N-O-P are you doing? Or Son of a bit-my-finger. Just sit down.* If you're chewing gum, he'll say something like, *Get rid of the gum, or I'm going to kick you, then I'm going to kick your dog.* And if you get on his nerves, he'll get on yours. He can be kind of weird, but he makes us laugh.

And he's a super math nerd. Fridays are jeans days for teachers, and he always wears some funny math T-shirt. He must have a dozen or more. Last Friday it was a black T-shirt with this slogan:

$$\pi$$

IRRATIONAL

BUT WELL-ROUNDED

And then there's this—he's gay. He thinks we don't know; we do. And it's not because he's an impeccable dresser; he's not, although he does look damn hot in those cords. It's not because his nails are always clean and neatly trimmed; they are, but that's not it either. And it's not because he sashays around the classroom; he doesn't.

It's because he follows AfterElton on Twitter. It's amazing what girls can dig up when they're motivated. And when it comes to Mr. McNelis, some of them are pretty damn motivated.

The girls think they can change him; I know they can't.

The solution to the puzzle suddenly presents itself in my mind. I use my pencil to scratch out then redraw two of the matches. Then I outline the new squares again with heavy lines.

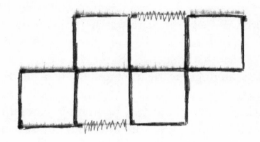

Mr. McNelis gets up and moves down the side of the room. He's allowed us to work in pairs or small groups, but I've chosen to work alone today. There's something about being in this room with him that makes me feel good, normal, relevant, but that doesn't mean I want to interact with any of my classmates. Not this week. He stops at a small group in the back—two girls and a guy in a football hoodie—and looks over their shoulders.

"Are there any days you can eliminate?" he asks.

They all look back at the question, then one of the girls offers up a Hail Mary answer. He smiles and tells them to keep working on it.

I scan the page and find the question they are on. It's a logic question. I think about what Mr. McNelis just said to the group and begin working my way through the problem backward.

I'm writing out the explanation when I feel his hand grip my shoulder. I look up and he winks. Something inside me shifts.

* * *

On Friday he passes out strips of paper and another packet of puzzles. His T-shirt today reads:

ARE YOU CRYING?

THERE'S NO

CRYING IN

MATH CLASS!

But I do want to cry.

Unlike my classmates, I'm dreading the bell at two thirty. I don't want to spend two weeks on death watch. I don't want to open gifts under the fat, eight-foot noble fir Aunt Whitney had delivered yesterday. God, I hate that tree.

The noble is an upgrade. So are the shiny new beads and angels and snowflakes.

The Scotch pine Mom and I spent an hour decorating with the accumulated odds and ends of Christmases past just two nights ago is back in the garage, lying on its side on the concrete, still clinging to its humble adornments.

The noble is so tall that the delivery guy had to trim several inches off the tip of the tree so it could stand upright. Then last night, Aunt Whitney wheeled Dad into the living room and she and Aunt Olivia and all the cousins decorated the new tree themselves, the whole time pattering on about how beautiful the angels are, my aunts reminiscing for the kids about all the fun they had decorating Christmas trees together when they were younger. I can just picture it—Olivia and Whitney (six and eight years older than dad, respectively) doting on their baby brother, dressing him up in reindeer pajamas, guiding him through the gluttony of a Westfall Christmas.

Mom and I watched mutely from the kitchen as we threw together another prefab meal for the masses.

When they finally left, Mom disappeared into the garage and a moment later let loose a primal scream. I was sure she'd been cornered by a monstrous rat or a rabid raccoon that had slipped in unnoticed. I sprinted for the garage, but before I could get to her, she calmly walked back in and closed the door behind her.

"What?" she'd said to me. That was it. Just, "What?"

I pick up one of the strips of paper and read the first question.

Make a Möbius strip.

I give one end of the paper a half twist and secure it to the other end, using tape from one of the dispensers Mr. McNelis has placed around the room along with multiple pairs of scissors.

Question: *What do you think will happen if you cut all the way along the strip in the middle?*

I don't bother to answer. I just cut the strip. The paper separates into one long strip, twice the length of the original.

I toss it aside and look at the next instruction.

Make another Möbius strip.

Done.

Question: *What do you think will happen if you cut all the way along the strip a third of the way from the edge?*

Answer: *I don't give a flip.*

I pick up the scissors and make the cut. What I'm left with are two interlocking rings.

Normally I'd try to understand how that one loop of paper had become two, but today I'm just thinking about the loops. I place my fingers on the inside of each loop and apply pressure outward. How much pressure will it take before one of the loops snaps? I increase the pressure.

As it turns out, not much.

Andrew

From the back of the room, I study Robert. He's playing with the second Möbius strip, now two interlocking loops. It's a cool party trick, and one that I still find fascinating even though I understand the principle behind it.

I was disappointed that Robert chose to work by himself yesterday, but I think I understand it. At least he was engaged. I'd even caught him watching me during class a few times. I found his attention curious, and both a little uncomfortable and a little flattering.

I've grown accustomed to being stared at by the girls; after all, I'm only six or seven years older than the seniors and nine or ten years older than the freshmen. And male teachers my age are uncommon enough in high school that we stand out.

I think the girls get from me what they want from the boys in their classes, what the boys haven't yet figured out that the girls need—attention. Just that simple. Only, the attention I'm giving them is just part of the job. If they see it as something else, if it makes them feel just a little better about themselves, then great.

I don't mention the fact that they are barking up the wrong proverbial tree.

But today Robert seems distracted, less engaged, angry even. He's doing the work, but his mind seems millions of miles away. I'd welcome one of those looks, if just to give him an encouraging smile, to let him know I understand.

But he doesn't look. He spreads his hands and the larger ring snaps.

I scan the room. Some of the kids are just starting on the paperclip magic where you loop a strip of paper into a zigzag and use two paper clips to hold its shape. When you give the two ends of the paper a sharp tug, the paperclips link together. Another cool party trick. I notice that Robert has skipped over that one, as if he already knows what will happen, and has moved on to the maze.

The next thought comes to me completely unbidden: *I wonder if Robert and Whore-Hay are sleeping together?*

I try to wipe my mind of that inappropriate thought, but it is as permanent as Sharpie on a dry erase board.

When the bell rings, Robert stays behind to straighten the desks the other kids have left willy-nilly and pick up scraps of paper from the floor. This is not unusual.

When the room is empty and it's only the two of us, I ask the same question I've asked the last two days in a row. "How are you holding up?"

He balls up the paper in his hands and takes a shot at the trash-can next to my desk. The paper bounces off the rim and onto the floor. I pick it up and drop it in.

"Did you know that some Christmas trees are evil?" he asks.

"No. I didn't know that."

He chews on his bottom lip, then says, "They are."

He picks up his things and leaves me wondering what the heck he was talking about.

In seventh-period Algebra, the kids are watching the second half of *Stand and Deliver.* Jennifer e-mails: *Choir practice tonight?*

Three date requests in one week. A new record.

Choir practice is not literally *choir* practice. It's code for beer and wings and nachos at Bubba's—a big open-air barn with a bar at one end and a stage at the other. About half the tables are between the bar and the stage and the other half spill out onto a brick patio under an extension of the metal roof. It's a place where teachers, admins, and other school staff go to let their hair down on Fridays, especially after test week or just before a holiday break or the last day of school. I've been once or twice.

It's a dangerous place. When teachers drink, they start behaving in some pretty unprofessional ways. Secrets are revealed, unhealthy alliances are formed, and gossip flows in direct proportion to the beer.

I learned quickly to limit my visits there. But it's Christmas break, and I don't pick up Kiki until morning, so what the L-M-N-O-P.

I e-mail an affirmative.

When the last bell rings at two fifteen, the kids rush the class-room door. I wrapped up things during the movie, so I'm planning to leave almost as quickly. I'm shutting down my computer when Robert sticks his head in.

"Hey," he says. "Hope you have a nice Christmas."

I want to say, "You too," but that seems all kinds of wrong. Instead I nudge the chair next to my desk with my foot and say, "Come on in. Talk to me for a minute."

He pulls the chair out a bit and drops into it, letting his backpack slide to the floor.

"A rough holiday ahead, huh?" I say.

"Yeah. Can't say I'm looking forward to going home. Maybe I could just hang out with you for the next two weeks."

I smile and he smiles back. "It's going to be okay, Robert. I know it's hard, but . . ." I stop and shrug.

"Hey, do you have a pencil and a piece of paper?"

"Um, sure."

I scrounge around in my desk drawer for a Post-it pad and hand it over. He takes a pencil from the school mug on my desk and neatly writes a phone number on the Post-it and hands to me. Then he says something that takes me by complete surprise:

"That's my cell number. You can call me if you want."

He gets up. I stand too. "Robert . . ." I'm not sure what I'm going to say, I just know that teachers don't call students. Not this teacher. "I can't call you. I'm sorry." I hold the note out to him.

"Mr. Gorman calls me all the time," he says. "It's no big deal."

I feel a little pang of something that I suspect might be jealousy. Stupid, really. Mr. Gorman is the band director. His relationship with kids is on an entirely different level. They spend long hours together on the practice field. I know he even drives the van to area and state solo and ensemble contests in Austin or Dallas or San Antonio. But still, I'm sure those calls are strictly band business.

"I'm sorry," I say again.

He takes the note and shoves it in his pocket. He bites his lip again, the way I saw him do when he talked about the Christmas tree that I still don't understand, and I think he looks embarrassed.

"It's okay," he says softly. He turns and leaves.

Shit.

If someone were to ask me what it's like to be a high school teacher, I'd have to say it's like having one foot on a banana peel. The potential is always there for a slip . . . or a push. Part of that slippery nature is knowing where to draw the line sometimes, the one between student and teacher, the one that delineates mentor from friend. The one that says, *I can go this far for you, but no more.* Since I started teaching, I've drawn that line repeatedly. And I've moved it, a little this way, a little that, more times than I can count.

But this is one of those immovable lines—teachers don't call students to chat. They just don't.

Still, I can't help feeling like I've just cut him loose and he's going under, maybe for the first time, maybe the second, maybe the third. I just don't know. I only know that the look on his face when I said no was one of lost hope and maybe even deep hurt.

I scribble my number on another Post-it and catch up with him in the hallway.

He looks down at his athletic shoes, and I know—I *know*—that I'm doing the right thing. "Look, I can't call you," I say, "but if you need me, if you need to talk or just let off some steam, you can call me. Okay?"

I hand him the Post-it. He looks at my number for a moment, then meets my eyes with his. "Thanks, Mr. Mac."

Robert

I enter Mr. Mac's number in my phone as I cross the parking lot. I don't know why he decided to give it to me, or whether or not I'll use it, but it feels good to have all the same.

Nic is leaning against my car when I get there. I shove my phone back in my pocket.

"Hey, what took you so long?" he says and gives me a brief hug, leaving enough distance between us to drive a school bus through. "I've been waiting for hours."

Apparently I've been forgiven for my lack of clairvoyance. "I thought you had plans tonight," I say, tossing my backpack in the front seat.

"I do, but I wanted to see my guy for a few minutes first."

His guy. Hmph. Nic talks about all his friends like they're his personal possessions. My guy, my girls. Tonight he's hanging out with his girls—cheerleaders, all of them. And I'm not invited. I imagine they're going to do girly stuff like paint their faces and their nails and talk about boys.

He's like their little mascot. I think it's degrading; he doesn't see it that way.

That last part—the talking-about-boys part—sticks in my craw a bit. Apparently having a boyfriend and lusting after hot guys is not mutually exclusive. Sometimes I wonder what I ever saw in Nic. He's cute, he's funny, he's smart. All true. And he's gay. A definite plus. Beyond that, though, we don't have much in common.

He's never even been to my house. He doesn't *do* sick people, he told me once. But when I told him my dad was dying three days ago, he'd gushed and cried and carried on like someone had just run over his pet turtle.

Nic does *do* drama.

"Look, I made something for your dad," he says. He pulls something out of his backpack and hands it to me. It's a book, carved up with the pages glued together. Most of the cover and a good many pages have been cut away, framing the page beneath, which he's painted over with something white that allows the words to seep through just a little. Some of the words are still completely exposed—a word here, a word there—and he's circled them with a black Sharpie. My eyes trail across the page—*you—are—loved.* Off to the side he's drawn a pink daisy with a yellow center and a green stem that weaves among the words. I turn the book over. On the back in red ink: *B+.*

"Do you think he'll like it?" Nic asks excitedly.

Your B+ art project? "Yeah."

"Oh, good!" He kisses me on the cheek. "I gotta go," he says, already backing away. "Can't keep my girls waiting." Then, almost as an afterthought: "You want to hang out tomorrow? I don't have anything else to do."

He doesn't wait for me to answer.

I pull my car up next to a Dumpster and toss the book in.

Andrew

"One beer," I tell Jen.

She eyes me and nibbles on a tortilla chip. "Were you always this stuffy, Drew?"

"Not stuffy. Just not stupid," I say in my defense. "This place is crawling with gossips. I'd just as soon not be one of their subjects."

"Aaah, come on. We've been locked up with hormonal teenagers for four months now. It's our turn to let it all hang out."

I laugh. "Sorry, partner. I'm not lettin' nothin' hang out tonight."

"You're no fun." She inches her chair closer to mine, then gathers her long blond hair and pulls it over one shoulder, twisting it in a move that I assume is intended to be alluring. I decide to change the subject.

"So, what are you going to do with that novel when you finish it?"

"I joined the Romance Writers of America. A hundred ten bucks, can you believe it? But they've got this special-interest chapter—Passionate Ink—for erotica writers. And I'm thinking... maybe my roommate had the right idea. She paid her way through college writing dirty novels. And, hey, I can write erotica. I've had sex."

I try not to grin too broadly as she goes off into a long, animated monologue about her publishing plans and pen names and the steamy scenes she wants to write. The music is loud—Journey, I think—and I lose some of her words in the beat.

I find myself thinking again about Robert. Would he actually call? And why me? Maybe he gave his phone number to all his teachers. Don't know, not going to ask. But I can't help speculating. And I can't help feeling that there's something about me that's more approachable than other teachers, some special quality that Robert intuits.

"Pride goeth before a fall," Jen says.

Most of her chatter has fallen on deaf ears, but this little indictment somehow grabs my attention. I look at her, and she nods toward Philip, who's making his way to our table.

"He thinks he's got this so under control," she says, snidely. She grins widely up at him as he approaches. I'd like to warn him, but I can see it's too late.

"Hey, you two, what are you up to for the holidays?" he asks. He pulls out a chair across from us and sits.

"Just hanging out with the family," Jen says brightly. "I bet your kids are excited about hanging out with their dad for two weeks straight."

He smiles. "Actually, Diana's got a honey-do list for me a mile long. It's going to be a working holiday for me. What about you, Drew?"

"I'm headed to Oklahoma to see—"

"Hey, is Liz here?" Jen interrupts. "I wanted to ask her about her trip to Mexico."

Philip looks uncomfortable. He glances around the room. "Don't know. Haven't seen her." Then he gets up and tells us he'll catch us later.

"You are shameless," I say to Jen.

"He deserves it. He's got four freaking kids at home."

"He's a nice guy."

"He's a douche." Jen grins and drains her mug. "I'm gonna get another beer."

Chapter 4

Robert

When I get up Saturday morning, I find Aunt Whitney in the kitchen surveying empty cabinets and drawers. She has taken everything out of them and stacked it on the counters. And she's obviously been here awhile; the old shelf paper is gone too, and new green spongy stuff has been precisely fitted to each shelf and drawer in its place.

It's just a shot in the dark, but I'm guessing Mom didn't ask Aunt Martha Stewart here to rearrange her kitchen for maximum efficiency. She's going to be pissed when she can't find the manual can opener later.

I take a glass and pour some milk. "Where's Mom?" I ask.

"Out running errands. I told her she should wake you up to do the errands, but she vetoed me on that. She acts like she can't get out of this house fast enough most days."

No kidding. Can't imagine why.

"You want something to eat? I made your dad a breakfast burrito." She sighs. "He barely picked at it. There's still some eggs and bacon left. I could put one together for you."

I mumble a no, thanks, but take a piece of bacon anyway.

"I think your dad's asleep now." She stoops to size up a bottom cabinet, then reaches up for a large saucepan and sets it on the shelf inside. "I think he was up all night again. He doesn't like being alone, you know."

He wasn't alone. Mom was right there in the bed next to him. It's a slight, another tiny dig on my mom—the bad mother, the bad wife. They hate her—for getting pregnant in college, for dropping out, for marrying Dad, for supplanting them in my dad's life, for existing. She'll never be good enough to bear the Westfall name. I know that, and so does she.

Aunt Whitney straightens up and leans against the counter. She studies me for a moment, then shakes her head slowly. "You look so much like your dad did at your age. You should be very proud of him, Robert. He's a very brave man."

I want to scream at her. *How? Tell me how having cancer makes you brave or good or noble?* But I don't.

Aunt Whitney sighs. "He would have been such a good doctor." Her voice catches in her throat.

She seems lost in her thoughts for a moment, then suddenly finds herself again. She examines the scarred nonstick pan she's holding. "God, some of this cookware is just a disgrace. I don't know why your mother doesn't invest in some good Calphalon." She forces the pan into a trash bag of other discards she's been collecting in the corner.

Andrew

"There's my girl!"

I scoop up Kiki and spin her around. She squeals in delight and pats my face like I'm one of her dolls.

Maya smiles and kisses me on the cheek. "So, what do you two have planned for today?"

I look at Kiki. "You want to go see Santa?"

"Ho-ho-ho!"

Maya laughs. "Good luck with that. My guess is you won't get her anywhere near the jolly old elf. But if you do, I want pictures."

"You hear that, Kiki?" I say to her. "Mommy wants a picture of you with Santa, and we can't disappoint Mommy, right?"

My daughter's cat strolls out the front door, and Kiki squirms to be put down so she can pet him. I drop her lightly to her feet. "So, you spending the day with Doug?"

"He's playing golf right now. Maybe later."

"Golf? Wow. How ... upper-middle-class straight."

"Quit. Not everybody can be you. And at least *he* wants to be with me."

Ouch. But that's Maya. Letting go has never been her strong suit. And now what should have been a friendly exchange of our child has become another awkward moment between us.

"He's a great guy, Maya. I don't know why you two don't make it official. Give the poor guy a break."

"Are you just trying to get out of paying child support?"

At least she can still make a joke. I take that as a sign of continued progress. I know it's been hard on her going from best friend to one-time lover to a married couple to this.

Kiki has thrown herself over the aging cat, who seems to have resigned himself to the assault.

"Are you taking care of yourself?" she asks.

"Yeah. I'm good."

"I don't like you being alone."

"Thanks, but I spend my days in a classroom so small I can't spit without hitting a teenager."

"Eew."

I laugh. "Trust me, after a day at school, alone is all I want to be." I don't look at her when I say this. "I'll drop Kiki off in the morning." I free the cat and scoop up the toddler.

"Are you going to your folks?" Maya asks.

Kiki pokes at my nose and giggles. "Yeah. I wish I could bring this one, but maybe Easter."

"Sure," she says.

Maya and I have a good relationship, but it's had its ups and downs. We both agree though that Kiki has been worth all the bad decisions. (I think of them as bad; I'm not so sure Maya agrees.)

Kiki looks a lot like her mom—rich brown skin, thick black hair, and huge eyes set widely apart. I love her more than anything. Maya knows that. We share her, perhaps not equally, but there's enough play in our agreement that I never feel shorted.

My own parents barely skipped a beat when I came out. There was some discussion about how they already knew, but I think that was just a lie to get past that awkward phase. Because even though sexual orientation is really about identity, there's no getting around the *sexual* part. If I'm gay, I'm interested in what's going on between guys' legs, and like it or not, my parents had to face that.

So, not surprisingly, they were shocked and more than a little confused when Maya got pregnant. When I announced we were getting married, they sat me down for a real talk, the don't-compound-one-mistake-by-making-another talk.

I listened patiently to their arguments, even considered some of them, but in the end I did what I believed was the right thing. I married Maya. We'd slept together only that once. We didn't even pretend to be a real husband and wife in that sense. For me, at least, we were friends and we were parents. I don't know why I ever thought that would be enough for either of us.

The mall turns out to be a mixed bag. Kiki refuses to go anywhere near the poser in the red suit. I won't traumatize her by forcing her onto his lap, but I drop to one knee just to make sure this isn't a momentary case of cold feet. After all, you're only two once.

"No like him," Kiki says, her bottom lip jutting out. She sticks her thumb in her mouth and I gently pull it back out again.

"But he's Santa. Like we saw in the movie, right? And Santa is nice. Don't you want to tell him about the doll you want for Christmas so his elves can be sure and make one just for you? You could tell him how much you like Rudolph, too, and that red nose. I'm sure he'd like to hear that."

"Hey, teach!"

I look up and see one of my students, a freshman. He's holding hands with a girl I don't recognize, and he keeps flicking his head to the side to clear his early–Justin Bieber hair from his eyes.

I'm trying to recall his name, but seeing him in a different environment makes him hard to place. And then I remember—second-period Algebra, back row, corner seat. "Hey, Alex. Doing a little Christmas shopping?"

"Nah. We're just hanging out."

"Well, have fun!" *And get a haircut,* I think. They move on and I turn back to Kiki. She looks glum and maybe a little sleepy. "You want to build a teddy bear?"

Build-A-Bear is crazy. There's a birthday party ahead of us with a gaggle of preteen girls, so it takes a while to get through all the stations. Kiki chooses a Dalmatian instead of a bear and dresses the stuffed animal in a froufrou little summer dress even though it's winter outside. At the sound table, she picks out a little box that plays "Who Let the Dogs Out" and giggles every time it goes *woof, woof, woof-woof.* When we're done, we print out the birth certificate and head to the counter to check out. I am exhausted.

"Mr. McNelis!"

"Kim! I didn't know you worked here." Kim I know immediately. She's another of those serious students like Robert. Same class, in fact. She's strictly academics though. I've wondered before if she knows what a cliché she is—Asian, smart, respectful. Even the serious, dark-framed glasses scream ambition. But she has a job, and therefore I must concede that she is more well-rounded than I thought. I have her pegged for valedictorian, or salutatorian at the least. I set Kiki on the counter and introduce her.

"Is this your doggy?" Kim asks Kiki, bouncing the dog on the counter so the skirt on its dress flaps up and down. Kiki smiles and hugs the dog to herself. "She's a cutie," Kim says, then to me, "She's a cutie too."

"Thanks. I think so." I pull out my wallet while Kim puts together a traveling home for the dog, aptly named Spot now.

"So, I didn't know you were married," Kim says, sliding the credit card receipt over for me to sign.

"Divorced."

I hand the receipt over and see her eyes widen as she says, "Oh." Then she flashes me a smile, a very big smile, and tells Kiki to take good care of that puppy. We leave, and I can't help thinking I've just missed something.

Robert

I think I would have gone out to dinner with Hannibal Lecter if it got me out of the house for a couple of hours.

With school out, the mall is packed with Christmas shoppers. But if there's one thing Nic likes, it's a big audience.

He hangs his heavy sunglasses from the V-neck of his sweater as we merge with the crowd. "I want to pick out some boots," he says, grabbing my hand.

His hand feels foreign in mine, and immediately I suspect it's just for show. It annoys me the way he's thrusting his chest out as we walk. He looks like a rooster. It's all so affected, like he's advertising—*gay boy here; come and get me*—when I know for a fact that if anybody took him up on it, he'd squeal and hide behind me like a little girl, and then I'd have to defend his honor. I hope I'm never called to do that because I'm not so sure I would.

A lone guy with heavily tattooed arms in a sleeveless shirt strolls past us. Nic appraises him with his eyes, then turns and walks backward. "Wow, do you see those biceps? Damn, break me off a piece of that." He gives an exaggerated shiver.

Really? Seriously?

"Um," he says, grabbing my arm and pulling me up short. "Let's go check out Hot Topic. I want to look for a beanie. I think I'd look good in one."

Right. I'd put money on the odds that Sleeveless in December just stepped into Hot Topic himself. I realize I don't care one way or the other.

"You go," I tell him. "I'm going to get us some sodas. I'll meet you there in a few minutes."

"No soda. It's bad for your skin. Get water, and make sure it's not just filtered tap water."

I take the escalator down to the first level. There's a Great American Cookies kiosk in the main thoroughfare just below Hot Topic. I'll get Nic his water, but I'm having a soda.

Waiting in line is Mindy, a drum major second to Luke and one of the shortest girls I know, and Anna, a senior tuba player. They both wrap me in a big hug when I get in line behind them. We're band; we're family.

"Is Nic here with you?" Mindy asks.

"He's upstairs."

"I'm sorry about your dad, Robert," Anna says, grabbing my hand and squeezing it.

I don't know what to do with the pity I see in their eyes. It's misplaced at best, and unwanted at worst. I smile wanly at her and mumble a thanks. She lets go of my hand, and she and Mindy pick up their conversation as I focus on the crowds breaking around the kiosk.

Across from us, a group of girls gather outside of Build-A-Bear, each clutching a cardboard bear house while a mom counts heads.

It's not until they move off toward the food court that I see him standing at the counter, holding a little girl on his hip. He smiles at the attendant, this girl from my math class, then signs the credit card receipt she places in front of him.

I feel my heart kick up the beat.

"So what are you doing for the holiday, Robert?"

"Huh?" Reluctantly, I look back at Mindy. "Oh, we're just staying home."

She seems to realize the flaw in her question and gets quiet. I glance back toward Build-A-Bear just as Mr. McNelis, holding both his daughter and the bear house now, emerges from the store and steps into the crowd. I watch him go.

When I get back upstairs, I sit on a bench outside of Hot Topic and wait for Nic. I think about texting Mr. Mac, just saying, *Hi. Saw you at the mall.* But I don't. Fifteen minutes and half a soda later, I'm still waiting for Nic. I check out the store, but he's not there.

Where are you?

Jamba Juice.

I find him sitting at a table with three of the cheerleaders. I'm sure I know their names, but I'm so irritated with Nic I can't recall them.

"Here's your water," I say, smacking it down on the table.

One of the girls giggles. He turns in his seat and frowns at the soda in my hand.

"I'm leaving." I turn and drop my soda in a trash bin, then head toward the nearest exit. I am so done with this. Nic catches up with me just as I step through the automatic door.

"Wait, Robert. Wait-wait-wait," he says, grabbing my arm. "Would you just wait? Jesus, I drove, remember?"

"So I'll walk home. It's five miles. I'm sure I'll survive." I turn to go, but he tightens his grip.

"Why are you acting like this? You're upset about your dad—I get that—but you don't have to take it out on me."

"I'm not upset about my dad. It's you . . . and your stupid bottle of water . . . and your Sleeveless in December guy . . . and your *girls.*"

"Oh, now you're just being dramatic."

The absurdity of the statement makes me laugh.

"And what are you talking about, Sleeveless in December guy? Are you talking about that guy who passed us upstairs? Oh my God. I was just looking. You can be so jealous sometimes."

My laughter dies in my throat. "You don't know anything about me," I say, then pull my arm free.

But he latches back on to me, with both hands this time.

"Okay. I'm sorry. Come back in. I'll buy you another soda, and a pretzel if you want." He pouts and runs his hand up and down my arm like he did when we first started dating, when he wanted me to go somewhere I didn't want to go or wear something I didn't want to wear. I resist the urge to flinch. "You're my guy. It'll just be me and you the rest of the day. Okay? Just me and you. Nobody else. We'll go to the bookstore and you can browse all you want. I'll even buy you a book for Christmas."

"I don't want a book. I don't want a present."

"Then we'll just browse . . . together."

Later I find myself wishing he'd just let me go.

Andrew

I don't know who's sleepier when we get home, Kiki or me. I put on *The Lion King* and curl up with her on the couch. A strand of dark hair falls across her face. I brush it away with my fingers as she clutches the dog more tightly to her chest. I drift off thinking this is heaven, or the closest I'm likely to ever get to heaven. Something about that thought leaves a sad imprint on my heart.

Chapter 5

Robert

This is Dad's last Christmas. It's the elephant in the room. It's the reason Aunt Whitney has pulled out all the stops—piles of presents, fresh garland wrapped around the banister and over the doorways, holiday music piped throughout the house, evergreen candles, a fire in the fireplace, and an animated Santa rocking in a chair next to it. And pies. Lots of pies.

The day is a throwback to Dad's childhood, an annual ritual he has refused to let go of despite the awkward strain it puts on Mom and me.

Still, I have to admit, it's all very pretty, and the house smells great. But no one thought to help us get Dad there.

He doesn't travel well, or easily.

Getting him from the bed to the wheelchair was bad. Getting him through the front door and over the threshold with his oxygen tank was worse. I was still in their bedroom gathering up Dad's pills when I heard Mom cry out: "I'm doing the best I can."

When I got to the living room, Mom, flushed and on the verge of tears, had tilted the chair back and was digging in to ram him through the door and over the threshold with brute force. Aunt Whitney always pulled him through backward. Reason enough, I suppose, for Mom to take the more direct approach.

Shit. "Wait-wait-wait. Mom." I sprinted over. "You're going to pitch him to the concrete if you're not careful. There's a three-inch drop to the sidewalk."

She shot me a look that said, *Don't tempt me.*

I pulled the wheelchair back enough to get through the doorway, then grabbed the frame in front and lifted it. Together we got him through and down the drop to the sidewalk without incident. Dad winced when the wheels landed, but he didn't say anything. I thought that was wise.

At Aunt Whitney's, we did it all again in reverse.

"You're here," Olivia exclaims when we make our way into the living room. She's sitting on the floor, supervising the kids who are rummaging through gifts, trying to locate the ones with their names on them. She jumps up to help us get Dad from the chair to the couch next to my grandmother. I give Grandma a hug. She barely touches me as she hugs me back.

Grandma—a prim, expensively coifed Southern widow of a prominent physician and the quiet matriarch of the Westfall family—still lives in Louisiana. She's been generous with me through the years, but distant. I'm like one of her charities that she donates to. I wonder sometimes if that will change after Dad's gone, if she'll see me as the last link to her lost son. I wonder if she knows it'll be about eighteen years too late.

"The kids are dying to open their gifts," Aunt Olivia says. "But I told them they had to wait until you guys got here." She calls out to Aunt Whitney and my uncles to join us.

Every year I dread this part of Christmas day—the gift exchange. Mom put her foot down years ago about exchanging gifts with extended family. It was just too much—the shopping, the expense. She asked that they not purchase gifts for us either. At first I resented her for that. Why shouldn't they give us gifts? They can afford it.

I don't see it that way anymore.

We sit awkwardly, pretending to enjoy watching our pajama-clad relatives unwrap presents. It infuriates Mom that we are subjected to this year after year, but it never changes. Aunt Whitney refuses to let anyone open a gift until we are all together. And Dad has refused to allow anything or anyone—not his wife or his child—to get in the way of his childhood tradition. They've fought about it for as long as I can remember. Dad always wins.

Mom's jaw tightens when Aunt Olivia hands her a small envelope with a red bow on it. Once again, they have refused to respect her request. Mom opens the envelope. Inside is a hundred-dollar gift card to Chico's. She never shops in that store; apparently, she should. The card is signed by both of my aunts and my grandmother.

For me there's an emergency roadside kit and two tickets to the Iron Maiden concert at the Pavilion. Metal music is not really my thing, but I love the outdoor amphitheater, and at least it's not The Beach Boys or Chicago or Jimmy Buffett. It's that kind of venue. I actually like both gifts, but not nearly as much as the car stereo Mom gave me this morning. I have to install it myself, but I'm cool with that. I don't look at Mom as I thank everyone.

Dad doesn't open his own gifts. They are piled all around him on the couch. Aunt Whitney sits on the floor in front of him, opening them one by one, exclaiming over each like he's a two-year-old.

"Oh, wow, a saint's bracelet. This is beautiful." She moves her fingers from square to square as she indentifies the saints thereon and their heavenly assignments. I can feel Mom's smirk from across the room. When she's done with muster, Aunt Whitney says to my dad, "Here, let me put it on your arm."

Another gift. "Oh, look what Mom got you. This throw looks warm too." She tosses it over Dad's lap.

Grandma tucks it under his leg. "You've always loved owls," she says thoughtfully, "even when you were a little boy."

It's hard for me to imagine my dad as a little boy, or my grandmother as a doting mom.

There's a new LSU cap, which Aunt Whitney places on Dad's head. His face is slack on one side, and when he crooks a weak smile, the look is ghoulish. There's a marked increase in his sluggishness today, almost a catatonia. Whether it's the cancer or the morphine, I don't know. Probably both.

I can't watch anymore. I head up to the media room. The

cousins are playing Rock Band. I settle onto a couch in the back, behind the captain's chairs, and pull out my cell phone.

"Are you texting your boyfriend?" Franny asks with a knowing grin. She thinks my being gay is so romantic.

"Yeah," I say.

Andrew

The first text hits my in-box during Christmas dinner. It's just the three of us—Mom, Dad, and me—so we don't stand much on ceremony. We're eating in front of the television, our plates balanced on our laps, doing our traditional Christmas thing—watching *It's a Wonderful Life.*

I fish my phone out of my pocket just as James Stewart crashes his car into a tree during a snowstorm. I don't recognize the number. I view the text anyway.

Hey.

Hmph. I thumb in a reply. *Who is this?*

Robert.

I smile to myself. I'm surprised, but I'd be lying if I said I wasn't just a little pleased.

Robert! Merry Christmas, my friend.

Merry Christmas to you too.

You caught me right in the middle of turkey and a movie.

Oh. Sorry. What movie?

"It's a Wonderful Life." Have you had Christmas dinner already?

Just about to. I've never seen the movie. Any good?

The first 20 times, yes. Now, it's just kind of habit.

"Is that Maya?" Mom asks.

"No. It's a student of mine." When she doesn't respond, I look up at her. "His dad is dying of cancer. I think he's a little traumatized by the whole thing, poor kid."

"A boy?" she asks. I detect a hint of something in her voice, a slight disapproval, perhaps, but I dismiss it as a figment of my imagination. "Yeah. A senior. He's one of my AP Calculus kids."

I slip my phone back in my pocket and take a bite of stuffing, ignoring the vibration.

Are you with your family today?
Yeah. In Oklahoma.
Oklahoma? Really? Drive or fly?
Drove.
Is it cold there?
So cold the snowman out front is begging me to take him inside.
So cold Santa had to jumpstart Rudolph?
When I put on my coat to take out the trash, it wouldn't go.
So cold the local flasher had to describe himself to women?

I laugh out loud. I'm walking Shep for my dad. It's actually not that cold outside—I'm pretty sure the flashers are still doing a brisk business. I love walking around my old neighborhood. The houses are smaller than I remember, the trees bigger. But it kind of makes me feel like a kid again.

I flex my thumbs. It's been a while since I've carried on such an extensive conversation using the keyboard on my phone. And Robert is quick with the thumbs. My texts, on the other hand, always take a little longer to compose.

The aging springer spaniel sits patiently while I thumb out another response.

Ahahaha. So what did Santa bring you this Christmas?

The pause drags out, and I'm beginning to think he's grown bored or I've said something wrong when the next text comes in.

So what do you like about AfterElton? The articles, right? Ha, ha.

At first I'm confused. And then I get it. My Twitter account. *Shit.* But I can't help being a little flattered, too, that he's checked me out.

The articles. Absolutely!

My response sounds coy, but it's the truth. AfterElton isn't some kind of online Playboy for gay men, after all. It's more of a pop culture news site, but the articles, columns, and such have a gay focus. The site has nothing to do with Elton John, but the name does refer to the musician's public coming out, a milestone for gay men.

It doesn't surprise me that Robert knows about AfterElton. It does surprise me that he knows about me.

But I'm more concerned that he avoided my question.

Do you have brothers and sisters? he texts.

Nope. Just me. Are you hanging out with Nic over the holidays?

Ah. You know about Nic. IDK. Maybe. Two numbers that multiply together to equal 1,000,000 but contain no zeros?

Math games. I loop Shep's leash on my wrist and make a few calculations with my calculator app. *64 x 15625*

You're brilliant.

I don't know about that!

Shep gets a very long walk. I return him to the warmth of the house somewhat reluctantly.

"Your dad and I are going to drive around and look at some of the lights," Mom says as I unhook the leash from Shep's collar. "You want to come with us?"

"Would it be okay with you if I take a pass?"

"Only if you promise to take this cobbler out of the oven when it's done."

"Apple?"

"Of course."

"Wow. You drive a hard bargain, Mom."

She laughs and swats me on the butt.

Apple cobbler, huh? Sounds yummy.

Even better with vanilla ice cream. What's your favorite dessert?

Apple cobbler with vanilla ice cream.

I find myself wondering—is he flirting with me? *Liar. Are you home yet?*

Just got here. Another Christmas bites the dust.

The cynicism that seeps into his tone every now and then worries me. I have to keep reminding myself that this is a really tough time for him.

Do you want to talk about it?

Yes. No. I think my thumbs hurt too much to speak right now.

I smile. My thumbs hurt too. I'm in my room now, the room I grew up in, surrounded by all my pre-adult relics. I pack the pillows against my headboard and lean up against them. It's late, but I was hoping Robert might want to open up, and if he did, I wanted to be there for him. Before I can reply, though, he sends another text.

So sleepy. Too much tryptophan.

Go to bed, friend. Sweet dreams.

I set my phone on the bedside table and slip under the worn comforter. I think for a moment about Kiki, and wonder what her face looked like when she saw all the toys under the tree this morning. I wish I could have been there. I called earlier, but she was too excited to talk on the phone. I know Maya has taken lots of photos and videos. She's already sent me a couple. I can't wait to see the rest of them.

And then I find myself wondering about Robert's Christmas. I can tell from what he didn't say that it had been a difficult day. My heart goes out to him. He's such a great kid, a good-looking kid, and suddenly I find myself thinking about Robert in ways I shouldn't—the way his blond hair kicks up a little in the front, the wooden choker he wears around his neck sometimes, the way he fills out the seat of his jeans, the way the back hem of those jeans is always chewed up.

I struggle to push those images out of my mind. While he might be crushing on me, I have no business crushing on him. Still, if I'm being honest, I do feel a little giddy when I read his texts.

Chapter 6

Andrew

I wake up in the morning to a quick, but disturbing series of texts.

You make me wanna listen to music again. How do I get you alone? And it goes on. I close that text and read the next two. More of the same.

Robert, I'm a little uncomfortable here.

Ha, ha. Good morning, Mr. Mac. They're just song lyrics. I'm sorting the music on my iPod into playlists. You like music, right?

I scan back through the texts and see that they are just that. Song lyrics. Some I don't recognize, but most I do. Adam Lambert. Heart. The All-American Rejects. I feel like an idiot.

How's your dad today?

Okay, I guess. The hospice nurse is here. I think she's helping him shower.

And you?

I can still shower myself.

You know what I mean.

☺ I'm okay.

Robert

Nic does a drive-by the next day. I'm trying to install my new car stereo, and I doubt he would have stopped if I hadn't seen him. He parks his vintage Mustang on the street and saunters over, then stretches out on the driveway.

"Trying to make your granny car cooler," he says, looking at me over his sunglasses.

So much for sweet Nic. My skin prickles in irritation as I wedge myself between the steering wheel and the front seat. I slide the head unit back into the dash cavity, careful not to bunch up or pinch the wires in back.

Installing the stereo has proven to be a pain in the ass. The instructions read like they were written by monkeys. I've had to go back to my room each step of the way to search for YouTube videos to clarify something that, in my opinion, should have been spelled out clearly by the people who made the damn thing. I'm sweating despite the temperature in the forties.

I prick my thumb on a sharp piece of exposed metal. A bead of blood seeps from the wound. I stick my thumb in my mouth to stop the bleeding.

Nic is pattering on about his new Kindle, the Rude jeans he's on his way to buy at Hot Topic with his Christmas cash (jeans he calls *sexy* and *to die for*), and the hot new guy at the tanning salon. Despite his annoying running monologue, I finally manage to get the connections right and everything back in place. I just need to get the screws back in, reconnect the battery, and try it out.

"Is your dad going to have a big funeral?" Nic says out of the blue. "I read that in New Orleans they sometimes march down the street after a funeral and play 'When the Saints Go Marching In.' I think that would be really cool since he's from Louisiana. And, oh God, it would be so sad, you know. It makes me want to bawl just thinking about it."

I don't respond.

"I'm not going to be there. You know that, right?"

I scoff as I try to get the angle right on the first screw and wonder again what I ever saw in this pretty boy.

"He's not even dead yet," I say sullenly.

"You're getting kind of fat, you know," he says, without skipping a beat. "You really should lay off the sodas and the French fries."

I yank down the hem of my shirt. "I'm not getting fat."

"Um, yeah, you are. Just a little though. A little pudge around the middle. And really, you should consider tanning. You're stomach is as white as a marshmallow."

I wonder for a moment if there is anything Nic likes about me. I'm about ready to jab the end of the Phillips head screwdriver right through his trendy designer sunglasses when he says, "Oh my God! I almost forgot. You're never going to believe who's tripping the light fantastic on the dark side."

"Who?" I ask, ignoring the strange juxtaposition of his words and feeling like I already know the answer to my own question.

"Your calculus teacher. Mr. McNelis. Damn, he's hot. I wouldn't mind tapping that."

Ironic, I think, *since you can't even stand the idea of French kissing.* I steady my hand, my throbbing thumb notwithstanding, and secure the screw.

I mumble something about not believing everything you hear, and reconnect the battery. When I start the car, the new stereo booms. I turn down the volume, then kill the ignition and close the hood.

A little black-and-white Boston terrier has appeared out of nowhere and is sniffing at Nic's legs, his tail wagging furiously. Nic knees him—"Get out of here"—and the scrawny dog scuttles backward. He advances on Nic again, a little more cautiously. This time Nic smacks him hard in the nose and the pooch yelps.

"Why did you do that?" I ask angrily.

"He's getting dog snot all over my jeans."

I crouch down on the driveway and try to coax the dog to me, but his tail is between his legs now and he holds back, wary. His ribs show through his dull, short coat. "Come here, boy. I won't hurt you."

"He's probably got rabies," Nic says.

"He doesn't have rabies. He just looks like he's lost." I stand up and take a step toward the dog, but he turns tail and dashes off.

"That's one ugly dog," Nic says, then flexes his ankles and studies his Rockports.

"I gotta go in," I say, closing my car door. "I need to help Dad with a shower."

It's a lie, but Nic runs off like his hair is on fire.

Andrew

By the end of the day I've accumulated so many texts that my inbox reaches its limit and I have to delete some. I start with the oldest texts and delete a lot of them, but I don't delete Robert's. I pretend that I don't know why.

The next morning, another long string of texts. More lyrics. I recognize them for what they are this time, but these are darker.

Hello, teacher, tell me what's my lesson. We should never be afraid to die. Boys don't cry.

Wow. What's the title on this playlist?

Pity Party. Hey, you drive through Huntsville on the way home, right?

You are correct.

Can I meet you there? At SHSU? I want to tour the campus. It's not top tier, but I can commute if Mom needs me here after, you know.

Wow. I didn't expect this. I'm planning to head out in about an hour. But that would put me in Huntsville at about ten this evening. A little late for a tour of the campus even if it weren't a colossally bad idea.

I don't know, Robert. Not a good idea.

Why? I'd go with Mom, but this, um, doesn't seem like a good time.

I don't respond right away.

Mr. Mac, I've got to get out of here for a while. Seriously. You take classes there, right? You could show me around. If you don't, I'll go by myself. It's no big deal.

What about Nic?

He wouldn't be caught dead on the SHSU campus.

Why am I not surprised? *Your parents okay with this?*

Mom's totally cool. Don't think Dad cares much about anything anymore.

Against my better judgment, I plan to meet Robert at two o'clock the next afternoon. I don't tell him, but I drive home that day as planned and sleep in my own bed.

Robert

Dad looked bad Christmas Day. Turns out, that was the beginning of a rapid downhill spiral as the cancer spread exponentially throughout his brain. He can still speak, but it's only with a great deal of effort, and Aunt Whitney says soon he won't be able to do that either. He's weaker, and he's confused, but he does have a few hours of unexpected lucidity this evening.

"I've called Father Vincent," Aunt Whitney says gravely.

Mom pulls the fish sticks from the oven. Her back is to Aunt Whitney, but her silence speaks volumes.

"You know, Kathryn, I know you are not a spiritual person, and that makes me very sad for you. But my brother is. He needs to make his last confession and receive absolution."

That's an understatement.

Aunt Whitney shoots me a look, and I fear I might have spoken out loud. But then she rattles off a couple of things she wants me to find.

When I've collected the stuff she's asked for—a crucifix, a vial of holy water that she purchased for Dad years ago—I take it to her in the bedroom. She's dusting and straightening everything in the room. On the highboy are three lit candles. A white tablecloth covers the puzzle on the card table at the foot of the bed. And the windows are open. I can't help wondering if she's airing out the room for God or so the priest doesn't have to breathe in death.

When Father Vincent arrives, he ushers us out of the room. The confession, not surprisingly, doesn't take long, and I wonder what the eternal penalty is for omitting sins to God on your deathbed. We are welcomed back to witness communion, the anointing with oil, and the last blessing. Father Vincent finishes with, "and may the blessing of Almighty God, the Father, the Son, and the Holy Spirit, descend on you and remain with you always."

My aunts are weeping (it's the only word for what they're doing) as they mutter an amen.

Mom and I stand off to the side, interlopers in this little ritual. All of this stuff is supposed to prepare Dad for his passage through the portal of death into eternal life. I shouldn't feel this way, but I'd like to dispense with all this hocus pocus and just shove him through and slam the door.

After Father Vincent leaves, Aunt Whitney gets Dad out of bed and props him in an armchair she's muscled in from the living room. Aunt Olivia brings a bowl of homemade chicken soup on a tray and places it on Dad's lap. He struggles with the spoon, and I wonder if it's the last time he will ever feed himself. I'd prefer to make myself scarce, but Aunt Whitney charges me with changing the sheets on the bed while Dad is out of it.

And that's when Mom makes her move. I can't blame her. Dad's going to die, but we have to go on living. And Mom's practical because she's had to be. Her questions are gentle enough, and not extraordinarily difficult—"Wesley, I need to know where your will is, what life insurance policies you have, passwords."

"Not now," Aunt Whitney warns when Dad becomes agitated.

Mom ignores her and presses him for answers. I snap out a clean sheet and settle it over the mattress. There's a sudden movement from Dad, and I look up as the tray and the bowl clatter to the floor, leaving noodles and bits of chicken scattered all over the carpet. Before anyone can react, Dad throws his good arm out, his fist clenched, and knocks the lamp off the table next to him. Aunt Whitney tries to calm him down, but he's grunting and growling as if all speech has left him. He struggles to get out of the chair.

Mom looks at him coldly and leaves the room. Aunt Whitney catches up with her in the kitchen a few minutes later.

"What is wrong with you? My brother is dying. You are the most insensitive, selfish *bitch* I have ever known."

Mom glares at her, then grabs her keys off the counter and slams the door behind her.

Aunt Whitney turns on me. "Are you running away too?"

Chapter 7

Andrew

I drive back up to Huntsville the next afternoon and park in the main lot right across from the steps that rise between the English and the Fine Arts buildings. It's nice out—cool, but sunny—and I lean against my car, tip my head back, and soak up some of the sun.

I have to squint when Robert pulls up next to me fifteen minutes later. He's driving a late-model Camry, and my guess is it has more air bags than a kid's birthday balloon bouquet.

"Nice car," I say as he gets out.

"Thanks. It was a birthday present from my grandmother. Sweet sixteen."

I smile and nod. "So . . . where are you really?"

He smiles back, guiltily. "At Nic's."

"Aren't you afraid he'll call your house?"

"Nic doesn't call my house. You didn't just drive in, did you?"

I feel my cheeks redden. "Come on. Let's have a look around."

I don't know the Sam Houston campus well at all. In the fall and spring, my graduate classes are online (although I'm not taking a class this spring; I plan to be busy with the admin training program). And when I do come up for graduate classes in the summer, I park outside the education building, go to my classroom, and straight back to my car an hour or two later. I had to look at a map of the campus just to come up with an easy-to-find place to meet.

So we explore together.

The campus is largely vacant. We see perhaps two or three people as we make our way from one end to the other. The SHSU campus is not unlike others that I've been on—old buildings, new buildings, a memorial garden here and there, a student center, multistory dorms. The hills are perhaps its most distinguishing feature, and the muscles in my thighs are burning by the time we circle back to the fountain in the heart of the campus.

There's a north breeze, and we have to stand upwind to avoid getting showered. The tile bottom glitters with coins.

Robert fishes in his pocket for some pennies and hands me one. He shrugs and grins at me. "Make a wish."

"Okay." I squeeze my eyes shut and make a wish, then toss the coin in. He smiles and does the same.

"So what did you wish?" I ask.

"Can't tell you or it won't come true."

I laugh and start to turn away.

"I wished that my dad would be dead when I get home."

That stops me. I search his eyes in the bright sunlight.

"What the L-M-N-O-P, huh?" he says, and smiles, but it's a pained look.

"Yeah. What the L-M-N-O-P? You don't mean that," I say, but I suspect he does.

He shrugs. "I cannot tell a lie." He kicks lightly at the bricks around the fountain with the toe of his athletic shoe, then grimaces, and I see his eyes are glistening. "I just want it all to be over, you know. The people always in our house, the smell, the resentment. Yesterday a priest came and gave my dad last rites."

We sit down on a bench a few feet away from the fountain. One thing I've learned working with kids is this: When they want to talk, you shut up. I twist on the bench to face him and prop my head on my fist. He watches a mockingbird land in the mist from the fountain, flutter its wings some, and then fly away.

"I know he's my dad and all," he says finally, "but I feel like he's just this thing that sucks all the oxygen out of the room. Like the world has stopped spinning and it can't start again until he's gone." He folds his arms across his chest like he's cold and tells me about the chicken soup.

"I just wanted to rip that oxygen tube away from his face and replace it with a pillow and just hold it down, you know. You would think he'd want to make sure that I was going to be okay, that his affairs were in order so we wouldn't have to untangle everything after he died. But all he can think about is himself. It's as if I don't even matter. And they talk about him like he's such a hero. I don't understand any of it. And I can't stand the way everyone acts like my mom is some bad person. She's not."

I rest my hand on the back of his neck. He slips into silence, as if he can't handle any more naked honesty today.

"You hungry?" I ask after a while. "I know a little place. Great Mexican food. I'm buying."

Robert

We leave my car in the lot and he takes me a few blocks down the street to Jack in the Box. I have my first good laugh of the day.

We take our tacos, onion rings, and drinks to a table next to the window.

"So," I say, tipping a wrapper down and allowing the taco to slip out a couple of inches. "What do you like about being a teacher?"

"Hmm. That's a pretty complicated question. Definitely not the pay. Definitely *not* the adoration of hundreds of teenagers. How about summers off and pizza or Chick-fil-A five days a week, thirty-six weeks a year."

"Well, at least you're honest." He smiles at me and I feel myself go a little gooey inside. "But you don't buy school lunch," I remind him.

"Oh, yeah. How do you know that?"

"Because you have a five-quart cooler sitting on the floor next to your desk every day."

"Five quarts, huh? That's a little anal, don't you think?"

I shrug, a little embarrassed. "The real question is"—I spin an onion ring on my finger—"what's in it?"

"The real question?"

"There is *some* speculation."

"About what's in my cooler? Really? So what does conventional wisdom say?"

"It's pretty much an even split between peanut butter and jelly and some kind of tofu crap. I peg you for a peanut butter and jelly guy."

"Jif. Creamy. And jam, not jelly. Peanut butter on one slice of whole wheat, jam on the other. Eaten whole."

"Who's anal now, Mr. Mac?"

He grins. "Can I ask you a favor? Can you stop calling me Mr. Mac? It sounds like you're talking to my grandfather. And, anyway, my last name is *Mick*-Nelis, not *Mac*-Nelis, like *Mick*-Donald's."

"It's not *Mick*-Donald's."

"Sure it is. That's how you pronounce the M-C."

"Oh, really? Then why don't they serve Big Micks instead of Big Macs?"

He looks at me a moment, then laughs. "Okay, you got me there. How about we just dispense with the whole issue and you call me Andrew."

Andrew? "What happened to Drew? It's, uh, on the school Web site."

"Okay, then call me Drew."

"No. I think I'll call you Andrew." The name feels a little foreign on my tongue, but in a good way; it's going to take some getting used to.

"So, are you really considering Sam Houston?" he asks me.

"No."

His eyebrows shoot up at my admission. I don't give him a chance to follow up. "I'm going to LSU. Premed, then medical school."

"Wow. That's a big deal." When I scoff, he follows up with, "You don't seem too happy about that."

I shrug again. "It was kind of decided for me. My grandfather left me a trust when he died. I'm the last of the Westfalls. He expected me to carry on the tradition. It's been understood that I would become a doctor since I was born."

"Is that what you want?"

"Does it matter?"

"I think so."

"No premed, no medical school, no trust. No trust, no funds for college."

Andrew leans back in his chair and studies me. I have a feeling I'm about to get a lecture, so I change the subject. "You wear an OU T-shirt on college day. Is that where you went?"

"Yep, I'm a Sooner. The pride of Oklahoma." He scoops up the trash from the table and pushes it through the swinging door of the receptacle a few feet away, then sits back down. I glance out the window at the fading light. I don't want to leave.

"Do you think I'm a bad person?" I ask.

He pushes his drink to the side and plants his elbows on the table, then rests his chin on his fists. "No. Definitely, emphatically, unequivocally no."

"You seem a little unsure."

He smiles. "Do *you* think you're a bad person?"

"Sometimes."

He doesn't say anything further. He's in listening mode and seems in no hurry to leave. So I start talking, trying to explain things I barely understand myself.

"Everything feels like it's more than I can handle, you know? I keep thinking, you can't hate someone who's dying, right? Especially your own dad. But I can't *not* feel this way. I want to close this chapter in my life and move on; I want him to die, but I'm so afraid that makes me some kind of monster."

"Robert," he says, reaching across the table and laying his hand on mine. His fingers curl around the edge of my hand and dig into my palm. "I don't know your dad, and I don't know what's happened in the past, but I do feel like I know you. You are not a monster. I suspect that what you feel or don't feel toward your dad has more to do with self-defense than it does any kind of pathology."

I look at his hand gripping mine, and I desperately want to turn my hand over and feel our palms meet, our fingers lace together. I force my hand to remain where it is. "He doesn't love me," I say, lifting my eyes to meet his.

"Are you sure about that?"

"He resents me. Sometimes I think it's because I have the opportunity to become what he couldn't. I don't know. The crazy thing is, he didn't want to be a doctor any more than I do. But in the Westfall family, if you're not a doctor, you're nothing. They blame my mom for getting pregnant, which is just stupid. She quit school—another Westfall sin—got a job, and supported us while dad played at being a student. The seizures started during his final year of med school, and he just never finished. He's never even held a job. But do you know that his sisters still tell people he's a doctor when they talk about him or introduce him. That status is everything to them; it's everything to him. And I'm . . . nothing."

He retrieves his hand and props his chin on his fist again and studies me. My hand feels naked, and an ache blossoms in my chest. A silence grows between us, like he's working out some problem in his head, and I'm waiting for the answer. Then he asks, "Do you know what chaos theory is?"

"Yeah. The butterfly effect."

"The math of messes," he says. "Tiny differences in starting conditions—the beat of a butterfly's wings, a temperature differential of half a degree, a bottle withheld a few beats too long, an ear infection that went undetected for a day or more—any little difference can lead to a totally different outcome later on. The entire *Back to the Future* movie trilogy was based on that very concept." He shrugs. "Who knows what little things made your dad the way he is. Maybe what he took from his experiences left him insecure and unable to develop into an independent, fully functioning adult and a loving father. I don't know.

"But the point is, you don't know either. And you probably never will. Don't beat yourself up for feelings you can't help because of the dad he couldn't be."

* * *

He offers to follow me home a little while later, with a very teacher-like admonishment: "No texting on the road, okay?"

But I'm not really thinking of him as a teacher anymore. I'm thinking of him as a friend.

Andrew

Tell a stranger that they're beautiful.
Stop listening to Adam Lambert, my friend, or you will go blind.
Ha, ha. Good catch. Hey, Andrew, thanks. For meeting me today, for listening.
It was my pleasure.

I feel a warmth inside as I push Send. There is a great deal of satisfaction in knowing that you've taught your students well, that they've mastered the objectives set forth in the state standards, but that's not what keeps teachers coming back to the classroom.

The pull is something a little less quantitative and a little more qualitative. It's the knowledge that you've really touched someone, the knowledge that you've made a difference. It makes all that other stuff worth it—the grading on weekends when you'd rather be hanging out with your family, the pay that (on average) falls some twenty-five thousand dollars short of the income needed to meet basic middle-class needs.

I picture Robert looking into the fountain, making a confession no kid should have to make. I've seen that kind of raw honesty only once before. It was when Maya told me she couldn't go on pretending to be husband and wife anymore. When she told me what it did to her every night when I retired to my room and closed the door. We thought we could make it work, for the sake of Kiki. But we couldn't. And I'd had no idea what it was doing to my best friend and the mother of my little girl. I moved out the next day and she started trying to build a life without me.

I don't know if all my talk about chaos theory really made a difference with Robert. It seemed intuitive at the time; now, I'm not so sure. Maybe he just needed me to be there, to allow him to get what he needed to off his chest, to let him know he didn't have to carry that burden around all by himself.

MAC-Donald's. Big MAC.

Don't rub it in, smartass.

Ouch! Your language, my eyes!

I don't give a damn what you think.

Nice. Eminem, right?

Chapter 8

Andrew

"Damn. You look great."

It's Monday, a week after we returned from break. I look up and see Robert standing in my doorway and screw up my face. "This old thing?" I say, tugging at the lapel on my jacket. "I feel like I'm trapped in a scene from *Wall Street*."

Robert's holding a tray from the cafeteria with two slices of pizza and a Powerade balanced on top.

"Come on in. Not eating in the cafeteria today?" I loosen the knot on my tie a bit.

"Can I have lunch with you?"

"Sure." I clear off a space on the corner of my desk, and he sets his tray there.

"Don't you teacher types have a lounge or somewhere to eat lunch?"

I smile in response. I'm actually glad Robert has stopped by. It's hard to really gauge how he's doing in class. And in his texts, even when he's being funny, I sometimes sense a subtext there, something darker. But he looks good today, relaxed.

"So, what's with the suit?"

"I'm applying to the administrator training program. I had an interview with the superintendent's council this morning."

"Aah. That explains why you weren't here when I stopped by earlier. So, what's for lunch?"

He stopped by earlier? I process that as I tear off a corner of my sandwich and hand it to him.

"Wow, PBJ. I thought you were just kidding." He looks at it with mock disgust, then pops it into his mouth. "Do you always eat at your desk?" he asks as he cracks open the Powerade.

"It's half an hour of grading that I don't have to do at home."

"How did I do on Friday's review quiz?" he asks, stretching across my desk to get a look at my computer screen.

"Uh, uh, uh," I say, swiveling the screen away from him. "You'll just have to wait until sixth period like all the rest of the goons."

He pulls an ankle across his knee and I notice he's wearing black athletic shoes with black no-show socks. The black contrasts nicely with his bare ankles.

"I saw your boyfriend a few minutes ago."

"Nic?"

"Whore-Hay."

"Aaaah." He laughs. "You know about that too."

"This place is like a petri dish of gossip, my friend. Keep that in mind. So how long have you two been dating?"

It's clear Robert doesn't want to talk about Nic when he skips backward over that question to the other comment. "Do teachers really gossip?"

I just avoid squirting water out of my nose. *Do teachers gossip?* That's the understatement of the year.

"Sorry about hitting you with that AfterElton thing. I just thought you should know. And just so you don't get the wrong idea," he continues quickly, "you've kind of been trending since one of the girls found you on Twitter."

Trending. Great. "So, what you're telling me is you're not some kind of crazed stalker kid?"

He laughs. "Me? No."

I fight to keep the disappointment from my face.

"Anyway," he goes on, "I guess everybody kind of knows which department you shop in."

That stops me. "Not everybody," I say, not entirely certain that this is true.

At least, I hope it's not true. Not that it's a big deal, but my personal life is mine. I prefer to keep it that way. Over-sharing is a definite negative for teachers. We've already gotten the spiel this year on social networking and being above reproach. I'm very careful that my Facebook and Twitter posts are as bland as a butter sandwich.

It hadn't occurred to me, though, that who or what I follow might rip open my little bag of secrets and spill the contents for all to gawk at.

I vow to do a little editing on my accounts tonight.

"It's no big deal," Robert says. He sets his half-eaten slice of pizza on his tray and wipes his hands on his jeans. "But I have to warn you." He flicks his eyebrows. "Some of the girls are convinced they can change you if they can just get you in a backseat somewhere for twenty minutes."

I feel a little sick. "Will you do me a favor? When you hear that stuff, you think you could redirect the conversation? You know, without mentioning..." *Shit.* The last thing I need is some rumor that I'm a teenage girl fantasy. "I just don't want anyone thinking about me in that context."

I can see he gets it when his eyes meet mine. "Sure. And just so you know, I haven't told anyone that I...that we...well, I just haven't. And I won't."

I study him for a moment and think that we are the very definition of complicity. *No, that is not true,* I chide myself. Complicity suggests that what we are doing is wrong. That's ridiculous. He looks to me for support. And I'm doing what we teachers do—I'm meeting one of my students where he is. That's all.

"So, back to Nic. Are you two, uh...?"

"Are we having sex?" he finishes for me.

I was going to say *exclusive.* But I don't correct him.

"It's okay, Mr. Mick. You can say the word."

I smile at his use of Mick. I noticed that he didn't call me Andrew. It's school. He's a smart kid. I'm glad I don't have to insist on that distinction.

"No. Definitely, emphatically, unequivocally no," he says, lobbing my words back at me. "He's not really my type, you know."

In fact, I do know.

"I've been thinking," he continues. "Maybe it's time we break up."

"Do me another favor," I say before I can stop myself. "Don't break up."

He doesn't seem surprised that I asked.

We finish lunch on safer topics—music mostly, the college application process, the new stereo he installed in his car over Christmas break, the admin training program. He doesn't mention his dad, and I don't ask. I know he'll talk when he needs to.

I'm disappointed when the bell rings.

"I'll see you sixth," Robert says as he heads for the door.

"Oh, by the way," I say, "ninety-eight."

He turns back. "Ninety-eight?"

"Your quiz. You made a ninety-eight. You missed a sign." I wink and he flashes me a smile, then tosses his tray in the trashcan at the door. He starts out, then stops and turns back.

"I just want to say thank you again for meeting me in Huntsville. It meant a lot to me to have someone to talk to. Someone who wouldn't judge me."

"You can talk to me anytime, Robert."

Chapter 9

Robert

The speakers crackle a little when I crank up the volume, and I know I've got a bad connection somewhere. It seems I have a lot of bad connections lately.

Nic, for one. I think about what Mr. Mac (Andrew—the name still feels a little odd on my tongue) said. *Don't break up.* What he's asking is tough, though I understand why he asked, I think.

The thought of breaking up with Nic is not a new thought. I've just been too lazy to do it. Actually, now that I think about it, that's not true either. A boyfriend gives me a reason to get out of the house. It gives me someone to meet for a movie or a burger, if said boyfriend isn't already booked up with his girls. It means someone to hang out at the pool with during the summer and a date to the homecoming dance in the fall.

I don't know why I didn't break up with him that day after Christmas. He'd been such a jerk. I think about calling Luke when I get home. It's been almost a year since we "dated," and I miss having someone like that to unload on. But it's not really Luke that I want to talk to.

Do you think I'm fat?

LOL. Who told you that?

Nic. He also says I look like a marshmallow.

I love marshmallows! Especially sandwiched between two graham crackers with a bit of chocolate. Yum.

I'm still trying to think how to respond to that text when a second one comes in: *Um, strike that last text. You are not fat.*

I smile down at my phone. I do believe that Andrew has embarrassed himself. I like that about him. In fact, there's not much about Andrew McNelis that I don't like. No, that's not quite right. There is *nothing* about Andrew McNelis that I don't like. Nothing at all.

Andrew

I'd like to break that little cheerleader's neck. It wouldn't take much force either; he's a scrawny, sassy little twerp. And the *nerve.* Robert's worth ten of that pompous little queen.

Maybe I shouldn't have asked Robert to keep dating him, but I can't help being a little nervous that there's too much of me out there. And from the way Robert's talked, their dating can hardly be described as *dating,* so maybe that's not so bad.

I reply to his text, and even as my thumb is hitting Send, I see the innuendo in my words and fire off a follow-up. I can feel the heat in my face. *You, teacher. You, adult,* I remind myself.

Yum? God.

I set my phone on the table next to me and start with my Twitter account since that seems to be ground zero. I'm not worried about my tweets, but I scan over a few pages just to be sure. Most of them are links to news articles and opinion pieces I've read in the *Huffington Post* or the *Daily Beast.* I can't help being a little political, but the links indicate a liberal bent that's not that unusual among younger teachers, even in this area. I scan through my list of followers and those I follow and block and unfollow anyone or any organization that might suggest to anyone that I'm a pervert in any way. I'm not.

When I'm confident that I am *above reproach,* I turn to my Facebook page.

BTW, you owe me 2 points.

???

My quiz. The sign. Not wrong. A sliver of wood fiber in the paper made the – look like a +. Can bring back tomorrow for you to check.

No need. Won't be the first time a piece of wood—

Check that. Damn, why does everything read like a sex joke now? I backspace over the last sentence and write: *The 2 pts are yours, plus 2 more for my sloppy grading.* I consider tossing in an extra two points for my Freudian-like slips.

Facebook. I don't post much, but I do find it a convenient way to share photos of Kiki with my mom and dad and to keep up with Kiki when she's with Maya.

Originally my friends consisted of old college buddies and my family, but in a moment or two of weakness, or perhaps guilt, I've accepted friend requests from colleagues. It's kind of awkward to see those friend requests just sitting there. You know the person on the other end is wondering why you haven't accepted. So over the year and a half I've been teaching, plenty of non-friends have made their way onto my Friends list.

I'm regretting that right now, although I have nothing whatsoever to hide. Still, I'd just prefer *not* to be on anyone's radar. I scan through the list. Among my old college friends is Jeremy. I notice he has a new profile picture up. He's got his arm casually slung over his partner's shoulder. Cute couple.

The way I see it, I have two choices—unfriend my colleagues or unfriend my friends. I choose to avoid the awkward questions in the teachers' lounge when someone discovers I'm no longer on their Friends list. My old college friends will understand. Actually, I doubt they'll even notice. We don't really keep up with each other. I hit the Unfriend button a few times and vow to start sharing photos with Maya and my parents via e-mail.

On a whim, I search Robert's name on Facebook. I find quite a few Robert Westfalls, but none who are high school students or who live in this area. *Good for you, Robert.* And then just for the heck of it I click on the Pages tab.

Well, well, well. A Robert Westfall fan page. I click on the link and have a look. A quick scan of the posts—the most recent just two days ago—tells me this is a fan club of three, all boys. Their profile photos scream freshmen; their comments scream band kids. I hit the Older Posts button and start at the beginning.

Erick Wasserman OMG! Did you see that flip? I almost peed my uniform.

Caleb Smith Me too. Damn he's hot.

Zach Townley He can run that sword thru me anytime.

Caleb Smith Ha, ha. Me too. He sat in front of me on the bus last night. I almost licked his neck.

Erick Wasserman Down, gurl. I got dibs on him.

I pick up my phone.
Are you aware you have a Facebook fan page?
No, I don't.
Yeah. You do. I'm looking at it right now.
Hold on.
You'll need to sign up for an account, then search your name and click on the Pages tab at left.
Too late, I realize I just showed him my hand. Maybe he won't notice.

While I wait for Robert to join the twenty-first century, I have a peek at the photos. Most look like they were taken at football games. And they're professionally done. The little stalkers must have bought them from one of those photography companies that photograph school events, then post the photos online for parents to purchase. Robert is in every one of these—a few in his band uniform, but most in costume. I can't tell what role he played this year, but the photos depict him all in black, his face painted in stripes and swirls. In a couple of photos he's carrying a sword.

Ah, and there's the flip. It's a still shot, caught mid–back hand-spring from a black podium on the field.

There's also a video. I click that too. He and another kid are standing on a gazebo stage that looks very much like the one at Northshore Park. They're doing some kind of impromptu rap, it seems. A rap of insults. A contest, maybe, the way they alternate back and forth and the way the kids below the stage groan and laugh at the end of some lines. I can't make out all the words. But I can hear the boy holding the camera loud and clear: "Come on, baby. Give it to us!"

Those kids are in my band! I'm going to kill them.
Aaah. Don't be mad. It's kinda sweet. You should be flattered.
Not flattered. Mad.
LOL.
Just wait until I see those little pervs tomorrow.
Don't be so hard on them. It's not their fault you're a stud!
Stud, riiight. So how did you find this anyway?
Just stumbled across it.

I'm still chuckling when I open my online grade book via the district's Web portal and give Robert his four points.

Chapter 10

Robert

I don't kill them. I want to kill them, and they're lucky that we don't have band the same period, but I don't seek them out.

At lunch Andrew pulls up the fan page again and reads some of the comments out loud. He laughs so hard that tears stream down his cheeks. And then in sixth-period Calculus, he has to leave the room for a minute when he gets the giggles right in the middle of some practice problems. There's a bunch of tittering in the classroom as my classmates speculate on what's so funny all of a sudden.

He just stumbled across it, I think as I head home later. Right. I didn't have to play around on Facebook long last night to know he totally searched my name. Somehow, that kind of makes up for the humiliation of having a fan page in the first place.

Aunt Whitney's and Aunt Olivia's SUVs are both parked in the driveway, so I park on the street. I feel a little spark of hope in my chest that maybe while I was at school, Dad checked out. What would Andrew say about that?

Mom shoves a tray of chicken tenders and Tater Tots in my hands when I come through the garage door. "Take these to your cousins, please. They're in your room."

"Why are they in my room?"

"Because I had nowhere else to put them," she says sharply. She looks frazzled and pissed.

"Where are Aunt Whitney and Aunt Olivia?"

"Holding court. Where else?" She dumps a pan in the sink and turns on the water, squirts too much soap in, then viciously starts scrubbing.

My room is dark and stuffy, the way it gets when there are too many bodies in there. One of my cousins—Franny probably—has found an old GameCube in my closet and the twins are sitting on the floor playing Super Smash Bros. Melee. Franny is at my computer, and Noah and Aunt Whitney's two kids—Jude, five, and Brian, eight—are doing God knows what on my bed. I flip on the lights. And that's when I see it—a black line circumscribing my room, cutting across framed certificates, the photos on my bulletin board, my closet doors, my band hoodie that's hanging from a doorknob, my bookshelf, my books.

I drop the food on my desk and storm back to the kitchen.

"They Sharpied my room!"

"What?" Mom says. She turns off the water.

"One of the kids took a Sharpie and ran it all around my room."

I'm showing Mom the damage when Aunt Olivia appears in the doorway behind us. "Oh my goodness," she says.

One of the four-year-old twins looks up guiltily. "I didn't do it."

"You little—"

"Robert," Aunt Olivia says sharply. "Mark would never do that. None of my kids would. I've raised them better than that. And watch your mouth."

I stare at her like she's lost her mind. If not them, then who? Perhaps she's suggesting I did it myself, in my goddamn sleep?

Mom takes my hoodie from the doorknob. "I think I have some Ink-Out that might get this out, or at least fade it." Her voice is tight, and it occurs to me at that moment that she is just as angry as I am, perhaps more angry. And then the smell hits me.

"Did one of you pee in here?"

The other twin, Matthew, looks up at me with these big pathetic eyes. "I had to go potty?"

"Where?" I demand.

Sharpie kid—perhaps happy to have the spotlight off him—points to the corner behind my papasan. I turn on Matthew. "Why didn't you go to the bathroom?"

"I did," he says, big tears welling up in his eyes. "Right *there*."

"Don't yell at him," Aunt Olivia says harshly, picking up a Sharpie from the floor along with a half-eaten Ding Dong. "He's a little kid. And as I recall, you were still wetting the bed at twelve."

I am speechless.

"Robert," my mom says quietly. She grabs my arm, but I turn and go, fumbling for my keys as I slam the garage door behind me.

The doctor told my mom it was nothing to worry about.

But it was humiliating. I didn't do sleepovers. I didn't go to summer camps.

Every time Mom had to wash my sheets, she'd try to reassure me that I would grow out of it. I had a hard time believing her, but she'd have those sheets washed, dried, and back on the bed, smelling mountain fresh so fast that I didn't have much time to dwell on it.

Dad never said anything.

Then one evening my computer wouldn't boot up. I had some research to do, and Mom told me to use Dad's. He was sleeping in anticipation of whatever it was he did all night long. He was nocturnal even then.

I was just about to log Dad out of his e-mail account and log me in just for a quick check when it struck me that there were no e-mails in his in-box. None in his sent box either. He e-mailed all the time, and everybody had e-mails lying around in their boxes. And then I checked Trash. There were pages of e-mails to Aunt Olivia mostly, and some to Aunt Whitney and Grandma.

Out of curiosity, and with a sense of dread, I opened the first e-mail. He'd written it to Aunt Olivia just that night.

> *Whitney thinks he needs to see a psychiatrist, too, or maybe a psychologist at least, but Kathryn's dug in. She refuses to take him. It pisses me off that she won't listen to you guys. You're doctors, for Christ's sake. I'm*

starting to agree with Whitney—she's a lousy mother.
I'd drive him myself if I could. I mean, he's twelve
years old and still pissing his bed. I can hardly stand to
be around him. His room stinks. He stinks. I can't help
it. My own son disgusts me. I wish he was more like
your kid, Liv. And then all that hip-hop dancing, or
whatever it is he's doing in his room. I swear
sometimes I think he's not mine.

My ears hear only screams.
I don't know that one.
I got ice in my veins, blood in my eyes.
Lil Wayne, right?

Chapter 11

Andrew

"You're welcome here anytime, Robert."

"You sure you don't mind?" he asks.

He looks tired, defeated. I'm a little tired myself. I had Kiki last night. She couldn't sleep and ended up on the futon with me. When she finally did fall asleep, it was crossways with her little feet dug into my side. Every time I drifted off, she'd wake me up again with a kick to my ribs.

I reassure Robert with a smile. "I'm pretty sure I don't mind. I didn't mind yesterday, or Tuesday, or Monday, and I won't mind tomorrow. But I do have to get these plans written for next week. They're due at the end of the day. So if you don't mind watching me work, then . . ."

I gesture to the chair and he sits.

He's unusually quiet, I notice, and I decide the plans can wait a few minutes. "You didn't turn your homework in yesterday."

"Yeah, I know. Sorry."

He doesn't offer any more.

"Did you do last night's homework?"

"Some."

"Robert, is there something you want to talk about? I hope you know by now I'm a pretty good listener."

He shakes his head. "Can I finish my homework in here?"

"Sure." I glance at the time on my computer screen. "You've got about twenty-two minutes before the next bell."

He moves his tray to a desk, then takes a calculus book from the class set on a shelf. I'm left to wonder what's going on.

"Holy shit!" Jen says from the doorway. "You're not going to believe what just happened!"

She's hugging the door frame and leaning into my classroom. I tilt my head toward Robert.

She mouths an *oops* and then gives me a *come here* gesture. I set my plans aside and, with a brief glance at Robert—he doesn't look up—meet her in the hallway.

She talks in low, excited little bursts. "Oh my God. Philip and Liz just totally got busted! Some parents called to complain. Apparently the kids were noticing. It's like this huge scandal. Mr. Redmon called them in. Philip just got reassigned to a middle school. And Liz is outta here at the end of the year. Everybody, *every*body is talking about it."

She barely pauses for a breath when her face switches from conspiratorial to confused, and she says, "Hey, does that kid eat lunch in here every day?" She hooks her thumb toward the open door.

"That's Robert Westfall."

"I know who he is. Twinkle toes. Why's he been hanging out with you? Got a crush on teacher?"

"Yeah, right." I feel heat creep up my neck. "He's losing his dad. Cancer."

"Oh. I feel small." Jen looks contrite for about two beats, and then she brightens. "Hey, if you ever get sick of playing nanny, send him over to me. He can cry on my shoulder while he eats his burrito." She flashes me a wicked grin.

Robert doesn't eat burritos. I don't say it, but I think it.

Robert is concentrating on his work when I reenter the classroom. I barely give another thought to Philip and Liz. What they do, who they sleep with, that's their business. Carrying on in front of students is pretty stupid, though.

We finish lunch and our work in companionable silence.

Robert

Mr. Gorman is weaving his way through the rush of kids in the math hallway Friday just before sixth period. He pulls up in front of me and stops me with a clap on the shoulder. "You're coming to the dance tonight, right?"

"Um, yeah, I think so."

"Good. Hey, we can use a few more chaperones. Let me know if you think of anybody?"

"I can ask my mom?" I offer.

"Your mom's a sweetheart, but she's got enough on her plate right now."

I see Mr. Mac step out of his room a few paces away. He's wearing a T-shirt that reads

I ACCIDENTALLY

DIVIDED BY ZERO

AND MY PAPER

BURST INTO

FLAMES

"Maybe Mr. McNelis can chaperone."

"Chaperone what?" he says, joining our twosome.

"Andrew, right?" Mr. Gorman says, extending his hand.

"Right. Um, Mr. Gorman, band?"

"Richard. It's our annual spring semester kick-off band dance. Great music, great kids, and all the homemade cookies and chips you can choke down. Interested?"

I look back to Andrew and will him to say *Yes.*

"Sure. When?"

"Tonight. Six thirty? We wrap up at nine. A lot of our kids are new drivers; we don't like to keep them out late, you know."

"Okay. I'll be there."

"All right," Mr. Gorman says. He claps me on the shoulder again as he joins the fray.

Mr. Mac gestures to the open doorway, and I head into class. "Band dance, huh?" he says quietly as I slip past him, a note of amusement in his voice.

Chapter 12

Andrew

As it turns out, more parents than expected turn up to chaperone. Richard tells me I'm off the hook but welcome to hang around for the fun. I choose to accept his offer.

Here's what I expect:

1. Loud music—rap, hip-hop, pop, alternative, dance, rock. ✓

2. Lots of flirting and some covert necking in the shadows. ✓

3. Line dances, a conga line, dance circles. ✓

4. The RW fan club ogling in the wings. ✓

Here's what I don't expect—Robert, dancing like Usher and Justin Bieber rolled into one with a little Shakira thrown in for flavor. I'm, frankly, a little stunned.

I try not to be one of the oglers, but when he takes the center of the dance circle and goes *low low low low, low low low low* to the Flo Rida song, I can't help watching and thinking, *Damn, that kid's got some strong thighs.*

"He's good, huh?" Richard shouts over my shoulder.

"Really good."

"I swear every joint in that kid's body is a double. You know he was voted homecoming king, right?"

"Yeah, I heard that somewhere."

"Well, there you go. He had the band vote hands down, and that's a block of kids that can sway any election." He laughs. "I'm really glad to see him here tonight. He's been kind of withdrawn the last couple of months, and, well, I've been worried about him."

"Yeah. Same here. Does he talk to you about what's going on?"

"He doesn't talk about his home life much. I think he's more concerned with disappointing me, if you can believe that. He never misses a rehearsal, never complains. I didn't even know his dad was sick until I got that e-mail. In fact, I wasn't even sure he had a dad; I've never seen him. I don't think he came to games or concerts. Makes sense now that I know about the cancer. I just never asked. I've got new twins at home, so I've been a little distracted." He pulls out his phone and proudly shows me a photo of two tiny babies. I acknowledge the passion and trials of new fatherhood. He takes another long look at the twins and puts his phone away, then shrugs. "I assumed Robert's dad was out of the picture," he says a little too loudly as "Low" fades out and "Cupid Shuffle" fades in. "Not unusual," he continues. "His mom's a rock though. They'll get through this."

"Come on, Mr. Gorman!" a pigtailed girl shouts, grabbing his arm. He tosses me a smile over his shoulder and joins the line dance. I wander over to the food table and get a cookie.

I'm enjoying watching Richard dance with the kids. It's always the same with older guys—the hunched shoulders that carry all the movement, the bent elbows and the fists that follow the shoulders. He's only in his thirties, I'm guessing, but hip-hop he is not. He's having fun though, and the kids clearly love him for trying.

I notice the RW fan club in the line behind Robert. When the dance turns him in their direction, he seems not to notice. I realize I'm marking out the song with my body, even though my feet stay firmly planted on the floor—*To the left, to the left, to the left, to the left.*

After just one line dance, Richard begs off and allows himself to be sucked in by a group of moms manning the door prize table. Keeping one eye on the dance floor, I tour the band hall and take in this corner of Robert's world.

What strikes me is how the kids have made this space their own, and how the band directors have let them. It's a mess. In one corner I find an artificial Christmas tree still decorated with different-colored Post-its on which kids have written Dear Santa notes. There are requests for ponies and sophomoric stuff like this one:

Dear Santa, Please bring me some clam shell boobs like the Little Mermaid has.

And this one:

Dear Santa, I'd like a unicorn, and a rainbow, and the color purple. But don't leave them under the tree or Luke will wear my rainbow, eat my purple, and assault my unicorn. He's like that.

I look, but I don't find one from Robert. I guess wishing your Dad would die is uncool, even for these goofballs.

I'm standing near the Igloos sometime later when Robert takes a break. He's sweaty and flushed as he reaches into one of the coolers and grabs a soda.

"Hey, Mr. Mac," he says, popping the tab on the can. He takes a long drink. "You don't dance?"

"I dance."

He grins and waves at someone across the room, then turns back to me. "It's okay, Mr. Mac. I can teach you if you want. Me teacher, you student for a change. Ha." He slaps me on the shoulder.

I can feel myself slipping into defensive mode. "I may be a teacher, but I'm not dead yet." I immediately regret the Monty Python words, but Robert just laughs.

"Ah, don't feel bad. Maybe Mr. Gorman could give you some lessons. His dancing is probably more your style anyway."

"That's low."

He gives me a mischievous look. "Prove me wrong, then. Show me what you got."

"Why do you just assume that anyone over eighteen can't dance?"

"Why would I assume they can?" He shrugs. "Seeing is believing. Put your money where your Nikes are."

"Go dance," I tell him with mock severity.

The dance is winding down, and I head out before I get roped into cleanup duty. A couple of the kids are heading out early, too, but otherwise the parking lot is quiet. Even though I hear the footfalls slapping the concrete behind me, I don't think anything of it until Robert calls out my name.

"Wait up!"

"Is the dance over?" I ask as he draws up in front of me.

"Nope. Well, almost." He's got this impish grin on his face, and I know he's got something up his sleeve.

"What?" I ask.

"You didn't think I was just going to let you off the hook, did you?"

"Let me off the hook?"

"Yeah. Come on." He gives my sleeve a tug, then jogs to his car, which is parked a little ways away under one of the parking lot lights. I follow more slowly, as I'm just a little wary about what he's up to. He unlocks the door, then climbs in and turns the ignition so just the power comes on. As I approach I see him plug in his iPod, then scroll through the songs until he finds what he's looking for. He hits Play, then turns up the volume and gets out.

"No," I protest. " 'Stereo Hearts'? Not fair."

He grins and leans against the car, folding his arms, then gestures for me to go.

I look around at the parking lot. There are still quite a few cars, but no people at the moment. "You're really going to make me do this, aren't you?"

"I'm sure going to try."

I figure I have two choices—refuse and say good night, or

dance. *Oh, what the hell.* "Okay." As Adam Levine's hook segues into Travie McCoy's rap, I spin three-sixty, crack my knuckles, and then I show him what I got.

The look on his face is first one of surprise, but soon he's watching my footwork, moving his shoulders and head to the music.

"Woo-hoo. Dance party!" someone calls out. We're joined by three other kids leaving the party, attracted to the music like moths to a light. Among them is one of my former freshmen, Aneecia Moore. She's a big girl, maybe five-ten, but damn she can move. She dances with me, then grabs Robert's arm and pulls him away from the car. Two more join our group.

When the song is over, the kids move on as quickly as they arrived. Aneecia turns to walk backward and gives a hoot. "Mr. Mc-*Nel*-is can dance! You been holding out on us, Mr. Mac."

"Yeah, yeah," I respond and wave her on.

When I turn back to Robert, he's smiling broadly.

"Do I pass muster?"

"Hmm. I'll get back to you on that."

"You'll get back to me on that," I mutter, smiling. I take out my phone to check the time.

"Is that your daughter?" Robert asks, craning his neck to get a look at the background photo.

"That's my Kiki," I answer, holding it out to him for a better look.

"She's very pretty."

"That she is."

"Do you have some more?"

He's going to wish he never asked that. I pull up my photo album and flip through the photos, explaining where each was taken and why. There's even a photo of Maya in a baseball cap and big sunglasses. Her hair is stuffed up in the cap and she's holding Kiki in the air. I snapped the photo just as she was turning away. You can't see her face, but her smile is mirrored in Kiki's. It's one of my favorite photos of them. When Robert asks about her, I say, "Long story. I'll tell you about it sometime."

I slip my phone back in my pocket, and that's when I see the guard practice rifle on his backseat. I can't resist. "Can I?" I ask, opening the back door to get it out. It's white with a black bolt and a black strap, and scarred—the end pads scuffed and pitted from repeated drops on the concrete.

I think it must be a law of nature—if you find yourself with a baton in your hand, you're going to twirl it. Same thing with a guard rifle. I give it a spin and a toss, then duck when it clatters down over my head.

"You okay?" Robert asks.

"Shit. That hurts."

"It's almost five pounds of wood designed to injure anyone within a three-foot radius of the tossee, including the tossee. If you want to play with my rifle, then you gotta learn to handle it."

"Oh, I do?" I say, biting back a grin despite the pain in my cranium.

"Yeah, you do."

He picks up the rifle and for the next ten minutes or so—despite good-natured taunts from other friends leaving the dance—he teaches me to do a single rifle toss, which consists of holding the rifle palm up in my left hand, and palm down in my right, then pushing the butt down with my right and up with my left and releasing when the nose is pointed at the ground. The rifle rotates once, and I catch it with my hands in the opposite position, the rifle pointing in the opposite direction. Or something like that.

It's tricky, but with some focused practice, I finally get it.

"Guard rocks!" someone shouts. Robert waves back.

He hops up onto the trunk and watches me with amusement as I flip the rifle over and over again.

"You want to know the top-ten reasons you should date a guard member?"

"Let's hear 'em," I say, giving the rifle another toss.

"Ten, we know how to keep people in line. Nine, we're always working on our technique. Eight, we wear tight clothes. Seven, we do it on football fields and gym floors. Six, we're used to poles of all sizes. Five, we strive for the perfect performance. Four, we work well with our hands. Three, we're very flexible. Two, we always want to be on top. And one, we love making people scream and yell."

He says all this with a straight face until he gets to number three. By then I'm laughing so hard that I lose my timing and miss a catch, almost breaking two fingers in the process. It's not that the reasons are all that funny. They're just so damn funny coming from him.

I shake out my smarting fingers.

"You want to learn a double toss?" he asks, still grinning.

Actually, I do.

Chapter 13

Robert

Mom's asleep on the couch when I get home, the TV on low. I turn it off.

From the hallway, I see Aunt Olivia in my parents' bedroom, sitting on the chaise, thumbing through a box of photos that Mom keeps on a shelf in her closet. She takes one out and lays it on one of the stacks she's made all around her.

Then, sensing my presence, I suppose, she looks up and motions me in.

Aunt Whitney is on the bed next to Dad. Her soft snoring and the constant hum of the oxygen compressor are the only sounds in the room. Dad seems to be asleep, too, but more likely he's unconscious, or in a drug-induced coma. The pressure in his head makes it impossible for his eyes to fully close, and I find looking at him to be increasingly disconcerting.

As I turn away, my eyes light briefly on the small notebook still lying on the bedside table.

"Your mom said you went to a band dance," Aunt Olivia says quietly.

Her question doesn't sound like an accusation, so I sit at the card table at the end of Mom and Dad's bed. The puzzle is almost complete. Immediately my eyes focus on a piece. There is the tiniest sliver of brown on the otherwise blue background. I place it in the puzzle to complete the cat's whiskers.

"Did you have fun?" she asks.

Best night of my life. "Yeah."

"Good."

"How's Dad?"

She pauses in her photo search and looks up at him. "He's calm. I don't think he's in any pain. The hospice nurse gave him a sponge bath today. And he's home." Her face contorts like she might cry, but instead she drops her eyes to the box of photos.

I look at the notebook again. I can't help wondering what Dad has written on those pages. Did he feel pressured to do it? Did they give him the words to say? Are they warm words of love? Or are they cold words of indifference? And why do I care? I turn my attention back to the table and fit another piece into the puzzle.

Aunt Olivia studies the photo she's holding. "You look so much like him when he was your age. Look at this one." She grips the box to her chest and shifts forward on the chaise to hand it to me, being careful not to knock the other photos off.

I take it. I'm a year old, maybe, lying on a quilt on the living room floor. Dad's got his T-shirt pulled up over his head like Cornholio in the *Beavis and Butt-head* cartoon. I'm looking up at him and laughing. I smile a little and hand the photo back and pick up another one from the pile—a photo of my dad and another man kneeling on the shore of a lake, holding up their catch.

"I recognize that cap he's wearing."

She smiles. "He loved that cap. He never went camping without it."

"He liked camping, didn't he?"

"Loved it."

"Who's he with?"

She tips the photo so she can see it better. "That's Patrick O'Kelley," she says, smiling nostalgically. "He's an old college friend of your dad's."

There's a boy kneeling between the two men. *Grown-ups only, Robert.* I feel a lump form in my throat. "Who's the kid?"

"That's Patrick's son. Sammy, I think. You met him a long time ago, remember? You're about the same age. I'm surprised you're not in the photo. Didn't you go on that trip?"

"No." I hand the photo back. "Are there any pictures of my mom in there?"

"Hmm," she says, curiously. "I haven't really seen any."

"Why is that? I mean, there are photos of Dad all over the house, but there aren't any of Mom."

I'm thinking about the photos Andrew showed me in the parking lot, the way his face beamed with pride as he shuffled from one to the next. There was even a photo of his ex-wife. His *ex*-wife. I still find it odd that he even has an ex-wife.

Aunt Olivia seems surprised by my question. "I don't know. I guess your mom doesn't like to have her picture taken."

That isn't true. I've never once heard Mom protest when someone turned a camera on her; maybe that's because no one, in my memory, ever has. On the other hand, there are hundreds of photos of my dad around the house—framed, in albums, in drawers, even in magnet-backed sleeves on the refrigerator door. Photos of me too. But not one of Mom.

When I tell Aunt Olivia that I don't believe that to be true, she sighs. "She was always the one with the camera. She took the photos. That's just the way it was."

"You know, I can't help thinking that if it were Mom dying, I wouldn't have any photos of her after she's gone. Nothing. Well, maybe one or two that my teacher took of us when I graduated from kindergarten and her old wedding photos."

"But your mom's not dying, is she? Your dad is. You can take all the photos of your mom you want after he's gone."

Her tone is sharp, unexpected, and it cuts at me. She's missed the point entirely. I sweep the puzzle off the table and leave, ignoring the shocked look on her face.

The rug rats have completely taken over my room. They're sacked out on the floor in this one amorphous bed that someone has created from assorted quilts and blankets. But one of them has made his way into my bed. The guest room is empty, but it's clear from the bags tossed up on the bed that this is where Aunt Olivia plans to spend the night.

I fold myself into the love seat in the living room and pull a throw over me. It's uncomfortable, but I hardly notice. I'm physically and emotionally exhausted.

I drift off to sleep thinking, *Andrew,* and wonder at how easily his first name plays on my lips now.

Andrew

I adjust the headphones snugly over my ears, drop the cord down my shirt, then fish it out the bottom and plug it into my iPod.

I don't want to sleep; I want to dance.

Chapter 14

Andrew

I promised Maya I'd pick up Kiki at nine, so here I am.

"Wow, you look like you've been run over by a dump truck."

I smile tiredly at Maya. "I feel like I've been run over by a dump truck."

She squints a little and tilts her head. "Have you been drinking?"

"Drinking?" I laugh. "No. I, um . . ." I hesitate. I chaperoned a band dance, for Pete's sake, but I'm tired and sore from twirling that silly rifle in the parking lot well after the lights went out last night. I learned the double toss, then the triple, then had almost mastered the quad before we moved to the horizontal toss. It was tricky and pretty stupid in the dark, but the moonlight and the whiteness of the rifle made it doable. And there was something very intimate about being alone with Robert in the dark, his hands on mine, his body close. We didn't talk about anything important. We just played with the rifle and laughed. God, what a beautiful sound, his laugh.

But somehow, telling Maya that I had some kind of Zen experience in a parking lot with one of my students until the wee hours of the morning would be even stupider than being in that parking lot in the first place. I could just tell her about the dance. That would be good enough to explain the tired muscles on my out-of-shape body, but I am feeling some serious warm fuzzies at the moment, and I want to share them, even if it means telling a slightly embellished version of my night. So I settle on a half-truth. "I went dancing last night."

Her eyebrows shoot up. "Dancing? Like, with a guy?"

"Maybe." I know I'm being coy, but frankly, I feel coy today.

"Really? So . . . is this guy someone special?"

"Special?" I realize I'm echoing her words and make a point to stop. "Yeah. I'd have to say he's special. Very special, in fact. But special for me? I don't know. We're just friends."

She eyes me for a moment, a knowing look, and a slow smile makes its way across her face and lights up her eyes. "You're in love!"

Maya always did know me, better than I know myself.

"Just friends," I insist, but I'm not so sure anymore. All we did was twirl that rifle and toss it in the air more times than I can count, but despite how tired I am, I feel more alive today than I have in years, maybe ever.

"Kiki's still eating breakfast. Doug's here. Want to come in and have some coffee?"

Kiki's face lights up when she sees me. She holds out a soggy Cheerio, and I bend down so she can put it in my mouth. Then I give her a kiss on her milky lips. "How's my best girl this morning?"

"Cheewios!"

"I know," I say, but decline when she offers me another one.

Maya hands me a cup, then pours some coffee as I sit down. Doug is at the stove whipping up something that smells like onions. He looks comfortable there, and I can't help thinking that he and Maya will make a nice couple, and that he'll be a good stepdad to Kiki. Maya swats him on the butt as she returns the carafe to the coffeemaker.

He looks over his shoulder at me. "I'm making breakfast. You interested?"

"Sure. Smells good."

"Maya tells me you applied for the administrator training program. Have you heard anything yet?"

"Not yet. I just had an interview Monday. I'm hoping to hear something this week."

"So the kids might be calling you Principal McNelis soon?"

I laugh. "Hardly."

Maya hands me a carton of half-and-half, a sugar bowl, and a spoon. I give her a wink.

"It's a two-year program. I intern in the last semester. They'll get me a sub, and I'll get to play administrator for a number of days. Then I'll start applying for positions. But from what I hear, though, the district tries to rough you up a bit before they'll offer you anything. Lots of interviews, lots of rejections. You just gotta be patient and keep at it. So, I figure it'll be at least four more years before I even make assistant principal."

"Ouch."

Doug's an engineer. He's only a few years older than I am, but he earns three times as much. That's okay. It means security for Maya and a chance for her to stay home with Kiki if she wants to after they marry, if they marry.

"Not that bad," I say. "I really love working with the kids. Every day's a new challenge. Each year's a new challenge. You never know for sure what you're going to be teaching or what kind of kids you're going to get. I hear it keeps you young. If the pay weren't so bad, I might be happy to stay a teacher the rest of my life."

Maya looks a little uneasy. She knows about my financial struggles, but she also knows I wouldn't have it any other way. I manage. I'm happy. That should be enough for anyone.

"Drew met a guy," Maya says.

"Oh-oh-oh," I sputter. "Thanks for keeping my secrets."

"You didn't say it was a secret," she says sweetly.

"Yeah?" Doug says. "Where'd you meet him? School?"

"He's just a friend," I say, evading the last question.

"They went daaancing last night," Maya singsongs.

Doug moves the pan from the stove to the table, far enough away from Kiki so she can't reach out and burn her little fingers. *Good move, Doug.*

"Could he keep up?"

"You know, I find it disturbing that you know so much about me."

He hands me a plate and grins. "You're a legend."

"I doubt that."

"Just pillow talk."

"Might I suggest you get some new pillows or this little one here"—I muss Kiki's hair—"is going to grow up an only child."

Maya blushes, but Doug doesn't skip a beat. "We do all right."

I bet. I already know Doug spends the night when Kiki is with me. Although, I'm pretty sure he spent the night last night, too, judging from his casual dress this morning—barefoot, TAMU sweatpants and a Fruit of the Loom undershirt—but I can hardly blame them since I was the one who changed my plans at the last minute. Maya's flexible like that; we both are. Anyway, Kiki's only two, and if it makes Maya happy, it makes me happy.

My cell phone vibrates in my pocket. I'd texted Robert before I even got out of bed this morning: *Can't move. Every muscle in my body hurts. Blame you.*

He must have slept in. I take out my phone and check the message.

Serves you right, old man.

I can still fail you.

Ha, ha. You know I'm kidding, Andrew! (No Mr. Mac. Did you see that? Huh?)

I saw ;)

When I look up again, Maya and Doug are exchanging an amused look.

"What?" I ask.

"You're smiling," Maya says. "Your new guy?" I take a piece of bacon and pretend I didn't hear the question.

Robert

"It smells like smoke in here," I say to Aunt Whitney as I pour a glass of milk.

She takes the carton from me, checks the level, and returns it to the refrigerator. "You sleep okay?"

"Yeah," I answer. "Pretty good." Just not nearly long enough. The rug rats were up early.

I pull my left arm behind my head, then my right, trying to work out some of the kinks. Andrew isn't the only one with sore muscles this morning. But every ache reminds me of last night, and I savor every twinge.

"Sorry I had to put the kids in your room," she says as she adds milk to her shopping list. "There really wasn't any other place. This house is pretty small."

She means it as a mere observation, I'm pretty sure, but the implication from years of just such comments still seeps through. The former-Westfall women live in large homes, homes that befit their status as physician-gods (Aunt Whitney, neurology; Aunt Olivia, otolaryngology, a fancy word for the field of ear, nose, and throat medicine). Ours is a hovel and clearly beneath their baby brother. I shake off the bad vibes and try to give her the benefit of the doubt.

"How's Dad this morning?"

She shakes her head. "He's a fighter. He's hanging on with everything he has, but . . ." She takes a deep breath and her eyes flood with tears. "He's actively dying, Robert."

"But you just said he's fighting it."

"What I mean is his systems are shutting down. It won't be much longer. As bad as he looks, I have to believe that he's completely oblivious, that death will be just a small hiccup between this world and Heaven." She smiles weakly and sniffs. "You sure you don't mind running to the store?"

"I don't mind."

"I'd go myself, but someone needs to stay with your dad."

I bristle. *Someone.* Right. "Where's Mom?"

"Don't know. Apparently there are more pressing demands on her time than staying by her husband's side." She adds fish sticks to the list and hands it to me. "Stop by the Hallmark store next door first and see if they have any puzzles there. Someone finished the other one last night."

* * *

At Hallmark, I pick up the most difficult puzzle they have—a twelve-hundred-piece double-sided mosaic with no defined parts or reference points. I hope they rot trying to put it together.

I hate everything about you.

Wow. I didn't think my dancing was THAT bad.

☺ *Do you have Kiki already?*

I open one of the coolers in the freezer section at H-E-B and pull out three bags of fish sticks and toss them into the cart with the milk, bread, and other items I've already accumulated.

I do.

What are you guys doing today?

Well, right now we're buying ice cream.

Baskin-Robbins or Cold Stone Creamery?

H-E-B.

I push my cart to the end of the frozen dinners aisle and make my way to ice cream.

He's holding his daughter in one arm and the cooler door open with his hip. With his free hand he's restacking cartons of ice cream.

It's a little cool out for shorts, don't you think? But, um, nice legs.

Very nice, I think. A light covering of brown hair that matches the hair that peeks out from the collars of his shirts. I watch as he juggles Kiki, his phone, and the ice cream. He's wearing khaki shorts and flip-flops with an OU hoodie. If I didn't know better, I'd have pegged him for a college student.

His face screws up a little as he reads my text. He one-handed thumbs in a response.

??? Are you some kind of clairvoyant?

He smiles at Kiki as he drops two pints of ice cream into the basket at his feet, and I hear him say to her as I approach, "Hey, kiddo, somebody thinks I have nice legs. What do you think?"

"I think she'd have to agree if that weren't just a little creepy," I say, positioning my cart next to his basket.

His head snaps to me. His smile turns a little sheepish, and his ears redden just a shade. And suddenly I forget all about puzzles and being a guest in my own house.

Kiki twists in his arms to get a look at me, and Andrew has to heft her to maintain his grip. The little girl that I know from the photos is holding a spotted stuffed dog in a summer dress. Little white sandals are strapped to its stubby paws.

Andrew places his cheek next to hers and speaks in a low, conspiratorial voice. "This is Daddy's friend Robert. He's sneaky, but don't hold that against him. He can Dougie like nobody's business."

Kiki giggles and buries her face in her father's neck.

"I like your doggie," I say. "What's his name?"

"You want to tell Robert your dog's name?"

Apparently she doesn't. So I guess: "Let me see . . . Ralph?" No response. "George? Bruno?" Andrew winces and tugs at the little dress as if to remind me that the dog is a girl. "Daisy?"

Kiki whips around and fixes me with gray eyes that remind me so much of Andrew's. She looks a little perturbed, insulted perhaps, when she says, "Spot!"

"Oooh, Spot. That's a great name. The dress. Of course. Silly me. I should have known." I give Andrew a look that says, *Thanks, pal.*

He winks, then scans the contents of my cart.

"So what are you doing here, my friend? I didn't know you had such a developed palette. That's a heck of a lot of fish sticks. I imagine if you took them all apart you might be able to reconstruct an entire guppy."

I turn my shopping list to him. "We've got kind of a crowd in our house right now."

His smile fades and he studies me for a moment. "Your dad . . ."

"No. Not yet. Won't be long though. They don't want to leave him, so I'm the designated shopper today."

"Can I do anything?"

You can take me home with you. Make me feel like I belong somewhere. "No, but thanks." I take a look at his basket on the floor. "Who gets the Cake and Ice Cream flavor?"

"Me!" Kiki cries out.

"And the Moo-llennium Crunch is for Dad, right, kiddo?"

She pokes him in the nose. I want to just look at them, to fix in my mind this sweet moment so I can take it out later and reflect on what it means to be adored. And then an idea occurs to me.

"Hey, let me take your photo," I say, holding up my phone that I realize is still clutched in my hand.

"Aaah, we like our picture taken, don't we, Kiki?"

I snap the photo and capture them, father and daughter, cheek to cheek, smile to smile. I show it to him. Kiki pokes her finger at the screen. "Daddy."

"Hey, let me take one for you with your phone," I suggest.

"Yeah? All right." He hands it over, and I snap a second photo, then return the phone to him. He looks at the photo, then shows it to Kiki. She takes the phone from him and shows it to Spot. While she does, he locks eyes with me, and I feel like we exchange some silent communication. To me, it goes something like this: *There's something going on here between us, and we both know it.* I wonder what words come to him.

"Well," he says with a quiet smile, "I guess we need to get going, right, Kiki?" He nods to my list. "It looks like you still have some shopping to do, and our ice cream is melting."

He grabs the handles of the plastic basket and hoists it up. Besides the two pints of ice cream and some wafer cones, there's a bottle of red wine. I'm acutely aware that even if I wanted to, even if he asked, I'm not legally old enough to have a glass with him. That reality takes a little of the buzz out of our meeting.

I shuffle my feet a bit. I want to say, "Don't go. Not yet." What I say is, "Have a good weekend."

"You too."

I'm turning to go when he says, "Hey, Robert."

I look up and he snaps my picture. His phone is gripped in the hand that's holding Kiki, so I doubt he even got a good shot of me.

"If you wanted a photo of me, you could've just downloaded one from my fan page."

He laughs. "Actually, I think this might be my ticket into your fan club."

"Right." I turn to go again, but he stops me once more.

"Oh, hey. Do you like burritos?"

"Burritos?"

"Yeah. You know, tortillas with beans or beef—"

"Um, yeah, I got that. Is this some kind of trick question?"

"Nope. Just a question."

"No right or wrong answer? You're not going to ding a quiz grade or anything?"

"No dings."

"Then, no, not really."

He seems pleased with my answer. I walk off wondering what all *that* was about. I feel my phone riding against my thigh in my pocket, and I feel like I'm taking a little piece of him with me. At the pizza case, I grab four Red Barons, then circle back around to the ice cream and grab a half gallon of Moo-llennium Crunch.

Chapter 15

Andrew

When I was a sophomore in high school, I had this English teacher—a man, Mr. Jacobson. There weren't many male teachers in my school (are there ever?), and the ones we did have taught math or science or business classes, often half time if they also coached.

But Mr. Jacobson taught English. It was a class where we talked about feelings, and I was sure feeling him. He was my first real crush.

As I recall, he was in his mid-thirties, married. He had a small cleft in his chin and a dimple when he smiled and these dark eyebrows. What I remember most is the way he'd run his fingers through his hair as he strolled around the classroom. As much as I could, I'd watch him, much like Robert watches me sometimes, and imagine that he was trying to find his way close to me. When he called on me, my insides would flip a little at the sudden attention.

I wanted him bad, and I'd spent endless hours sitting on Maya's bed playing *what if*. What if he divorced his wife and suddenly realized he liked boys? What if I just told him what I felt about him one day, and he suddenly confessed that he'd always thought I was special?

That went on for the better part of the school year, and then one day after spring break, the varnish started to crack, just a little at first.

I noticed things I'd never noticed before. The way his shoes were always scuffed and the heels worn down on the outsides, like he didn't much care about his appearance. The way the cleft in his chin formed a dark crease that looked like a pine seed might take root there like they did in our gutters when you didn't clean them for a while. The way he always smelled of garlic. The way his eye teeth dropped down a little too far and the way one of his incisors was smaller than the other. And worst of all, the way his hair stood up when he ran his fingers through it, like it was dirty and thick with oil.

After a while, I began to wonder what I ever saw in him. I not only quit following him around the room with my eyes, I quit raising my hand. I even found it hard to look at him when he called on me.

I will never admit it to another living soul, but I've fallen for Robert. Hard. Maybe it's because I'm finally facing my true feelings for him that I'm thinking about my old English teacher. Am I Robert's Mr. Jacobson? Is that the way it will be with him? Crushing on me today, too aware of my flaws tomorrow?

I have considered that after his graduation, I might approach him, ask him out, like a real date. I'd wait a month or two just so there's no question about our teacher/student relationship. I know that kind of stuff happens. After all, six years isn't an unbridgeable chasm.

Would he say yes? Or would I have become by then just another what-did-I-ever-see-in-him crush?

He'd move on to college. Meet lots of great guys his own age.

I flop back against the throw pillows on the futon and study his photo. He was right; there are lots of photos on his fan page I could download, but this one is different. This one I captured myself.

Kiki curls up next to me. She's warm and cuddly, and I'm pretty sure this is going to be a nap for two today. I kiss the top of her head and look at Robert's photo again.

"What do you think, Kiki? You think your daddy's silly for falling for one of his students?"

She reaches up and pats my face with sticky fingers. "Silly Daddy," she says sleepily.

"Yeah," I say softly. "That's what I think, too, baby girl."

Robert

Moo-llennium Crunch turns out to be this interesting blend of vanilla ice cream, chocolate and caramel chunks, and three kinds of nuts. My younger cousins don't much like nuts, but they don't read labels. All they see is ice cream.

Aunt Whitney fills their waiting cones with heaping scoops, then disappears into Dad's room. In one minute flat, the ice cream is melting in the sink, the cones discarded the instant the offending chunks were discovered.

Mom's putting away the rest of the groceries.

"Where'd you go this morning?" I ask, trying to decide if what I'm chewing is walnut or pistachio.

"Target. I had to get a new vacuum cleaner."

"What happened to the old one?"

She huffs. "I moved it into your room this morning so I could vacuum up all the popcorn on the floor, and then Mark smashed his fingers in your closet door, and while I was running cold water over them in the kitchen sink, Brian found some matches. Apparently he struck a few and blew them out, then dropped them on your floor. Then afraid he'd get in trouble, he vacuumed them up and the entire bag caught fire. I guess at least one of the matches was still smoldering."

"You're kidding, right?"

Mom laughs, a humorless sound. "I wish I were, Robert. I really wish I were."

"Did you tell Aunt Whitney?" Brian is her kid, eight years old, and a little stinker.

"I did. She wanted to know what I was thinking leaving matches around where little kids could get to them."

I scoff. "It's *my* room. Did he burn my carpet?"

She looks at the fish sticks and rolls her eyes. "I don't think so. It's flame retardant. But the vacuum is trashed. I had to drag it out to the back porch to douse the flames."

I hold the freezer door open so she can cram in the bags and boxes of pizzas. The shelves are already packed with corndogs, chicken tenders, and Kid Cuisines.

"Are they ever going to leave?"

She shuts the freezer door and leans back against it and folds her arms. She looks so tired. I think she'd cry if she had the energy. "Hang in there, okay?"

There is no place in our house that isn't littered with little people or their little-people discards, except perhaps my dad's room. But the litter in that room is like a whole different level of hell. I take my ice cream outside and lie across the trunk of my car.

The sun is bright, and I have to shield the screen of my phone with my hand to see his picture. His smile makes me smile. I think about texting, but something holds me back. The bottle of wine maybe.

The phone rings suddenly. Nic.

Don't break up.

That's what Andrew told me. I wondered then and I wonder now if that was some code for *me-teacher, you-student, don't get any ideas.*

I close my eyes and let the sun warm my face for a moment as the phone rings for the second time, then the third. I won't break up with Nic. I'll give him that. But I won't answer either. I wait until the call rolls to voice mail, then text Andrew.

Ask you a question?

ZZZzzzZZZzzz

Sorry.

Ha, ha. I'm up. Is it a trick question?

Why am I still dating Nic again?

Aaaah. My bad. We'll talk on Monday. I'm bringing subs for 2. Bring your appetite . . . and your homework!

It's a date.

I consider the text before I push Send, almost scratch that last line, then think, *What the L-M-N-O-P,* and send it anyway.

Chapter 16

Robert

Monday morning. No clanging bells, no rattling pots in the kitchen, no rug rats clamoring for food. Their dads picked them up yesterday. A welcome hush has settled on the house. I find Aunt Whitney sitting cross-legged on the bed next to my dad, his useless left hand gripped in hers. Her eyes shimmer with tears. She sniffs as Dad's chest heaves with the exertion of drawing in even a small amount of air.

I let my gaze settle on his face, the open but vacant eyes, the grotesquely stretched skin, the foam that is just beginning to form around his nostrils and his lips.

Aunt Olivia has pulled the armchair from the living room up next to the bed. She checks the bag clipped to the side rail. "He's just not producing anything anymore." She looks over her shoulder at me and wipes her eyes. "You're not going to school today, are you?"

"I've got sectionals this morning and an English test this afternoon."

"Make it up later," Aunt Whitney says sharply.

Aunt Olivia's voice is softer: "Robert, your dad may not be here when you get home. You see this?" She holds up the bag she was looking at a moment ago. "His kidneys have shut down."

"Is that why he's foaming?"

She glances at his face. "His lungs are filling with fluid." Then she turns back to me. "This is your last chance to be here for your dad."

The way he was here for me?

I stay under the radar over the next half hour, showering and dressing quickly and quietly. In the kitchen, I grab a couple of blueberry waffles and drop them in the toaster.

"You want something more than that?" Mom asks, coming into the kitchen. "I can make you some bacon and eggs."

"No, thanks." The truth is I feel a little sick this morning. Two dry waffles and some water is about all I can handle. I can't watch this. I won't watch this. And then there's Andrew. "I'm going to school," I say, looking up from the toaster to check her reaction.

"Good. You don't need to be here for this."

"What happens when he dies? I mean, what do you do with him?"

"Honestly, Robert, I don't know. I've never done this before. I'm sure your aunts know what to do."

The waffles pop up. I take them out with my fingertips and drop them on a napkin to cool. "Why do you do that?" I ask. "Let them run the show?"

She bites her lip and looks at me like I just slapped her face.

Andrew

From the cubbyhole that constitutes my school mailbox, I extract a stack of papers—attendance verification forms I need to sign (*No black ink, please.*), grades for two new students (both algebra), an invitation to meet with financial planners in the upstairs lounge this afternoon (as if I had any money to invest), the current issue of *Pi in the Sky* (a note from the librarian paper clipped to the cover—*Mr. McNelis, Great article on math games. Thought you might like some new material.*), a certificate for ten dollars off a meal at some new restaurant, and an envelope with my name on the front in Jen's distinctive loopy writing.

I set my cooler on the floor, tuck the rest of my mail under my arm, and open the envelope. Two tickets to the Iron Maiden concert tomorrow night at the Pavilion and a note, this one on a sunflower Post-it rather than the business yellow the librarian used.

Throw a girl a bone already. Pretty please?

"There you are," Jen says from the doorway. She slips behind me to her own mailbox.

"Did you just grab my ass?" I say in a low voice. We're the only two at the mailboxes, but just through the open cubbyholes is a workroom. I can see Mr. Redmon at the copier.

"Don't tell me you didn't like it," she responds in an equally low voice.

I laugh and hand the tickets back to her. "School night."

She snatches them from my hand. "It's an early concert. I promise, I'll have you home and in your Barney pj's by eleven."

"Don't be mean. I outgrew Barney last year. I'm wearing Spider-Man now."

"God, you are such an old fuddy-duddy."

I laugh. That's me. "Come on. I'll buy you a cup of coffee."

I call out a bold "Good morning" to Mr. Redmon through the cubbies; he calls one back. Then we sneak out the back door so we don't have to cross through the reception area again. It's still early—six thirty—but you can always count on there being at least one parent waiting to talk to the principal about some injustice that's been served up to their kid, no matter the hour. I counted three when I came in.

We cross paths with Robert a little ways down the hallway. He's holding the strap of his backpack over his shoulder with one hand and lugging his saxophone with the other. He catches my eye and holds it just a beat too long before letting his gaze drift down to the cooler in my hand, then he smiles and says, "Good morning."

We watch him disappear down the music hallway.

"I could swear that kid's hot for teacher," Jen says.

My heart skips a beat, then picks up its pace. "You should be flattered," I tell her with a broad smile that I'm pretty sure doesn't reach my eyes, though I try.

"Um, I wasn't talking about me. I'm not his type, you know."

* * *

The coffee is still dripping when we reach the lounge. Jen catches the drips with her cup while I try to maneuver the spout so that the coffee splashes into her cup and not on the counter, then fill my own.

"So, when do you hear about the admin program?" she asks.

"Today, I hope. It starts in February, so they can't wait too much longer."

"Oooh, you know, you could be my boss one day. That'd be kind of hot, don't you think? I wouldn't mind so much getting summoned to the principal's office if you were sitting behind the desk. I might even break a few school rules just so you can spank me."

I squeeze the little plastic single-serve container of half-and-half a little too hard, and it squirts onto the counter.

"You have quite the imagination," I say, mopping up the spill with a paper towel.

"That's what I've been told," she says, ducking her head down and fluttering her eyelashes at me.

Ahem. "Gotta run!"

I drop the paper towel in the trash receptacle at the door and escape before Lolita can throw me to the ground and hump me right there in the teachers' lounge.

It's been two weeks, but some of the kids still seem to be on Christmas break. Settling my freshman Algebra students back into a routine has been a challenge. Stephen Newman has been especially trying. He bounces in this morning with his pants hanging halfway down his ass to show off his *South Park* boxers, no doubt a Christmas gift.

Stephen likes attention, a lot of it. Twice he interrupts my lesson on solving quadratic equations by completing the square with some inane comment. Now he's stretched out in his seat with his T-shirt hiked up, and he's carrying on a bizarre conversation with Kristyn Murrow next to him . . . using his belly button as a mouth, squinching it together with his fingers to simulate moving lips. She titters across the aisle from him.

"Stephen," I say, wrapping up the equation on the whiteboard and turning to him. "If you keep getting on my nerves, I'm going to get on yours, buddy. You got that?"

Astonishingly, he responds with his belly button. "I got that, sir. Yes, sir."

The rest of the room snickers. I look around sharply and they quiet down. I wait while he pulls his shirt down and hunches over his desk.

It's a relief to get them started on their homework a few minutes later. Next year I'm petitioning for Algebra 2 classes. Freshmen. Sheesh.

A couple of new e-mails came in during my lesson. The one from Mr. Redmon has been flagged *high priority.*

Yes!

> *Mr. McNelis—*
> *Please stop by my office during your planning period*
> *this morning.*
> *Mr. Redmon*

I would be happy to, Mr. Redmon.

I take a sip of coffee. It's lukewarm. I decide to nuke it between classes. I want to be on my game when I meet with him third period.

I can't wait to tell Robert. The thought skips through my brain and settles into that little compartment where I keep all things Robert. I sit back in my chair and scan the room, but I'm thinking about that intense look on his face when he danced, the way his arm felt pressed against mine as he looked at the photos on my phone, the sweet way he interacted with Kiki in the grocery store.

When the bell rings, I realize I'm smiling like an idiot.

When second period ends, I hustle to the main office. Mrs. Stovall, Mr. Redmon's secretary, motions me to a love seat adjacent to her desk. Jen calls this the *deep-shit sofa* where they leave you to piss your pants before your inquisition begins. I think she exaggerates. Not all visits to the principal's office are bad things.

There are three red folders spread uniformly on the desk next to Mrs. Stovall's computer. Clipped to each folder is a temporary badge on a lanyard. Mrs. Stovall (not *Ms.* unless you want her to cut you with one of her looks) is on the phone still trying to locate the subs she needs for the day. A sub shortage means other teachers have to fill in on their planning periods, and the district has to pay them. It's cheaper and less disruptive to have a sub. But there are never enough of them to go around.

She's clearly in a bad mood so I sit quietly and imagine sitting at the desk behind that door one day. It's a hard job, I know that. The hours are brutally long, but the pay is at least a living wage. And the position is a bully pulpit, an opportunity to shape the culture of a school. I already have some ideas about how my own school will be different.

I'm lost in my thoughts, so I'm a little startled when Mrs. Stovall tells me I can go in.

"Drew," Mr. Redmon booms as I step into his office. "Have a seat. Sorry to keep you waiting. I was just talking to my son. He graduates from MIT this May."

"I didn't know that. That's great. Smart kid."

"Yeah. He's the last one. Once we get this one out of school, my wife and I are going to take a long cruise in the Greek islands."

I smile just as his fades a bit, and mine subsequently falters.

"Drew, this is really difficult for me to talk about."

What? I quickly catalog my qualifications for the admin program. I have a strong academic record, my kids' test scores are solid, I've proven myself in the classroom, I've tutored and even participated in the annual chili cook-off, I'm a man, I even had a teacher friend in English check over my application to make sure I hadn't made any inadvertent grammatical faux pas. And the interview had been lively.

Until this moment, I'd considered myself the perfect candidate. I can't believe they're not admitting me into the program, and that is exactly what I'm thinking when Mr. Redmon slams me in the chest.

"I want you to know that your sexual orientation has never been an issue for me."

My heart stutters to a halt.

"But"—Mr. Redmon studies his hand—"a band parent called

this morning about another issue and mentioned that you were in the back parking lot Friday night with Robert Westfall."

My heart kicks up a wild beat and my fingertips tingle. I force my face to remain neutral, my voice nonchalant. "Mr. Gorman asked me to chaperone the band dance."

"I find that curious, Drew. Usually parents chaperone those dances." He holds my gaze for a moment before continuing. "Look, I have no objection to you chaperoning a band dance. I do, however, question your judgment in spending time alone in a parking lot at night with one of your students."

I start to open my mouth to defend myself, but I clamp it shut at the last second. Any protest would stink of guilt.

He studies me as I struggle for some kind of neutral response, then drops another bombshell. "Robert Westfall has been having lunch in your classroom for the past week." It isn't a question.

My first thought is, *Jen.* But any number of people pass by my classroom during any given lunch period. It could have been anyone from the copy room aide to another student. The door always remained wide open. I haven't been trying to hide anything, exactly.

I steady my voice before I speak. "He's having a rough time. I think he sees me as a big brother he can talk to. That's all."

"That ends today, Drew," he says sternly. "This instant. Let me remind you that perception is everything in a public school. You're young. You're a nice-looking man; he's a vulnerable teenager. And *you* are not a counselor. That is Ms. Lincoln's job. I've already asked her to call Robert in today for some counseling. Might I suggest that you stick to algebra and calculus. You have a bright future ahead of you. I don't want to see you screw it up."

I mumble, "No problem. Thank you," and stand, willing my knees to lock beneath me. He hands me a sheet of paper. I take it, but I'm afraid to look at it.

"By the way," Mr. Redmon says as I open the door, "I don't have the admin training list yet, but I'm sure your name will be on it."

"Great." I offer him a bright smile and close the door behind me. In a faculty bathroom, I shoot the deadbolt and sit on the toilet.

My hands tremble as I take out my cell phone and delete all text messages from both my in-box and my sent box. From my photo album, I take one more look at Robert's face before I delete that too.

At lunch I quickly exit with my students and lock my classroom door behind me. Jen is surprised when I show up in the lounge. She's sitting at a round table with other math teachers and pats the empty seat next to her. I take it.

"You know," I say with a big fake smile on my face, "I might take you up on that concert after all."

I open my cooler on the floor and retrieve one of the sandwiches, a bag of chips, and a Powerade, careful to keep the lid half closed.

She flicks her eyebrows at me. "Well, all right, then."

I force myself to eat, to swallow, to laugh at all the right places, and when Jen places her hand on my knee, I leave it there.

I try not to think about my student, standing outside my locked classroom door, wondering what happened.

In Calculus I feel Robert's eyes on me. I can barely think straight as I work through problem after problem on the board. I don't let them start their homework early as I usually do. And when the bell rings, I call Stacy Woodward up to my desk to give her the letter of recommendation she asked me to write for a summer job she's applying for. I chat with her for a few minutes about the job and her college plans.

Robert lingers, and when Stacy gushes a thank you and heads for the door, he approaches my desk. I try to look busy, shuffling papers that don't need shuffling, jabbing the pens and pencils that litter my desk back into the holder.

"I thought we were going to have lunch together," Robert says.

"Oh, hi, Robert. Sorry. I had to attend a meeting. I hope you got something from the cafeteria."

I can see on his face that he's uncertain whether to believe me or not. Finally, he seems to decide not. His face screws up with his question: "Are you mad at me?"

"Mad at you? Of course not." I keep my voice bright and slap him lightly on the shoulder as my seventh-period students begin making their way through the door. "You better get going or you'll be late for class."

His eyes hold mine for another couple of beats until I look away. And then he goes, and I'm left standing behind my desk, feeling like I've just kicked him in the gut.

When the bell rings at the end of seventh period, I don't wait until my duty ends to leave. I lock my door and head to the parking lot.

Robert

I hurry through the rapidly clearing hallways to my seventh-period class. I don't understand. I thought that maybe he'd been called away on an emergency, that perhaps something had happened to Kiki.

I took that worry with me to fifth period. When I arrived in his classroom sixth period, I expected to see a sub, but he was there, just like every other day. He greeted everyone, just like every other day. He took roll as we completed our warm-up, just like every other day. He lectured and worked problems on the board, just like every other day.

He didn't look at me. Not once. And I don't know why.

And when I stayed behind after class and asked if he was mad at me, he acted just like a teacher—fake cheer, distance thinly disguised as warmth.

Lunch was *his* idea, I remind myself angrily as I take my seat in economics.

"Mr. Westfall," Ms. Flowers says quietly before I can even pull my mechanical pencil from the rings of my spiral notebook. She hands me a white office pass with my name on it and a check mark in the little square next to the word *Counselor.* "Ms. Lincoln would like to see you."

I lay my notebook on the desk and start to get up. "She wants you to take your things with you," she adds.

* * *

Ms. Lincoln greets me with a sympathetic smile and gestures to a chair in front of her desk. She seats herself in the chair next to me. "How are you holding up?"

"I'm okay," I answer.

"I spoke to your mom a few minutes ago."

"Is my dad . . . ?"

"No. But I think you should go home."

My heart sinks a little. "I only have one more period."

"Robert . . ." She shakes her head but doesn't finish.

I meet her eyes and wonder what she thinks about me. I heft my backpack back onto my shoulder, but I don't get up.

She sighs. "I know this is a really hard time for you and for your mom. You should be with your family right now. School can wait."

I nod my head. I know she expects this.

"Is there anything you want to talk about before you go?"

I shake my head, and she pats me on the knee.

"I want you to know that my door is always open. You can talk to me about anything. I'm here for you, okay?"

I wonder for a moment what she'd say if she knew how desperately I wanted this chapter to end and the next to begin. Would she understand? Or would she refer me for some psychiatric counseling on the grounds that I am a psychopath, unable to form an attachment with or feel empathy for my dying father?

She takes the pass from me and scribbles something on it, then hands it back. "Go ahead and check out, then go home."

I stand, my knees weak at the understanding that now I will have to witness death. Ms. Lincoln means well. But I know Andrew never would have sent me away. At least, a few hours ago, I thought I knew that.

I don't understand.

He doesn't respond.

I've always thought of death as coming in one of two ways—quick and bloody, or slow and gentle. It comes neither way to our house.

Dad's eyes are still open, still vacant, but now he's blowing huge wads of foam from his nostrils in great but irregular bursts. My aunts huddle around him. Aunt Whitney gently wipes the foam from his face.

Over the next seven hours, the foam dries up, and Dad's breathing becomes so shallow, so intermittent, that it's hard to know sometimes if he's breathing at all. Near midnight, he grows still. Aunt Olivia places the round disk of her stethoscope on his chest.

Aunt Whitney is curled up next to him and whispering in his ear, speaking for him the words he can't speak for himself. And even though her voice is soft, I can hear her pray: "Into thy hands, Lord, I commend my spirit. Holy Mary, Mother of grace, pray for me. Protect me from the enemy and receive me at the hour of my death."

"He's gone," Aunt Olivia says quietly. She sniffs as she gently closes Dad's eyes, then places her cheek on his chest and sobs. I see tears in Mom's eyes as she sits quietly on the end of the bed, ever the outsider, and I'm surprised to feel the pricks in my own eyes.

When Aunt Whitney and Aunt Olivia pull back the sheet to bathe Dad one last time before the funeral home people show up, I have to leave the room. Even though he's gone, I'm still embarrassed for him, for me, for my mom.

It's a relief when the hearse pulls into the driveway. We wait stiffly in the living room while the attendants take care of business. When they emerge a few minutes later, they are soft-spoken, kind, and respectful as they wheel the black vinyl bag cocooning Dad's wasted body out to the hearse. It's one o'clock in the morning, but a few neighbors are standing around. Aunt Olivia reaches for me as one of the attendants closes the back doors. I shrink from her touch and pull my keys out of my pocket.

No one tries to stop me as I get in my car.

Chapter 17

Andrew

I'm distantly aware that my sleep is fitful—I startle awake, then drift off, then startle awake again. I'm dreaming that I'm standing at my classroom door, jiggling the key in the lock, but it won't open. I pull it out, check the key to see that it's not bent and that none of the teeth have been broken off. I insert it again and twist, but it holds fast.

A sharp rap on the door, and I bolt upright. Another sharp rap.

I grab for my phone on the end table next to the futon. Three AM. My first thought is Kiki. Heart pounding, I flip on the lamp and open the door without even checking the peephole.

Robert is standing there, his eyes slightly swollen and downcast, his hands stuffed into the front pocket of his hoodie. And all I can think to say is, "You shouldn't be here."

He swallows hard and seems to grapple for something to say. Finally, he settles on, "Can I come in?"

By way of answer, I step out onto the porch. He hesitates, then takes a step back, and I pull the door closed behind me. I couldn't have hurt him more if I'd slammed the door in his face and called security.

It's chilly out and I hug my arms to myself. I feel exposed standing under the porch light, but I know that to let him in is to commit a far graver error. The paper Mr. Redmon handed me as I got up to leave, the litany of cautionary behavior that served as a warning, looms large in my mind:

1. Maintain your boundaries.

2. Don't touch students to show affection.

3. Avoid being alone with students.

"Why?" he asks, faintly. "I thought we were friends."

I think about all the hours I spent in front of the computer this evening researching—the names, the faces, the charges, the lives destroyed by acts of indiscretion. Amy McElhenney, twenty-five, accused of having a sexual relationship with an eighteen-year-old student and charged with a second-degree felony. Randy Arias, twenty-seven, facing a twenty-year prison sentence if convicted of an improper sexual relationship with a seventeen-year-old he planned to marry with her mother's consent.

The 2003 Texas law under which they were arrested was intended to apply to students under seventeen, but some self-righteous blowhards had fought to amend the law, making it a felony now for educators to engage in sexual relationships with students of any age.

It's a law that makes criminals out of consenting adults, and while not without its critics, it is the law. Amy McElhenney, Randy Arias, Mary Kay Letourneau, Rachel Burkhart—their names and their public records stand as beacons of caution about letting one's baser desires overrule the strict code of conduct for teachers.

The pain and confusion and, yes, maybe the anger in Robert's face digs at my resolve, and I have to steady myself by imagining my name and mug shot on a site titled The Fifty Most Infamous Teacher Sex Scandals. I'm grateful that this happened now rather than later, when it might have been too late. Because if I'm being honest with myself, my relationship with Robert has not been as professional or as innocent as I claimed.

I take a deep breath and determine to get this over with.

"Mr. Redmon called me in today." He looks up at me for the

first time, surprise flickering in his eyes. "A parent told him we were in the parking lot Friday night."

"So? We were just playing around with my guard rifle. Didn't you tell him that?"

"It's not what we were doing so much as the fact that I was with you at all."

"What does that matter? We're friends. Didn't you—"

"No. Because I can't *be* your friend." I scrub my hand over my face, trying to clear my head. "Look, Robert, it's a violation of the student-teacher relationship. The state calls it a differential of power." I realize I'm parroting my research, that I'm talking down to him like a teacher to a student, but that is what we are, that is what we have to be. "I could lose my teaching certificate. I could even go to jail."

He looks at me like I'm making this stuff up. I don't blame him; it feels that way to me too. "We weren't *doing* anything," he says. "They don't fire people or throw them in jail for talking."

He's right. But the way he emphasized *doing* reminds me how easily talking becomes something more if you're not careful. I have a daughter who is proof of that.

"It's a public high school," I say to him. "Mr. Redmon is right. Perception is everything, Robert. If it even looks like there might be something going on—"

"Nothing is going on. *Nothing.*"

His words slice through me, and Kiki's voice echoes in my head: *Silly Daddy.* Yeah. No kidding. *Shit.* I feel like I've really let him down. All he wanted was a friend, and I'd screwed that up by imagining there was something more. And now there is no going back.

"Robert. I'm your teacher. That's all I can be. I can't be your counselor or your therapist or your—"

"I only asked you to be my friend."

"I can't."

He glares at me like I've just shed my sheep's skin and revealed the wolf beneath. "You could if you wanted to." He huffs. "You just—"

"I can't have lunch with you anymore," I say quietly. "I'm sorry. Ms. Lincoln—"

"Ms. Lincoln doesn't know me." He looks away at the empty parking lot. A fine drizzle is just starting to fall.

I don't want to say what comes next, but I know I have to.

"I need you to do something for me." He tilts his chin to the sky and closes his eyes, waiting for the anvil to fall as he surely knows it must. "I need you to delete all my texts and any that you sent me." His jaw clenches. "And I need you to delete my photo. I can't text with you anymore."

He doesn't respond. The drizzle gathers in droplets on his tense face and dampens his hair. It torments me to see him hurting like this and to know I'm the cause.

"I'm still your teacher, Robert. I can still be there for you in that way."

He opens his eyes and blinks a few times. "If you're worried about my Calculus homework, Mr. McNelis," he says coldly, "don't be. It'll be on your desk tomorrow along with every other student's."

I wince a little at his formal address, but I nod. He has a right to his anger. I'm the adult; I let this happen. I reach behind me for the doorknob.

"Be careful driving home. I'll see tomorrow."

He begins to turn away, then pauses. "My dad died. A couple of hours ago."

"I'm sorry," I say, trying to imbue my words with more meaning than simple sympathy for his loss.

"Yeah. Me too." He turns and walks, then jogs to his car across the lot.

Robert

The driveway is empty when I get home, but the house is ablaze with lights.

I ease past the oxygen compressor that's now blocking the path to the garage door and let myself in. The dryer is tumbling, and the washing machine next to it is filling with hot water. I open the lid and recognize the sheets from my mom and dad's bed. The smell of bleach is strong.

I make my way through the otherwise quiet house. There are no dishes in the sink, no throw pillows on the floor, no crumbs on the couch.

I find Mom in her room. She's managed to dislodge the king-size mattress by herself. It's lying half on the second box spring and half on the carpet. The box spring that sits closest to Mom is out of the frame and leaning against the highboy.

"Where have you been?" she asks softly, looking up at me from her kneeling position on the floor.

"Just driving."

"I wish you would have called or answered your phone. I've been worried. You okay?"

I shrug. "What are you doing?"

She sighs, then tucks a loose strand of hair that's freed itself from her messy ponytail back behind her ear. She looks around the room like she's never seen it before, then she leans back over the bed frame and applies the Phillips head to a screw.

"I'm just cleaning up."

What she's doing is removing all traces of disease and death that have slowly taken over her bedroom over the past year or so, starting with the oxygen compressor and the sheets. And now she's moved on to the side rail bolted to the bed frame.

"Let me do it," I say, taking the screwdriver from her. She drops back on her butt and scuttles backward until she's leaning against the fish tank.

I remove the first of the screws and lay it on the carpet. From the corner of my eye, I see her pull a trash bag from a roll sitting next to her chaise. She opens the cabinet below the tank and starts dumping everything into the bag.

The second screw is only half out, but I stop and watch her for a moment.

"Mom, what are you doing?"

I start to ask what she thinks the fish are going to eat when my eyes stray upward, and I realize there are no fish swimming in the tank. The water still bubbles from the various filters, the live plants still sway in the current, but there is no other sign of life. Then I notice the large net lying on damp carpet next to the tank. I quietly lay the screwdriver on the lip of the bed frame and go to the kitchen.

Dad was meticulous about caring for his fish. The tank was always spotless, the water clear, the fish colorful and healthy. At the first sign of ick or any number of ailments that fish tend to get, he'd isolate the sick fish in a separate tank and treat it with antibiotics or whatever fish medicine his amateur diagnosis pointed him to. Sometimes it recovered; sometimes it didn't.

When it became clear that a fish wasn't going to make it, he'd scoop it into a Baggie with a little water and put it in the freezer, where he believed it quietly and humanely froze to death.

I pull open the freezer door. A large Ziploc bag, a gallon size, sits on a shelf, the fins and eyeballs of thirty or so fish pressed against the plastic, frost just forming along the amorphous outline.

I close the door and gag into the kitchen sink.

Then I get a garden hose from the garage. In the bedroom I unplug the filters, then drop one end of the hose into the tank and draw the other across the room. I open the window, lift out the screen, then suck on the hose just as I've seen my dad do so many times. Just as I feel the water bubble up to my lips, I hang the hose out the window and let the air pressure on the surface of the tank push the water through the hose.

As the hose siphons off the tank, I take the trash bag and dump it in the container in the garage.

We don't say a word.

After I remove the side rail, we maneuver the box spring back onto the frame, then heave the mattress on top.

Mom runs her hand across the bare mattress. A stain darkens the quilting on Dad's side, blood from a bad jab or maybe just a cut. I don't know. I don't want to know.

I sit on the floor, suddenly exhausted, my eyes grainy. I pick up the small notebook on the bedside table and turn it over in my hands, but I don't open it.

"Why did you marry Dad?" I ask. "I mean, I know you were pregnant with me, but you still didn't have to marry him."

Mom takes a deep breath and lets it out slowly, then lies back on the bed. Her bare feet dangle over the edge.

"He was handsome and charming and boyish. He was from a good family. He had a great future ahead of him." She shrugs. "And he asked me."

"Are you sorry you did?"

"I don't know. Sometimes I think I was really bad for him. Not that I was a bad wife, that I didn't do enough, but that, I don't know, that I did too much. He went from being the baby of the family to being my baby. I think I was too willing to take the reins when he wouldn't, to make decisions, to be both mother and father to you. Maybe if I hadn't, he would have."

"Did you hate him?"

"Wow. Is that what you think?"

"I think that's what those fish think."

She gets quiet and curls her toes tightly. Then she sighs heavily and flexes them. "I shouldn't have done that. Yes, maybe I did hate him. Or maybe I just hated what I became after I married him. He was like a child. I think that's partly why I fell for him in the first place. He needed me; I took care of him. I think maybe he resented that, even though he had no choice, and I resented him for not loving me for it."

"Did he love me?"

She rolls over onto her stomach and shimmies around until she's facing me, then rests her chin on the palm of her hand and studies me. "Yes. Of course he did."

I want to believe her.

"Can I give you some advice?" she asks. "Never marry a man who loves himself more than he loves you."

I feel tears well up in my eyes.

"Oh, baby." She gets up off the bed and sits on the floor next to me, but she doesn't pull me to her. "Nic is a nice kid. But he's not the one for you. Date, have a good time, but don't make the same mistake I made. When the right man comes along, it won't be like this. You'll know. Don't settle for anything less."

When I finally quit bawling, Mom finds a rubber mallet in the garage, and together we knock out the safety handrails that were installed in the shower a year ago. We knock out a few tiles with them. It feels good.

I wonder what my aunts will think when they see the demolition, and I realize that I don't care. Their license to make decisions for this family has been revoked.

Chapter 18

Andrew

My head is pounding, my eyes feel like someone dumped a bag of sand into them, and my mind keeps losing track of the problems as I work them on the board. From behind me I hear a snicker. I take a deep breath and write:

$$3x^2 + 8x + 4$$

My intention is to show how to factor by grouping, but the snickering behind me distracts me to the point where I can no longer ignore it.

I turn and lean against the aluminum rail below the whiteboard. Stephen Newman has his foot out of his athletic shoe, and he's poking his socked toes under Kristyn Murrow's thigh. She slaps at his foot and giggles while I watch, unamused.

"Mr. Newman," I bark. He draws his foot back and snaps to attention with exaggerated and annoying precision. He relaxes his face into a false expression of piety, but when giggles erupt around him, he cracks into a big goofy grin.

"How would you solve this problem?" I ask, tapping the board with my marker.

"I guess I'd tell me to shut up and get out," he says, referring to the other problem in the room. More giggles.

Ah, they know me too well.

"Then shut up and get out," I say.

He stands and makes his way to the door, arms clamped to his sides, head down, the very image of shame, although I have no doubt that that child has never in his life felt a shred of shame. He does, however, know the game.

I dart a look around the classroom, and the other kids get quiet, but the smiles remain.

Stephen baby-steps out of the classroom and closes the door behind him, then immediately reopens it and steps back in. "I apologize for disrupting the class, Mr. McNelis. May I please return to my seat?"

He doesn't wait for me to answer, but takes his seat again, then flashes me a smug smile.

God, save me from freshmen. I turn back to the board and get through the lesson as quickly as I can.

In the last ten minutes, I get the kids started on their homework and collapse at my desk. I'm nauseated from lack of sleep and too much coffee and a double heaping of guilt.

I scan my e-mail for the one I know will come today. And there it is, just below a heads-up for a fire drill scheduled for fifth period.

To: **Fabiola Cortez, Bob Benson, Annet Nguyen, Richard Gorman, Susan Weatherford, Andrew McNelis, Bette Flowers**
From: **Lynn Lincoln**
Subject: **Robert Westfall**

Teachers—
I'm sad to inform you that Robert Westfall's father passed away late last night. According to Mrs. Westfall, it was a peaceful passing. Robert will not be in class the rest of the week as the family deals with their loss. When he returns, he will need your support, your under-standing, and your flexibility as he catches up with his

coursework. Please keep the family in your thoughts. I
will provide you with funeral details as soon as I
receive them. Thank you as always for all you do for
our students.

Ms. Lincoln
Twelfth Grade Counselor

I lean back in my chair and close my eyes and try to imagine what he might be doing right now. Do his fingers itch to text me the way my fingers itch to text him? Do I dare text him at least a word of sympathy, an acknowledgment that I'm thinking about him? Would he welcome my text? Would he even read it? Would I be opening a door that I'd only have to close again later?

I'm mulling over these questions when someone farts loudly and the class erupts in laughter. *God, I'm not in the mood for this.* Fortunately, the bell rings and the kids hustle on to their next class.

I poke around in my desk drawer for something to nip this headache, but all I come up with is a still-sealed box of Imodium, a little gift from the woman who heads the math department. The anti-diarrheal had been in my welcome basket last year, tucked among dry erase markers, Hershey's chocolate Miniatures, pencils, and assorted notepads. There'd been a small bottle of Motrin also, but that bottle is long gone. I actually consider the Imodium for a moment before shoving it to the back of my drawer.

Hey, Jen. You got some Tylenol or some Motrin?
I have Midol.
Good enough. *I'll be right over.*

"Kidding," she says when I enter her classroom. She holds out a small gold pillbox with the lid flipped up. "Pick your poison," she says, discreetly dumping the contents into my hand behind her desk. I have no idea what's what, but I choose two matching pills and funnel the rest back into the box.

"Gates open at six thirty," she says as I toss the pills into my mouth. She hands me a water bottle. "You want me to pick you up or you want to pick me up?"

I take a sip of water and use that moment to try and get my bearings. *Gates?*

"Hey, Ms. Went!" a student in a Houston Texans hoodie calls from the center of the room. "Can I go to the bathroom?"

"That's what passing period is for. Take a seat, John."

"But I have diarrhea."

And I've got some Imodium for you, kid. Diarrhea. The only diarrhea that kid has is coming out of his mouth.

Jen rolls her eyes. "Go. Make it fast," she says to him, then turns back to me.

Gates—Pavilion—Iron Maiden. Right. "Um, I'll pick *you* up," I say. "Six o'clock?"

I return to my full classroom as the bell rings and wonder what I was thinking accepting her invitation.

There's no need to mark Robert absent sixth period. The attendance clerk has already entered a PN (parent notification) in the online record for him for the rest of the week. I open my Web page and make a few additional notes in the class calendar so he'll know exactly what he's missed if he's keeping up. And knowing Robert, he's keeping up. Will he notice the more detailed notes? Will he read between the lines? I hope so. I really hope so.

Robert

I'm still thinking about those fish in the freezer when I curl up on my bed for a nap. I have a couple of hours before we head to the funeral home, and I plan to spend them sleeping. But those frozen eyeballs keep floating across the inside of my eyelids. I'm not surprised that Mom turned them into fish sticks the first chance she got.

Mother's Day, four years ago. I remember it like it was yesterday, like all the dramatic moments in my life—the day I lost my first tooth in a rush of blood when the kid down the street accidentally slammed me in the mouth with his Buzz Lightyear, the day I took my driver's test and bumped the curb parallel parking and failed, the day Luke called me on the phone and asked if I'd like to meet for a soda, the moment I realized I was just a no-fly zone between him and Curtis.

Dad was up, showered, and dressed early that morning. He told Mom he needed to run some errands, and I can't blame Mom for expecting that those errands had something to do with the fact that this was her day, even if she had to drive. But I could feel the temperature in the car drop when Dad said he needed to go to the fish store.

He charged over two hundred dollars that day—money I doubt we had to spend—on some live plants, a couple of rainbows, a clown fish, and a plecostomus, plus a new whisper filter and an all-glass deluxe hood (custom fit to reduce evaporation).

It was then, as Mom and I shuffled around the store for over an hour, pretending that this wasn't awkward, pretending that this was a day just like any other, that I finally understood her reaction to me another Mother's Day, a few years earlier.

Like a Russian nesting doll, I open that memory too.

I'd been running errands with her that morning when she'd suggested we stop by the mall for a Mother's Day gift. I had a few dollars saved up from mowing lawns over spring break, but it was money that I'd planned to spend on some new games for my Xbox. So, lacking any fatherly direction, I had innocently responded, "I'm not spending my money on you."

She'd turned the car around, headed straight home, then sent me to my room. I could hear her crying through the closed door. I didn't really get why she was so upset at the time; I was just mad that she wouldn't take me to get my games.

I got it that day in the fish store, the humiliation of being dismissed by her own husband on Mother's Day and by her own son, who was seemingly growing up to be just like him. But I wasn't like him; I was just clueless. And if I'd had a driver's license at the time, I would have taken the keys and Mom and just left Dad there. I would have taken her to lunch, bought some leftover flowers at H-E-B, tried to make her feel special.

Instead I closed myself in my room when we got home. I made her a Mother's Day card on Publisher and printed and carefully folded it, then signed my name at the bottom. But before I could give it to her, the fighting started. Even through the closed door, I could hear them.

"I don't believe you," she yelled. "I am his mother, and you are his father, and it's *your* job to teach *your* son what it means to show appreciation to the women in his life. *Your* job to help him pick out a card or flowers or make a *god*damned piece of toast for me."

I can still hear the ice in his voice when he told her, "You're not my mother."

He just didn't get it. He never did. I suspect those frozen fish were more self-aware at the moment of their demise than he ever was. Someone or something had to pay for the hurt he'd inflicted on her that day, the way he'd simply dismissed her. The fish were just guilty by association.

I actually believed that when Dad died, my aunts' influence ended. But as I sit next to Mom and across the table from Aunt Whitney and Aunt Olivia, I realize how wrong I was.

The funeral director sits uncomfortably at the end of the dark, highly polished conference table. He shifts the knot in his tie a little, then thumbs through the papers in front of him as Mom glares across the table.

They've already bullied Mom into a 2,700-pound, lined concrete burial vault that is guaranteed to protect Dad's mahogany casket—with a Memory Safe drawer for securing private mementos and messages and a Memory Shelf for the subtle display of keepsakes and photos—in perpetuity.

Now they want to hire a bagpiper.

"We cannot afford all this," my mom argues. I can see she's embarrassed at being forced to fight for economy and angry at the suggestion that she's being cheap.

Aunt Whitney's face is stony. "That's what Wes's life insurance is for."

I glance at Mom. Her face is flushed, her jaw tense.

"No," she says finally. "No vault, no bagpipes, no five hundred prayer cards. We'll have a simple funeral."

Aunt Whitney looks at her like she's a cockroach she'd like to smack with her shoe. "My brother is *not* having a pauper's funeral. I'll pay for it myself if I have to. But I just want you to remember something." She points her finger at my mom. "This is *my* kids' money that you'll be spending here. What I have to put into this funeral to give my brother the dignity he deserves takes away from *my* kids."

Mom pushes back her chair and storms out of the room. I follow her into the vestibule.

She's crying and hugging herself, and I'm suddenly so angry at my aunts I can't see straight. I don't like seeing Mom like this, broken. She's always been the adult in the house, the strong one.

"Fuck them," I say.

She smiles a little as fresh tears spill down her face.

I look out onto the cemetery grounds beyond the glass doors. The plots are divided into two sections—those with flat markers, and those with headstones and monuments purchased by families who apparently cared enough about their loved ones to drop the cash. I can't help but notice all the flags and trinkets and photographs that mark the flat graves. Maybe the other section is similarly adorned, but it's hard to see past all that granite.

"You can put him in a pine box for all I care," I say. "If they want anything more, then let them pay for it."

In the end, Mom signs over almost the entirety of Dad's measly whole-life policy and pushes the papers down the table to the funeral director.

I drive Mom home in silence, then lug the aquarium out to the back porch, and with Dad's scarred, hand-carved, wooden tribal cane from Africa, reduce it to tiny shards of glass and dented metal. I cut my right thumb when I pick up the pieces and bleed all over my band hoodie.

A double Band-Aid stems the flow, but the bleed-through leaves a watery red smudge on my keypad a little later as I delete the text messages in my in-box one by one, reading each one one last time before I let it go forever. There are 199, one short of the maximum my phone will hold. I've already pared them down repeatedly, saving only the most recent and the most personal. I don't keep any of them now.

N

Just another homework assignment that I will dutifully complete because he's the teacher, and I'm just the student.

The most recent text, however, is from Nic, sent minutes after school let out for the day, about the same time my mom was signing away any small hope I had of pursuing a college education of my choosing.

OMG OMG OMG. Your dad! I just heard. I wondered where you were this morning. You must be completely devastated!!! I know I am. Krystal and I are going to make you something tonight to make you feel better. Oh, and if you get a new suit for the funeral, be sure to buy one with skinny legs. Trust me on this.

On a low shelf that runs along the far side of my desk, next to a sticky ring of something red (Hawaiian Punch, maybe) are the Iron Maiden tickets my aunts gave me for Christmas. I hadn't mentioned them to Nic.

I pick them up and notice the date. I know that if I step outside, I'll be able to hear the relentless bass two miles away. But I don't go outside. I drop the tickets in the wicker basket next to my desk, delete Nic's text, and go to bed early.

Andrew

When I told Jennifer I'd take her up on the concert, I wasn't thinking about actually *going* to the concert. I was running for cover, hiding my privates like a kid in a locker room who's just been pantsed.

Despite another dose of pain killers and a glass of wine at home, I am still strung tighter than a drum, irritable, and wanting to be anywhere but in a car on the way to a concert with Jennifer Went—especially a concert by a band that's not only a little long in the tooth, but is known for squirting fake blood from a papier-mâché mask on stage. It's unfair to Jen, but I can't seem to shake my bad mood. She attributes it to a bad day at school. I don't dispute that.

"Come on," she says, reaching between the seats for the blanket she tossed back there when I picked her up. "I'll buy you a beer, then give you a back rub. You'll be chillin' and enjoying the music in no time."

Not likely.

It's hard to chill at a metal concert, but I don't argue when she takes my half-empty cup of Shiner Bock later, sets it aside on a level square of trampled grass, and insists I assume the position.

I read somewhere that the lead singer—Bruce something-or-other—could raise the dead with his powerful vocals. I don't know about that, but his *powerful* voice and the thundering bass drum and crashing symbols are like spikes in my brain. Still, I think I actually doze as the band blisters through its first set, Jen's thumbs digging into my muscles, easing the soreness that still lingers from Friday night's guard practice. I don't even complain when she slides her hands up under my shirt and works her way up and down my spine. I just let myself experience it, and let my mind drift, unguarded, to a blue-eyed, blond-haired kid with chewed-up hems on his jeans and a killer smile.

I see him close his eyes and bite his lower lip as he pops and locks to the music, the sweat beaded up behind his ears as he spins and comes up on his toes like a skateboarder, then loses his balance and stumbles forward, the grin when he challenges me to prove myself in the parking lot. I feel the warmth of his hands when he positions mine on the rifle, the solidness of his body when he embraces me before saying good night. I won't say that I imagine the fingers that have slipped beneath the waistband of my jeans are his, and I won't say that I don't.

I will say that when a couple of my students call out a hello to us as they head to the concession area for sodas during the band's break, I don't turn over. Still lying on my stomach, I take a sip of warm beer and reluctantly let go of his image.

Chapter 19

Robert

People I barely recognize, and many I don't recognize at all, mingle in the vestibule. There are lots of hugs, quiet conversation, and quieter laughter. A sixteen-by-twenty framed photo of my dad in his younger days sits next to the guest book. Before the wake, every single person who signed their name seemed to find it necessary to comment on how handsome he was as they sniffed and took a prayer card from the stack.

Near a large potted palm, my dad's old college roommate chats up the priest, who is apparently congratulating him on a beautiful eulogy, despite the fact that said roommate hasn't seen Dad in ten years. The second eulogy was given by my uncle Michael (Aunt Whitney's husband) who's never spent one moment alone with my dad. The third and fourth were given by my aunts, who both sobbed as they told about the brother they cherished, the husband who was devoted to his wife, and the father who was devoted to his son.

I didn't even know who they were talking about.

I huddle outside the men's room door and watch these strangers. From their midst, Mr. Gorman emerges and makes his way over to me. He hugs me warmly, the way I imagined a father would hug his son. "You okay, buddy?"

"Yeah."

"If there's anything you need . . ."

"I know."

Uncle Thomas weaves his way through the crowd. I introduce my band director to him. The two men clasp hands, and Mr. Gorman expresses his condolences.

"You ready?" Uncle Thomas says, turning to me. "Everyone's gathering at the casket now. Your mom sent me to get you."

"I'm not going."

"Of course you're going."

"No, I'm not," I say pointedly.

Mr. Gorman shifts uncomfortably. "I'll be at the funeral tomorrow, Robert," he says. I nod and thank him. He squeezes my shoulder and leaves.

"They're waiting for you," Uncle Thomas persists. "This is your last chance to say good-bye to your dad before they close the casket."

I shake my head. I don't know why I don't want to view my dad's dead body. I just know that at the moment my feet are rooted to the floor. I don't belong there.

As if he can read my mind, Uncle Thomas reminds me why I feel like such an intruder.

"Don't be a pain in the ass. This is something you do for the family."

"I *am* the family," I say, stonily.

Chapter 20

Andrew

I know I'm sticking my neck out, but I don't care. The guilt is eating me up on the inside. The need to be there for him, overwhelming. They don't own me, and there are no do-overs. I will never be able to make up for abandoning him on this day.

Mrs. Stovall is not at her desk. With a confidence I don't feel, I knock on Mr. Redmon's open door. He's typing but glances up briefly and motions me in. I get right to the point.

"I'd like permission to attend Mr. Westfall's funeral this afternoon."

Mr. Redmon's eyes remain fixed on his computer screen. "No. We're short on subs today."

"I can get someone to cover my sixth- and seventh-period classes."

He ignores me, but I am not giving up so easily. This is nonsense.

"Robert is my student. He talked to me a lot about his dad. I feel like I'm letting him down if I don't at least make an appearance at the funeral."

Mr. Redmon settles back in his chair and finally looks up at me. "Robert Westfall has seven teachers, Mr. McNelis, in case you've forgotten. I can't release seven teachers to attend a funeral. Ms.

Lincoln, Mr. Hough, and Mr. Gorman are already going. There's no need for you to be there. I suggest you send a card to the family."

The argument is stupid. I doubt even one of those other six teachers, with the exception of the band director, has expressed any interest whatsoever in attending the funeral. And Logan Hough? The twelfth grade assistant principal? I doubt Robert even knows him. He's not the kind of kid to spend a lot of time in the AP's office. I tell Mr. Redmon this and suggest I go in Logan's place, but he doesn't budge.

"I'm not releasing you. That is my final word."

I know what he's thinking, and it pisses me off.

"I could ride over with Ms. Lincoln or Mr. Gorman."

I wait for him to respond to my suggestion, but he ignores me. After a long moment, I stalk out of his office, furious.

The funeral is scheduled to begin at one o'clock. Mr. Westfall is Catholic, so the services will be held at St. Mary's. In the next few minutes before my planning period ends, I call the church. If I can't be there for the funeral, maybe I can be there for the family gathering after the burial. I jot down the information the church secretary gives me.

Until this morning, I hadn't even considered trying to attend the funeral. It was Kiki who changed my mind.

She'd been especially hard to disengage when I dropped her at Ms. Smith's Village. She clung to me, she cried big two-year-old tears, she begged, "Daddy, no leave."

Robert had said he wanted his father to die, but I wonder if somewhere down deep inside, he's crying too. *Daddy, no leave.*

I've really known Robert for only a little over four weeks, but I feel like, in some ways, I know him better than anyone else. I feel like he's shared with me his deepest hurt.

I need to be there.

When the final bell rings, I usher the kids out, lock the door, and use the MapQuest page I printed to find my way to him.

The family is gathered at the home of Robert's aunt, Dr. Whitney Bloom. The house is in a transitioning neighborhood where large, ostentatious homes on small lots dwarf the 1950s-style one-stories of older residents who are still holding out. Two homes on the street are under construction. The cars packed in the driveway and the photo attached to a gas lamp point the way to the house.

I find a place to park on the curb six houses down and walk back.

Through the thick leaded glass, I can see the mourners. A middle-aged man in a dark gray suit opens the oversized, heavy steel door. I reach out my hand. "I'm Andrew McNelis, Robert's Calculus teacher."

"Oh. Thank you for coming," he says, gripping my hand firmly, then swinging the door open wide.

"Robert's here somewhere. I didn't see you at the funeral?"

"I couldn't make it. Is it okay if I'm here?"

"Of course it is. Come on in. There's plenty of food in the kitchen; please go help yourself. I'll see if I can find Robert."

I thank him and migrate toward the food, but I'm not hungry. Still, I don't know these people, and standing around with my hands in my pockets is awkward, so I take a plate someone hands me and lay a few slices of ham and a roll on it and wander back into the living room.

It's cool but sunny outside, and someone has propped open the French doors. Two young boys, twins, a few years older than Kiki, are taking turns dunking a junior-size basketball into a Little Tikes hoop a few feet away from the pool, while the adults sitting at the patio table look on. They seem relaxed, and I think, were it not for the black suits and dresses, this could be any poolside party.

No one pays any attention to me, and I don't want to intrude on the gathering of family and friends, so I continue through a wooden gate that leads to a covered area just outside the garage.

I almost don't see Robert. He's sitting on the concrete pad, his back pressed against a stone column. He's staring out at the construction the next lot over. As I settle onto the concrete next to him, he looks up, surprised. His face is pale and pinched.

"I didn't think you'd be here," he says.

I offer him some ham, but he shakes his head. "Have you eaten anything today?" I ask.

"Not hungry."

I set the plate on the ground next to me. "Your dad must have had a lot of friends. That's quite a crowd in there."

Robert smirks. "They're my aunts' friends, colleagues, I don't know."

He looks back at the construction. I study his profile as the silence stretches out. He's gotten a haircut recently, his sideburns trimmed with neat precision. But he looks exhausted, like he can barely keep his eyes open.

"Are you sleeping?" I ask.

"You know, I didn't even know we were coming here until Father Vincent invited everyone at the end of the service." He scoffs. "Mom and I spent all day cleaning the house yesterday, and now everyone's in there telling Aunt Whitney and Aunt Olivia and my grandmother how sorry they are for their loss. They look at me like I'm just some random kid who was dragged to the funeral by his parents."

"What about your mom?"

"She disappeared right after we got here. I think she's upstairs taking a nap. It's been a hard couple of weeks on her."

He stretches out his legs for a moment, then pulls them back to his chest.

It makes me angry to think how self-centered these people are. This day should be about this young man, comforting him, offering him words of encouragement, but here he sits, alone in a carport, and nobody inside even seems to notice his absence.

"Why did you come?" he asks. "I thought Mr. Redmon read you the riot act?"

"Yeah, well. Mr. Redmon may be the boss of me at school, but he doesn't own me. I couldn't get away for the funeral, but I wanted to be here for you, even if I am a little late."

"Ms. Lincoln and Mr. Gorman came. Mr. Hough too."

"I know. Did they talk to you?"

"They didn't come to the cemetery, but they did come through the receiving line after the funeral. Ms. Lincoln sent a little magnolia tree with one bloom for us to plant in the yard."

I smile. "That's a nice gesture."

Robert is still wearing his suit, but he's pushed his sleeves up to his elbows, and when he stretched his legs, I noticed that he's holding a small notebook. "What's in the notebook?" I ask.

He looks down at it for a moment like he's just seeing it for the first time, then turns it over twice in his hands.

"One of my aunts gave this to my dad before he got so bad he couldn't write anymore. It was so he could record his memories, words of wisdom, his hopes for my future . . . his love."

He bites his lower lip, then looks away. I take the notebook from him and open it. I flip through the blank pages and silently curse the man who dared to call himself a father.

He's beginning to twitch. I lay my hand on his shoulder. "Robert . . ."

He suddenly pushes himself to his feet and stumbles over me, fishing his car keys from his pocket. I catch up with him at his car. "Robert."

He turns, his face stricken. "I have to get out of here."

I nod and hold out my hand. "Let me have your keys. I'll drive."

He hesitates, then hands them over.

I hit the unlock button, then get him settled in the passenger seat before climbing behind the wheel. When I crank the engine, Muse's "Uprising" explodes from the speakers. Robert doesn't even flinch at the loud music, and he doesn't complain when I drop the volume.

I don't think about where I'm going when I pull his car into the street. I just drive, glancing across the console at him when I can. He's folded his arms tightly across his chest, and he's twitching more violently, almost like he's cold. And I know he's hurting, for the father he's lost . . . or maybe the one he never had.

A short time later I find myself pulling into a parking space in front of my apartment. Somewhere in the back of my mind, I know this is a bad idea. But I'm not thinking about consequences; I'm thinking about a young man who's falling apart.

The efficiencies are aligned along the back parking lot, the bottom units each with a front door and a broad window overlooking the concrete front porch. The last time Robert had stood on that porch, I'd sent him away.

I wrap my arm around his shoulders and walk him to my apartment as he furiously wipes at his eyes. But once I unlock the door and show him in, he turns and falls into me.

"It's okay, baby." The words are out of my mouth before I can check them. I close the door behind me and hold on to him as he sobs into my shoulder, his fingers gripping at the back of my shirt. When his anguish dissolves into something like hiccups, he turns his face to my neck.

"Come on," I say, pulling away. I settle him on the futon, then bring him a small glass of wine and sit on the sofa table in front of him.

He takes a sip, grimaces, then drinks the whole thing down. I reach for the bottle and refill his glass. He stares into it, but he doesn't drink again. "I'm sorry," he says quietly.

"Don't be. Everybody needs a good cry every now and then."

He sniffs and swipes at his eyes with the heel of his hand. "When was the last time you cried?"

I want to make him feel okay about letting go, but it seems important that I be honest with him. So I tell him the truth. "I don't know. I guess it's been a while. I almost cried this morning when Kiki wouldn't let go of my pants leg. I had to shake her off like a dog. That hurt like hell."

He smiles a little, but it lasts only a moment.

"Do you want to talk?" I ask.

He shrugs and swallows hard. "I thought I'd be relieved when he died," he says finally, turning the glass around in his hands, "but I just feel so damn empty." He looks up at me. "So damn . . . insignificant."

"You're not insignificant."

He searches my face, and for a moment, his eyes settle on my mouth. I feel like some invisible elasticity between us, like a rubber band that has been stretched, is about to release. And then his eyes find mine again, and he says, "Thank you."

He looks around at my apartment. From where he sits he can see every inch of it, with the exception of the bathroom and the inside of the closet. "Where do you sleep?" he asks.

"You're sitting on it."

"I'm in your bed?"

"I'm going to pretend like you didn't say that."

He laughs a little, the first really happy sound I've heard him make in almost a week. I realize how much I've missed that. It feels like the sun rising on a cold winter morning.

"Can I use your bathroom?" he asks.

"Are you going to nose around in my cabinets?"

"Probably."

I smile back at him and nod my head toward the bathroom. While he's in there, I look for something to feed us. The toilet flushes and then the faucet turns on and then off again as I pull out leftover burger patties and buns from the night before and set them on the counter. I can hear him opening the medicine cabinet, the cabinet under the sink, the shower curtain. I think he's doing it all loudly so I'll know. I have no secrets, but I'm amused by his blatant snooping.

I turn on the toaster oven. I'm just slicing a tomato when I hear the rush of water in the tub. The distinct bubblegum smell of Mr. Bubble wafts under the door.

"Dang this stuff makes a lot of bubbles," he calls out.

I laugh to myself and turn the toaster oven on low, wrap the meat in foil and toss it inside.

I'm watching some breaking news on CNN when he emerges half an hour later. His white dress shirt is unbuttoned and hanging loosely over his trousers and he's holding a Binky up by the plastic handle, a grin playing across his face.

"Ah, so that's where I left it," I say, plucking it from his hand and into my mouth as I make my way back to the kitchen. I lay the Binky on the counter. "Feeling better?" I ask over my shoulder.

"Yeah. Has Tom Cruise come out of the closet?"

I glance back at the TV. "If he did, I don't think it would be breaking news. What do you like on your burger?"

"Whatever you got."

I settle next to him on the futon. He takes the stacked paper plates and separates them on the sofa table. I hand him a cold can of Coke. He sets the can down next to his plate and picks up the ticket stubs from a pewter tray where I dump my pockets at the end of the day. "The Iron Maiden concert," he says, looking at them. He fans them out in an unspoken question.

"I went with a colleague."

"Male or female?"

I wonder if this is a loaded question. "Female, actually. Ms. Went."

He sets them back in the tray and picks up the blank notebook I had placed there. I curse myself for not throwing it away. Robert fans the pages. His eyes are slightly puffy and the edges of his lower eyelids are tinged red. He sets the notebook back down and takes another sip of his soda.

On CNN, Wolf Blitzer is soliciting Sanjay Gupta's opinion of some protests somewhere in the world.

"Aren't you worried about my being here, in your apartment and all?" he asks.

"A little."

"Then why did you bring me here?"

I think about this a moment before I answer. A few days ago this would have been out of the question. A few days ago all I could think about was my career, my reputation, how a scandal might affect my daughter.

But when he'd showed me that notebook, something about those blank pages had written something on my heart, and there was no unwriting it. I could have taken him to a Starbucks half an hour away to talk, someplace where no one was likely to recognize us. We could have sat in his car in a parking lot somewhere. But I'd taken him here, right into the lion's den, so to speak.

The fact is, he was crashing, and he needed a soft place to land. It was just that simple.

"Because," I say, turning to him, careful to keep my eyes above his shoulders, "I'm more concerned about you at the moment than I am about me."

He locks eyes with me, and I think he's going to cry again, but then his eyes drift down to my mouth, and an alarm goes off in my head.

"Eat or you're going to hurt my feelings."

As he picks at his burger, I realize I have no appetite either. I focus on the TV, but I am keenly aware of him next to me. "How about some ice cream?" I ask after a while.

"Moo-llennium Crunch?"

"Ah, you were paying attention. Lucky for you, I haven't opened it."

I stack our plates and dump them in the trash under the sink and find a couple of bowls. I've got the ice cream carton open, and I'm looking for the scoop with the sugar cone handle that Kiki likes when my phone signals a text.

If I said you had a beautiful body . . . ?

I laugh when I read his text. I know what comes next. "Country Western? Argh, you're killing me." I glance over my shoulder. He's leaning against the facing that delineates kitchen from living/sleeping quarters.

"They're not lyrics," he says.

I know that. I can see it in his eyes, soft and pleading. I smile at him again like he's joking around and turn back to the ice cream. "One or two scoops?" I ask stupidly.

"Can we just talk about this?"

No, we can't. I scoop up some ice cream and release it into one of the bowls.

"Please look at me," he says quietly.

"Do you want ice cream or not?" I ask lightly.

"Please."

"Robert, do me a favor, will you? Button your shirt."

"Why?"

"Do you really have to ask that?"

"No," he says, "but I want to hear it from you."

I realize I've got a white-knuckled grip on the edge of the counter. In the bowl, the lone scoop of ice cream is melting around the edges. I can't do this. I can't look at him. He sees right through me. Part of me is glad that he knows, and part of me is terrified about what he'll do with that knowledge and whether or not I can put on the brakes if it comes to that.

"If I button my shirt, will you talk to me?" he pleads. When I don't respond, he says, "I'm buttoning it, okay?"

After a moment, I pick up the scoop from the counter and set it back in the carton, then turn to him, my eyes fixed on the linoleum floor.

"I think there's something going on between us. The way you look at me." He pauses, and when he speaks again, I can hear the frustration in his voice. "I just want to talk about this. Why can't you look at me? I'm not a kid. I'm eighteen. And look around. There's nobody here. Just us. *Dam*mit." In my peripheral vision I can see him hold his hands out, then drop them limply again to his sides. "I think I'm in love with you, Andrew, and I think, maybe . . ." He mutters a *fuck*. "Just tell me I'm wrong, and I'll never mention it again. We can go back to where we were. Pretend like this never happened. But I need to know. Please. Please, just tell me."

I don't respond. I don't know how to respond. I won't deny it, but how can I confirm it either? The silence stretches out between us. I'm afraid to look at him.

The heater kicks on.

Finally, he turns away. "I'll drive you back to your car," he says quietly.

"Robert . . ." He stops, and I lift my eyes to him. I want to reach out to him. Instead, I grip the counter behind me more tightly. I'm about to make an admission I have no business making, but I can't let him go like this. I take a deep breath and allow myself a small smile. "The minute you walk down that aisle with a diploma in your hand, I'm going to be all over you like glaze on a donut. But until then—"

I don't get to finish because he's there, his hand over my mouth, his eyes searching mine. Every neuron in my brain, every nerve ending in my body fires at once. A war wages in my chest—the teacher who knows this is wrong, and the man who aches to hold him close. With his free hand he touches my cheek, my jaw, my neck. I won't touch him. I won't. But I know this too: I won't stop him from touching me. He releases my mouth.

"Robert . . ." It's a plea. For what, I'm not sure. He uses both his hands to draw my face to his, and when he presses his mouth to mine—tentative at first, and then desperate—I can't help but respond in kind. It's wrong, and it's right, and it takes every ounce of my willpower to finally bring it to a stop.

"Shit," I mutter, pressing my forehead to his and grasping his wrists to pull his hands from my face. "We have to stop."

"I don't want to stop," he says breathlessly, pulling his hands free. His mouth is on my neck now as one hand works its way up my shirt. My stomach retracts, and I feel the gap between my waistband and my abdomen. A groan escapes. I can hardly think as his hand grabs at the hair on my chest.

When the rational part of my brain finally surfaces again, I put the palm of my hand against his chest and create a narrow distance between us. "We *have* to stop."

Robert

"I don't want to stop." I withdraw my hand and reach for the buttons on his shirt, but he locks his fists around my wrists.

"Stop," he says firmly.

He's breathing heavily, and when he shivers, I can't help but smile.

"Okay," he says, closing his eyes for a moment and pursing his lips. When he opens them again he smiles back at me and shakes his head slowly. "So much for my timeline, huh?" He takes a deep breath and blows it out through fluttering lips. "I'm taking you home."

I don't want to go home. I don't want to be anywhere that he's not. He doesn't give me a choice, though. He slips past me, grabs my keys off the table, then opens the door—"After you."—but he's still smiling. It's this impish, guilty little smile. I growl my frustration and walk through the door.

I drive, but every chance I get, I glance over at him. He watches me, thoughtful, still smiling. All I can think about is what it would be like to get him naked. I wonder if he's thinking the same thing.

I pull into Aunt Whitney's street. It's not quite dark yet, and a number of cars are still parked in her driveway and at the curb. I ease the car down the street until I locate Andrew's. I pull up to the curb behind him and put the car in park.

He's still smiling like the Cheshire Cat. I laugh. "So what do we do now?"

He exhales, then looks off down the street, then back at me. Still smiling. My heart swells because I had something to do with that smile. "New rules of engagement, okay?" he says.

I'm not sure what he's talking about, and I'm not sure if I should agree, so I just wait.

"First," he says, finding my hand on the gear shift and linking his fingers with mine, "you delete every text, immediately. Sent and received. If my name is still in your contacts, get rid of it. You can memorize my number. No friend requests on Facebook, don't follow me on Twitter, and no more lunches in my classroom."

"Okay."

"And no more lingering gazes in the classroom. You want to look at me . . ." He pauses a moment and looks away, shaking his head like he can't believe he's saying this. When he turns back, his face is more serious, but soft. "You look at me in your dreams. As far as everyone else is concerned, you are my student. And that is all you are. Four months, baby. Okay?"

He called me baby. I nod, and a tremendous relief floods through me.

"And I want you to keep seeing Nic, at least for a while, okay?"

I let out a groan and drop my head back against the headrest. That is asking too much.

"I mean it, Robert. You're going to go on being that little twerp's boyfriend until graduation. Got it?"

I let out a huff. "Okay."

"And I'm going to spend more time with Ms. Went."

"What? Mr. Redmon already knows—"

"Mr. Redmon doesn't really know anything. And neither do those kids. And if they think they do, then I'm going to give them a reason to doubt."

"Anything else?"

"We play it cool, okay? No taking risks. I can't bring you to my apartment again, not yet, and you can't just drop by. I don't want Maya asking a lot of questions if you make a surprise visit when she's there. She already knows there's a guy. But I haven't told her everything."

Everything, as in the fact that I'm still a high school student? He doesn't have to spell it out for me. But then I fix on the other bit of information. *She already knows there's a guy.* I smile at that thought.

"And besides," he adds, gripping my hand more tightly, "I cannot guarantee that I will continue to behave honorably if I spend time alone with you."

He glances up and down the street, then leans across the console and kisses me. Behind him, his hand finds the door handle. He pops it, and he's gone.

Four months. Glaze on a donut.

Chapter 21

Andrew

Yes, I know I've crossed a line. But . . .

1. Robert is eighteen, a fully consenting adult by law.
2. He initiated the relationship; he pursued me. I am not complaining; merely making an observation.
3. In four more months, our teacher-student status won't even exist anymore.
4. I'm crazy about him. I can't help that he came into my life four months too soon; he stole my heart when I wasn't looking. That I don't want it back even if he's willing to hand it over.
5. If I had a chance for a do-over, or an opportunity to make corrections like I give my students when they screw up a test, I'd take a pass.

I even think that Maya would approve of the person I've chosen, though she might not be too keen about the circumstances. I think I can trust her, and I consider taking a left at the next traffic light and heading over to her house.

Maybe I just want someone to share the burden of my secret

with. Maybe I want to be told that the heart trumps the law. But I don't make the left turn.

Being careful means that no one, *no one,* can know. In June I will shout it from the rooftops—*I love Robert Westfall!*—but for now, I have to think of ways to sweep a branch across my tracks.

I call Jennifer Went. Let them gossip about that for a while.

"Hey, partner!" she answers, brightly.

"Hey," I respond. "You up for a movie tomorrow night?"

Robert

It's dusky out, but finding Dad's grave is easy. I follow the crushed grass to the mound of fresh dirt that marks his resting place. The plants have been removed—probably softening all the stark places in Aunt Whitney's house—but the cut flowers and sprays remain, arranged around the grave and over it. I want to know who they are from, but all the cards have been removed.

I know my aunts and my grandmother will miss my dad. He's their baby brother, their pet, her son. His absence will leave a huge hole in their lives.

I loosen a calla lily from a spray and run my fingers over the waxy petals.

I think about the way my heart thudded in my chest when Andrew held me to him as I cried, and the way my eyes stung at how good it felt to know he wanted me as much as I wanted him. The way his skin felt, the way his lips felt, the way his hand felt gripped in mine.

I'm more concerned about you at the moment than I am about me.

I swipe at a fresh tear that rolls down my cheek.

Sprinklers switch on in the section across the narrow road from me, and crickets begin to chirp as the dark gives way to the sodium vapor lamps warming up and buzzing at the edges of the cemetery.

I drop the lily in the dirt, then I pull the notebook from my pocket where I'd stuck it as I left Andrew's apartment. I toss that in the dirt, too, and take a deep breath to steady myself.

I'll keep you my dirty little secret.

Ha, ha. I believe I've seen that one before. Delete, okay? Xoxo

Chapter 22

Andrew

I don't have Kiki this weekend, but Jennifer doesn't need to know that. We take in an early movie—some romantic comedy she picked out—share a bucket of popcorn, then I drop her off so I can purportedly pick up my daughter by nine.

If Jen notices that I'm distracted, she doesn't let on. I doubt she notices.

Robert returned to school today even though he was expected to be out the entire week. I'd had to pinch myself a couple of times during class to keep everything nice and loose. He'd done good, almost too good, to the point that I'd found myself willing him to look at me. And here I was worried about him giving us away.

I was the one I had to watch.

But damn, he looked good. Not any different than he looked any other day, but any other day I hadn't known what it felt like to have him so close to me, to put my mouth on his, to shiver under his touch.

He didn't linger after class, he didn't stop by after school, and I found myself thinking I had imagined everything.

"You sure you can't come in for a minute?" Jen asks, looking up at me with unabashed hope in her eyes.

We're standing outside her apartment door, which is, thankfully, on the other side of town. I resist checking the messages on my phone.

"Sorry," I say, shrugging my apology for emphasis. "I'm afraid I'm Daddy first." Which isn't exactly a lie.

She slips her arms around my waist, and I know I'm supposed to kiss her good night. "Did you like the movie?" I ask.

"Yeah. It was good. But, I don't know. I think Jennifer Aniston is a little overexposed. Don't you?" She says all this in a husky voice, like she'd like to be a little more exposed herself.

"Well, next time, no Jennifer Aniston."

I can see the *next time* register in her eyes, a promise that she files away, perhaps only to take out and examine for hidden meaning when she curls up in bed tonight.

I don't particularly like the deception. But I consider it a necessary evil. She's young and pretty. She'll get over it. In fact one day, she'll soothe her raw emotions with words like *prick* and *douche* and that's okay with me. I'll spot her a couple of *pricks*.

"Gotta go," I say, unlocking her wrists behind me.

"When do I get to meet your daughter?"

"Um, soon."

"Okay," she says, and sighs heavily, a long note of resignation.

"I'll call you tomorrow, okay?"

With that I let go of her hands and return to my car.

I miss you.

I smile and delete his text.

A lot of singles live in my apartment complex, so it's not surprising that the parking lot is fairly empty this early on a Friday night. Without any real conscious thought, I find myself scanning the spaces for Robert's car. I'm both relieved and disappointed when I don't find it. Maybe he went out with Nic tonight. Maybe he's hanging out with some band kids. Maybe he's just sitting at home waiting to exchange some sexy texts with me. As I pull into a parking space opposite my apartment and get out, I realize I'm okay with the last two thoughts, but I don't like the first one at all.

The light is out on my front porch, and as I fumble for my apartment key in the dark, I make a mental note to buy a new lightbulb tomorrow. The first key I try turns out to be for my classroom door. Before I can identify the right key, my cell phone signals a text. I snatch it from my pocket so quickly I almost fumble it to the ground.

Make me your radio.

I lean back against the door and read the text again in the dark.

"How was your date?"

His voice startles me, and I almost fumble my phone for the second time. I look around and find his silhouette sitting against the wall on the far side of my concrete porch, not four feet from me. "You scared me half to death," I say, trying to calm my skittering heartbeat. "What are you doing here? Is everything okay?"

"Yeah," he says, getting to his feet. "I just wanted to—I thought—" He doesn't finish, and even though I can't make out the features of his face in the dark, I know him well enough now to know he's chewing on his lip again. It's that hesitation, that uncertain quality in his voice that I'm becoming increasingly familiar with. So when he asks, "Can I come in?" I can't say no. "Are you going to behave yourself?" I ask playfully.

"I don't think so."

I laugh quietly. "Come on."

I shut the door behind us and lock it just as he proves he can't, in fact, be trusted to behave himself. He presses me up against the door with his own body, and for a few moments, I forget what a bad idea this is. I've checked my hands at the door, literally, but one of his grips the back of my head. And it strays . . . down the length of my arm, up the back of my shirt, down again over my ass. I feel my nerve endings spring to life. The sense of déjà vu makes me grin, breaking the lip lock he has on me.

"What's so funny?" he asks.

"Nothing." And then it clicks. "Did you unscrew my lightbulb?"

"I might have."

"A life of crime always starts with the little things."

"Then lock me up before I can cause more harm."

I might just do that. In his right hand, he's clutching a small bouquet of what I think are carnations. I smelled them somewhere between getting pressed against the door and getting felt up, but I've been a little too busy fighting the urge to throw him to the ground to comment on them. Now seems like a good time.

"You brought me flowers?"

"Isn't that what a guy does when he's courting his paramour?"

"Paramour?" I take the flowers from him and run the petals through my fingers in the dark. "Is that one of your SAT words?"

I expect him to laugh; I expect him to make some witty comment; I expect him to reengage my mouth. He does none of those things. Instead, he grows quiet for a moment, and then using both hands this time, addresses the buttons on my shirt.

The primal part of my brain allows him two buttons before the scared-shitless part engages. "Hey, hey, hey," I whisper, capturing his hands in mine and smacking him in the nose with the carnations in the process. "PG-thirteen, remember?"

"I don't want PG-thirteen. I'm eighteen, and I want you."

"And you'll have me . . . when you graduate. Glaze on a donut, right? In the meantime"—I flip the light on to dampen the obvious sexual tension growing between us—"we keep it above the waist . . . and fully clothed."

He groans in frustration. I feel his pain to the tip of my toes.

"Come on. You can watch a rerun of *Tosh.O* with me."

"Are we going to watch from your bed?"

I try to give him a scowl, but I don't think I quite pull it off. "You are trouble," I say.

"No, I'm not," he replies, grinning.

I leave him to turn on the TV and rummage around in the pantry for some popcorn. Frankly, I had my fill of popcorn at the theater, but Robert needs something to keep his hands and mouth busy, so more popcorn it is. I find a couple of boxes behind the nutritious whole-grain Lucky Charms that Kiki and I keep secret from Maya. "Butter or caramel?" I call out. When he doesn't respond, I look around the wall to the living room. He's got the remote in his hand, and he's scrolling through the onscreen guide, in his boxer briefs. They're a soft gray flannel, nicely filled out all around. I help myself to a good look before I *ahem.*

"What channel?" he asks innocently.

"Why are you in your underwear?"

A mock seriousness overtakes his face. "Because I know how much it bothers you when I take off my shirt. So I didn't. Kudos for me, right?"

I shake my head slowly. "Right." I turn away, smiling at his brazenness. "Sixty-one," I call back. "And put your pants on."

As the popcorn heats up in the microwave, I futilely attempt to cool off, but he's so damn cute and so sexy. And that's when the light goes out in the living room. "Too much glare," he calls out before I can react. *God help me.* I leave the kitchen light on when I bring the bowl of popcorn in a few minutes later. He picks up the remote again, points it at the TV, and presses the Power button.

"Did I miss something?" I ask, setting the bowl on the sofa table.

"Can we just talk?"

"Not in the dark with you still in your underwear."

He holds my eyes for a long moment, then gets up and pulls his pants back on. I instantly regret saying anything, but I'd never admit that. He settles back on the futon, and warily, I join him.

I think I know where this is going, but I ask anyway: "What do you want to talk about?"

"I'm eighteen," he says simply.

"No."

"You don't even know what I'm going to say."

"Yeah, I think I do. Four months, Robert. We can wait four months."

"Last night I stopped by the cemetery on my way home."

I take a deep breath and mentally kick myself for forgetting that his dad has been in the ground barely twenty-four hours. I feel like an ass.

"Are you okay?" I ask.

He shrugs and his eyebrows draw together. "I don't know why I went. I just keep trying to feel something for him. Not anger or hurt or anything like that, you know. But loss, I guess. I mean, I wish I could say that I'm going to miss him, but . . ." He shakes his head. "I feel like I've been cheated all my life of something that should have been mine. That's what gets me. I've been trying to remember the last time my dad touched me—the last time anyone touched me like they really meant it. I know Mom used to. And then I went all adolescent on her in junior high, and, well, let's just say she overcompensated. I think she's afraid to even hug me now. It's my fault, but I miss it, Andrew. I miss it so much it aches sometimes, you know?"

I do know. *I do know,* I want to tell him, but I let him talk. And he does, with a gut-wrenching honesty that tears at my heart.

"I want to be held. Is that so wrong? I want to be held, and stroked. I want to know that someone loves me. I want to feel it on my skin." He looks at the ceiling and exhales, then meets my eyes again. "But nobody touches me anymore. Not even when I have a fever. Mom just hands me a thermometer now." He drops his eyes and his ears redden. "Even when you kiss me, you don't touch me. It's like I'm a leper or something. I can hardly keep my hands off of you, but it's not the same for you, is it?"

He has no idea what he does to me, what he's doing to me right now. I want to make him feel better, make him smile again, lighten the mood. So I smile when I ask, "Why do I feel like I'm being subtly manipulated?" I mean it as a joke. But it's stupid and ill-timed, and I instantly regret the words.

His face goes slack. "Is that what you think?" he says.

No. Yes. I don't know. Manipulation suggests there's something dark behind his intentions, but I see only light in Robert. And God knows I've more than met him halfway already.

Abruptly he gets up, and he's at the door before I realize he's leaving. He turns the deadbolt and has his hand on the doorknob by the time I reach him. I brace my hand against the door to stop him from opening it.

"Robert . . ."

He presses his forehead to the door. "Just let me go."

"I can't." With my free hand I reach up and tentatively stroke the back of his neck. "I didn't mean that. I thought you knew me better. You want to know what I really think? I think you've opened your heart to me, and you make me want to open mine to you. I think that if I start touching you, I won't be able to stop. I think that I don't want you to go, but I'm terrified of what will happen if you stay."

He turns to face me, but his eyes are on the floor. "It's okay, Mr. Mac. I'm just gonna go."

Mr. Mac. Ouch. "It's not okay," I say, lifting his chin and forcing him to look at me. I reach past him again and reengage the deadbolt. I'm going to touch him. And I'm going to keep touching him until he knows.

Robert

Tears sting my eyes as I hold him to me. He didn't have to do this, but damn it feels so good. He's breathing heavily into my neck and shivers as my fingers trail up and down his spine. After a long quiet moment he turns his head to the side and grapples around on the floor until he comes up with my T-shirt. "Sorry," he says as he dries me off, and I think he's actually embarrassed that he ejaculated on my stomach.

He sits up and finds his boxers on the back of the couch and slips them on. Then he hands my boxer briefs to me and turns away to gather up the rest of our clothes and to give me some privacy, which is kind of sweet considering there isn't any part of my body that he is not intimately acquainted with now. I smile, and over his shoulder he smiles back at me, then stretches out on the couch again and settles his head in my lap and gazes up at me. The hair on his chest is slightly matted with sweat. I run my fingers through it.

"Thank you," I say.

He responds by taking my hand and pressing it to his mouth.

"Do you have any idea how many times I've looked at that little hint of hair above your top button and wondered what it led to? You'd be doing calculus problems on the board, and I'd be unbuttoning your shirt in my mind."

"And all that time I thought you were thinking about differentials and derivatives and harmonic progression."

"I *was* thinking about harmonic progression. I'm thinking about it right now."

He rolls his eyes playfully at me, but then he presses his lips together and his expression grows serious.

"Uh-uh," I say, pinching his lips together with my fingers. "There are no police banging on the door, no lightning strikes, no regrets. And if you keep frowning that way, you're going to hurt my feelings, not to mention my manhood."

He smiles at that, then links his fingers with mine. "If anybody finds out, Robert—"

"They won't. You have my word. I won't let that happen."

He flattens my fingers with the palm of his hand, then draws them down to his mouth again and kisses my palm. "I am a bad teacher."

I laugh. "No, you're not. We just found each other a few months too soon, that's all. By June, it won't even matter anymore."

He reaches up and takes my wallet from the pocket of my jeans cast recklessly on the back of the futon. He opens it and thumbs through the contents. "Hmm, what is this? American Red Cross Lifeguard Certification. You're a lifeguard?"

"Last summer. The swan pool."

"Which one is that?"

"Ridgewood. Do you ever take Kiki to the pool?"

"I might this summer. Are you lifeguarding again?"

"I don't know. Maybe. Would you be wearing a Speedo?"

He laughs and his head bounces lightly in my lap.

He shuffles the card to the back of the stack.

"How was your date tonight?" I ask, but what I want to ask is, "What's wrong?" Was it really just minutes ago that his body was moving so beautifully against mine, his hands everywhere at once, as if I were some text written in Braille that he needed to memorize? But already I can feel him slipping away. He's scared, I tell myself. But he has nothing to be afraid of.

"Oh, yeah. My date. I'd almost forgotten." He's studying my school ID card.

"Did you kiss her good night?"

"Nope."

"Did she try to kiss you good night?"

"Nope."

"Did you hold her hand?"

He rolls his eyes up to me. "Do I detect a note of jealousy?"

"Maybe."

He looks at my American Express card, which Mom had issued in my name when I started driving. She wanted to make sure I was never stranded without the means to pay for gas or a tow or whatever. Behind the American Express are a medical insurance card and one from the auto insurance company on what to do in case of an accident. I'm about to take the damn cards and fling them across the room when he gets to my driver's license.

"March twenty-eighth. You have a birthday coming up in two months." He studies the license for a moment, then suddenly mutters, "Fuck. You're seventeen?"

I shrug.

"You told me you were eighteen," he says, sitting up suddenly. He stuffs everything back in my wallet and reaches for his shirt.

"I rounded up."

"Oh, you rounded up all right. Almost two months' worth." He flings my clothes at me. "Get dressed."

I gather up my shirt and jeans, but I don't get dressed. "It's no big deal."

"It *is* a big deal. It is a *huge* fucking deal. Oh *shhhit*. You shouldn't *be* here. I shouldn't be here *with* you. Seventeen? Oh, God. Get your clothes on. This did not happen." He yanks on his jeans, then his shirt. His hands tremble as he struggles with the buttons, and I'm reminded of the way they trembled when he really touched me for the first time.

But this hurts to watch. I get to my feet to help with the buttons, hoping to calm him down some, but he twists away and backs up, throwing up his hands as if to show he is not touching me. The move stings. He turns away and shoves his feet into his loafers by the door.

"I'm seventeen. So the fuck what? I'm still the age of consent. And I consent. Believe me. I totally, with everything I am, consent."

"Do you not understand?" he says, rounding on me. "I just committed a crime. I could lose my job. I could lose my career. I could lose my daughter. You can't even *vote*."

"It's not even an election year," I say quietly.

He zips up his jeans but doesn't bother to button them, then grabs his keys off the table. "Lock the door behind you, okay?"

"You're just gonna walk out? Just like that? Pretend like this never happened?"

He stops and screws up his face, then bangs his head on the door. He's gripping his keys so tightly that his knuckles have gone white. "This didn't happen. You got that?" Then he slips out without another word.

Chapter 23

Andrew

I wasn't thinking with my dick. I wasn't thinking with my dick. I wasn't thinking with my dick. Goddammit. I slam the heel of my hand into the steering wheel.

I was thinking with my heart.

A horn blares, and I realize I've just run a stop sign. I'm driving too fast. I ease off the accelerator. The last thing I need is to get pulled over minutes after committing a felony.

Seventeen. Ah, *fuck*. I slam the steering wheel again. I had this all figured out. PG-13. PG-13. PG-*fucking*-13. I made the rules; it took me barely twenty-four hours to break them. How did I let that happen?

I keep asking myself that question as I speed through the dark streets. Still driving too fast. I back off the accelerator again.

The truth is, I already had one foot over that line when I got back to my apartment. I know that now. Was it seeing Robert ignore me in class? Was I trying to prove to myself that he really wanted me, that I wasn't some old-fart teacher with worn-out soles on my shoes and stains on my pants?

And he brought me flowers. How was I supposed to resist a beautiful guy who brought me flowers, a beautiful guy who just needed to be touched?

Because he's not just a beautiful guy, asshole. He's a student. Your student. And that's a sacred trust you do not violate no matter what he says, no matter what he needs. No matter how he feels about you, or how you feel about him. You do not violate that trust.

Panic rises in me again. I can salvage this. It will never, *never,* happen again. But can I trust Robert to keep his mouth shut? He's a fucking kid. And he has every reason in the world to be pissed right now. And if he goes shooting off his mouth, I am fucked.

I don't even know I'm headed there until I pull up in front of Maya's house. It's dark, but I need to talk to someone. Who better than my best friend in the world? The one who knows me better than I know myself.

I call before I get out of the car so I don't scare her to death knocking. A lamp flips on in the house. I'm waiting outside the door when she opens it.

"Hey, Drew," she says sleepily. She brushes her hair back from her face and studies me. "Are you okay? What are you doing here? It's almost midnight."

"Can I come in?"

"Sure."

She steps aside and I make my way to the small family room. Even in the dark I could find my way around the house. It's just as it was when I moved out. There are new throw pillows on the couch, and the rug is new, but otherwise not much has changed. I drop onto the couch and stretch out on my back. "Is Kiki asleep?"

"Uh-huh." She picks up my feet and settles on the opposite end of the couch, then pulls my feet back into her lap like she used to do when we were married, and before. It's comfortable, and safe. "She's got that Dalmatian gripped so tightly around the neck he'd be one dead dog if he'd ever been a live dog."

"He's a she."

"He's a cross-dresser. Kiki insists he's a boy dog."

I smile. "Did she have a good day at Ms. Smith's Village?"

"It was okay, I think. She's having a harder time lately. I think the two-year-old room is a little rough. There's a lot of sparring over the Chatter Telephone and the Corn Popper. But she'll be all right. I have a feeling you didn't stop by to ask about Kiki's day, though."

She stretches out her legs on the couch, too, and we trade off foot rubs just like old times.

"If anything happened to me, you and Kiki would be okay, right?"

She gives me a puzzled look. "That's kind of out there. Did something happen?"

"I'm just asking. You know, if something did happen to me, you'd have Doug. You'd get married. Kiki would grow up with a dad. He's financially stable. He could give her everything. Send her to college."

"Okay, first of all, you're being a little weird. And second, I don't know if Doug and I are really headed that way. He's kind of . . . a work in progress. I'm not so sure I want to be the one to civilize him."

I snort a laugh. "A work in progress?"

"Yeah." She wrinkles her nose. "This is just between you and me, right?"

I don't even have to answer that question. We've always been each other's confidante. She trusts me; I trust her.

"Okay," she says. "He wears this scented deodorant that makes my eyes burn. And he sleeps in his socks."

"Okay, so buy him some unscented deodorant and tell him to take off his damn socks."

"And he likes to wear these white Fruit of the Loom briefs like he's four or something."

I smile at her across the expanse of the couch. I love this girl. I always have. "Come on, Maya. Aren't you being a little hard on the guy? Buy him some sexy underwear."

"Why are we talking about this anyway?" Maya says, then suddenly she becomes alarmed. "Oh my God, are you sick, Drew? Is something wrong?"

"No. I'm not sick."

She relaxes. "Then why are we talking about *what ifs*. Something's going on."

"I'm just wondering." My cell phone signals a message, the third since I got here. I take a quick look at the number.

"Is that your friend?" Maya asks.

"No. Some gibberish. I've been getting a lot of it. I think some-one spammed my phone number."

"Here," she says, reaching for the phone, "I'll block the number for you."

I slip the phone back in my pocket. "I can do it later. So tell me what else about Doug drives you crazy?"

"I don't want to talk about Doug anymore. I want to talk about you. Are you having some kind of breakdown, some kind of mid-life crisis at twenty-four?"

I smile. "No."

"Does this have something to do with your new boyfriend?"

"No new boyfriend. It just didn't work out." The fact of this statement hurts.

"I'm sorry," she says gently. "You know, this is the first guy you've been interested in since Kevin."

I don't want to talk about Kevin. The very mention of his name makes my skin crawl. But she's right. There hasn't been anyone since my college freshman crush five long years ago. I can tell from the way she's looking at me that she still believes Kevin broke my heart. I've never told her that he'd done much worse than that. He'd taken my innocence, and then he'd broken me. And now I've broken Robert.

"Have you ever thought about moving back, Drew?"

Her question comes out of nowhere and leaves me unbalanced. My first thought is no. We've been down this road before. It didn't work then; why would we think it could work now?

She retrieves her feet and sits up, folding her legs under her. "We could do this. Kiki misses her dad. I miss my best friend. You could save that rent on the apartment. You could buy a better car." She's talking fast now, animated, like she's been thinking about this for some time. "Your room is just like you left it."

My room. Her room. Kiki's room. A place for everyone, and everyone in their place. "We tried this before, Maya. It didn't work out so great. You want something I can't give you."

She laughs a little, then props her elbow on the back of the couch and cradles her cheek in her hand, her expression pensive. "You know, I've been getting that for a while now, and I've decided it's a little overrated."

No, it's not overrated. And maybe that's the reason I'm already clutching at the offer, letting it reel me in to safer waters.

She's still talking, working out the details as she goes. "It's not like we're going to get married again. And you can still have your own life. You can still date. Go dancing. Bring a guy over for dinner." She smiles and reaches for my hand. "And I can still have my life too."

She says the last like she's just throwing it out there to seal the deal. I pretend like she means it.

"Come on, when does your lease expire?" she asks.

And suddenly I'm in tenth grade again, running for cover behind Maya's American Eagle jeans and Aéropostale T-shirts. And I can't believe I'm actually considering her offer. Or is it really a lifeline?

"I'm on a month-to-month. I just have to give them thirty days' notice." I can't believe that I'm actually saying this, that I'm actually thinking about doing this.

"Then what's stopping you?"

Nothing at all. "If I can get a U-Haul, I can move back in tomorrow."

She jumps up and does a little happy dance right in the middle of the living room floor. "I'll get your room ready."

"Are you sure about this, Maya?"

But what I'm really asking is, *Am I sure about this?*

Robert

"How was your date?" Mom asks.

She's laying a clear plastic liner on the bottom shelf of a cabinet above the counter. A quick survey of the kitchen confirms what I suspect—she's continuing the systematic undoing of every improvement made to our house in the last year, including those made in the last few weeks.

I shrug.

Even though the cabinet held coffee and filters and mugs just this morning, I know it as the glass cabinet. Mom takes the glasses from me one by one, and places them on the shelf. Each time she turns to me for another glass, I feel the scrutiny, and I'm aware of my rumpled clothes.

She's asked me the sex question before, and I've truthfully denied it, but there's always a first time, right? Maybe she can see it on my face. Maybe she smells it on my shirt despite the cotton barrier of my hoodie. Maybe there's something in my eyes that screams *broken in*.

"Are you okay?"

I nod and fix my eyes on the shelf above, trying to remember what used to be there. Plates. They're stacked next to the sink. I retrieve as many as I can carry.

"Do you want to talk about it?" she asks, taking the plates from me.

"Can I say no?"

"Yeah. You can say no." She pretends to straighten the plates, which are already nestled into each other in a perfect stack. "Can I say I'm a little surprised? I didn't think you liked Nic that much."

Tears prick at my eyes. "What next?"

She points to a matching set of bowls. "I'm really sorry, Robert, that . . . you know . . . that I never had the talk with you."

"It's okay."

"I don't suppose your dad did either?"

"I know everything I need to know, Mom, okay?"

I finger the paper flowers that Nic's mom dropped off yesterday morning before the funeral, along with a pan of tamales. Nic didn't come. He told me he wouldn't. I wonder how long it took him and Krystal to make the flowers and what kind of grade he got on *this* project. God, when did I become so cynical? Maybe the gesture was sincere. Maybe I should be more appreciative of the effort. But I just can't muster it. Nic doesn't really care about me. Nic cares about himself. And I can't help but believe that the flowers are more about how great he is than anything resembling sympathy for me or my family. It's funny that the only flowers in our house that mark Dad's death are fake flowers.

"How long have you had an iTunes account?" I ask, scanning down the list of songs on her computer. I turn up the volume a little.

Mom smiles and steps down from the three-step ladder she's been using to reach the higher shelves. "About, um"—she glances at the time on the microwave—"fifty-two minutes."

It looks like she downloaded the top forty. I doubt she's even heard of the artists. She's moving on.

"Robert, we haven't really talked about your dad. Do you want to . . . ?"

No. I don't.

I change into a fresh T-shirt before getting in bed, but I keep the one I wore to Andrew's, the one he mopped my stomach with, next to me on the pillow.

I can't help texting him, even though I know it's a one-way conversation:

You had my heart inside your hand.

I wonder where you are tonight.

I've never called Andrew, but by two AM and after dozens of texts, I can no longer help myself. But I think even as I retrieve his number and press Call, I know.

The cell customer you are trying to reach is not available.

Chapter 24

Andrew

The furniture is rented, so the packing goes quickly. It's unsettling how few boxes it takes to close up one chapter of my life and start another. It's almost like that last chapter didn't count. I didn't bring much with me when I moved out a year ago. I'm not bringing much back now.

I've been thinking about Kevin again. They're not happy thoughts, and I wish Maya hadn't mentioned his name. Because hearing his name means living it all over again—the desperation, the heartbreak, the shame.

When we were in high school, Maya and I used to sit on the fluffy pink throw on her bed and talk about boys. Who was cute. What it would feel like to actually kiss one. What it might feel like to fall in love.

That didn't change when we went off to college together and moved into dorm rooms.

Maya is incredibly beautiful. She had lots of potential suitors, but she always found fault in them. For me, it was all about just one guy. Kevin McPherson.

I had this romantic idea that the fact that our last names both began with *Mc* was a sign that we were destined to be together.

Kevin was a grad student, some five years older than me. He was a teaching assistant in charge of my biology lab.

I remember the way my eyes used to follow him around the room, like Robert's eyes followed me, the way I lingered behind after every class, helping put away lab materials, straightening stools, anything to be alone with him for a few minutes.

A month or so into the school year, he asked me to help him take some trays into his office. He locked the door behind us, calmly set the trays on a counter, then backed me against the door and groped at my crotch. I was so excited he was paying attention to me, and I was finally going to find out what sex was all about, that it didn't occur to me that something was wrong when he pushed his jeans to his knees—"Is this what you want?"—then pushed me to mine.

It escalated from there. By the end of the semester I had made five visits to the university health clinic—abrasions that bled and scared me to death, hemorrhoids that itched and made going to the bathroom painful—each visit more humiliating than the last.

But here's the thing that causes me such shame: I actually thought he cared about me. How stupid is that? It didn't matter what he told me to do; I did it. Then I told myself it was because he wanted me so desperately.

But Maya, she knew something wasn't right. She begged me to quit seeing him, but even when the semester ended and he cut me loose, I continued to call, text, show up at his apartment, plead, beg.

I didn't get it.

One day when I knocked on his apartment door, desperate to see him and find out what was wrong, he invited me in. I was hopeful that maybe we could work this out, until I saw the guy sitting on his couch. He was wearing a mesh T-shirt, a massive hard-on, and nothing else. He stroked himself as Kevin introduced him as his new friend, Sam. Then Kevin gave me a slimy smile as he dropped to his knees and took that prick in his mouth. I remember being rooted to the spot, unable to move, unable to breathe.

It took me more than a year to get over the humiliation and self-loathing.

It took Kiki.

I heave a box into the small U-Haul trailer. There's enough room left for double my possessions, but they are what they are.

I've tried not to think too much about moving back in with Maya. The biggest plus is that I'll be with Kiki now every day, not just Wednesday nights and every other weekend. The second is that I won't have to pretend that I want to date Jennifer anymore.

But I am worried. I love Maya; that much is true. But I know it's hard for her to separate her feelings for me. Friend, lover. She wants both, even though she pretends only one is enough. But I've made a commitment.

It took only minutes this morning to complete the forms in the management office, pay the last month's rent, and make arrangements to return the keys and have the furniture picked up. The U-Haul was easy too. Apparently there's not a lot of moving in January, and I had my pick of trailers. I chose the smallest one—a four-by-eight cargo trailer.

I finger the carnations Robert brought me. They are still on the kitchen counter where I left them last night, now dry and wilted. I regret not putting them in water.

I've left the bathroom for last. I take an empty box and set it on the counter. Then I look at Robert's note again. He wrote it on a small whiteboard I suctioned to my bathroom mirror when I moved in to remind myself of meetings and appointments. I never used it.

But Robert did before he let himself out last night.

You lied too.

I'm not sorry.

I tried all night to think what he meant, what I'd lied to him about. But mostly I was thinking about the way he felt, the way I felt when my skin touched his.

I didn't mean for this to happen. But am I sorry it happened? I don't know the answer to that.

I pull the whiteboard from the mirror and lay it gently on top of the hand towels and toilet paper and toiletries and fold the cardboard flaps over it. I tape the box closed, then mark it *personal* with a Sharpie.

Then I sit on the toilet and read his texts one more time. There are thirty-seven, the last one sent at one o'clock in the morning when I finally blocked his number. My heart aches for him as I read through them, deleting each one as I go. I know what that hurt feels like, because I'm feeling it too.

Robert

Hey, Nic. Can we talk?
Sorry. I've got my girls over.
I need to talk to you. I'll come over there.
Um, no.
Too damn bad. I'm coming anyway.

"Why are you here?" he asks, like he can't believe he had to leave *his girls,* walk down the stairs, and open the damn door for me. He's leaning against the door frame, dressed in cut-off jeans and a tight, sleeveless Nike wick-away T-shirt. He doesn't sweat. And he doesn't have any muscles to show off. But that doesn't keep *him* from showing off.

Why *am* I here? Maybe I'm trying to salvage something with Andrew—make things right with Nic so he can relax and quit being so fucking afraid. Or maybe I want to know why our relationship stalled at *Boys ask me out.* But now, seeing that mixture of irritation and boredom on his face, I'm angry at myself for all the time I've wasted on him. And I'm just angry.

"I have something I need to tell you."

He rolls his eyes dramatically. "What?"

"You're an ass. Get yourself another boyfriend." I start to turn

away, then stop. "Oh, and you look like an idiot in those shorts."
Then I do go. I'm halfway down the sidewalk when he catches my
elbow.

"You're just jealous of my girls, aren't you?"

"Yep. That's it."

Chapter 25

Andrew

Stephen Newman is passing some notes around. He thinks I don't see him. I do.

Kids aren't nearly as covert as they think they are. But teachers learn to pick their battles. Sometimes it's best just to ignore a behavior until it dies. And when it doesn't, the district policy is to name the infraction and redirect: *You are talking; you need to get back to work.*

But I have found that making a game out of discipline is more effective as long as I remain the adult. In any event, you never let them see you sweat. If you do, you lose.

Sometimes, though, you just have to suit up and take on the offender.

I wait until one of the notes makes its way to the edge of the classroom, then I write an equation on the board and ask the students to solve it on their own.

They moan and groan, but eventually they turn their pencils to the task, and when they do, I nonchalantly make my way around the room. When I reach the kid who last got the note, I pause and hold my hand out. At first he acts like he doesn't know what I want, but when I don't move on, he pulls the folded note from under his spiral and hands it to me. He's grinning, and trying not to. There's snickering all around the room.

I don't open the note. I've learned that that is a bad idea. That any reaction from me will be the wrong reaction. It's best to just take the note and get back to business.

I walk by Stephen's desk. He looks up at me with these innocent eyes. I want to wrap my fingers around his neck and squeeze until his eyeballs pop out. But I don't do that either. I keep my face neutral and tap on his notebook. "Get to work."

When the class from hell finally leaves my room, I open the note. It's a cartoon drawing, a face, male, judging from the hair, the features overwhelmed by a gaping mouth and a rather large penis perched just at his lips.

Above the face is a caption. *Mr. McNelis.*

I'm gonna kill that little twit.

I'm short with my second-period class. They look a little nervous and don't give me much trouble. By the time I get to my third-period conference, I know I need to get it back together. I check e-mail, make a few notes on my calendar, then, as if on autopilot, I open Facebook and search Robert's fan page.

I'd never post or comment at school. I just want to look. Something I haven't done since we sat at my desk over lunch and looked at it together. I try not to think about that.

There are new photos now. Robert in the band hall retrieving his sax. Robert at his locker, in the lunchroom, standing in the hallway outside a classroom that I suddenly realize is mine. The photo's been cropped, but I can just make out the sleeve of my sweater. Robert is holding a half-empty Powerade in his hand.

Those little creeps aren't just taking photos on their phone during the school day—a definite violation of school rules—they're actually stalking Robert. Why else would they be in my hallway during lunch?

In the photo, Robert's smiling. God, I want to see that smile again. But, somehow, I don't think he'll be smiling sixth period. I can't wait to see him, and I'm dreading it at the same time.

"Hey, partner," Jennifer says from the doorway.

I quickly X out of the screen. "Hey," I say, turning to her with a bright smile.

"You didn't call me."

Shit. I'd hoped to avoid this little scene today, but I guess there's no sense in delaying the inevitable. I clear my throat and hope she's not packing a gun in her bag.

"Yeah, about that." I try to look contrite. "Jen, I moved back in with my ex-wife."

Her face pales. "You moved back in with your ex-wife." She grips the door frame really hard, and my balls creep up to my belly button. "Really? And how long have you been planning that? Why would you ask me out if you were even considering getting back together with your ex? I mean, what the hell was that all about?"

It strikes me how very little she knows me, even after sharing a wall for a year and a half. "I'm sorry."

"Yeah," she says sharply. "Me too, asshole."

Chapter 26

Robert

I won't look at him. I will sit in my seat, I will do my work (although I may or may not turn it in), I will keep my mouth shut, but I *will not* look at him. And that's what I do on Monday. And that's what I do on Tuesday. And that's what I intend to do on Wednesday when Ms. Lincoln catches me in the hallway before sixth period.

"Robert, how are you doing?"

"Great. Fine." I'm already running a little late. Somebody stuck a bunch of confetti hearts through the vents in my locker, and when I opened it, they fluttered to the floor. I lost a minute scooping them up and shoving them back in. And now Ms. Lincoln wants to talk.

"I really need to get to class."

"Okay," she says, smiling gently. "I just want you to know that if you need to talk, you can come to my office anytime. Just fill out a counselor request form, or just stop by."

I mumble a thank you, then jog to Calculus. The bell rings just as I reach the door.

"You're late," Andrew—*Mr. McNelis*—says. He's standing at the whiteboard, his dry erase marker poised in his hand. "You need to get a pass."

I am not late, and I am not getting a pass. I take my seat.

The classroom falls silent when he turns on me. "Go!"

So I go, but I knock the dry erase marker out of his hand as I do. He follows me out the door and closes it behind him with enough force to make me shrink back.

"What was that all about, huh? I am still the teacher in this classroom. And you are the student. I will *not* have you or anyone else challenging me. You're late. You get a pass. End of story."

"I was at the door," I say, angry too.

He drops his voice even more, but he's in my face, and I hear every word loud and clear. "You know, *this* is why teachers don't date students. *This* is why teachers don't give their phone numbers to students. *This* is why—"

"I'll get the goddamned pass," I say, cutting him off. I don't want to cry. At least I don't want him to see me cry. I turn to leave. He stops me with a hand on my arm.

"Robert . . . I'm sorry."

I jerk my arm free.

The band hall is a cacophony of chatter and music. These are friends. This is where I'm most comfortable. Usually.

Caleb Smith, freshman trumpet and Robert Westfall fan-club groupie, has his head in my instrument locker. Unbelievable.

"What are you doing?"

He jerks his head out so fast he bangs it on the metal opening.

"Oh, hi." He flashes me a big guilty smile. "Robert Westfall. Um . . . oh . . . is this your locker? Oh my God, I'm so stupid. I thought it was, uh, Erick Wasserman's. I was, um, looking for something for him."

I glare at him, and he shifts uncomfortably from foot to foot. But the smile is stuck on his face, and now he's beaming.

"The alto sax lockers are over there." I jerk my thumb in the general direction.

"Oh. Okay. Sorry."

He slinks away, past Luke Chesser, who gives him a friendly hey. As drum major, Luke has to like everybody. Luke leans against the locker next to mine and watches me pull out my bari sax case.

"Hey, man, what was that all about?" he asks.

"That is a charter member of my fan club. He and Erick Wasserman and Zach Townley started a Facebook fan page on me. And they didn't even bother protecting the page, so anyone can see it. The little twerps."

"I don't think you can protect a fan page, but really? I'm gonna have to go check that out."

I set my case on the floor and open it. "Please. Don't. And now they're following me around school. I can't turn a corner without bumping into one of them."

"Aaah. You should be flattered."

"So I've been told."

"You want me to talk to them?"

"No. I don't know. Maybe if I just ignore them they'll go away."

"Yeah. Maybe so." He stoops down next to me. "Hey, I haven't gotten to tell you yet how sorry I am about your dad."

"Thanks." I examine a crack in my reed. *Change the subject.* "I'm just curious. Did Curtis ever get that smell out of his truck?"

He laughs and drops back on his butt, stretches out his legs, and crosses his ankles. "You know, now that you mention it, I do still get a whiff of rotten eggs every now and then. I don't think he's fully forgiven me for that."

"I'm glad things worked out for you two."

"Me too."

I have my sax together and I'm tightening the ligature on a new reed when suddenly I just don't feel like playing anymore. "Hey, you want to go get a soda or something?"

There was a time when Curtis wouldn't let Luke get close to him, despite the fact that everybody knew they were crazy in love with each other. It was actually Curtis's idea for Luke to ask me out. I was to be the buffer that protected them from each other. It was a dumb idea that was destined for failure from the get-go. There's more to the story, but the bottom line is that Curtis hurt him, and Luke paid him back one night in spades. He egged and floured his truck while I played lookout. I remember telling Luke as he wadded up the empty five-pound bag of flour, "Remind me never to piss you off."

We sit in the same booth we did on our first "date" about a year ago. It hadn't taken long for Luke to come clean about why he'd asked me out. He shared a lot of secrets with me during those weeks we pretended to be a couple. He trusted me, and I trust him now.

So when he says, "What's going on?" I unload.

"Oh, *shit!* You and Mr. McNelis?" His voice is too loud. I glance around nervously, and he drops his voice and repeats, "Oh, shit! You and Mr. McNelis?"

I shrug, but I can't help smiling a little as I pick up my soda and take a sip.

"Okay, give me a minute here. *Wow.*" He fans himself with his napkin, then grins at me. "Okay, okay. I'm good. Dang, he's cute. How old is he?"

"Twenty-four, I think."

"That's just three years older than Curtis."

"He's freaked out about it. And now he won't even talk to me except to yell at me in class."

"Curtis did that kind of stuff. For a different reason. But it sounds like Mr. McNelis is just scared, like Curtis was. Don't be too hard on him." He slips his straw up and down in the plastic lid on his cup. "Glaze on a donut, huh?"

"Yeah."

"Four months. Big deal."

"I don't think he even wants that anymore."

"I wouldn't be too sure about that." He picks up an onion ring and pinches it flat. "You know, we could always egg his car."

There is that. Luke could always make me laugh.

"Four months," he says, thoughtfully. "I waited a lot longer than that for Curtis to come around. Did you know he sent me a message on a Cracker Jack prize at the first football game?"

"Was that the game security hauled you two out of the stall in the men's room?"

"Yep." He laughs now. "I got suspended for two games, and

Curtis got thrown out of the stadium. We were just talking—well—arguing. Oh, God, I was pissed about that. I do all that work to make drum major and then have to sit in the stands for two half-time performances." He shrugs and his mouth settles into an impish grin. "But, in the end, he made it up to me."

I bet.

"Listen," he says, folding his arms on the table and leaning in. "I'm here for you, okay? And if you want me to pretend to be your bitch for a while and make him jealous, well, I owe you one."

"Curtis would break my neck."

"Probably."

By the time we head to the car, some of the air has been let out of the balloon of my righteous indignation. I'll play the game. And if that doesn't work, I'll egg his car.

Chapter 27

Andrew

Why did I take up that stupid note?

They say, don't ask a question if you don't want to hear the answer. Same thing goes for notes in a classroom. You never know what a note is going to say. Kids reveal all kinds of personal stuff to other kids. They tell tales on each other. And sometimes they take jabs at adults. But the problem is, once you take up a note, you own that information. You can choose to address it or not, but you own it, and they know you own it.

I choose not to address the cartoon. What am I going to do anyway, take it to Mr. Redmon? I don't think so. The only thing I can do is forget about it and reassert my authority in the classroom, which might have been easy enough if they weren't all picturing me with a giant penis in my mouth.

Suffice it to say that my first-period class is out of control this morning. I can't turn my back on them without a flurry of giggles and sucking noises. So finally I resort to using my document camera and working problems on a sheet of paper. That way I can face them while I instruct.

It helps. Some.

The test on this chapter is next Tuesday. It's the most difficult chapter in the book, and I want to give them two full days of review.

"All right," I say, writing a problem on the sheet of paper:

$$13x^2 + 22$$

"When it comes to solving quadratic equations, we know we have some choices here. Can someone list them for me?"

Stephen Newman raises his hand. I know better than to call on him, but no other hands go up. *Thanks a lot, guys.*

"I think you should just go straight to factor by grouping. You know, like with like. Grouped." He punctuates his suggestion with a big self-satisfied smile. In fact, smiles erupt all around.

Do not react. Do not react. Do not react.

I jot down *factor* in the margin. "That's one way. Can anyone list the other three?" I scan my audience and watch the smiles dissolve on their faces. Not a soul raises their hand.

"Okay. I'll just write them down for you. You can use the quadratic formula, you can complete the square, you can take the square root, or you can factor using one of several methods, including grouping as Stephen has already mentioned. Stephen, stop talking or I'm going to kick you, then I'm going to kick your dog."

"I don't have a dog," he spouts off.

"Then I guess I'm just going to kick you."

"Right." He slouches back in his seat. It's a dare.

I turn back to the problem and manage to get through it and a few more before the bell rings. "Complete the chapter review over the weekend," I say as they shuffle out. "Mr. Newman."

He stops and sneers at me defiantly.

"I've had enough. I'm calling your father."

"Go ahead. My dad doesn't like fags." He gives me a smug smile and strides out of my classroom, tossing a wadded-up piece of paper in the general direction of the trashcan.

I feel like I'm drowning.

I want to talk it out with Jennifer, but that's completely out of the question. She's not talking to me. In fact, this morning in the teachers' lounge, she poured a cup of coffee while I waited and tried to engage her in small talk, and then she emptied the carafe into the sink and told me, in no uncertain terms, to go fuck myself.

Yesterday when I sat down at her table at lunch, she got up and moved. I'm not sure what the half-life is on a woman scorned, but I'm pretty sure she plans to school me on that.

I pick up the paper Stephen tossed and then check my e-mail as my second-period class starts to file in and take their seats. An e-mail from Mr. Redmon catches my attention.

Mr. McNelis—
The committee has denied your application for the
admin training program. Please feel free to reapply
next year.
Mr. Redmon

I am pissed. No, I'm more than pissed. I am furious. Outside Mr. Redmon's office, Mrs. Stovall tries to intercept me. "Is he expecting you?"

He damn well ought to be.

"I only need to see him for a moment."

I stride past her desk before she can react and stick my head in his doorway. "Can I speak to you for a minute?"

"I was just about to e-mail you. Have a seat." He picks up a pencil and taps it on his desk as I settle across from him. "I got a call from Stephen Newman's dad a few minutes ago. He wants Stephen moved out of your class."

Well, that would be a godsend, but I already know that kind of thing rarely happens. If it did, kids would be shuffling classes all year long.

I assume a concerned look. "Did he say why?" Like I don't know.

He takes a deep breath and blows it out loudly. "Well, he feels like you're picking on Stephen."

"That's ridiculous. I don't treat Stephen any differently than I treat any other student. If anything, I've given him more latitude than most. He's immature and he's disruptive, but I feel like I'm handling it. Are you going to move him?"

"No. But let me just caution you, if you *are* singling out Stephen, this is not going to go away. We dealt with this when his older sister was a student here. She was a good kid, but we walked a fine line. Mr. Newman is very involved in his kids' lives and in their education. Just remember that. You might need to cut Stephen some more slack. His grades in your class are pretty low. I expect you to find a way to remedy that. Maybe some tutoring after school. Or maybe you need to adjust your teaching methods. Quite a few of your kids have low grades."

I'm aghast. And I'm livid all over again. But I hold my tongue.

"I assume you stopped by to ask about the admin training program?"

It takes me a moment to redirect my thoughts. "Yes. I don't understand. Why was I denied?"

"I don't know. I assume it's because the committee feels like you're not quite ready."

Bullshit. They take on second-year teachers all the time.

"Apply again next year," Mr. Redmon says, turning back to his computer. "I'm sure you'll get in."

I know a dismissal when I hear one.

I'm still seething when sixth period rolls around. I'm worried about battling with Robert again (I don't want that), but he walks in and quietly lays three days' worth of homework on my desk, then takes his seat. When I work at the board, he watches, listens as I explain and work through problems. He doesn't raise his hand, but other than that, he's like every other student in the classroom—focused, well behaved.

As I watch him get started on his homework the last ten minutes of class, it's hard to believe that the hand that holds his pencil and the one that anchors his notebook are the same hands that just a week ago were eagerly exploring every inch of my body. That the lip that he's biting is the same lip that pressed so firmly against mine. That I know exactly what's under that *I'm too saxy for my band* T-shirt, and that I know that underneath those jeans he's probably wearing boxer briefs, gray, and filling them out quite nicely.

He glances up and catches my eye. I look away, and then beat a slow track around the room, checking to see that my students understand what they're doing, and at the same time, wondering what I'm doing.

What did I lie to you about, Robert? What?

Chapter 28

Robert

There are dents in the carpet where the fish cabinet stood. I know Aunt Whitney sees them; her eyes are smoldering with anger. I'm considering inviting her to tour the bathroom as well, but at that moment, Mom emerges from the closet. She removes the heavy flight jacket from the hanger and hands it to Aunt Whitney.

The jacket belonged to my dad's father, my grandfather, an Air Force physician before he retired and took up a highly lucrative private practice in Louisiana. I hardly knew him. He died a few years after Dad's diagnosis, after it became clear Dad wouldn't live to see his own son grow to be a man. A car crash, I think. The fur collar looks like it's been chewed by rats, and there are white lines in the leather from years of creasing. Dad wore the jacket a lot when I was younger. I assumed it would be handed down to me one day.

But Aunt Whitney wants to keep it in the family.

It's not the jacket. I don't care about the jacket. It's the slight. *I* carry the Westfall name. My cousins are Blooms and Abbotts. And yet, through some twisted logic, they are more family than I am.

Aunt Whitney folds the jacket and smoothes the leather before laying it on top of the owl throw and the few trinkets that she's also reclaiming. She scans the room, then runs her hand along the foot rail of the bed. "I'd like to have the bed frame back, too, when you're finished with it, of course. It belonged to my grandmother."

Mom steadies her gaze, and I suddenly understand the phrase *stare daggers*.

"You know what, Whitney?" she says, "I'm finished with it now."

She yanks the spread off the bed, scattering Aunt Whitney's stack, and discards it on the chaise. Then she lifts the corners of the sheets and gathers them up in a big wad. Before Aunt Whitney can close her jaw, Mom has completely stripped the bed and is wrestling the mattress off the box springs.

There's only one thing to do—I grab the other end.

"This is hardly necessary, Kathryn."

"You want the bed, you got the bed."

She watches us in stunned silence as we remove the box springs, then dismantle the frame.

"I can't just stick a bed in my car," she gasps when she realizes we're serious. "Michael will have to borrow a truck and come get it."

"Well," Mom says as we feed the headboard through the bedroom door, "it'll be out on the front lawn. Tell him to help himself."

When we come back in, Aunt Whitney is on her phone, pacing in the living room. As Mom and I remove the footboard and then collapse the rest of the frame, we catch little snippets of her conversation, things like *absurd* and *vindictive* and *ungrateful*. As we gather the frame up, Mom busts a laugh, and I can't help but join her.

When it's all laying in a heap on the lawn, there's one other thing I'd like to toss on top if I could—my last name. I'm sure as soon as she thinks of it, Aunt Whitney will ask for that back too.

As she backs out of the driveway, I pray her wheel will slip off the drive and into the ditch. But it doesn't. She drives off with a glance that screams, *You're crazy*. And maybe she's right.

The bed is still there when the sun goes down. It's gone when I wake up. Whether Uncle Michael picked it up or some flea market troller, I don't know. And I don't care.

194   •   *J. H. Trumble*

Andrew

"I get to pick out the book tonight," I tell my daughter. "Let's see what we've got here." I prop Kiki up on her bed and choose some books, then climb over the guardrail and settle next to her. Maya appears in the doorway.

"Okay, how about . . . oh, this is a good one—*Math Curse*."

"No!" She pushes the book out of my hand.

"Okay, then, um, *The Greedy Triangle*. This is one of my favorites."

Kiki doesn't even bother with a no. She just shoves the book out of my hands. "I want Wobert!"

Me too, baby girl. Then, *What?* My mind has to be playing tricks on me now. I shake it off and shuffle through the next couple of books. "How about this one—*Ten Apples Up On Top*, or *365 Penguins*."

This time Kiki swivels around on her butt and kicks the offending books off the bed.

"I want Wobert!" She pushes out her bottom lip.

"She means *Robert the Rose Horse*," Maya says, clearly amused at the little scene. "Her teacher told me it's her favorite book right now. We picked it up at the library on the way home. It's in the basket. You probably deep-sixed it when you shuffled through to find all those math books."

"What? Me?" I smile at her and roll onto my side and locate the book.

"Wobert!" Kiki squeals like she just got a new pony for real. She snuggles up to me in her striped Carter's with the pink heart embroidered on the front and pops her thumb in her mouth. I gently remove it.

"I'll leave you two to your story," Maya says. "When you're done, we can watch a movie. Night, sweetheart."

"Night, Mommy." Kiki throws out her arms, and Maya comes in for a quick kiss.

"Okay. *Robert the Rose Horse*."

The book turns out to be about this little horse with a big allergy—roses. Every time Robert gets near a rose . . . *KERCHOO!*

Kiki knows when the sneezes are coming. Her eyes get big, and she waits in breathless anticipation as I dangle the moment just enough beats and then let loose with a big sneeze. She giggles and then delivers her own line: "Bess you, Wobert." I smile each time she says it.

It's an old book with illustrations by P. D. Eastman. The robbers have guns. Oh, well.

On our third read, the fun starts to wear a little thin. By the end of the book, Kiki has her thumb in her mouth again, and nobody is blessing Robert anymore. I find that sad.

"Okay, baby girl," I say, closing the book at the end. "It's time to go to sleep." I ease past the guardrail and she snuggles under the covers and sighs. I tug her thumb from her mouth again and lay her tiny hand on the pillow. "Night, baby."

"I love Wobert," she says softly.

"Me too."

"Asleep?" Maya asks when I return to the living room.

"Down for the count. So, what are we watching?" I settle on the other end of the couch.

She names some movie and I say, "Great," but I'm not really paying attention. She curls up next to me, which I find both comfortable and not, like putting on a cashmere sweater on a hot summer day. We've been here before. I can't help feeling like I've made a huge mistake already.

Maya has set a bowl of popcorn on the table in front of us. I stare at it for a long moment, remembering. Then the movie starts, and I have to force my eyes to the screen, but I'm not watching. The truth is, I just want to be alone. I force myself to sit for as long as I can, and then I pat her on the knee and get up.

"I'm going to bed."

"Aaah, come on. The movie's only half over."

"Sorry. It's been a long day."

She pouts. She looks so much like Kiki when she does it. But it doesn't melt my heart in the same way. I stretch, yawn, and make my exit. I actually think about locking my door behind me, but dismiss the thought as silly. Maya wouldn't invade my privacy.

Before I turn out my light, I unblock Robert's number.

I'm so sorry. I want to start over.

I stare at the text so long that seven times the screen goes black, and seven times I have to press a button to light it up again. I want to press Send, but I don't. I press Discard instead and turn out the light.

Chapter 29

Robert

"Wake up, lazy bones. You've got a guest."

I roll over and groan. "What time is it?"

Mom opens my blinds. "It's eleven. Get up. I don't want to be left entertaining Nic for half an hour."

Great. It is way too early in the morning for this.

Nic has never been in my house. And I'm shocked that he steps inside when I open the door two minutes later. He's wearing his purple Rude jeans and a tight Tapout T-shirt like he's some kind of martial arts devotee. His sunglasses are pushed up on his head. Not too far, though. Just enough to be cool.

I wonder again why I ever found him attractive.

"What do you want?" I say, shoving my hand through my mussed hair. I'm still in flannel pajama pants and a T-shirt. My only concession to my former boyfriend is that I brushed my teeth.

"I want to know why you're mad at me." He props his fists on his hips and shifts his weight to one foot. His face takes on a petulant look that isn't winning him any points. "Is it because I didn't come to your dad's funeral? You know how I feel about sick people and stuff like that. I sent you those paper flowers though. Krystal and I worked three hours on those. I would think you would at least appreciate my effort."

"Thank you for the flowers, okay? We good?"

"You're mad because I had my girls over. Okay, I get that. You're jealous." He rolls his eyes and huffs. "So how about I make Wednesdays just for you? And maybe every other Saturday?"

"I do my service project on Wednesdays, and Saturdays I'm busy."

He fixes his eyes on me. "Why are you being so difficult?"

"Why do you even care? I'm nothing to you, and you're nothing to me. Why don't we just admit that and move on!"

"Oh, now you're just being a dick."

I throw my hands up, exasperated. "Just go," I say, opening the door. For a few beats, he doesn't move. He stares down at his boots, and I almost feel sorry for him. I squeeze my forehead with my thumb and middle finger. "Nic—"

"Your loss," he says, cutting me off.

"Too bad for me, then."

He gives me one last long look that I can't read, then he strides out of the house. I slam the door behind him.

Mom's in the kitchen, chuckling over a couple of slices of bread she's just popped in the toaster.

"You heard?" I ask.

"I never liked him. You know that. I'm just kind of sorry that he was . . . you know."

I thumb through a stack of mail on the kitchen counter. There's an envelope addressed to me. "When did this come in?" I ask, opening it.

"Yesterday, but I didn't pick up the mail until this morning. Who's it from?"

"Ms. Momin."

Inside the envelope is a handmade card with a drawing of me, I think, playing a recorder. Underneath the drawing in a pretty purple ink: *We miss you!* The card is signed inside with a bunch of random-looking marks. I can't read the names, but I know who they are—Patrick, Sophie, and Jo-Jo. The only one I can actually read is Ms. Momin's.

"Let me see," Mom says. I turn the card to her. "That's so sweet.

I bet those kids really do miss you. It's been, what? Seven weeks? You don't have much longer to accumulate all your service hours."

I miss them too.

Nic's paper flower bouquet is still in a vase on the counter. Mom snickers when I toss it in the trash.

Andrew

There are good things and there are bad things about living with Maya again. When I went to bed last night, it was all about the bad things. This morning, I can smell pancakes and it's all good. Kiki grins at me when I stick my head in her door.

"Daddy!" She holds her arms out to me, and I scoop her up.

"I think your Mommy's making pancakes. Yum."

"Yum," she repeats and pokes at the scruff on my chin.

"Let's go get some."

I shift her around to my back like she's riding a pony and gallop into the kitchen with her. I'm not surprised to see Doug. He and Maya are going to some art show today, which means I get Kiki to myself. But I can see that he is surprised to see me. I pretend not to notice and greet them with a good morning.

Doug's eyes travel down my boxers to my bare feet and back up again. He turns to Maya. His voice is low, but not so low I can't hear it. "What's going on?"

Maya's face looks so guilty she might as well say we're sleeping together, which we are not. I can't believe she hasn't told him yet. She had to know he'd see me this morning.

"Andrew moved back in," she says flippantly, like all ex-husbands live with their ex-wives. "He's sleeping in the spare bedroom. His old bedroom."

Doug glares at her for a few beats, then drops the spatula he's holding on the counter and stalks out of the kitchen.

"Doug," Maya says. "Shit." She runs after him. She leaves the front door open, and I can hear them arguing in the front yard.

I look at Kiki over my shoulder. "Uh-oh."

She giggles.

"I guess we're making the pancakes, baby girl." I set her on the counter, but far enough away from the stove that she can't reach it, and flip the pancakes. They're burned. I toss them into the sink and pour some more batter in the pan.

"Daddy—"

"Shhh," I say to Kiki, putting my finger to my lips.

She grins and puts her fingers to her lips. "Shhh." I grin back.

I'm eavesdropping. But, really, I can't help myself. I'm sure the neighbors are getting a good show too.

"Why are you acting like such a jerk?" Maya asks.

"Don't I get a say in this?" Doug fires back.

"No. You don't. He is the father of my child. There is nothing going on between us."

"Then why is he standing in your kitchen in his underwear?"

"He just got up. I don't know."

"You know what? I think you're still in love with him."

"You're crazy."

I flip the pancakes. "I think I may have underestimated Mr. Doug, baby girl. He's not as clueless as he looks."

I'm kidding around, but deep inside I know he's right. I know another thing, this can't end well. But that doesn't keep me from enjoying their little spat.

"Do you want to take me to the art festival or not?" Maya asks Doug outside.

"Are you sure you can break away from your little family unit?"

"You're pissing me off."

A car door slams.

I can't wipe the grin off my face when she returns to the kitchen. I try, but I just can't.

"You heard?" Maya says.

"He'll get over it. Go. Have a good time."

"I don't even know if I want to go anymore. He's being such a jerk." A brief pause. "But then again, you do look kind of sexy in those boxers. Can't blame him for being jealous."

Immediately I'm uncomfortable. I move the pancakes from the pan to a plate, then pour more batter. I make a mental note to put on some pants when I get up in the morning. I add that to my mental list of bad things about living with Maya.

I feel her behind me a moment before she slides her hands around my hips and gropes me. "I don't have to go. I can spend the day with you guys," she says in my ear.

"Maya, don't."

She doesn't remove her hand immediately as if a few more strokes will change my mind. It doesn't.

"Doug's waiting. You need to go."

I feel her stiffen behind me. She removes her hand. Then, as if this isn't the most awkward minute we've ever spent together, her voice gets all cheery, and she gives Kiki a big hug. "You two have a good day," she says. She kisses me on the cheek. I throw a half smile her direction and wish her the same.

As I pour the last of the batter into the pan, I'm thinking how different this would have turned out if that had been a certain seventeen-year-old's hand feeling me up through my drawers. The thought makes me hard in a way that Maya's hand couldn't, and I'm glad my daughter is only two.

Chapter 30

Andrew

Before the first bell rings Monday morning, I count the number of school days left—seventy-nine. I'm not sure I can even make it through today. When did this quit being fun? And now I have to tutor Stephen Newman. Lucky me.

He and a couple of his friends breeze into class about two seconds after the bell rings. They've been standing outside for three minutes or so. I'm writing the day's objectives on the board and pretend I don't notice. When I turn to look at the class, he's slouched back in his seat with that smug, self-satisfied expression. I refuse to be baited by this little jerk. I manage to get through class by biting the inside of my lower lip until it bleeds.

"Stephen," I say as he gets up to leave.

He comes to my desk, but when I start to speak, he turns his back on me and fist bumps his buddies out the door. Then he calls out to Kristyn Murrow, "Hey, girl," and waggles his tongue at her. She giggles and disappears out the door. When there's no one left in the classroom he turns to me.

I am not amused.

"I'd like you to come in for tutoring. You've got a sixty-eight average in Algebra for this nine weeks. I'll work with you until you get on more solid ground. I do algebra tutoring after school on Mondays—today. I can get you ready for your test tomorrow, and maybe, if you put in the effort, you can hang on to that eligibility."

"I can't make Mondays. I have . . . other things to do."

Sure you do.

"All right, then. I tutor calculus on Thursdays. I can work with you then on test corrections."

"Nope. Thursdays are no good either."

"Then why don't you just suggest a day," I say, irritated.

"Wednesdays. After football practice."

Wednesdays. Of course. That's the one day of the week that Maya works late. I'll either have to leave Kiki at Ms. Smith's Village late that day, or Maya will have to juggle work and a kid until I can get out of here. God, I am starting to hate this brat.

"What time are you done with football practice?"

He shrugs like I'm boring him to death. "It's off-season. Four thirty."

So I have to stay at school an extra three hours to tutor a kid who not only doesn't seem to care one whit about his grade, but who is trying his damnedest to make my life miserable. I hear these stories all the time from other teachers. Somehow, I thought I was immune. Silly me.

"Then I'll see you Wednesday at four thirty."

He looks me up and down like I'm a piece of shit, then ambles out of the classroom like he's got all the time in the world but wants to waste a few more seconds of mine.

It doesn't surprise me when he's fifteen minutes late Wednesday. I had already given up on him. I'm just shutting down my computer when he slouches into the room. His hands are empty. No paper. No pencil. No calculator. No respect.

So that's how we're going to play the game, huh?

I have some quadratic equations already written on the board. I stand and hold out a dry erase marker. "You made a forty-nine on yesterday's test. I'll allow you to do test corrections after we review. You can bring that grade up to a seventy. After that, with some sustained work, we can get your average above the failing mark."

He stares hostilely back at me.

O-kay. "Why don't you come up here and we'll work these problems on the board together."

"You're kidding, right?" he says to me and guffaws.

Don't take the bait. Don't take the bait. Don't take the fucking *bait.*

"All right. Then I'll walk you through them." I review the different methods of solving quadratic equations, then talk through a few problems. But I might as well be talking to the wall. He stares out the window the entire time, mouthing what looks like a rap song. I stop midproblem and wait until I have his attention. When it becomes clear that I'm not going to *get* his attention, I return to my desk and finish packing my things.

Stephen gets up and sneers at me. "Guess I'll see you next Wednesday."

Robert

"He's back, guys!" Ms. Momin closes the door behind me and ushers me into the living room where my group waits.

They are already seated in a semicircle. Patrick is the only one who gets out of his seat. He extends his bent arm out to me. It wavers and I have to grab his fist and steady it for a fist bump. "Hey, Patrick. How you doing, man?"

"Bah!"

"Yeah. I'm back. Have you been practicing?" I pull my recorder from the velour slipcase.

"Yah. Yah." The words explode from his mouth in a staccato burst.

He drops into his seat again as I squat in front of Sophie. Her eyes are fixed on something or nothing behind me. "Hey, beautiful. I missed you." She doesn't respond, but I know she hears me.

Ms. Momin coaxes her to look at me and say, "Hi, Robert." It takes a lot of coaxing, but eventually her head swings sharply my way and bounces a little like a bobblehead. She fixes her eyes on me briefly and says something that approximates "Hi, Robert."

I pat her knee and crab walk to the chair next to her. Jo-Jo. He's whimpering.

"Hey, Jo-Jo, you ready to play some music?" He draws in a deep, deep breath and lets it out with a shudder. He's going to burst into tears; I back off.

I pull my chair up close and I look up at Ms. Momin, who's wrapping Sophie's fingers around her recorder. "What have y'all been working on?"

She smiles over Sophie's head. " 'Mary Had a Little Lamb.' "

"That's a great song!" I say to my group.

As Ms. Momin explained to me in December, these kids don't do well with change. I learned that lesson the hard way when I tried to introduce "Jingle Bells." They like the familiar. They like the repetition. And every time we play it, it's like the most beautiful thing they've ever done, like it's the first time.

"Okay, everybody put your mouthpiece in your mouth." After a few tries, Patrick manages on his own, but Ms. Momin and I have to help the other two. And when they're ready, we play.

You'd think I'd get sick of this after months of the same old routine, but the look of triumph on their faces each time we finish the song leaves me humbled and grateful for the experience. I've missed these kids.

Parents are just arriving as we wrap up. I help the kids get the recorders back in the slipcases tagged with their names and then stack them on the table for Ms. Momin to put away later.

This is the first time I've seen the parents since Dad died, and I have to endure a few minutes of sympathy and promises to let them know if there's anything they can do for me.

"You are so good with them," Ms. Momin says as I help her return the chairs to the dining room table. "How are you doing?"

Ms. Momin is beautiful. She's young, with these huge brown eyes and long dark hair. I think if I were into girls, I'd find it very hard to be in the room alone with her right now.

"I'm okay," I say.

"We only have two more sessions before your service hours are complete. Honestly, I don't know what we're going to do without you."

Chapter 31

Andrew

This is what pisses me off.

The next week I stay after school *again,* three extras hours, without pay, on a non-tutoring day to tutor a sarcastic little brat who used his hour last week to fuck with my head. Maya has to move her group back an hour so she can pick up Kiki from Ms. Smith's Village and take her to a doctor's appointment, which I had planned to do, and said little brat doesn't show up. He doesn't say anything in class. He doesn't stop by after school. He doesn't leave a note in my mailbox.

He just doesn't show.

At four forty, I leave. And then, just to cover my ass, I leave a note on the door, just in case he does show.

The house is quiet when I get home. It occurs to me that I haven't been in the house alone once since moving in. I don't turn on the TV to check the news as I usually do. I just want to soak up the quiet and unwind, or I swear to God, I'm going to hunt down a live chicken and bite its head off.

So I'm not particularly thrilled when someone knocks on the door, and I'm really hoping I don't have to play nice with parents or babysit any kids until Maya gets home.

I paste a smile on my face and open the door.

"Sorry, I'm—" Robert looks up at me from the step down, and my knees actually go a little weak. "What are *you* doing here?" he asks.

For a moment I think he's followed me here, but he looks just as surprised as I am, and I dismiss the thought.

"I was about to ask you the same thing," I say, my heart hammering in my chest.

"I work with some kids here, every Wednesday, with Ms. Momin."

No. No way. No fucking *way.* Maya's talked about her group, but she's never mentioned any names, or if she has, they just didn't stick with me. I can't believe it. Robert, my Robert, has been coming here for months? And now he's here and I'm here and there are so many things I want to say to him. But all I can think to say is, "Come on in."

I hold the door open for him and he slips past me like I'm going to punch him or something. "Your group's been postponed until six. Maya said she called everyone."

"Maya? My phone's dead. Wait, you know Ms. Momin? And, why are you here?"

I wipe my hand down my face. Wow. It occurs to me later that this moment is the very definition of serendipity. "Maya—Ms. Momin—is my ex-wife." I'm embarrassed to admit the next part. "I live here now. I mean, I used to live here, and I moved back a couple of weeks ago."

"You were married to Ms. Momin? *She's* your ex-wife? *She* was the woman in that picture?"

I shrug.

His face screws up as he tries to grasp what I've said. "Wait. What do you mean you moved back in? You don't live in your apartment anymore?"

I shake my head.

"Why?"

"Do I really need to answer that?"

"Yes," he says, his voice cracking. "You do."

I'm still holding the door open. I close it, and that in itself makes me nervous. Because he's so close, and we are so alone. "Robert, I'm so sorry. I didn't—"

I don't know what he sees in my face, but he throws himself at me. I stagger backward into a small table and a lamp tumbles to the floor. I think he means to hurt me for hurting him, but he grabs my face in his hands and jams his mouth against mine.

It takes about five seconds to undo all the distance I've managed to put between us in the last two and a half weeks.

My hands are under his shirt and he's pulling it over his head and whispering things like, "How much time do we have?" and I'm answering, "Not much," and he's saying, "Then we'll hurry," and I'm saying, "God, I want you," and he's saying, "You've got me," and I'm hoping like hell Maya doesn't pull into the driveway for another twenty minutes at least.

There's no time to get completely naked, and no need. We're naked enough. And there's plenty of need already. By the time the garage door goes up half an hour later, we're dressed, I've righted the lamp and lit the candle that Maya likes to burn when the kids are here to help them relax, and Robert's moving the dining room chairs into a semicircle.

"Hey," she says to Robert as I scoop up Kiki. "You're early. Didn't you get my message?"

"Um, yeah. I just got here. Is it okay if I'm a little early? I can always—"

"No, of course not. I guess you've met my ex-husband."

"Yeah," I say before he can respond. We haven't worked out our story yet, so I'm doing it on the fly. "We've had a few minutes to get acquainted."

Robert smiles a little too broadly, then turns away quickly to retrieve his recorder from the table.

"Well," I say to Maya, trying very hard not to look at Robert and imagine him with his jeans around his thighs again. "How about I take this one for some chicken tenders somewhere?"

"Just no McDonald's," Maya says, giving Kiki a kiss on the cheek.

Maya's *no McDonald's* sets off a chant. "McDonald's, McDonald's, McDonald's." Kiki's jumping in my arms, and in my peripheral vision, I see Robert watching and grinning. Boy, I'd like to take him for a Happy Meal.

"All right, all right, all right," Maya says. "Just no chicken nuggets, okay. Who knows what's in that stuff."

As I watch my daughter pick her way through two chicken nuggets—she's quite persistent—I realize that I am too far gone to turn back now. I'm crazy about that kid. And four months—three now, I think—is too damn long.

In retrospect, lying about knowing Robert was probably a bad idea. There was really no reason to lie. I have students; he has teachers. No big deal. I just felt a little naked standing there and my knee-jerk response was to lie. No harm done, though.

When Kiki runs off to play with another little girl on the Mc-playground, I send him a text. I don't have to worry about him getting it during his group session; his battery is dead. But I want it to be the first thing he sees when he charges his phone tonight.

I surrender. Please delete.

I'm back home and in bed when he texts back.

Robert

Ms. Momin has always been super nice to me. And I feel a little guilty about ejaculating in her entryway.

I'm also finding it hard to focus on the kids today because I keep remembering the way his hands felt on my skin, and I'm sitting here in front of three special-needs kids and a woman who is my sort-of boyfriend's ex-wife, and I'm primed and ready to go again. I shift uncomfortably, hoping she sees me as too much of a kid to ever let her eyes drift between my legs.

"Good job, guys!" I say when we finish *the lamb was sure to go.* Patrick is out of his seat again and flailing his arms about and almost beans Sophie.

"Take it easy, Patrick," I say, capturing one of his bent arms. He puckers up his mouth like he's waiting for the word he wants to say to build up inside him, then explodes with a "Bah!"

"Yeah, it was really good."

"Bah!"

Ms. Momin winks at me over Sophie's head, and I wonder if

she's ever had Andrew's penis in *her* mouth. And just when I'm starting to get things under control again, suddenly I'm not.

Stop thinking about it!

I keep hoping Andrew and Kiki will get back before we finish, but they don't. And maybe that's for the best. But if I don't get my hands on him again soon, I'm likely to lose it and give us both away.

By the time I get home and plug in my phone, I'm already making plans. His text—*I surrender*—drives away any lingering doubts. I text back.

LOL. About time. I'm deleting.

Chapter 32

Andrew

Not even Stephen can ruffle my feathers today. He could drop his pants and tell me to kiss his ass first period, and I'd still be smiling.

When he asks why I wasn't there for tutoring yesterday, I beam as I tell him I didn't think he was coming, and the next time he's even one minute late, I won't be there either. *You little piss ant.*

I almost stay in my room during lunch, hoping maybe Robert will stop by, but that's about as stupid as you can get. So I lock my classroom and hurry off to the lounge, just in case.

I've continued to set my lunch down next to Jennifer every day, even after she went off on me. I admit, it's just to piss her off. I expect her to go away in a huff today, just as she's been doing for almost two weeks now, but she doesn't. In fact, she pulls out the chair for me and pats the seat like we're best friends again.

She's up to something, I know it. I just don't know what to do about it. I can leave and not know what she's up to, or stay and at least have a chance at heading her off.

I smile and sit.

She takes a bite of her salad and casts a smug kind of smile at me.

"So how are your classes?" I ask.

"They're all right."

Okay. I squirm. Around the table are my colleagues. I wouldn't call them friends, but they are people I work with every day, and we are generally friendly. I focus my attention on them. My department chair, a middle-aged woman named Ilene, says, "I hear they didn't approve your application for the admin program."

Old news, but apparently new to Ilene. There are no secrets in public schools. Well, there's at least one, and I intend to keep it that way.

"No. They sure didn't. That's okay," I say cheerily. "I'll apply again next year."

"Well, I just want you to know, I gave you a great recommendation."

"Thanks, Ilene."

"Let me know if you apply again next year, and I'll—"

She doesn't get a chance to finish, because Jennifer chooses that moment to ask rather loudly, "Why didn't you tell me you're gay?"

All conversation in the room comes to a screeching halt. And all eyes in the room fix on me.

The peanut butter kind of sticks in my throat, and I have to take a sip of Powerade to force it down.

"I, um, guess you didn't ask."

"Don't you think maybe you should have told me that *before* you asked me out?"

I set my sandwich back on the plastic wrap spread and dust my fingers while trying to remain calm, trying to look nonchalant, and trying not to be sick to my stomach. Finally, I look at her.

"Can we talk about this some other time?" I keep my voice low, hoping she'll follow suit. Like that was going to happen.

"You know what? No, we can't. Not that I care who you bang, but I don't appreciate being humiliated, and I don't appreciate you playing your little games with me." She shoves her chair back and snaps the plastic lid back on her salad, then snatches her water bottle off the table. "You need a cover, go to Penney's. I hear they're having a sale."

She takes her lunch and storms out of the room. For a moment, no one speaks, then slowly the conversation returns. By the end of the lunch period, it has almost reached a normal volume. I don't engage in the conversation, and no one tries to engage me. When the bell rings, I flee to the relative safety of my room.

Her question is a fair one. If I worked anywhere else other than a public school—an engineering firm, an accounting office, an insurance company—I wouldn't have thought twice about admitting to my colleagues that I am, in fact, 100 percent queer. But public school is a world unto itself. It's okay to be gay; you just don't talk about it. It's an unspoken rule, but it's pretty hard and fast down here. It's one of those things you just know. I honestly don't care if my colleagues know; I just didn't want to be the subject of their gossip. So much for that.

I haven't quite gotten back to my happy place by sixth period, but seeing Robert walk through that door does give me a little boost, and I have to remind myself to play it cool.

Today he smiles and says, "Hey, Mr. Mac," and I swear I want to kiss him right then and there, not because I want to kiss him right then and there, which I do, but because it's normal kid-to-teacher stuff—a smile, a greeting, the use of my name in diminutive. No winks, no full-body scans. Normal feels safe.

At the end of the period, he straightens the desks in his row, then gives me a shy smile (which I find so endearing, considering where that mouth has been) and drops a note on my desk.

Chapter 33

Robert

Longest week ever. It's hard to play student when you're this hot for teacher.

I'm the first one to the parking garage Friday evening. I find a spot in the shadows at the end of a dead-end row on the top floor where there aren't many cars, and get out, then I take a quick stroll around the floor just to be sure there are no bodies in the cars that are there. I'm leaning on the trunk when Andrew finds me and parks about eight spaces away.

He glances around, then hustles over to me. His huge smile mirrors mine. "Great place to rendezvous. So, what's the surprise?" he asks.

I tilt my head toward my car and hit the Unlock button. "I'm taking you out tonight."

"I don't—"

"I'm not taking any chances, okay? Trust me."

"All right, then." He opens the door. "Let's go."

When I get back in the driver's seat, he says, "I've missed—" But that's all he manages to say before I am over the console and all in his space. We are not going there in this parking garage, but I have to kiss him and I have to touch him and I have to hold him and I have to soak up everything he gives me back. And he does give back.

And then we do go there, because we can't not.

"Curse this damn console," Andrew mutters.

"Well, if you hadn't given up your apartment, I'd be stretched out naked on top of you right now instead of giving you a hand job in the front seat of my car."

I feel his grin against my neck.

"As long as it's your hand, baby, I'm good with that."

"You called me baby again. Like."

When a car comes up the ramp on the other side of the floor, we reluctantly disengage. But I think I can focus on the road now.

"Where are we headed?" he asks as we leave the parking garage.

"Downtown."

"Are you sure you're checked out to drive on freeways?"

"Oooh, that's cold."

He laughs and buckles his seat belt. "I am at your mercy tonight."

"I'm going to remember you said that."

On the way, I get to pump him for information—pets he had growing up (an ancient basset hound named Einstein), favorite way to waste an afternoon (pushing a two-year-old on a swing at the park, which I think is cheating), best movie he's seen in the past year (*Donnie Darko*, rented from Netflix—I didn't get the movie and neither did he, but he can't get the image of the evil bunny out of his head, thus best movie for its staying power).

"First guy you kissed?"

He doesn't answer for a couple of beats and I throw a quick glance his way.

"You," he says finally.

"You're lying. You're telling me you never had another boy-friend?"

"You didn't ask me about a boyfriend. You asked me about a first kiss."

I need to keep my eyes on the freeway. The traffic is heavy for a

Friday evening, most of it heading north, but plenty heading south too. Still, I can't help another glance.

He takes a deep breath and flutters his lips. "Oklahoma makes Texas look liberal. I didn't date in high school. Facebook and My-Space weren't very big back then, so I was pretty much encapsulated in my little world. I only knew a couple of other guys, but they were not my type, trust me on this."

I smile at the road ahead.

"So my first boyfriend, I guess, was in college."

"Why *you guess?*" I ask.

He shrugs.

"And you never kissed."

"Nope. We never kissed."

I try to wrap my brain around that—a boyfriend, but no kiss. I want to ask more questions—questions like, *Just what did you do?*—but I don't know if I'm ready to hear the answers. At least I don't want to hear them while we're hurtling sixty-five miles an hour down one of the worst freeways in the state. His tone tells me there's a story there, and it might not be a very pretty one.

"So tell me about Ms. Momin."

"Maya. You want the CliffsNotes, or you want the whole unabridged version?"

"I want the forty-minute version."

"Okay. She's been my best friend since junior high. We were close. Really close. We *are* close. We even went to college together. I think now she always had a crush on me, but I didn't really see it for a long time. I guess things really started to change after Kevin."

"The college boyfriend?"

"Yeah. I'm not sure I want to tell you this next part."

I glance at him. "Thirty-nine minutes. I want to hear."

He flutters his lips again and seems quite serious. I slide over into a more open lane.

"Maya was like my sister. No, not like a sister. Ick. More like a buddy, a pal, you know. I mean, she used to sit on the toilet in the bathroom and talk to me when I took a shower. It was no big deal. That's just kind of how we were."

If he sees me raise my eyebrows, he doesn't react.

"So, after Kevin, I was feeling kind of damaged." He stops and stares out the window.

"And?"

"And, then one night we were having a sleepover like we did all the time. I was feeling pretty down, and, well, she pushed and I didn't fight her."

He seems embarrassed, like this is some great revelation. Like I don't know where babies come from.

"After that, things really changed between us. There were no more massages—"

Massages?

"—no more conversations in the bathroom while I showered. It was awkward. About five weeks later, she found out she was pregnant. It changed things again. We just kind of went back to being best friends; no benefits. She had Kiki, we got married, we moved in together, things got awkward again, I moved out. And that's about it."

"And now you've moved back." I glance at him. "Why?"

"Because she asked. Because I was scared."

I think about the way he reacted when he saw my birth date on my driver's license. It had been such a one-eighty. For a while, he'd been focused on me, just me, his heart pounding in unison with mine as he gave in to all that passion. But even as he lay on the couch, his head in my lap, I could feel the fear creeping back in. And then, suddenly, he couldn't get away from me fast enough, like I was a flame he was standing too close to.

But to move in with Ms. Momin?

"Has it ever occurred to you that she's manipulating you?" I ask. It's actually hard for me to reconcile the Ms. Momin I know with the Maya he's talking about. It's like they're two different people. When I think in terms of Maya, the manipulation is so obvious. When I think Ms. Momin, not so much.

"No. I don't think so. It's just an arrangement that works for both of us right now, or at least it seemed like it at first. There's nothing going on between us. She has a boyfriend. It's all cool."

"You really expect me to believe that?"

"Okay, well maybe it's not all cool. She groped me last weekend."

"Holy shit! She did not." I feel like I'm going to go blind even thinking about Ms. Momin doing that.

"I think I've really screwed up, Robert. And now I don't know what to do about it. It's not Maya. It's Kiki. When I moved out the first time, she was too little to know anything. But now she's had her daddy there long enough for us to develop routines again. I know it would be hard for her if I leave. She's old enough to know if I'm gone, but too young to really understand why."

I feel partly responsible. If it hadn't been for me, he wouldn't have moved back and wouldn't be in this position right now.

When I say so, he reaches over and fiddles with the short hairs on the back of my neck. "Yeah, thanks a lot, pal. Next time I relieve you of your clothes, be the grown-up and walk away, okay?"

The club is near the university's downtown campus. Andrew is still wary, but I convince him that he won't see any former students here. Last year he taught strictly freshmen, and since it was his first year, it's highly unlikely that anybody here will know him. And I don't know anyone who's attending school at the downtown campus. I don't know if either one of us is 100 percent confident in my assessment, but the allure of dancing together is enough to make us at least pretend we are.

Andrew hooks his arm around my neck as we make our way through the college crowd gathered on the sidewalk out front. He's wearing one of his Friday T-shirts (*Math Geek*), jeans, and Vans, and he looks like I just plucked him out of his dorm room. A group of co-eds break to let us through. Someone wolf whistles.

"I hope you brought your Usher tonight, stud," he says in my ear.

"Oh, I brought him. You hauling out your tired old Mick Jagger again?"

"Low," he says, pretending to strangle me. "As a matter of fact, I'm unleashing my Adam Lambert tonight since you seem to like him so much, friend."

"Aren't you afraid I'll go blind?"

"You might. But then you'll have to feel your way to me later tonight."

I stop and he swings around to face me, grinning. "Okay, we're going back to the car," I say, turning to go.

"Uh-uh," he says, grabbing my hand before I can take a step away. "We're dancing. You can feel me up later."

"One condition."

"What's that?" he asks.

"You don't call me 'friend' anymore."

He studies my face a moment, then, "Come on, baby, let's dance."

I don't know which I enjoy more—dancing or watching Andrew, who has completely unplugged from the grown-up grid for the night. He dances close to me on the packed floor. We grind, we make out during slower songs. I've completely forgotten that this is my teacher until a curvy girl with a lip ring and pink hair approaches us between songs and says, "I know you," to Andrew.

He stiffens, and I can tell from the look on his face that he's searching his memory bank for an image that matches the face and hoping to hell he doesn't find one.

"Dunn Hall, right?" she goes on, pointing a finger at him. "You were at the fall mixer with Kruger. You hooked up with some drunken redhead as I recall." She appraises me, then looks back at Andrew with raised eyebrows.

Andrew raises his brows back at her. "I'm flexible," he deadpans.

"Hmm," she says, giving him a full-frontal scan with her eyes. "See you at the spring mixer, hot stuff."

"Yeah," he says. When she turns to go, he grabs my hand and tugs me in the other direction. "Let's get out of here," he says in my ear.

Hot Stuff and I spend the next hour seeing just how flexible he really is in the backseat of my car.

Pretty flexible.

We're basking in the afterglow when I tell him, "I have a confession to make."

Andrew

Is this what I missed in high school? Making out in the backseat of a car in a dimly lit parking lot? Banging our heads on the armrest when we try to stretch out on a seat that is about two feet shorter than we are? Holding our breaths every time we hear a voice, every time a door slams or a light sweeps across the windows?

I'm an adult now, but here I am sneaking around like the kid I wasn't as a teenager. I'd prefer a nice king bed, or at least a futon, but I'm not complaining.

And then Robert tells me he has a confession to make.

"Oh, please don't tell me you're sixteen," I joke. But the truth is, I'm terrified that that's exactly what he's going to confess, and that would mean adding statutory rape to my growing list of felonies.

He grins, then gropes around on the floorboard until he comes up with his phone. Apparently, it slipped out of his pocket when I shimmied his jeans down. He pushes a button to light up the screen, then thumbs around for a moment before turning the screen to me.

In the photo I'm leaning against the aluminum rail below the whiteboard in my classroom, my arms folded across my chest. I appear to be listening to someone. "Shame on you, taking a photo of your teacher during the school day. I might have to punish you."

"Yeah? What might that look like?"

"Don't tempt me or I'll show you."

His smile fades in the dim light and his face grows serious. "After you left that night, I just wanted something to hold on to," he says quietly. "Even when you were being such a jerk to me. I just wanted to keep a piece of you with me."

I trace his eyebrow with my finger, and then I take the phone from him and delete the photo. "No more photos. You can hold on to me from now on."

On the drive home, I get to ask the questions. Pets he had growing up (none because of his dad's allergies), favorite way to waste an afternoon (Xbox, what else, he's seventeen—grrr), best movie he's seen in the past year (*Brokeback Mountain,* a cliché, he admits, but he bought the DVD and can't help watching some of the scenes again and again).

I'm a little afraid to go there when he's driving, but there are other things about him I really want to know. So I ask. "Were there ever any good times with your dad?"

He keeps his eyes on the road and doesn't answer right away. I shouldn't have taken the conversation there. I should have asked about his early crushes or why he likes being in the band guard or what brand of shampoo he uses.

And I'm about to do just that when he says, "Can I say no?"

"You can say anything you want."

"I want to say no, then, but, you know, there had to be some good times, right?" He glances at me, but quickly returns his eyes to the road. It's around eleven PM and traffic is lighter, but I still worry that my question has distracted him. He puts on his blinker, checks his mirrors, then eases into the left-hand lane to go around a slower-moving car. "It's not that there were bad times. There just weren't *times.*" He glances at me again.

"Let's talk about this later, okay?" I say.

He smiles wanly at me. We're quieter on the rest of the drive home. I take some time to study his profile and think that I will never tire of looking at him.

"You're staring at me," he says, but he smiles when he says it.

I don't look away until he exits the freeway.

He stays off the main thoroughfares and opts instead for some side streets. We're only a couple of miles from the pavilion's parking garage when something darts into the road. Robert doesn't even have time to swerve or hit his breaks. He hits it dead on, and then there's a sickening thump as he runs over it.

"Oh, shit," he says. He yanks the car to the shoulder and slams on the brake, then he's out of the car and jogging back.

It takes me a minute to find his hazard lights. I turn them on and pull his door closed. When I get out, he's kneeling on the dark road. His hands are over the dark lump like he wants to touch it but doesn't know where or how. "I didn't see him." His voice catches. "I swear I didn't seem him. He was just there."

As my eyes adjust to the dark I can see that it's a good-size dog, a golden retriever, I'm guessing, from the length of the fur.

"We have to get him to a vet," Robert says shakily. I can see that he's looking for a handhold, a place where he can get his arms under the dog and lift him up, but there's so much blood and gore, that I know he won't be able to pick up the animal without leaving parts of him on the road. The dog is panting shallowly.

"He's not going to make it, Robert."

"No. He's—if we just—oh God—the vet—they can save him." His voice is desperate and hitches every few words.

"They can't save him."

The dog lets out a rush of air and grows still.

Robert scrambles to his feet and vomits in the grass on the side of the road. I hold his shoulders as he spits to clear his mouth. And then he's crying. "I didn't mean to hit him. He was just there. He just came out of nowhere. I couldn't stop."

"I know," I say, rubbing the back of his neck. "There's nothing you could have done."

"I couldn't stop," he whispers. "We have to move him."

This is the hard part. That dog isn't getting moved without a shovel. And I'm pretty sure I won't find one in Robert's trunk. We have no choice but to leave him on the road until the county can clear the mess. I know it's a daily thing for them. If it weren't, the streets would be littered with dead squirrels and armadillos and possums and the occasional domestic pet. I'll call them with the location when we get back, but right now, I have to get Robert off the road.

"We can't move him," I say gently.

"We have to move him." He hiccups. "If we don't move him—" He doesn't finish. He swipes at his eyes with his forearm. Images of the dog being run over again and again flash in my head. I know Robert is seeing that too.

A car turns onto the street and pulls up behind us. Robert turns his back to it and stumbles back to the car.

A teenager leans out the window. "You need any help?" I don't recognize him, and I hope to hell he doesn't recognize either of us. I'm counting on the dark to ensure that.

"No, we're okay, but thanks."

"Dead dog. That sucks," he says. Then he pulls around us and speeds away.

Robert has slid down the passenger side of the car, and he's sitting in the grass now, hunched over, his shoulders shaking. I crouch down in front of him. "We've got to go, Robert. It's dangerous sitting on the side of the road like this."

"I can't just leave him. He belongs to someone."

"I'll get his collar, okay? I'll call and let his owners know what happened. They'll come get him. Okay?"

He buries his face in the crook of his elbow and his shoulders heave. "He just ran out in front of me." His voice is small and filled with anguish.

I run my hand over the back of his neck, then return to the dead dog. I'm worried that someone will come speeding down the road and wipe us out too. I pinch the buckle on the dog's collar and release it. There's a bone-shaped tag dangling from the heavy nylon. I pull the collar off and my hands come away wet with blood. I wipe them on the grass, then find a leaf I can use to pick up the collar again. I drop it in the trunk.

Robert is still crying. It's the kind of crying I can describe only as a purge, like something's been ripped open inside him, and I suspect this is about more than a dog.

"Come on," I say, pulling him to his feet. He falls into my arms, and I hold him for a minute before settling him in the passenger seat. On the two-mile drive to the parking garage, he uses his sleeve to wipe his face repeatedly, and finally just buries his face in his collar. He's facing the side window like he's embarrassed, but he can't stop the crying.

It's close to midnight and the fourth floor of the garage is largely empty. I pull up next to my car and cut the engine. There are only three others on this level. I get out just long enough to get the phone number off the collar.

Holding on to Robert with one arm, I dial the number. I'm relieved when a man answers. I don't want to have to tell a kid we just killed their dog. I explain what happened, give the location, and tell him how very sorry we are. He asks if we're okay, and I say yes. But I think that's kind of a relative term, because there's nothing okay about Robert right now.

I put down the phone and pull him to me a little more snugly. Somehow that makes him cry harder.

Chapter 34

Robert

I wave to Mom the next morning as she heads off to Goodwill with a trunk full of Dad's clothes.

The sun is trying hard to warm the February air, but I'm still getting the occasional goose bumps on my arms. I stretch out my legs on the lawn chair for maximum warming. My eyes ache from crying last night, and I spare a moment to think about the dog who'd be happily munching on some kibble right now if I hadn't been on the road. There's nothing I can do to undo what happened. I whisper an I'm sorry to the sky, then I redirect my thoughts to Andrew and the sweet way he took care of me after it happened. I think I would have given anything to fall asleep in his arms last night.

30 crows in a field. Farmer shoots 4. How many in field now?

I have to squint to read his response: *4. All dead. Rest flew away. Too easy. 50 divided by a half?*

100. Pls, you insult me.

He's getting faster at his texting, so when the next one doesn't come right back, I try to think of another puzzle. Before I can, my phone vibrates.

OK, smarty pants. What comes next in this pattern?

1
11
21
1211
111221
312211
13112221

Okay, that one's hard.

I give.

Read aloud. Each line describes the one before. One one. Two ones. One two, one one. Got it?

That hurts my brain, but I got it.

Show off. T or F? I have webbed toes.

You do NOT have webbed toes. You have very sexy toes. T or F? I have camptodactyly.

I am intrigued.

Googling.

Camptodactyly. Bent pinkie fingers. Both hands. They bend inward, and I remember thinking once when I was standing at Andrew's desk while he looked over something for me that playing a woodwind instrument might be a challenge because the keys are fixed and positioned for straight fingers. I'm not sure they could accommodate a bent pinkie. He would have to be brass or percussion. In any event, we are going to make music together, bent pinkie or not.

Yeah, about that . . .

LOL. Genetic. Kiki has it too.

A car coming up the street catches my eye. Ugh.

Nic in my driveway, 30 seconds. Pls advise.

Tell him to piss off. You belong to me.

Taylor Swift?

No. Andrew McNelis.

I smile and tuck my phone away as Nic pulls into the driveway, obstructing my view of the neighborhood. He can't sour my mood though. There is nothing he can do or say that will bring me down from this cloud I'm floating on, despite the accident last night.

He gets out, adjusts his sunglasses, and stalks over to me.

"You're seeing someone else."

Nothing, except that.

I don't respond. I don't know what he knows, and I'm not going to fill in any gaps for him, so I say nothing.

"I can tell, you know, the way you've been all happy lately." He's got his fists on his hips and his weight on one leg the way he does. And he's actually pouting. "So who is he?"

I breathe a quiet sigh of relief and shrug.

"Does he go to our school?"

Again, I say nothing.

"Is he hotter than me?"

I have to force my face to remain neutral because I so want to crack a smile.

"You're doing this because you're still mad at me, right? Okay, then I'm sorry. I'm sorry I didn't come to your dad's funeral. I'm sorry I haven't let you—you know. We'll go out tonight. I'll drive. We can go to a movie. We can, like, I don't know, maybe hang around in my room afterward and make out."

Even with his face half hidden by his sunglasses, he looks like he'd rather be doing anything but that. And for that I actually have to thank him. I'm glad we never went there. I'm glad I got to experience so many firsts with someone I'm crazy about, and not just with someone who would let me.

And I feel kind of sorry for Nic too. Although, I don't really know why. He just seems kind of desperate for something, but he doesn't really seem desperate for me. I decide to let him go gently.

"I'm not seeing anybody, Nic. I just don't think we're right for each other. You deserve somebody you really want to be with, and admit it, I'm not that guy."

"But everyone thinks you dumped me," he says.

I should have known. He doesn't want to get back together with me because he likes me and misses me; he wants to get back together so he can be the dumper and not the dumpee. That almost pisses me off, but then I find it really kind of pathetic.

"If you want, I'll tell everyone you dumped me. I'll even try to look broken up about it."

"You'd do that?" he says, pushing his sunglasses up on his head.

"Yeah."

He shuffles around a bit and looks a little guilty. Then he shoves his hands in his pockets and lifts his shoulders. "Well, okay, then. I guess I'll see you around."

Yeah. Piss off.

He drives away, and I'm so glad Andrew didn't insist I play that game. I'd sooner jab my eyes out with hot pokers.

Speaking of which, Andrew's sent six messages in the time it took to unload Nic for good—all Lady Gaga lyrics. The last one: *I want your psycho, your . . . you know.*

I laugh and thumb in a reply.

Andrew

"Who are you texting?"

I'm sitting on the back deck soaking up some rays while Kiki plays in the little turtle sandbox I set up for her on her second birthday. I lay the screen flat on my stomach and look over my shoulder at Maya. She hands me a mug of coffee.

"Just a friend."

"That's an awful lot of texting for just a friend." I drop my feet so she can have the other chair. "Is it your old friend or a new friend?"

I look at her and I see it. Jealousy. Hurt. She says she can handle our living together. She says we can have our separate lives. But she can't, so we can't. What was I thinking moving back in? Why did I think this time it would be different?

My phone vibrates on my stomach, but I ignore it.

"Maya, we need to talk."

She presses her lips together and turns her gaze to Kiki, who is piling up mounds of sand, trying to build a hill, I guess.

"I'm sorry, but this isn't working."

She tucks a strand of hair behind her ear and closes her eyes for a moment, then turns back to me and smiles like she's so fucking happy she can't believe it. "Look, I don't care if you have a boyfriend. I'm happy for you. *Really*. I just want to know about him. You're acting so secretive about everything. I kinda feel left out, you know. You're my best friend."

"What about Doug?"

"What about Doug?" she replies. "It's none of his business. He doesn't own me."

"No, but I think he cares about you a lot." I want to give her an out. Not make this about the two of us. Not make this about her and what she is and isn't doing that's pushing me away again. "I think I'm just in the way. I should never have taken you up on your offer. Look, give me a couple of—"

"If this is about what happened the other morning—that was a total mistake. I don't know what I was thinking, but I promise you it won't happen again."

I try to protest but she keeps talking, intentionally fast, I think, so I can't get a word in. And amazingly, in a matter of a couple of sentences, she transforms from the suspicious, possessive person of a few minutes ago to the Maya that I've loved for so many years.

"Look, I'm an idiot," she says, leaning forward and clasping her hands around her mug. "It must have been some kind of flashback or something, but really, I don't want you to go. I don't like being here by myself, and I'm just not ready to make that kind of commitment to Doug. And Kiki really loves having you around. And I'm glad you're dating, I really, really am. So, please, say you'll stay. *Please*. For Kiki?"

Not fair. I look at my daughter. I see now she's been building a bed for Spot. She lays him down on the mound a little roughly and shakes her finger at him. "You go sleep."

"She didn't get that from me," I say to Maya.

She laughs.

Robert was right. I am being manipulated. I know that. There are negatives to staying, but there are positives, too, I tell myself. And then I hear myself agreeing to stay.

"Yay," she cheers, her eyes bright. "Okay, so tell me about this mysterious guy. Things are working out after all, huh? What does he do?"

Shit. I wasn't expecting to have to make up a plausible bio on the fly, and for a moment, I can't think of a single occupation but my own, so what the hell. "He's a teacher."

"Yeah? Math too?"

"Um, no. Science."

"Where'd you meet?"

Oh, man, if I'm going to make up a whole imaginary biography for this imaginary teacher friend, I'm going to have to keep it simple. I take a sip of coffee before answering. "School."

"Your school?"

"Yeah."

"What's his name?"

"I'm not telling. Because then you'd just look him up in the faculty directory, and I'm really not willing to go there yet. We're just kind of getting to know each other."

"There can't be that many hot, young, male teachers at school. Do you think I can't figure it out on my own?"

Hadn't really thought about that. "Okay, maybe he's not at my school."

"Are you kidding me? Why all the mystery here? You used to tell me everything."

Not this time.

"What's he texting you about?" she persists.

"Nothing much."

"Come on, let me read a few."

I level my gaze at her as I take my vibrating phone off my stomach and slide it into my pocket. She pushes out her bottom lip and pouts, just like Kiki does. That used to really get to me.

"You're no fun," she says. I think she realizes she's pushing too hard. She settles back in her chair and takes a sip of her coffee and watches our daughter. "Can you believe she's going to be three soon?"

"I know." And I really am happy to be spending this time with her. But what I wouldn't give to have my own place right now.

I study Maya's profile. She's beautiful, really. Strong, but pretty features, as if everything about her face is absolutely deliberate. It's that Middle Eastern part of her that is both enhanced and softened by her Irish genes. Yet, no matter how often I'd wished that Maya and I could be a couple for Kiki's sake, I couldn't love her in that way.

And it strikes me, too, that no matter how much I fight it, I can't *not* love Robert.

I try to calculate the number of days left in the school year. Too many. I'm getting that warm feeling inside thinking about him. I tell Maya I'm going to the bathroom and I'll be back. This is one warm feeling I can't just ignore.

You make it hard for me to be in public.

Ha, ha. I refuse to apologize for that!

Chapter 35

Robert

I log in to Facebook. I haven't even added a profile picture to my page. And then—I probably shouldn't, but I do it anyway—I add a relationship status to my profile: *In a relationship*. It feels really good. And then it feels really stupid, and I change it back.

I check out Andrew's page, but it's protected. If I send him a friend request, he'll just ignore it; so I don't, so he won't have to. Then, just for the heck of it, I check out my fan page.

Those little turds. They took a photo of me talking to Luke in the band hall the other day. And not only that, but there's a photo of me looking very chummy with Erick Wasserman at a football game, when I know for certain I never sat next to him. I am baritone sax. He is alto. We don't sit together. Creeps.

Caleb Smith Dudes. I almost touched him. I was soooo close.

Oh my God, I about wet my pants.

Erick Wasserman Where, dude? Where?

Caleb Smith Band hall. And then he left with Luke Chesser.

I wanted to be Luke soooo bad.

Zach Townley I want to be his sax. He can finger me any time.

Caleb Smith He can blow my horn.

Erick Wasserman I want to blow his horn.

Zach Townley Ha, ha. Hey, I saw him last night. At the pavilion.

Caleb Smith Oh my God. Did you just die? Who was he with?

Zach Townley Don't know. Some guy.

Caleb Smith Nic Taylor?

Zach Townley No way. They broke up.

I feel sick. Mom sticks her head in my room, and I quickly minimize the window.

"Robert. Just so you know, your aunt Whitney's on her way over."

"Do we have time to move?"

"We could try."

If only she weren't kidding. "No. Please, I can't take any more Aunt Whitney. Is she bringing the brats over?"

"Probably."

"Then I'm leaving." I have plans anyway, but Mom nixes that real quick. Apparently, Aunt Whitney has specifically requested that I be here. I protest, but Mom tells me just to hold my nose and let's find out what she wants. I'm actually surprised that Aunt Whitney would brave another visit after the bed incident.

I have no choice but to shoot Andrew a text and let him know I might be a little delayed.

Lonely . . . waiting for you.

I smile at the abbreviated Heart lyrics.
Me too.

By the time Aunt Whitney pulls into the driveway, I'm pacing. I open the door for her. *Let's get this show on the road.* Sure enough, she's got both her kids and Aunt Olivia's, and she's clutching Happy Meal boxes in both hands. She holds them high as the kids jostle past her into the house, then she sends me to get the drinks from the car. When I get back inside, the kids are settled around our dining room table and the younger ones are arguing over their Mc-action figures. Franny is missing, and I suspect she's taken her food into my room.

I pass out the drinks. Mark immediately knocks his over, sending Mom dashing for paper towels. Matthew sees a spot of ketchup on his burger and bursts into tears. I take his top bun to the kitchen to scrape off a layer of bread. I consider using the knife on Aunt Whitney, who's sneaking fries from Jude's stash as he, unaware, carries on a battle across the table with his older brother.

The door to freedom is just paces away.

Finally, the kids are settled and she gets to the point. "I've been so busy with your dad these last few months that I haven't been keeping up. I know you got early acceptance. I want to make sure you've confirmed with LSU that you *are* coming. And we need to make living arrangements for you. I can't believe we haven't done this already. I don't even know if we're going to be able to get you in a dorm—"

Since when did *she* become my mom? "I haven't even decided whether or not I want to go to LSU, or med school for that matter. I got accepted to A and M too. I'm thinking about veterinary medicine."

"Veterinary medicine?" She laughs. She *actually* laughs at me. "You can't be serious. One, you're never going to make a decent income working with animals. And two, the trust is strictly for four years of premed study at LSU, four years of medical school, and two more if you decide to specialize."

"Are you telling me, no medical school, no trust?" I already know this is the case, but I want her to say it. I want her to speak the words. I want her to own the message.

"That's exactly what I'm telling you."

"Then I'll get a job and pay my own way."

"Yeah, I hear volunteer work at the animal shelter pays really well."

"Fuck you."

She slams the drink she's holding down on the table, making the kids jump, then she rounds on me. "You know, I don't know why my dad thought the Westfall name was worth the investment he wanted to make in you, because frankly, you're not worth it."

"Whitney—" my mom says sharply, but I cut her off before she can finish.

"No, Mom, let her say it."

Aunt Whitney looks from my mom to me, then drops her eyes and shakes her head slowly. "I'm sorry." After a moment she lifts her eyes again and fixes them on me. "I know you have some romantic notion about working with animals, but it's time to put away childish things, Robert. You're going to LSU, and you're going to honor your grandfather's legacy."

The hell I am.

You don't realize what a small world it is until you try to get lost in it.

"So he really Photoshopped a photo of you and him together?" Andrew asks as we explore a large two-story house under construction in a new development a few miles away.

"Yep."

"You know, that's starting to make me a little nervous. Maybe you should confront them about the page. Tell them to take it down. You can complain to Facebook if they don't."

"Yeah, I thought about that. But at least with the page I know what's going on."

"And so does anyone else who looks at it."

"As far as I can tell, it's just the three of them. I'm gonna wait. Maybe they'll get bored and move on. But I don't want to be wondering what they're up to."

"Speaking of being up to things . . ." He presses me into some not-yet-painted drywall in the master bedroom.

"You have a pretty strong libido for an old man," I say.

"You call me an old man again, and I'm going to hurt you."

I want to laugh, but I'm thinking about Aunt Whitney's visit again.

"Do you think I should take the money and go to medical school?"

"I don't know. The money *would* be hard to turn down. Eight years of tuition and living expenses. That means you'd not only finish with a highly lucrative career, but you'd finish debt free."

While that is true, it's not really what I wanted to hear.

"Look," Andrew says, tugging on the short hairs in my sideburn, "no one can make that decision for you. You've got to decide what's most important to you, then pursue it with everything you have. Make it happen."

The sound of a car engine cuts through the still air.

"We have company," Andrew says, pushing out his bottom lip and sighing heavily.

On the way back to his Civic, however, he has an excellent idea.

Chapter 36

Andrew

Tuesday morning I call Mrs. Stovall to let her know I've fallen gravely ill and won't be in. She says she hopes I feel better—even though the tone of her voice says she doesn't believe for a minute that I'm sick—then assures me she will find a sub. I tell her my plans are on my desk (right where I left them Monday in anticipation of my grave illness).

At seven thirty, I'm pretty sure it's safe to return, but I wait another half hour just to be sure. At eight o'clock on the nose, I head home. The garage is empty. I leave the door open and park in the driveway.

All clear. Get over here, baby.

As I wait, I calm my nerves with a litany of assurances that our secret day together will remain a secret. Neither Kiki nor Maya showed a hint of coming illness this morning. There is nothing broken in the house that might mean an unexpected call from a service-person. The homes in the neighborhood are small, modest, and owned by mostly single people, all of whom work. Maya is in an all-day training session half an hour away with lunch provided. And the weather is beautiful. It's going to be okay. It has to be okay.

Robert is not far away. In three minutes he's pulling into the garage. I push the button as soon as he's clear and the door closes behind us. Within seconds he's in my arms again.

It's the first time we've had this kind of freedom, and we take advantage of every moment of it, starting in my bedroom. By the end of second period—even when I'm playing hooky, the teacher in me can't help but measure time by my school schedule—we're pleasantly sated. By fourth period, we're on the couch challenging each other to Devilishly Difficult Sudoku races in our underwear. I win the first, he wins the second, but on the third puzzle he keeps gripping my erection with his toes. I call foul and he accepts a boxer penalty. We never finish that third puzzle.

It's my idea to play Truth or Dare in the shower during fifth period. I throw a washcloth over the drain, and the water slowly backs up to make a shallow tub. We plant ourselves opposite each other on the tile floor, our knees drawn up, our feet locked together in the middle. Sophomoric as it is, the game serves two purposes: It involves no physical activity beyond talking (a much-needed rest), and it allows me to get an answer to a question that's been dogging me for weeks.

So here's my twist on the game, as I explain it to Robert: You can only choose Truth.

"Okay," I say to him. "Truth or Dare."

He rolls his eyes and grins. "Truth."

Here goes. "That first time, you know, you wrote on my whiteboard that I lied too. What did I lie to you about?"

His grin slides away. "Dare."

"No. You can't choose Dare. That's not the way we're playing the game. Truth. Let's hear it."

He eyes me through the spray and pushes his wet hair back from his forehead. I'm beginning to think that he won't answer, and then he does. "When I asked you why you brought me to your apartment, you said you were more concerned about me than you were about yourself. And then you freaked out over a two-month discrepancy and . . . you just walked out on me." He bites down on his lips and looks away. I don't respond until he looks back at me. He shrugs like he's just admitted some big secret he's been holding on to. And I guess he has.

"I got scared," I tell him.

"Are you scared now?"

"Yeah. But I'm here. And I'm not going anywhere. Okay?"

He nods his head, and gives me a wan smile. I return it.

"All right. Your turn," I say.

"Truth or Dare."

"Truth."

"Have you ever had a crush on another student?"

"No."

I think my quick response may have been too quick. He looks unconvinced, as if that word *no* is just a knee-jerk response not tied to any kind of truth, the kind of knee-jerk response I see in the classroom all the time. I say, *Stop.* Kid says, *What? I didn't do anything.* It wouldn't matter if I'd captured the entire thing on video. The response is always self-righteous indignation.

Is that the way I sounded to him just now? One way or the other, I intend to find out.

"Truth or Dare."

"I don't want to play anymore," he says. He stretches out his legs and draws one of my feet into his lap, then threads his fingers through my toes.

"Come on. One more."

He sighs, a note of resignation. "Truth."

"What's bothering you?"

His eyes meet mine, and I'm not so sure I want to hear the answer anymore. I steel myself for whatever's coming.

He takes a deep breath and lets it out as he flexes my toes back and forth. "I guess I'm afraid that everything's going to change one day. That you'll outgrow me. That I won't be able to afford college unless I go away and do something I really don't want to do. That if I go away, you'll meet somebody else. That somebody will find out and the whole thing will blow up in our faces. And that if it blows up in our faces, you'll go away."

"That's a lot to worry about."

The afternoon passes by too quickly. Robert leaves at two, a little before the end of seventh period, and after a long, tight embrace that we are both reluctant to end. Dressed in corduroy slacks and a light knit pullover, I head over to pick up Kiki at Ms. Smith's Village. On the way, I text Maya to tell her I'm not tutoring today.

Robert

"The school called and said you were absent today."

I'm holding my phone with one hand as I let myself in the garage door with the other. Damn, I should have called the school myself this morning.

"I just didn't feel good when I got to the parking lot, so I turned around and came home. I should have called you. Sorry." I'm trying very hard to sound pathetic.

"And you didn't answer your phone either."

"I think I had it on vibrate," I mumble convincingly. "I went back to bed and slept all day." Which is exactly what I'd like to do right now. In fact, I'm already kicking off my shoes and pulling my shirt over my head as we talk.

When she gets home, I've got the quilt drawn over me and I'm reliving the day in my head, but I'm also thinking about the future. What's going to happen next August? Baton Rouge is hours away. Five or more. Even College Station is almost two hours, although it's unlikely I could come up with the tuition for A&M this late.

Mom leans into my room to let me know she's home.

"Hey, Mom?" I say as she starts to leave. "What if I don't go to LSU? What if I don't study medicine?"

"If that's not what you want to do, Robert, we'll figure something out. Okay? Don't let Aunt Whitney or your late grandfather bully you into something that's not right for you. But I do think you're going to have to make a decision pretty soon."

Andrew

Maya tosses her bag and her keys on the counter and gives Kiki a hug.

"Mommy, look!" Kiki holds out a fistful of shredded parmesan cheese that she's been throwing into a salad bowl, mostly.

"I like cheese," Maya says, taking a small bite from Kiki's hand. "How was *your* day?" she asks me.

"Good. How was yours?"

"Well, they haven't cut my job yet, so pretty good, I guess. Thanks for picking up Kiki. No tutorees today?"

"Nope."

"Yay you. What's for dinner?" She crosses the kitchen to where I'm turning chicken breast cutlets on a small grill.

"Chicken Caesar salad. Okay with you?"

"Perfect. I'm going to go change, okay?"

When she comes back, she's dressed in plaid flannel pajama pants and a snug white T-shirt. I'm cutting the chicken into thin slices to throw on the salad. Kiki has moved on to croutons.

Maya reaches into a cabinet and pulls out two shallow salad bowls. "Did you take a shower when you got home? Your bathroom's all wet."

Why were you in my bathroom?

"No, actually. I started to. I turned on the shower, then forgot all about it." I nod toward Kiki like I blame her.

"So how did the towels get all wet?"

She doesn't sound suspicious. They're just questions, I tell myself. Questions that she wouldn't even have if she were respecting my privacy. "I didn't have the curtain closed good and by the time I remembered the shower, there was water all over the floor. I mopped it up with the towels. I'll throw them in the washing machine in a bit."

"Oh," she says.

I'm about as clean as a person can get, but after dinner and after I read to Kiki (*Robert the Rose Horse,* of course, of course) I stick with my regular routine and shower again. I send Robert a quick text first.

Sooo tired ;)

I delete the sent text, then lay the phone face down on my bed and get into the shower. When I come out ten minutes later, my phone is face up. I notice it immediately because I always place my phone face down—it's a weird habit—and there is zero chance that I didn't this time. I even specifically remember thinking if anyone were to come into my room, they wouldn't see the screen if for some reason it were lit up.

I pick up the phone and check my messages. Robert has texted, but only his number shows up now, and the message hasn't been read. I'm relieved, but I can't believe that Maya is snooping in my room. This is *not* okay.

I pull on some clothes. I'm ready to confront her when something grabs my ankle. And then a giggle.

"What are you doing under my bed, baby girl?"

Kiki crawls out clutching Spot. I pick her up. She's wearing Little Mermaid pajamas tonight and her dark hair is tousled. "*You* are supposed to be in bed, little one."

She sticks her thumb in her mouth and smiles around it. "I hide."

"I know you hide. You scared your daddy half to death." In more ways than one.

Chapter 37

Andrew

I sleep like a baby, and by the time I get to school the next morning, I'm ready to face those freshmen. I stop in the men's room. The face I see in the mirror is a little too happy for school. I try to relax my smile, to look serious and stern as I must be in about forty minutes. But trying not to think about yesterday actually focuses my mind quite sharply on the smallest of details, and I'm not only smiling again, but I'm getting a hell of an erection.

I force myself to think about Stephen Newman for a couple of minutes. He's an anti-aphrodisiac if there ever was one. I keep this in mind as I leave the restroom.

The sub has left a mess on my desk. There's a scribbled note that she couldn't follow my plans (and she's not a math teacher anyway—she was told she wouldn't have to teach math to sub in math), so, essentially, she gave all my students a free day.

Wonderful.

The only thing more difficult than managing a classroom full of fourteen- and fifteen-year-olds a few weeks before spring break is trying to manage them after a sub has turned them loose for a day. I can just imagine what kind of trouble they were getting into while she read a book or surfed the Internet on my computer or checked her friends' statuses on her iPhone.

I glance at the name at the bottom of the note so I can ask that she not be assigned to my classroom next time. *Bob Wilson.*

Oh.

So, anyway, I'm not particularly surprised when the students in my first-period class enter like a troop of baboons. And I'm certainly not surprised when Stephen Newman struts in a few beats after the bell. I can't ignore this again. He's clearly drawing a line in the sand just to see if I'll step over it. But he's messing with the wrong guy. It's him or me. Either I hold him accountable for his actions (despite his dad calling foul), or I lose this class for the rest of the year.

"All right, let's settle down and get out your homework," I say. "Stephen, you're late. Please go get a pass from the AP's office."

He stops and throws his hands out like I'm out of my mind. "I'm not late," he says with indignant outrage. "I was inside the door when the bell rang."

"You're late. Go."

"You're crazy. What? You got something against football players?"

"I'm not playing with you," I say calmly. "Get a pass, or I'll give you a referral."

The rest of the kids are watching. He turns to the door and mutters just loud enough for everyone to hear, "Fucking cocksucker."

I shouldn't react. I should either:

1. let him go, get my class started, then write an office referral to give him when he returns with that pass, or

2. tell him to wait outside, get my class started, then write an office referral, calmly hand it to him in the hallway, and send him on his way.

Yeah. That's what I *should* do.

Here's what I actually do.

I fling the dry erase marker in the general direction of my desk and say, "Get the hell out of my classroom, you little snot."

As I shadow him into the hallway, I hear giggling and *oohs* from the kids. I shut the door hard enough to rattle the glass. He spins around, defiant, his chin up and his eyes narrowed. I get in his face. "You are not going to disrespect me in my classroom, do you understand me?"

He scoffs and looks away.

"You think you're real cute, don't you? Think you're hot stuff? Big, tough football player? You're just the class clown. You think they're laughing with you? They're laughing *at* you, buddy. You're not cute. You're not funny. You're just a little shit, and I've had enough of your crap. You got that?"

"My dad—"

"You know what? I don't give a shit about your dad. If you're in my classroom, you're going to behave, or you're going to leave. And if you're late, you're going to get a pass. Do I make myself clear?"

His lip curls and he looks off down the hallway.

"Do I?"

I'm vaguely aware that Jennifer has stepped outside of her door. We do that, act as witnesses for each other when something's going down. I don't know how much she's heard. I'm not even sure at this point exactly what I've said. I just know I'm so goddamned mad I can hardly see straight.

Stephen refuses to answer, and I can't stand to look at him another second.

"Get out of my face. And don't come back until you've been signed off on by an AP."

Jen watches him stalk past her, then turns to me and mouths, "Little fucker."

I smile and decompress just a little. There's one thing I can always count on: the support of other teachers. Because they've all been there.

The chatter quiets when I return to the classroom. I don't have any more trouble from the kids the rest of the period. But I don't have any engagement either. They work quietly on a couple of problems while I complete the referral and e-mail it to the AP's office. I may have won the battle, but I'm damn sure not winning the war.

Before the class period ends, I get an e-mail from the principal.

> Mr. McNelis—
> Please stop by my office during your planning period to
> discuss Stephen Newman.
> Mr. Redmon

Great. This kid hijacks my class, and now he's hijacking my planning period.

Mr. Redmon motions me to a chair and gets right to the point. "I got a call from Mr. Newman about an hour ago. You want to tell me what's going on in your classroom?"

I shrug. "I referred Stephen to the office today. He was late, he was disrespectful, I sent him out."

"His dad says you humiliated him in front of the other kids."

And he called me a fucking cocksucker.

"I just sent him out. Look, Mr. Redmon, he's turning my class into a zoo. I can't teach algebra if—"

"What have you done to solve the problem? Have you redirected Stephen?"

"Of course. Repeatedly."

"Have you called his father?"

He already knows the answer to that question, and it irritates me that he asks. I answer in the negative. In my experience, despite my earlier threat to Stephen, calling parents about their misbehaving teenagers rarely solves problems. Nor does sending them to the office. I know that. Problems are solved in the classroom. And solving them means having an effective plan for dealing with kids, and then working the plan.

I had let Stephen push my buttons and subsequently threw the plan out the window, and now I'm paying for it.

"His father is asking again to have him moved out of your class."

I bet he is.

"Of course," he continues, folding his arms across his chest, "we don't do that. But I'm disappointed that you haven't spoken with his father. I've set up a conference with him and with Stephen tomorrow morning, six thirty. I plan to be there as well."

"All right." By which I mean, *What choice do I have?* I stand.

"I just want to caution you," Mr. Redmon says as he gets up and begins pulling on his suit jacket. "This is not a parent you want to mess with. If you have a problem with this young man, you need to get over it by tomorrow morning. I will support you one hundred percent, but you better have your ducks in a row."

He pats me on the back and walks out with me. He stays behind to talk with Mrs. Stovall, and I head back, getting more and more angry with each step.

I have lunch in my classroom, getting my *ducks* to line up.

"Want some company?" Jen asks from the doorway.

"I thought you hated my guts."

She shrugs and steps into the room. "I got over it."

I gesture to the chair next to me, and she sits, setting her salad on my desk.

"So, why are you eating alone in your room again?"

"Parent-teacher-principal conference in the morning. I need to gather some info."

"That sucks."

That's an understatement. From what I've heard about this dad, this is not going to be one of those positive experiences where we all unite together to get a kid back on track. I need to be prepared. And I'm not without fault here, which only complicates the problem.

"Okay," she says, her eyes lighting up, "so you want to hear the latest gossip?"

"Does it have anything to do with me?"

She laughs. "No."

"All right. Hit me with it."

"Okay, you know Melissa Sparks? She's technology, com apps or something like that."

I only vaguely know who she is, though I probably couldn't put name to face if I saw her in the hallway. I nod anyway as I retrieve Stephen's grades and send them to the printer.

"Anyway, she's friends with Guy Sutherland in language arts. So, he found out his wife is sleeping with his best friend and he's depressed and all that shit, so she gives him some of her antidepressants. *At* school. That's a felony, baby. So the deal is, they both get called into Mr. Redmon's office. I don't know how he knows about it, but, you know, you can't keep anything secret around here. Right?" She smiles. "He says he won't report the transfer of a controlled substance to the authorities as long as it doesn't happen again and it doesn't leave that room. If there is any talk about it at all, he'll have no choice but to call in the police."

I choke down a bite of my sandwich. "Then why are we talking about this?"

"I don't know. Good stuff, huh?"

My phone vibrates in my pocket. I keep it on just in case Kiki's school calls. I check my message.

I'm thinking about you.

No txtng at school. Me too. ☺

"Is that your ex-wife?" Jen says.

"Yeah." I put my phone back in my pocket.

"So, is she down with this gay thing?"

This gay thing? "That's why she's my ex-wife."

"So why are you living with her again? I mean, I know the pay sucks, but where are you going to entertain your men friends?"

"Who says I have any men friends?"

"A good-looking guy like you has got to have men friends. If you don't, well, I could hook you up with some."

"I bet. But, no, thanks. I've got that under control."

But actually, control is something I don't have, not when it comes to Robert. It's hard to be in a classroom with him for an hour and not give away the fact that I have carnal knowledge of him. I find myself looking at him when I shouldn't. Smiling when my mind wanders. My mind wandering when I should be focused on my students.

I worried at first that he might give us away. But he's much better at this than I am. He's so good, in fact, that it starts messing with my head.

I find myself walking the room more often, chatting with students as they work through problems just to give me an excuse to stop by Robert's desk and chat with him. I place my hand on a kid's shoulder as I walk by, just so I can do the same to Robert. I put problems on the board and ask students to go up and work them, just so I can stand in the back of the room and watch him unobserved.

And then he kind of smiles out of nowhere, and I know he knows.

I want to see him after school, but I have tutoring with Stephen, and then I need to pick up Kiki from Ms. Smith's Village and keep her out of Maya's hair for a little while. I don't dare come back until the group is finished. Maybe I can run out to the grocery store this evening and "run into" him there again. Maybe we can meet at Ridgewood Park for a few minutes of serious making out.

When the bell rings, he packs up, then stays behind to straighten the desks. He casts a quick look at the door after the last kid leaves.

"You're bad," he mouths to me, then flashes me a grin.

Robert

Andrew, Andrew, Andrew. I like that he's so aware of me in class. But he's so obvious. At least, *I* think he is. But maybe that's because I know what's going on between us. Maybe to my classmates it's just class as usual.

I really want to see him tonight, but I don't think that's going to happen. Then again, maybe he'll get home early and I'll see him before I leave the group session.

I stop by the band hall to pick up my sax. I could stand to practice some tonight.

"Oh, hey, Robert," someone calls out as I squeeze through the crowded doorway. It's Luke. He weaves his way over to me and throws an arm over my shoulder as he walks with me to my locker. "Hey, I didn't know that you and Erick Wasserman were such *close* friends."

"You saw."

He cracks up and leans against the locker next to mine. "Dang, that *is* a fan club. Those three have got it bad for you."

"Look," I say, nodding toward my three stalkers huddled together on the other side of the band hall. All three are watching me, but when Luke looks their way, they scatter.

"Better you than me, man," he says. "So, anything new in your love life?"

I don't answer, but I can't stop the grin from spreading across my face.

"Yeah?" Luke says. "Things are working out? Holy cow, I still can't believe you and Mr. McNelis."

I give my head a subtle shake and take a quick survey of everyone around us. No one seems to be listening.

"Sorry," Luke says, dropping his voice.

Andrew

I'm watching the clock. I swear to God, if that kid is one minute late, I'm out of here. So I'm especially irritated when he walks in fifteen minutes late and slouches into a desk like he's about to kick his shoes off and watch a rerun of *South Park,* which apparently is showing outside my classroom windows.

Unbelievable.

"So, I'm meeting with your father tomorrow morning. You want to give me a preview of what the problem is?"

He smirks but doesn't look at me.

"Great. Okay. Well, you haven't turned in your homework all week, so I'm going to assume that we need to review this unit from the beginning. Would you say that's true?"

Nothing. I wait, a nice fat pregnant pause, just for him. And still nothing.

"You know what? You're a piece of work, Stephen. My little girl is spending two extra hours in day care today, just so I can waste my time here with you. If you're not going to engage, why do you even bother coming?"

Now he does look at me. "I'm surprised you could even get it up for a girl."

I want to deck this kid *so* bad. I swallow my retort. "I think we're done here."

He gets up and gives me a look of disgust as he struts past me to the door. "See you in the morning, Mr. McJerkoff."

I grab the sleeve of his jacket before I can check my anger. "You little prick."

He tries to shrug me off at the same time I let go, and he stumbles and drops to the floor.

"You okay?" I ask, offering my hand.

He slaps it away and gets up, shrugs his backpack back onto his shoulder, then gives me the finger.

I can't wait for our meeting in the morning.

Robert

I'm going to miss these kids, I think as I move the chairs back to the dining room table. But I don't think I ever want to hear "Mary Had a Little Lamb" again.

Ms. Momin is in the driveway helping Jo-Jo's mom get him into the car. I can hear him laughing and snuffling even inside.

As I pack up the recorders, I let my eyes linger on the couch and try to imagine myself there with Andrew again. I can't stand all this sneaking around. I wonder—if I told Mom, would she understand? Would she let us hang out together at our house? Nice thought, but not likely. Still, I find myself imagining him stretched out naked in my bed and feel myself start to stiffen.

"That's the last one," Ms. Momin says from the doorway. I give her a smile and stack the recorders on the hearth. She holds the door open for me. "So, one more session, next week, right?"

"Um, yeah."

"Great." I slip past her, and then she says, "Hey, Robert, I'm just curious. What math class are you taking this year?"

I hesitate and consider lying. "Calculus."

"Oh. Then you must have Ms. Echols."

She knows. "Um, no. Actually, I have Mr. McNelis."

"You do?" She's holding on to the edge of the door. Her eyes shift to the street, then back to me. "You didn't tell me that last week. In fact, you acted like you'd just met."

"Yeah, I know. Sorry. It's just kind of weird running into your math teacher outside of class, you know."

I can't dial fast enough.

"Hey, this is a surprise," Andrew says when he picks up.

"Where are you?"

"Right at this moment, I am riding a black stallion."

Whatever I expected, it wasn't that, and it kind of knocks me off my track. "Um, should I be jealous?"

He laughs. "Hardly. I'm on the merry-go-round at the mall with Kiki. And frankly, I'm a little nauseated."

"I think your ex-wife knows."

"Knows what?"

"About us."

For a moment all I hear is the music of the merry-go-round and the chatter of voices in the background. Then Andrew says, "No way."

"She asked me who my math teacher is."

"Did you tell her?"

"Yeah."

"Good. Look, I know it may sound like she's suspicious, but it was probably just natural curiosity. She knows you're a senior. She knows I teach seniors. At some point she probably realized I might be your teacher."

"But we acted like we didn't know each other."

"Okay. There is that."

"I told her it was just weird running into you like that outside of school."

"Makes perfect sense to me."

"I don't think she believed me."

"Okay, let's just assume for a moment that she knows. What? That I'm your teacher? That it was awkward running into each other at my ex-wife's house? She doesn't know anything. Maya's been my best friend for more than ten years. If she knows something, if she's suspicious, she'll say something to me. She's always had my back. Okay?"

I'm not so sure, but I say, "Okay," anyway.

"Hey, I'm the one who's supposed to be paranoid here. I'll let you know if you need to worry. And, hey, I kind of like you calling me."

Since he likes it so much, I call him in the morning too.

"You are going to make me late," he says quietly when he answers. No *hello*. He just jumps right in. I like that.

"I just wanted to say hi."

I can actually hear him smiling through the phone. "Hi to you too."

"Do you always leave for school this early?"

"No. I have a parent-teacher conference this morning. My favorite thing to do, you know."

"Somebody giving you a hard time?"

"Oh, you could say that."

"Anybody I know?"

"A kid named Stephen Newman. He's a freshman and a pain in the ass."

"I know his sister. She was a flute player."

"I'm sorry."

I laugh. "If he gives you too hard a time, just let me know. I'll beat him up."

"I'll keep that in mind. But I don't think we'll have to resort to that. He's a big talker, but he's pretty harmless."

I draw my phone a little closer to my mouth. "Can I see you tonight?"

"I was hoping you'd ask that. Got a place in mind?"

"I'll think about it."

"And I'm going to try very hard *not* to think about it." He laughs. "You are going to get me in so much trouble. I got to run. I'll see you sixth."

"Try not to grope me in class, okay? Kids might start to talk."

Chapter 38

Andrew

The meeting is being held in a small conference room behind the receptionist's desk. "They're waiting for you," she says.

"Thank you very much."

I am smartly dressed in a pair of dark gray slacks and a white, long-sleeved button-down with a tie. And I am right on time. Nevertheless, when I open the door I apologize for keeping them waiting.

"I'm Andrew McNelis," I say, extending my hand. Mr. Newman looks at it like I might have peed on it first. Like father like son. I withdraw my hand and greet Stephen (who also looks at me like I'm urine-soaked) and Mr. Redmon as I take a seat. This is going to be fun.

I lay my records out on the table in front of me. Mr. Redmon starts the meeting with some small talk. "Mr. Newman was just telling me that Stephen has been tapped for varsity next year."

"That's great," I say, looking directly at Stephen. *They must need a freakishly short ball boy.* He glares back at me. Neither he nor his dad responds.

Mr. Redmon clears his throat and suggests we get started. He asks me to talk about what I see going on in class and about Stephen's grades.

Fortunately, I have come prepared. I address his grades first since that's the most objective issue and the least likely to call my professionalism into question. I've printed out three copies of his grades and slide one over to Mr. Redmon and one to Mr. Newman.

"Stephen is not turning in his homework. I've received only three partially completed assignments since we returned from the holiday. Not only is that pulling his grade down, but I believe the lack of practice is really hurting his performance on quizzes and tests. The last test he took"—I remove that from the folder and pass it across the table—"he made a forty-nine on. As you can see, he didn't even attempt about a quarter of the problems. I gave him as much partial credit as I could on the other problems he missed. I also gave him the opportunity to make test corrections after a review with me. That could have brought his grade up to a seventy, but he declined."

I rest my case.

Mr. Newman barely glances at the papers in front of him. When I'm done, he pushes them back across the table. I take them, stack them neatly, and return them to Stephen's file.

"My son doesn't like you," he says, which are the first words he's spoken since I arrived.

"I understand that, but I'm not here to be popular with kids, Mr. Newman. I'm here to teach algebra."

Mr. Redmon clears his throat again. "Mr. McNelis, Stephen believes that you have singled him out, that you are treating him differently than other students." He consults the paper in front of him. "He's says you've humiliated him in class, that you've threatened to kick him, that you've told him to shut up and get out, and that you've stood him up for tutoring. He also says you called him a prick yesterday."

That little prick.

"Mr. Redmon, I think I'm a pretty good classroom manager. Some of what Stephen has described is merely part of my management system. The kids understand it for what it is. When I tell a student I'm going to kick them, and then I'm going to kick their dog, absolutely *no one* takes that literally. The same goes for telling them to shut up and get out. I'm sure I say something like that a couple times a day, and have for over a year. It is not meant in any way to shame students. *They* know that. And I believe Stephen knows that too.

"As to why he's coming to you with this now," I continue, "I can only assume he's expressing his anger at being held accountable. He's been increasingly disruptive in class."

"That's a lie," Stephen cuts in.

I continue without pause. "I have had no choice but to deal with his disruptions, including referring him to the office yesterday. I have a class to teach, and I cannot teach if a student insists on hijacking the entire class."

"Everybody's talking in class," Stephen sputters. "And everybody's goofing off because we're bored. He doesn't teach us anything. And he just doesn't like me."

Mr. Redmon addresses me, ignoring Stephen's outburst. "Have you spoken with Mr. Newman about Stephen's behavior?"

"Actually, no. I think it's more effective if I work directly with my students. Unfortunately, in Stephen's case, I believe we were headed for parent intervention."

I can tell from Mr. Redmon's demeanor that he appreciates the fact that I have dotted my i's and crossed my t's and that our discussion so far has remained professional. It makes his job a lot easier.

"Did you call Stephen a prick during tutoring yesterday?"

"Absolutely not."

"Liar," Stephen says again.

You know what, you little shit? Two can play this game. And I've had a hell of a lot more practice than you've had.

"I don't really understand why Stephen is so angry with me and why he is choosing to act out in class." I say this looking directly at Stephen. I love the expression *act out*. It makes him sound like a two-year-old. "But I assure you I don't treat him any differently than any other student. If anything, I've given him more latitude with tardies and such just to avoid getting into a battle with him over petty issues. And I certainly haven't called him names.

"I am happy to do anything I can to get him back on track. In fact, I've already rearranged my own personal schedule to accommodate his football practice. I don't know what more I can do."

Take that, *twerp.*

Mr. Redmon thanks me and releases me back to my classroom. He is clearly planning to remain behind to continue speaking with Stephen and his father. I offer my hand to Mr. Newman again just to emphasize what a pompous ass he is, and just as I expect, he refuses to shake.

Afraid of the gay?

I retrieve my hand, give him my biggest smile, and leave the room.

I can only imagine what's being said in there. If Mr. Redmon is half the principal I believe him to be, he's supporting me 100 percent, just as he said he would. If he believed everything kids told their parents about teachers, there'd be none of us left.

Last year Ms. Young—one of our more senior teachers with thirty-five years in the classroom and six months from retirement— was accused of inappropriate contact with a student because she, allegedly, tried to kiss one of the boys in her class. Yeah, she did. When kids misbehaved, she threatened to kiss them. That was *her* classroom management plan. First, she warned them. With the second warning she pulled out her fire-engine red lipstick and slathered it on her thin lips. There was no third warning. The next time a kid misbehaved, she gave him a big ol' smooch on the cheek. She rarely had to correct a student three times.

I get back with plenty of time to spare before first bell, and I have to admit, I'm feeling pretty good. Numbers don't lie, but kids do, all the time.

"How'd it go?" Jen says from my doorway.

"Good. We'll see what happens tomorrow."

Robert

It's dark and it's pouring rain; we take advantage of both to make out in a far corner of the H-E-B parking lot. Andrew is soaking wet and his skin is cold and goose bumpy. I'm doing my damned best to warm him up. Nobody's undressing today, though. We're taking a risk as it is, but we're not *that* stupid. That doesn't mean that we're hanging out in the backseat like altar boys, though.

"Can you get away for a night this weekend?" he asks. "I'll get a hotel room downtown—a late Valentine's Day present, or maybe an early birthday present."

"Really? All night? Like with a bed and everything? And a lock on the door? And no pictures of your ex-wife anywhere?"

"Uh-huh."

"I don't know. Are you sure your heart can take it?"

"You know, you keep that up and I'm going to . . ."

"You're going to what?"

"I'm going to dock you ten points on your next test."

"Gasp. Abuse of power. Sorry, Teach."

"Don't say that, okay?"

Chapter 39

Andrew

I lean back in my desk chair and close my eyes. God, I'm tired.

Robert and I stayed out later than we'd planned—ten o'clock, not that late—but when I got home, Maya ripped into me for not calling and for standing up my daughter.

"You know," she'd said angrily, "your daughter likes routine. And she was expecting you to read to her tonight." I felt like I was in high school again being scolded by my parents for missing curfew. She wanted to know where I'd been. I told her, "Out with a friend." She didn't seem to like that answer very much.

When the bell rings, I start, then rub my eyes and get to my feet. The kids start trickling in. I'm just finishing writing the day's objectives on the board when Stephen shows up . . . on time. And the real kicker, he actually acts human. And do I detect a small measure of contrition?

I allow myself a moment of pride at my eloquent presentation of the situation yesterday and the subsequent taking down a peg of one Stephen Newman.

The kids have a quiz today. After we go over homework, I pass out the quizzes and instruct the kids to place them in a basket on my desk when they're done and get started on tonight's homework.

I park on the stool in front of the classroom to monitor, but I'm foggy-brained, and at least once I almost lose my balance and tumble off the stool. I need caffeine, and I need it badly. But there's no leaving the room.

The first kid to finish is one of the girls—Safina Ahmad. She drops her quiz in the basket and catches my eye. I motion to her. "Would you do me a big favor?" I ask quietly. "Would you take this cup to the teachers' lounge at the end of the hall and fill it with coffee?"

"Sure." She takes the cup.

"And there are some little containers of cream and some sugar packets. Would you bring me a couple of each?"

She smiles and quietly lets herself out of the room. Not only is Safina bright as hell and poorly placed in this class, but she's one of those kids who loves to help out her teachers. And she's one I can trust to go into the teachers' lounge and not get into some mischief on the way.

When Safina gets back, I mouth a thank you and give her a wink, then set the cup on my stool to add cream and sugar.

The kids are starting to finish in larger numbers now. Two and three at a time are at my desk. I notice that Stephen is still working. No doubt he's just doodling since he hasn't done any homework on this unit and has wasted every class period. But he's not acting like a jerk. I take that to mean that his dad gave him the *what for* after our meeting, and I wouldn't be having any more trouble from him. Maybe after this quiz I can get him back on track and help him salvage what's left of the school year. In high school, kids should be using summer school to get ahead, not to recover credits. Even an immature little brat like Stephen Newman.

In the back corner of the room, I see Tyler Hicks stretching his scrawny self in his seat to see over Izzy Garcia's shoulder. I'm pretty sure that's not going to do him much good. I clear my throat and he darts a look at me, then hunches over his quiz again. I keep my eye on them until Izzy turns in her quiz.

That's when I see the note being passed hand to hand. I consider letting it go, but I figure I'm on a roll, so I might as well ride this baby as long as I can. I pick up the note and make a big show of dropping it in the trash unread.

Another quiz, second period, practically puts me in a coma, despite the coffee. By third-period conference, I have to move around.

I grab some more coffee, check my mailbox, stop by the attendance office to sign a few forms, then just to keep busy stop by the library to check out some picture books for Kiki. The librarian, Ms. Wetzel, purchases them for teachers in English classes to use in teaching literary elements.

She pulls a couple of new ones from her not-yet-available-for-checkout shelf and checks them out to me because, she says, I'm *too cute for words*. She's about eighty. She talks to me like I'm eight. Sometimes I think she thinks I'm checking out the picture books for myself.

On my way back to my classroom, I reach for my phone to check the time. It's not in my pocket. I try to remember when I last had it, but I just don't know. Sometimes I place it on my desk during class, so I check there first, under papers, around my computer, in my desk drawers, under my desk. Then I resign myself to retracing my steps. Lounge, mailboxes, attendance, library.

No phone.

In the few minutes I have before fourth period, I go out to the parking lot and check my car. Nothing. That's just great. I probably left it at home this morning. I'm going to feel naked all day without it.

And I do. Countless times I reach for it, and then remember it's not there. I even call myself from my classroom phone. Nada.

During fourth, I pull a book from my shelves—a biography of Galileo—and tuck a note inside, leaving about a quarter inch exposed: *Phone missing. Don't text. Will call later.* On the outside I attach a Post-it: *Robert Westfall.* Then I look up Robert's schedule and add *Room 242.* Out of an abundance of caution, I put a rubber band around the book, then shanghai the first kid to finish the quiz, Annie Dunn.

"Would you take this to Robert Westfall, room 242. He left it in my classroom this morning."

When Robert comes into class sixth, he waves the book at me. "Thanks for returning my book, Mr. Mac."

"You're welcome, Mr. Westfall."

I search everywhere when I get home for that damn phone, but it's just gone. I use Maya's phone to call myself. Nothing.

It is beyond frustrating to lose a phone. Do I wait and keep looking? Or do I just drop another couple hundred dollars or so that I don't have and buy a new one? I decide to wait until Saturday morning at least.

When Maya takes a bubble bath that evening, I borrow her phone and call Robert.

"Hello? Ms. Momin?"

"Not Ms. Momin."

He laughs. "I didn't think so. Still no phone?"

"Nope. If it doesn't show up by tomorrow morning, I'm going to have to buy a new one. In the meantime, though, we have some plans to make. And we have about ten minutes to make them."

I hate hanging up when I hear Maya pull the drain on the tub because I know there will be no communicating with him until tomorrow. I delete the call dialed and replace the phone exactly as I found it.

By two o'clock Saturday afternoon, I've got a new phone, disabled the SIM card on the previous one, and downloaded all my contacts. It costs me almost two hundred dollars for a similar refurbished phone since my contract isn't up for renewal yet. I don't carry insurance, because I don't lose my phones.

Maya is vacuuming when I get home, and Kiki is napping in a pile of clean laundry on the couch. I move her to a cozy, oversize chair and sit on the couch to fold. Maya turns off the vacuum cleaner. "Did you get a phone?"

"Yep. What a pain."

"Hey, Doug is out of town. How about I rent a movie from Redbox and we have a pajama party tonight?"

"Wow. Sounds like fun, but I'm going out tonight. In fact, I'm leaving about five."

"A date?"

"Yeah."

"What time are you going to be home?"

I'm folding a towel. I make a trifold the way Maya likes it and set it on the back of the couch. "I'm not going to be home tonight, Maya."

I pick up another towel and focus on making neat, tight folds.

"Are you staying at his place?"

I don't particularly like her tone. I am not a child. I do not need her permission or approval. I don't answer. Maybe that's what sets her off.

She snaps the vacuum handle in the upright position and storms out of the room, but just as she reaches the hallway, she turns back. "Why is he texting your phone?"

Goddamnshitmotherfucker. She *was* in my room. She looked at my phone. Hell, for all I know, she took my phone. I am livid. No, I am beyond livid, but I force my face to remain neutral, or if not neutral, at least confused and maybe a little indignant. I'm not sure how well I'm accomplishing any of those.

"What are you talking about, Maya? And what's with all the questions? Weren't you the one who insisted we were still going to have our own lives? I think your actual words were, 'You can still date. Go dancing. Bring a guy over for dinner.' So what was that? Just some kind of bullshit to get me back in the house again?" I pick up another towel and wad it up. "Well, I'm back, but I'm not too damn happy about it right now."

I get to my feet and fling the towel at the couch. "I'll be back tomorrow, early afternoon. I'll take Kiki to the lake to feed the ducks, and you can have the afternoon to yourself. Okay?"

She says, "Okay," but she doesn't mean okay. She makes me feel like I'm committing adultery. Like I'm committing statutory rape.

We avoid each other for the next few hours. It's a relief to zip up my small duffel bag and kiss my daughter good-bye at five.

"I hope you have a good time," Maya says, but her tone sounds more like she hopes I get a disease and die. As I pick up my duffel bag, I make a decision. On Monday, I'm going to look for an apartment. We're better friends when we're apart. When we're together, it's just toxic. And I don't want to have to drive an hour to spend a night with my boyfriend again.

She recognized his number. *Fuck.*

Robert

I tell Mom I'm spending the night at Luke's. She just tells me to keep my cell phone on and have a good time.

Chapter 40

Andrew

It's hard to stay in a bad mood when Robert's dancing dirty hip-hop on the bed in my striped dress shirt and nothing else, and singing, "Shawty had them Apple Bottom jeans, jeans . . ." It's cute and damn sexy.

It's his way of making me forget about my fight with Maya.

It's working pretty well.

There'll be time to deal with Maya tomorrow.

The bed is not nearly firm enough, but he manages the ball changes and turns easily enough. The spins and the slides are a little tricky, though. So when he attempts a three-sixty spin, his feet get tangled in the bedspread and it's more of a stumble, but he catches himself. I pull him down to me before he can do it again.

"I think you forgot your pants," I say, running my hand up his thigh and over his ass.

He looks down like this is news and gasps. "I'm naked," he mouths, pointing down.

"I know," I mouth back. "You know," I say, taking full advantage of said nakedness, "the next time you dance on a bed, it'll be mine."

He flicks his eyebrows at me. His smile lingers a moment longer, then morphs into something more serious. "I brought condoms."

"You did?" His comment has taken me by surprise, and I don't know how to respond. I knew this would come up one day; I just didn't think it would come up this day.

My hesitation plays out on Robert's face. I move my hand to his sideburns and play with the short hairs there. "We don't have to," he says after a moment.

I take a deep breath, and when I let it out, I fix my eyes on his. "I haven't had good experiences with that."

"The guy you never kissed?"

I pause a moment before answering. "Yeah."

"Will you tell me about it someday?"

"Someday." I hate disappointing him. I hate giving Kevin that power. He took so much from me, and now I'm letting him limit my intimacy with Robert. I don't want that, but I'm afraid, and I'm not even sure of what. "Is that kind of sex important to you?" I ask.

He hesitates before answering, as if he's examining the question and his feelings in order to respond honestly. I love that about him. Finally he presses his forehead to mine. "No, it's not important to me, but *you* are."

O'Donnell Street Pub is not far from the hotel. It's an Irish pub and a small live-music venue located on a dimly lit side street near downtown, but very popular with those who've been lucky enough to discover it. The crowd is mostly young, professional urbanites. I've been here twice with Maya, and I've never seen anyone I know. I have tickets for the nine o'clock show.

This is the first time I've taken Robert out on a real date, and I want it to be something special.

A waitress greets us as we settle in at a small round table for two along a wall adjacent to the stage. "What can I get you gentlemen to drink?"

"I'll have a beer," Robert says with an admirably straight face.

My eyes widen but I don't mention that he is not old enough to order beer. "Make that two. Guinness Stout."

"Two beers, you got it. I'll need to see some ID, please."

Robert pats his pocket. "Oh, gosh. I left my wallet in the car," he says sheepishly. "I'll just have a Coke."

I produce my ID and she gives it a quick look without skipping a beat. "One Coke and one Guinness Stout coming up." She flashes Robert a smile that seems to suggest I'm not the only one who wants in his pants. My heart swells with pride.

"What?" Robert says when she leaves.

"A beer?"

I think that's the end of it, but when the waitress sets our drinks on the table, then returns to the kitchen with our dinner order, Robert switches the mugs. "You're driving."

I sigh. "My list of crimes is getting long and longer."

"Ah. You worry too much," he says, laughing. "Let's just have a good time."

In truth, I'm not that worried. Robert was right—there've been no lightning strikes, no cops banging on my door. And even if Maya thinks she knows something, she'd never betray me. I'm sitting here with a guy I love more and more every day, and I couldn't feel more carefree, more fulfilled if I tried.

"I like this place," Robert says, looking around. "Who are we seeing again?"

"Idgy Vaughn. She's from Austin. I think her music has been described as country confessional."

"You're kidding, right? I mean, you—me—country music?"

"Come on. Be a little open-minded. You'll like her."

Boy, that turns out to be an understatement.

Our steak and mashed potatoes come just as the band begins their first set. We move our chairs so we're both facing the stage. I order another beer, which Robert promptly confiscates.

I'm not sure at just what point I realize he's a little tipsy. Maybe it's the first time he touches his middle finger to his thumb, places them in his mouth, and lets loose an ear-splitting whistle at the end of a song. Or maybe it's when he starts singing the chorus. Or maybe it's when he jumps up at a break between sets, staggers a little, and says, "Let's get a CD," then drapes himself over me and howls like a hound dog. To be fair, the last song was "Redbone Hound" in which Idgy and most of the audience howled like a hound dog. Only, when the song was done, they stopped.

I put my finger to my lips as we make our way to the side room where Idgy is signing her CDs. "Shhhh."

Robert drops his voice and howls more quietly.

"Who shall I make this out to?" Idgy asks, smiling up at us.

"To Robert," I say, to which he says, "That's me." He says it to Idgy, and then he says it again to me.

"I know that's you," I say.

And then he starts gushing. "I love you, Idgy Vaughn. This is the best concert ever. *Ever.*" And then he howls—*Ah-Rooo!*

She smiles at him, then raises her eyebrows at me, and pushes the CD back across the table.

He would like another beer. I don't think so. I ask for two Cokes.

"Are you having fun?" I ask him.

He looks at me and grows absurdly serious. "You have the most beautiful eyes."

I roll them at him.

The band starts their next set on a somber note. Idgy tells about a small graveyard that she could see from her bedroom window growing up. The graves hold the bodies of twelve little girls who died a horrible death when their angel costumes caught fire during a Christmas play and they all burned to death. It happened so quickly that neither the nuns nor the mothers could get to them in time. The song is based on that tragedy. And it's sad. I even tear up a little when I hear it.

But for Robert, it's a two-beer-dead-dog sad song. Halfway through, I glance at him and see that his chin is twitching and tears are spilling down his face. I move my chair closer to his and put my arm around his shoulders. He folds himself into me and sobs for those little girls and those moms with empty arms and those dads who weep and the nun who lost her hands. I don't quite know what to do but hold on to him.

A couple at the table next to us look over with concern. "Is he okay?" the woman asks quietly.

"He's fine," I say assuredly, although I'm not so sure I believe this.

When he doesn't settle down by the end of the next song, I decide the best thing to do is just take him back to the hotel. He's still clinging to me as we make our way through the tightly packed tables. Idgy calls out, "We've lost one. I hope he feels better."

At the door, Robert suddenly stops and diverts unsteadily to the men's room with a rather loud, "I have to take a piss."

Thankfully, the men's room is empty. He braces his forehead against the tile wall. I wait close by just in case he tanks.

"You okay?"

He sniffles, then buries his eyes against his arm. I'm glad that he's centered himself in front of the urinal because he is not watching where he's peeing.

A bearded older man with a graying ponytail enters. He eyes us then goes about his business.

When Robert finishes, I coax him off the wall, and he drapes himself over me again.

"You need to put your dick away and zip up your pants," I tell him quietly.

He looks down and studies himself through blurry eyes and says, "What are you doing out?"

I stifle a laugh and do it for him. I can feel the older gentleman's scrutiny, but I don't dare look up. I clear my throat. "Come on. Let's get you back to the hotel."

We barely make it halfway down the narrow, broken sidewalk to the parking lot before he says, "I don't feel so good," then pukes in the weeds along a chain-link fence. I rub his back while he spits and cries. "Those poor little angels."

I look at his pinched face and think that every single thing he does just etches him a little more deeply on my heart. Of one thing I'm fairly certain: He's been badly wounded, and every now and then something—an empty notebook, a dead dog, a song—rips open the scab and he bleeds. I want to just hold him and make all the bad things go away.

I brush a damp washcloth over his forehead.

"I'm sorry," he whispers.

"You don't have anything to be sorry about."

"I ruined the night and now I can't even get it up."

This makes me smile because in truth, I'm a little worn out, and I like lying here next to him, quiet and sleepy. The heat is off and the room is getting chilly. I reach behind me and set the washcloth on the bedside table and turn out the light. Then I tuck the covers around us, press my cheek to his shoulder, and allow myself to drift off.

Chapter 41

Robert

"How did it go?" I ask.

"Well, the locks weren't changed, and she's still allowing me to be alone with my daughter."

Andrew's at the lake with Kiki right now, feeding ducks. I wish I could be there too. I feel cheated. I passed out and slept away our entire night together. I didn't even get to wake up with him. When I woke, feeling like I'd been dividing by zero, it was already ten o'clock in the morning, and Andrew was in the shower.

"Look who's up," he'd said when I pulled the shower curtain aside and stepped into the spray with him. I can still see the little soap bubbles clinging to him in all the right places and his smile when I wiped them away. And then he howled.

He calls out to Kiki to be careful with the big duck.

"I have one group session to go. Maybe I should just not show up."

"Oh, that won't confirm her suspicions." He laughs into the phone. "Nope, you gotta show. Act totally normal. If we just keep it up and don't give her any other reason to think otherwise, she'll start doubting what she saw or what it means. I'm done worrying about it.

272 • J. H. Trumble

"Hold on. That big mallard is about to trample my daughter for that bread."

I listen while he takes on the duck. I'm pacing on my driveway, but I should be there with them. Movement down the street catches my eye. A dog. As he gets closer, I notice he's limping. A little closer and I realize it's the little Boston terrier that had been sniffing around Nic that day I installed my stereo.

I quietly head out to meet him. His eyes are focused on the road, so he doesn't see me until I've closed the distance between us. Then he looks up and falls over himself in his rush to get away from me.

I try to calm him with my voice. "It's okay, boy," I say gently. "I'm not going to hurt you."

"Who are you talking to?"

"It's a stray dog. He's hurt, but he's skittish. I'll call you back, okay?"

I end the call and slip my phone in my pocket. The dog is back on his feet and hopping madly away. I grab him and he reaches back and nips at me. But it's just a nip. His bulging eyes make him look even more terrified than he already is.

I run my hand over his trembling hips and legs. They feel okay. I have to pick him up to check his feet and this sets off a new panic. He squirms, and it's like trying to hold on to one of those liquid-filled rubber squishy toys.

"Take it easy." I can see right away that the pads of his feet are all chewed up. The back right is the worst. The entire pad is hanging by a narrow piece of skin and bleeding. "Where you been, little fellow? Have you had a long walk?"

His skin is stretched tightly over his prominent ribs, and now that I've got him tipped back I can see the rash on his belly and on the insides of his back legs too. It looks raw and painful. I turn him right side up again and tuck him securely under my arm, then take out my phone and snap our photo.

My new dog.

Aaah. What a cutie. You'll make a great doggy daddy.

What shall I name him?

Kiki says Spot.

Chapter 42

Andrew

Screw it. I'm keeping that photo on my phone. And third period, I'm going to start apartment hunting. A few more months and this nonsense is O-V-E-R.

I look at the ugly little black-and-white face with the bush-baby eyes. *You may be terrified now,* I think, *but you are one lucky pooch.* I think about the angels that burned and how Robert cried over them. He may have a weak stomach, but he has a compassionate heart.

And once again my own heart swells with pride.

I feel like this is one of those days where everything is new again, like it's truly the first day of the rest of my life. And it feels good.

I greet my students with a cheeriness I haven't felt in quite a few months. There is nothing they can do to kill my mood today. I feel empowered, in control, and ready to engage them with the beauty of math.

And it goes pretty well. I still have some damage control to do; I accept that.

Then, a few minutes into first period, a student steps into my classroom with an office request for Stephen Newman. He's instructed to bring his things.

Stephen goes and he doesn't return, and I'm thinking the day is getting better and better, and then I chastise myself for that thought. I am above that. Still, I make a mental note to check his behavior record later in the day to see what he's being disciplined for. In my experience, when a kid is misbehaving in one class, he's misbehaving in others. Best to get it all out on the table and get as much mileage out of it as we can.

By third period I'm in my head, picturing Robert sleeping over in my new apartment, waking up in my apartment, dancing on my bed with his pants off. It's a pleasant thought, and I'm smiling to myself as I Google apartments in our area and jot down addresses and phone numbers.

"Mr. McNelis."

It's Lauren Crew, a first-year AP responsible for eleventh graders. She's standing in my doorway. I find her formal address funny since we were on the same math team last year.

"Hey, Lauren. What can I do for you?"

"I need you to come with me, please."

Mr. McNelis *and* a please. That's when I take a good look at her. She's gripping her walkie-talkie in her hand and her face is grim. I know that face.

"Okay," I say. Fear floods through me.

Logan Hough, the twelfth grade AP, is waiting in the hallway. He's looking at his feet, then at Lauren. He doesn't look at me until I speak to him.

"What's going on, Logan?"

"Sorry, I don't know, Drew. We were just instructed to escort you to the office."

"You're kidding, right? Why didn't you just send me an e-mail? I know my way."

He doesn't answer.

I don't wait to be *escorted*. I lift my chin and stride smartly down the hallway. They fall in step on either side of me.

I will not fall over and play dead, and I will not collapse into a heap of Jell-O, even though I feel like Jell-O inside. Someone saw us this weekend. Or maybe I've misjudged Maya. I can't believe she'd do this. I try to remain calm, but I am gripped by panic and my knees threaten to fail me as we head to the office.

For the most part, the halls are clear, but we do cross paths with a handful of other teachers. They look at me walking between two APs and quickly avert their eyes. It'll be all over school before the end of the period.

There's a police officer standing off to the side when we enter Mr. Redmon's office. Logan closes the door behind us and Mr. Redmon begins to introduce the officer, but I cut him off.

"Mr. Redmon, what's going on?" I ask. He stops and then drops his eyes.

"Are you Andrew McNelis?" the officer asks.

"Yes." I know they've found out. All I can think is *second-degree felony, second-degree felony, second-degree felony.*

"Mr. McNelis, can I see your cell phone, please?"

I hesitate. "Do you have a warrant?"

He studies me a moment, then says, "I can hold you right here until I get one. We can drag this out, or you can cooperate. Your choice. I'm fine with it either way."

I remove my phone from my pocket and hand it to the officer. He takes a moment to verify what I already know—nothing in any in-box, sent box, or drafts. No contacts except family, Ms. Smith's Village, the school's main number, and roadside assistance. No calls dialed, missed, or received that would link me to Robert. Photos of Kiki and Maya.

Ah, shit. And one of Robert.

The officer pauses at something on the screen, then turns it to Mr. Redmon. "Do you know who this boy is?"

Mr. Redmon steps around his desk and looks at the screen. "That's one of our seniors. Robert Westfall."

"It's a photo of him with a dog," I say emphatically. "A dog. A little stray dog he took in. He sent me the photo. That's it. I told you, Mr. Redmon, he sees me as a big brother. I've tried to keep a professional distance from him. I can't help it that he still reaches out to me."

I'm rattled. What do they know?

The officer places my phone on Mr. Redmon's desk and picks up another, one I hadn't noticed.

"Mr. McNelis, do you recognize this phone number?" He thumbs a few buttons on the phone, then reads off a number. The phone he's holding is not Robert's phone and I'm confused.

"Yes, that's my cell phone number."

And that's when everything changes.

The officer produces a zip tie handcuff.

"Mr. McNelis, please place your hands behind your back. You are under arrest for solicitation of a minor for sex, indecency with a child, and child pornography. You have the right to remain silent. If you . . ."

"*What?* I don't know what you're talking about," I say, angry. And then I realize something else. This may not be about Robert at all. I'm doubly confused. "Who's accusing me?" I demand. "I have a right to know who is accusing me. This is insane. I haven't done anything wrong." I'm talking to the officer, talking over him, but he continues to inform me of my rights as if I haven't spoken at all.

I turn to Mr. Redmon. "I want to know what, exactly, I'm being accused of."

When he tells me, I'm left speechless.

The officer tightens the zip tie around my wrists.

My head is a jumble of discordant images as I try to reconcile the accusation with reality. I have never, *never* sent a sexually explicit message in my life, and I damn sure didn't send one to that kid. And there is no way in hell calling him a prick can be misconstrued as soliciting sex, as indecency, or as child pornography. This is batshit insane. I will crucify that kid when I get a lawyer.

I struggle against the cuffs.

"This is outrageous. This is where I work. You cannot parade me out of here in handcuffs like a criminal. I have done nothing wrong. Whatever that kid told you, it's a bald-faced lie. I want to see your proof. Mr. Redmon," I say, turning to him again. He has to know how crazy this is. "There is no way I would ever do such a thing. That kid has it in for me. You *know* that."

The officer indicates a chair and tells me to sit.

I don't want to sit. I want to defend myself. I want them to listen. I want them to show me whatever proof it is they think they have, but they've clammed up.

The officer puts his face close to mine. I can smell his morning coffee on his breath, and I want to gag. "Sit, or I'll make you sit," he says like he would actually enjoy forcing me down.

I don't give him the chance. "Can I at least call my ex-wife? I have a daughter, for God's sake. She needs to know."

"You'll get a chance to make a phone call soon enough."

A squad car is parked at the curb just outside the school's front door. When the bell rings to start fourth period and the halls clear, I'm escorted to it, past secretaries and other staff members who drop their heads and suddenly become very busy. It's humiliating, but I am so angry I barely notice.

Robert

The first hint that something's up comes during fourth period— band. It pretty much amounts to this: Someone's been arrested.

One of the bassoonists was doing some research and got a glimpse of the police escort through the READ posters fixed to the library windows. I don't think too much about it. The drug dog was probably here today and someone got busted.

In fifth-period English, Ms. Weatherford spends a good twenty minutes of class time just outside her door talking in a low voice to a colleague. We're supposed to be reading on our own—*The Catcher in the Rye*—but there's a lot more whispering than reading going on.

It's the first time I hear *teacher,* and I go cold.

When I walk into Calculus sixth period, I know, even before I see the sub at Andrew's desk. I drop my things and ask if I can go to the bathroom, then I call his phone. An unfamiliar voice answers.

"Sorry, wrong number," I mumble.

Chapter 43

Robert

Ms. Momin pulls into the driveway at dusk. I'm waiting on the front porch.

The garage door rumbles down, and I can hear her chatting cheerfully with Kiki. A minute later the front door opens. I stand and turn to her.

"Is he okay?"

She fixes cold eyes on me and folds her arms. "He's in a holding cell right now. I've already contacted an attorney. With any luck, he'll appear before a judge tonight for an arraignment. In any event, the attorney thinks he'll be out in forty-eight hours. I haven't talked to him."

"What's he charged with?"

From inside, Kiki calls out, "Mommy!" Ms. Momin calls back that she'll be right in and pulls the door closed behind her a little more. She looks at me again. "I want to know what's going on between you and my ex-husband."

I knew this was coming. "He's my calculus teacher."

"Don't lie to me, Robert. You've lied to me enough. Were you with him Saturday night?"

I don't answer.

She smirks, but in a way that looks like a prelude to tears.

"I want to know what he's being charged with," I say quietly.

"They're saying he sent sexually explicit text messages to a student, among other things."

"He wouldn't do that."

"He wouldn't?" She lets that settle on me, then huffs. "I don't know anymore what he would and wouldn't do."

"How can you say that?" I'm angry now, and I don't care that she knows. "He's a good, decent person."

"He's a teacher," she hisses. "And you're just a boy, a student, *his* student. And you! Do you have any idea what you've done? What you've cost him?"

"I love him, and—"

Her breath catches.

"—he loves me."

Kiki appears at her mom's side, her face a pout. "Mommy, I hungry," she says around the thumb in her mouth.

A tear spills down Ms. Momin's cheek. She brushes it away as she runs a hand over her daughter's hair. "I'm coming, baby."

Kiki notices me just then. Her pout transforms into a bright smile. She plucks the thumb from her mouth and holds out her dog to me. "Spot."

I reach out to pet her dog, but Ms. Momin snatches it back. "Stay away from Drew. Stay away from my daughter."

She pushes Kiki back inside the house and makes like she's going to shut the door in my face, but I take a step forward and put my hand on the door.

Her look is at first one of alarm, then hatred. "Don't," she warns. "Don't you dare try to insert yourself into our lives. Do you really think you're the only one?" She scoffs. "You're not the first pretty boy that he's fallen for. You're just the first one *stupid* enough to believe you actually had some kind of future with him."

"I don't believe you."

"You don't need to come for group Wednesday. I'll e-mail your counselor and tell her you completed your hours." She backs away and shuts the door in my face.

He didn't do it, and I intend to prove it.

* * *

"I heard it's going to be on the news tonight at ten," Luke says as we head up the stairs to his room. "It's all over Facebook already. Some kid is bragging about taking him down."

"Who?"

"Some freshman."

Something clicks. "A kid named Newman?"

"Stephen Newman. Yeah. How'd you know?"

"He's Anna Newman's little brother. The kid who's been giving Andrew a hard time in class."

"That's Anna's little brother? No kidding. Well, the story is that Mr. McNelis sent him a text with a dirty picture."

"That's bullshit."

"Well, apparently Stephen got some photos and some racy messages, and they came from Mr. McNelis's phone. Somebody made an anonymous call to Mr. Redmon, Mr. Redmon called Stephen in, looked at his phone, and he unloaded."

He shakes his mouse and his computer screen lights up.

"He didn't send them, Luke."

"I believe you. But then how did they get sent from his phone? You think somebody hacked him?"

He opens Facebook and points out some of the posts. "These are just the ones that other kids reposted. I'm not actually his Facebook friend."

One in particular catches my eye.

That faggot's getting what he deserves. Ha!

"Nice guy, huh?" Luke says.

Suddenly, I know exactly what happened. "He stole his phone."

"Somebody stole his phone?"

"Yeah. He wasn't sure. It disappeared Friday morning. At first he thought he lost it, then he thought maybe his ex-wife had taken it. He didn't have his SIM card disabled until the next day just in case he found it. If that kid took his phone, he could have sent the pictures himself, right?"

Luke studies me for a moment, then shrugs. "Yeah, I guess. You really think he'd do something like that?"

"You read the posts. What do you think? Andrew wouldn't do this, Luke. I know him."

He nods and turns back to his computer. "Let's see if we can see who Stephen's friends are." He opens his page and shakes his head. "Uh, uh, uh. Look at this—he doesn't even have his page protected. Shame, shame. Friends, let's see." He opens up the entire list and scans through the photos. "Looky here. Your number-one fan."

He points his cursor to a photo near the bottom.

A fan club has to be good for something. I'm counting on that right now as a familiar voice answers the phone.

"Caleb, hi. This is Robert Westfall."

"Oh. Robert. Hi. Um, what's up?" He covers the microphone, but I can still hear a muffled, *"It's Robert Westfall. Oh my God!"*

"You got a minute?"

Muffled talk: *"He wants to know if I've got a minute."* Then, as if he hadn't been about to pee his pants, "Sure. Whatcha need?"

"A favor. You're friends with Stephen Newman, right?"

"Yeah. Why?" he asks cautiously.

Someone rings the doorbell. I leave it for Mom.

"Good friends?"

"No. Not really. We rode the same bus in junior high."

I realize I've been holding my breath. I let it out. "I need you to do something for me."

"Sure. Anything," he says eagerly.

I honestly think he means that. I tell him what I need, and he promises he'll get it done.

Mom sticks her head in my room. Her face is white. "Robert, I need you in the living room."

I try to read her expression as I say, "I really owe you one, Caleb."

"Robert, did something happen?" she asks as I end the call. "There are some police officers at the door."

My heart sinks.

The officers begin to introduce themselves as we enter the living room.

"What is this about?" Mom asks, cutting them off.

"Ms. Westfall," one of them says, turning to her, "we believe your son may be involved in a relationship with Andrew McNelis."

She looks at me, her face a question. "Who's Andrew McNelis?"

I glare at the officer.

"He's one of your son's teachers, ma'am. Math, I believe."

"Robert?"

"Did he tell you that?"

"I'm not here to discuss with you what he did or did not say to us. I am merely asking you a question. You should know that we have his cell phone in our custody."

That means nothing to me. "Are you arresting me?"

"What?" Mom's face blanches even further if that's possible, and she takes my elbow like she'll fight for me if it comes to that.

"We're just here to talk, son."

"Well, I'm not interested in talking."

"There's a photo of you on his phone." He lets that sit there for a moment. "Did you send him that photo?"

I can't believe Andrew kept a photo of me. After all his talk about being careful. What else did he keep? Text messages?

When I don't respond, the officer says, "We can subpoena you."

Mom steps between us. "Then you need to do that. My son is not answering any questions tonight."

The officers exchange a look, but after a brief standoff, they allow Mom to show them out.

When she returns, I'm sitting on the couch, nervously picking at my cuticles. She sits opposite me and waits. Finally she gives up. "It's true, isn't it?"

My eyes flood with tears. "He's in trouble, Mom. Some jerky kid set him up. He's being accused of something he didn't do."

She wrinkles her brow. "Are you telling me that this is not just about you? Oh, Robert."

I don't sleep. And every time I turn over, Spot II starts and his little heart races.

"It's okay, boy," I say each time. His belly is full and round, but his ribs are still achingly prominent. I run my hand over his soft fur and he relaxes again.

The ten o'clock news had run the story just like Luke said. Mom and I had watched it together.

The field reporter didn't mention any student names but used Andrew's name repeatedly, then cut to a video of him being escorted from the police cruiser to the jailhouse. That is the reel that keeps looping in my mind—his hands secured behind his back, a police officer gripping his arm. But Andrew didn't walk with his head down like a common criminal, nor did he tip his nose in the air in haughty defiance.

I was proud of him, but angry and frustrated that I couldn't do a damn thing for him.

Mom moved to the couch next to me and put her arm tentatively around my shoulders.

"What do you know about the students involved?" the anchor woman in the studio asked.

"All I can tell you, Hannah, is that there are two students, both minors. Sources tell me that both are, in fact, students of this teacher."

"Wow," Hannah said to her coanchor. "I'd say that Mr. McNelis is facing some very serious charges." Her coanchor shook her head and said, "You know, stories like this are so disturbing. What are these teachers thinking? It seems like every week we're hearing about another teacher being accused of sexual misconduct. You send your kids to school, you expect them to be safe"—she turned to the camera—"and then you hear about things like this."

"I know what you mean," Hannah said.

"They've already convicted him," I'd said angrily to Mom.

When I can't bear to think about him in jail anymore, I turn my attention to Stephen Newman. He set him up; I know it as surely as I know that Andrew would never send a sext to anyone, even me. It's the only thing that makes sense.

I still find it hard to believe that anyone could be that cold and vindictive though. To ruin an innocent man's life and then to brag about it? I swear to myself, he will not get away with it.

Spot II makes a noise that sounds like a bark through sleep-paralyzed vocal cords. His little legs twitch like he's running. I notice that one of his pads is bleeding again and there's a watery blood spot on my sheet. "Shhhh, boy," I say quietly. "You're okay." I place my hand on his head and he jerks awake and yelps. When he realizes he's in no danger, he nudges my hand with his wet nose.

I get up for a washcloth and some hydrogen peroxide, then hold it to his paw until the bleeding stops again.

Sometime in the middle of the night I finally allow myself to think about what Ms. Momin said.

Do you really think you're the only one?

Chapter 44

Robert

I turn that thought over in my mind the rest of the night. By morning I know my answer.

I get to school early, hoping against hope that Caleb has been able to elicit some kind of confession from Stephen. I sit on the floor and lean against the sax lockers and wait.

I'm thinking about Andrew—Did he sleep? Is he safe? Is he afraid?—when Luke drops down on the floor next to me.

"Did you see the news last night?" he asks.

"Yeah." I twist my head to look at him.

"How you holding up?"

Before I can answer, Caleb calls to me from across the band hall. He's holding a piece of paper high in his hand. My heart thuds in my chest, and I hope to hell that's what I think it is. We get to our feet. "I've got it," he says excitedly. "I didn't think he was going to respond, and then this morning I got up, and, well, look for yourself."

Luke reads over my shoulder. "You got him."

"That motherfucker," I say softly.

"Caleb, I love you." I grab his face and plant a kiss right on his mouth. He beams and maybe swoons a bit, but I'm already running across the band hall.

I'm out of breath when I burst into the front office. I barely register the receptionist's surprised look or Mrs. Stovall's "Ex-*cuse* me" as I slip past them to Mr. Redmon's door.

"I have proof that Mr. McNelis did not send those text messages."

Mr. Redmon looks up from his computer screen. I enter his office and place the screen shot of the private Facebook conversation on his desk. "Andrew—Mr. McNelis didn't do it. Stephen admits right here that he set him up. And it all makes sense. Andrew—I mean, Mr. McNelis—his phone disappeared Friday morning. I can prove that. He sent me this note during fourth period to let me know it was missing so I wouldn't—" I stop. *Shit.*

I lay the note on his desk next to the other paper. "Stephen took his phone, then he used it to send texts to himself. Then he made an anonymous phone call to you that morning. He made it so you would call him in and then he acted like he'd been too afraid to tell anyone when all along there was nothing to tell. He made it up. They have to let Andrew go. You have to make them see that."

Mr. Redmon drops his eyes to the two pieces of paper on his desk. He picks up first the Facebook screen shot, then Andrew's note, then stacks them neatly together.

I don't get it. He should be jumping all over this evidence. Instead, he sits quietly and stares at the papers. I want to shake him. "Mr. Redmon, he's innocent. He didn't do anything wrong. He would never do anything like that. He's a good person. Pick up the phone," I plead. "Just call them. Please."

"Robert, sit down," he says, looking up at me.

"Call Stephen in. Ask him. Search his house. You already have all the evidence you need right there. You can't let this happen."

Mr. Redmon props his elbows on his desk and presses his mouth into his clasped hands, then rests his chin on them. "You speak very passionately on his behalf, Robert. I assure you, I will turn this over to the police. But I need you to be honest with me about your relationship with Mr. McNelis."

"We're friends," I say too quickly. "That's all."

"I wasn't born yesterday, Robert. I assume you are aware that we've already spoken with Mr. McNelis about the time he's been spending alone with you."

I shake my head, desperate to make him believe the lie.

"There's a photo of you on his phone. And a call came into his phone yesterday afternoon from your cell number. Let me ask you again: Have you been involved in a relationship with Mr. McNelis?"

"No," I say emphatically.

"Robert." He sighs heavily. "The police will subpoena you. I understand that they have some pretty solid evidence that you were with him Saturday night."

I am mute with shock. He's lying. He has to be lying.

"You can't protect him from this, Robert. He is a grown man, and he has violated a sacred trust. He used the power of his position to take advantage—"

"He took advantage of nothing."

"He used his power—"

"I wanted to be with him," I snap. "*I* pursued *him*." I suddenly realize what I'm saying, but I'm helpless to stop. It's too late for that. "No one made me do anything I didn't want to do," I say more quietly. "I'm not a child. And in just a few more months I'll graduate and none of this will even matter."

The weight of what I've just confessed presses down on me, and I sit, numb. "Mr. Redmon, you have to see that—you can't—he's not—" I don't know how to make him understand.

Mr. Redmon leans back in his chair and wipes his hand down his face. "All right." After a moment he gets to his feet. "I want you to wait here for a few minutes. Okay?"

When he returns, it's with Mr. Hough. He has a form with him. He tells me he needs to take a statement from me.

Chapter 45

Andrew

Crews from two of the four local TV stations are waiting outside the jail when they release me. They dog Maya and me and my lawyer all the way to our cars, shouting questions and getting no answers. Maya takes charge, elbowing reporters out of her way, telling me in a no-nonsense voice to keep moving.

As she pulls the car into the one-way street, I see the signs advertising bail bondsmen. There's one on every seedy little dump for blocks. I wonder for a moment which one she used. I feel like I'm in a nightmare I can't wake up from. I watch from the window as the grungy city slides away. I want to go home.

"Kiki's with a sitter," Maya says, turning on her blinker to enter the interstate. "She doesn't know."

I acknowledge that information with silence.

"I picked up your car this morning. Karen next door drove me up to the school."

I feel her glance at me. I notice that a few early wildflowers are just starting to bloom in the scruffy patches along the freeway. I try to remember their names—crimson clover, red poppy, Indian paintbrush, bluebonnet.

"One of your teacher friends called. Jennifer, I think. She said to tell you she's taking care of your classes."

My classes. My students. Funny. If anyone had told me this is how my teaching career would end—fingerprinting, a mug shot, a command to jerk off in a room so my erect penis could be photographed—I would have laughed. It was just that absurd. I almost refused. They couldn't force me. But if I could prove that I did not send that photograph, that the penis in that photograph was not attached to me, then I had to try. The officer had uncuffed my wrists and handed me a *Boys' Life* magazine. A *Boys' Life*. I can still hear him snicker.

But I couldn't do it.

It didn't matter in the end. I don't know how, but by the time Maya had arranged bail, I had already been cleared of any charges relating to Stephen Newman, but those charges had been replaced by another—improper relationship with a student. No amount of jerking off could exonerate me on that charge.

They'd pulled my credit card bill and then pressured Robert into a confession.

I don't blame him. I'm only profoundly sorry for dragging him into this mess.

"It's going to be okay, Drew," Maya says, patting my knee.

I don't think so.

When we pull into the driveway, the sitter opens the door and Kiki runs to me. I scoop her up. "Hey, baby girl." I choke on the words and bury my face in her hair. She doesn't understand, and in a moment she's crying too.

"I'll take her," Maya says, reaching for her. But I clutch her to me, her wails covering my own, quieter sobs.

Maya quickly pulls a few bills out of her purse for the babysitter, who is standing by in awkward silence. Then she takes my elbow and ushers me into the house. Inside she peels Kiki from my arms and quiets her with some juice and crackers in the kitchen. I retreat to my room.

Sometime later she knocks on my door and comes in, then sits on the bed next to me. "Can I make you something to eat?"

I shake my head and close my eyes, hoping she'll just go away and leave me alone.

She begins to shift a little closer to me but stops when I roll over and turn my back to her. After a moment, I feel her pull her legs up onto the bed and settle closer to me anyway, and then her thumbs press into my shoulders.

"You just need to relax, baby," she murmurs. "Everything's going to be okay. How about I draw you a bath?"

I answer her with silence.

"Oh, Drew. You're home now. And I promise you, I'm going to be with you every step of the way. We're a family. We'll get through this together. One day we're going to look back on this and—"

"Can I borrow your phone?" My voice is rough, like I haven't used it in a while.

Her hands freeze on my back for just an instant, then resume their kneading. "I've already called your parents. They know you're home and you're okay."

That's not what I want, and she knows it. I can hear it in her voice. "Please, Maya," I plead. "I need to use your phone."

She removes her hand from my back and the bed shifts as she gets up. I hear her huff. "Do you have *any* sense of self-preservation?"

I wince at her shrill, angry tone.

"Do you have any idea how this has affected me? How it's affected your daughter? You stay away from that kid, or so help me . . ."

I roll my face into my pillow.

"I'm sorry," she says quietly. "But you have to understand that your relationship with Robert Westfall is over. You're going to be damn lucky to escape a prison sentence as it is. If you contact him again—don't do that to your daughter. Think about somebody other than yourself for a change. This thing you had going, it could never last. You know that, don't you? He's a bright young man with a big future ahead of him. If you care anything at all about him, you'll let him go."

I feel like I'm suffocating in her presence, and then I hear the door close behind her.

Robert

"I just want to talk to him. Just for a minute."

Ms. Momin steps out onto the porch and pulls the door closed behind her. "He doesn't want to see you, Robert. He goes before a grand jury in a couple of months. If they know you've been here, it will only make things worse for him. Don't come again. Do I make myself clear?"

"Will you at least tell him something for me?"

She pushes the door open behind her and slips back in without another word.

Andrew

Maya is just coming in the front door as I'm coming in the back with Kiki. I can see on her face that she's upset.

"What's wrong?" I ask.

She smiles. "Nothing."

Jen takes a good look at me when I open the door later that evening. "You look like shit," she says.

I take the box she hands me. "Thanks, Jen. You didn't have to do this."

"Your sub's been poking around your desk, and no one else was breaking down the door to protect your stuff, so here I am."

"What are they saying about me?"

"About what you'd expect. Pervert. Stupid. Incompetent. Sleaze. Creep. Everybody knew there was something *different* about you." She makes those finger quotes when she says *different*.

"Thanks for making me feel better."

"Aah, come on, Drew. It's not the end of the world."

"Isn't it?" I take the box to the kitchen counter. She closes the door and follows me in.

"You know, this whole mess would make a great novel."

"Don't even think about it."

She laughs. "Don't worry, I'll change the names. So, um"—she pauses then gives me an impish grin—"what's he like in the sack?"

I can't believe she just asked me that.

"Come on. Throw me a bone." She lifts a tie from the box. I always keep one—*kept* one—in my desk drawer just in case. She wraps the tie around her fingers and flicks her eyebrows at me. "Is he as hot naked as he is in those jeans?"

I look at her for a moment in disbelief, then take the tie from her.

"Okay," she says, undeterred, "so this is just research. So, let's just say that gay men engage in three different acts. I think one and two are a given. But what about number three?"

I stare at her, trying to make sense of what she's asking me, and then I get it. "Are you asking me if we had anal sex?"

"Well, yeah," she says, grinning.

I feel my eyes fill with tears.

"Oh, shit," Jen says. "Okay, don't cry. Crap."

I press the heels of my palms to my eyes and will them to dry up, but it's no use.

"What's going on?" Maya asks, coming into the room.

I drop my hands and turn my head away, blinking a few times. Then I introduce Jennifer. "She's in the classroom next to mine."

"Oh," Maya says coolly, then continues on to the kitchen.

"I'll show you out," I say to Jen.

She follows me to the door, but I don't open it right away. I study my bare feet, reluctant to let her go because right now, she's the best link I have to him.

"I didn't know," she says quietly. "I'm sorry."

I swallow past the lump in my throat and look up at her. "Have you seen him?"

"Yeah. I've seen him."

"Does he look okay?"

She shrugs. "Kinda quiet, but that's nothing new."

Chapter 46

Andrew

It's March twenty-eighth. A Monday. Robert's eighteenth birthday.

Kiki is pushing Spot around the house in a toy stroller and babbling to him like he's a real baby. I smile when she stops so I can pet him. We've withdrawn her from Ms. Smith's Village now that money is so tight. It gives me something to do with my long days and keeps me from going completely mad. I'm not under house arrest, but it sure feels like it.

"Spot thirsty," she says to me in her most grown-up voice.

"He is? Well, maybe we should get him a drink." I go to the cabinet and remove a sippy cup, then pretend to fill it with apple juice from the refrigerator.

She takes it from me with a very serious look on her face, then gives the stuffed dog a two-second drink. "Daddy thirsty too," she says, handing the cup back to me.

"I am." I pretend to take a drink, which seems to delight her.

She scuttles off with Spot, and I'm left clutching the cell phone in my hand. My own phone is still being held in evidence; this is a cheap prepaid phone that Maya bought so I'd have a way to call her or 911 if necessary. I haven't dared use it for any other purpose.

I have never felt this low in my entire life. Not even after Kevin.

I feel worthless—no career, no job, no income, no choices, no life. I feel like Maya is my mother, and I'm some impetuous child who's had to be harnessed for his own good.

Just last night, after Jen left, Maya told me she'd contacted a Realtor about putting the house up for sale. She wants us to move back to Oklahoma and start over. She's already talked to my parents about moving in with them for a while after this school year ends, just until we can find new jobs, just until we can find our own place to live, just until we can get back on our feet.

All this *we, we, we* is making me crazy. I don't want a *we* with Maya. I want a *me*. Even so, I do sometimes think about it now. Just giving in. Being what she wants me to be—husband, lover. Sometimes it feels safe, like a place where I can hide from all the bad things. But at other times, I feel like I can't breathe when she's in the room. No. Right or wrong, I'm in love with that kid, and there's no going back. I'm not so sure where forward will lead me, but back is not an option.

His birthday.

"Kiki! Hey, baby girl, you want to go for some ice cream?"

Maybe I *am* impetuous, and maybe I will regret this later, but it's his birthday, and he will have flowers. In the H-E-B floral department, I choose a small clear round bowl tightly packed with hot pink roses, light pink carnations, and white daisies with green centers. The flowers are bright and beautiful, just like him, and they smell like happiness, which is exactly what I wish for him on his birthday. Just that—happiness.

I set the basket with the chocolate ice cream on the floor and take a small card from the display. I've been thinking about what I want to say since we got in the car. I borrow a pen from the florist person and scribble a quick note, then tuck the note into an envelope and stick it in the little pitchfork jutting out from the flowers.

"This is our little secret, right?" I say to Kiki.

She holds her finger to her lips and says, "Shhh."

"That's right. Shhh."

We're checking out when a woman in black jogging pants with a matching zip-up jacket leans over the counter past the bagger and fixes me with cold eyes. "That little girl deserves better." She storms off. The checker avoids my eyes as she hands me the receipt.

We leave the flowers in the shade on Robert's front porch, and then hightail it home.

Robert

"Happy fucking birthday to me."

"I'm sorry," Luke says. "You want to go get something to eat? My treat? You don't turn eighteen every day, you know."

I bang my head against the band lockers, then get to my feet. From across the room, I see Caleb heading our way. "Thanks, but I just want to go home."

"Have you talked to him?"

I shake my head. "No. Maybe Ms. Momin is right. Maybe he really doesn't want to see me."

"Hey," Caleb says, planting himself in front of us. "I just wanted to say happy birthday."

I look up at him. "Thanks, Caleb. Where's the rest of my fan club?"

He smiles sheepishly. "I took the fan page down. It was kind of a stupid thing to do. I hope there're no hard feelings."

"Thanks."

He fidgets around. A month ago I would have found this irritating. It's not so irritating.

"I also wanted to tell you that, well, I told off Stephen Newman the other day. He said something pretty rude about Mr. McNelis. I wasn't going to let him get away with it. I mean, if you like him that much, he must be a pretty good guy."

"Yeah."

There is one thing I'm looking forward to on my birthday—getting home to Spot II. His paws and his belly have healed, and he acts now like I'm God himself when I get home each day. This is why I'm so disconcerted when I pull into the driveway and see Nic waiting for me on the front porch. He's holding a glass bowl of pink and white flowers, real ones this time. He hands them to me when I get to the porch. An envelope peeks up from the center.

"I haven't seen you in forever," he says, pushing his sunglasses up to his forehead and squinting at me.

"I saw you at lunch just yesterday, Nic."

"You know what I mean. Anyway, I wanted to say happy birthday."

I move past him to unlock the door but he grabs my arm and stops me.

"You broke up with me because of him, right? Well, I want you to know that I forgive you for that. He totally took advantage of you, and it's not your fault that you're a pushover. But that's okay. I like that about you."

I jerk my arm away and open the door, then whip back around. "Get off my front porch." I shove the flowers back in his hands. He starts to protest, but I say, "Don't," and he rolls his eyes at me.

"Why do you have to be so dramatic about everything?" he says.

I want to laugh in his face. Instead, I turn my back on him, enter the house, and shut the door.

Chapter 47

Andrew

Maya gives me a hard time about leaving the house that evening.

"Look, I'm just running to the store for some razors."

"I can pick them up for you tomorrow when I go."

"I don't need them tomorrow. I need them tonight." I pick up my keys from the counter and shove them in my pocket.

"Do you even have any cash on you?"

She knows I don't. "I'll use my credit card."

She huffs. "You know this is a bad idea. Do I need to remind you what a small community this is? You are not a very popular man right now. You can't just go to the store anymore, not until all this stuff blows over."

"And I can't hide out in this house every *god*damn day for the rest of my life. I have to get out of here."

"Well, maybe you should have thought about that before you dropped your pants with that kid."

I don't believe her. I storm out of the house and slam the door behind me.

* * *

In a back corner of the H-E-B lot, away from all the sodium vapor lights, I find a spot and pull in. The clock on the dash reads seven fifty-two. I kill the engine and watch for his car.

At ten, I tuck my tail between my legs and go home.

Maya doesn't bother to ask me about the razors.

Chapter 48

Andrew

Just as my lawyer predicted, the grand jury declines to indict me because of Robert's age and his affidavit that our relationship was completely consensual.

Three months after my arrest, I am cleared of any criminal charges, but my teaching career is finished. I've been terminated by my school, and the state is in the process of revoking my license.

Crews from all four of the local TV stations this time are waiting outside the courthouse when we exit. My lawyer covers me on one side, Maya the other, as we hurry to our cars.

We try to pretend like it's just a normal evening. We have dinner together. I read Kiki as many stories as she wants, and when her eyes droop, I tuck the covers around her and kiss her good night.

Maya's waiting in the living room. When she hears me come in, she looks up from the spiral notebook she's been keeping since I was first released from jail. The pages are filled with lists and plans and projections. I guess committing everything to black-and-white on paper empowers her. It's funny, though . . . I've always found a certain kind of beauty in lists. But the only thing I find in her lists is despair.

"I just talked to my principal," she says with a small smile. "As soon as she can find a sub to finish out the school year for me, I'm free to go. It's just a couple of weeks. Shouldn't be a big deal." She looks at me and her smile falters, but she continues with even greater energy. "And I talked to the Realtor this morning. She's had a couple of bites and thinks if I'm willing to drop the price a little, she can get a contract by the end of the week."

I sit on the edge of the couch and clasp my hands together. I don't know what she expects me to say. So I say nothing. Frustrated, she looks back at her notes like she's missed something, and if she can just remember what it is and record it in her list, everything will be okay. Tears edge the lower rims of her eyes.

"Talk to me," she pleads.

Her phone rings. She looks at the number, then disconnects the call. I glare at her. "Was that him?"

She sniffs and glares back. "No."

I hold my hand out for the phone, but she slips it into her jeans pocket.

"Let me have the phone, Maya."

"It wasn't him," she snaps. "Why can't you understand that? He's a fickle young man and he doesn't—"

"Give me the *god*damn phone!"

"No!"

So I try to take it from her.

"Stop it," she says, twisting away from me.

"I want the phone. Why won't you let me talk to him?"

"Because," she screams at me, breaking free. Then she pulls the phone from her pocket and flings it at me. "Because he hasn't called you."

I don't believe her. I retrieve the phone from the carpet where it landed after bouncing off the couch and open her Missed Calls folder. The call was from some one-eight-eight-eight number. I open the All Calls folder and scan through them, too, but I don't see his number anywhere.

"It's time to move on, Drew," Maya says, crying softly. "We've got to—"

"You're right, Maya. It *is* time to move on. But not together."

Numbly I hand her the phone and collect my keys from the counter.

"Where are you going?" she says, suddenly wild-eyed.

"I've already reenrolled Kiki in Ms. Smith's Village. They're expecting her tomorrow morning. Mom and Dad paid her tuition for the next two months. As soon as I can find a job, I'll catch up on child support."

Maya's lip trembles and tears spill down her cheeks. "You don't have to do this. Drew—no—don't—please—wait. We can make this work."

"We can't make this work, Maya. I don't want to make this work. I want—I just—" I stop and will myself to hold it together. "Will you tell Kiki something for me?"

"You're just going to walk out on me and your daughter? Just like that?" She's angry, and I don't blame her.

"Tell her that her daddy loves her, and he'll see her soon."

Her breath hitches and she wipes at the tears on her face. I've left a small bag just inside the hallway. I shoulder the strap and let myself out.

I've debated and debated whether or not to see Robert before I leave. It's been so long. I don't even know if he wants to see me; I don't know if I want to see him, because seeing him will just make everything so much harder.

I pull up to the curb outside his house and put the car in park, and I sit. One window is lit up, but I've never been in his house and have no idea if that's his bedroom window or not. So many emotions jumble at the back of my throat, and I find it hard to swallow. When he didn't rendezvous with me, it hurt like hell. I admit that. And I'd been so certain that was him who'd called earlier. How could I have been so wrong?

Through the white shade I see some movement in the room. Two people. Then the shade shifts and a little black-and-white dog works his way between the shade and the window. "Hey, Spot," I say softly.

I wait, hoping Robert will retrieve the dog and I'll get to see him, but after a minute or two, the dog backs his way out and disappears into the room.

I put the car back in drive and head out.

It takes about fourteen hours to make the eight-hundred-fifty-mile drive to my folks' house. I drive straight through the night, stopping only for gas. I've made myself a promise—when I get there, I'll allow myself to feel.

I keep my mind busy. Outside of Huntsville, I try to calculate the time it takes to destroy a man's life. Maybe two seconds to swipe a phone. Another fifteen to jot down a phone number and a note (*Anybody going to Saturday's concert? Call me.*) and pass it around the room just so I'd take it up and everyone would know I took it up. Five minutes to take a couple of photos and fake some text messages. A half a minute maybe to make an anonymous phone call. Another five minutes to walk from my classroom to the office and claim he was too ashamed to tell anyone about my "advances." Eleven minutes. Less time than it takes me to shower most mornings.

Outside of Dallas, I try to calculate my debt. Student loans, attorney's fees, car loan, back child support, credit cards. I can't even wrap my brain around the number. It might as well be a million dollars.

I'm crossing into Oklahoma as the sun rises on the passenger side of my car. For the last hour or so I've been thinking about all the reasons why I couldn't stay—Maya, no career, no job, the public humiliation. Those things have kept me up at night for weeks, but there was something else, something I just couldn't live with.

It was the fear of seeing that light go out in Robert's eyes when he realized I wasn't as clever or as smart or as good-looking as he'd once thought I was. That fear that one day I'd no longer be someone he looked up to, someone he admired, respected. I'd just be another loser with worn-out soles on my shoes and cheap twill pants.

Maybe to him I already was.

I pull into a Shell station and maneuver close to a pump and get out. It's hot and I think we're in for a scorching summer. I stick the nozzle into my gas tank and lock it. I'm surprised to see a pay phone on the outside wall of the station. I leave the pump and call Mom and Dad to let them know where I am.

Mom answers. "Are you okay, sweetheart?"

Hearing her voice rips something open in me. I start to say yes, but my voice catches. I swallow hard and croak, "I'll have to call you back, Mom."

"Drew, where are you?"

I somehow manage to tell her, then I fumble the phone back on the hook and grip the edges of the privacy wings as all the feeling I've been holding back finally overwhelms me.

Robert

I don't understand. I will never understand.

I'm furious that Ms. Momin blocked my number, but he could have found a way to contact me. And then when I stopped by last night, she told me he was gone. Her eyes were red, and I could tell she'd been crying.

"Just leave him alone, Robert," she'd said. "If he wanted to see you, he would have seen you. You have no idea what this has done to him."

"Where did he go?"

"You just don't get it, do you?" she'd said. "You practically destroyed him. He's lost his career, he's lost his reputation, and you think he's just going to pick back up with you now that he's free? It's not going to happen."

I didn't want to believe her, but he had no reason not to see me last night. He could have, but he hadn't. I understood that we couldn't be in contact while he was waiting for his hearing with the grand jury, but that was over. And yet, he'd left without so much as a good-bye.

"Hey, man." Luke takes the chair next to me as I'm numbly going through the motions of warming up. He opens his clarinet case and begins snapping the pieces together. "I saw the news last night."

"Yeah." I stop and adjust my mouthpiece for something to do.

"So, what happens next?"

"Nothing. He left last night."

"Is he coming back?"

I look at him, and I burn with jealousy. I remember how Curtis fought for him. I really thought Andrew would fight for me. I thought what we had was solid, real.

I think about those months before he was arrested. The time we spent together, the things we talked about. I really felt like his equal. And now, I just feel like a student who once had a crush on a teacher.

"No. He's not."

Chapter 49

Andrew

I've lost track of the days. My time at home has been a blur of sleep, self-pity, more sleep, Rice Krispies Treats I don't eat and hot chocolate I don't drink, overly cheerful chatter from my mom, and silence from my dad. My jeans, when I bother to put them on, are loose, and I don't care.

I can hear Mom and Dad outside my door, arguing quietly. The bright sunlight seeps through the blinds. Groggy and with a pounding headache, I drag the clock into bed with me and press the button on top to light up the display: 3:00 PM.

I can feel an intervention coming on. It won't be the first.

When the door opens I pull the quilt up over my head. Just as quickly, someone yanks it back.

"Drew," my dad barks. "Enough. Get up. Get dressed. We're going for a walk."

I don't want to walk. I don't want to talk. I don't want to do anything.

Mom pretends to be busy scrubbing the sink as Dad silently hooks the leash on Shep's collar and hands it to me. "I'll have an early dinner ready when you get back," she offers as he opens the back door and gestures for me to walk through it.

Shep takes the lead and I trudge along behind him. Dad walks with his hands in his pockets. When Shep stops to lift his leg to a curb, Dad turns to me. "You need a shave, and you need a haircut."

He waits for a response from me, but he doesn't get one.

He takes a deep breath, then lets it out with an, "Aw, hell." Shep starts to walk on and I start to follow, but Dad takes the leash from me, and I dissolve into tears. I haven't cried since they picked me up at that gas station some two weeks ago or so. I drop my head and hug my arms to myself. I don't want to do this, but I can't help myself anymore.

"Goddammit, Drew." He hooks his arm around my neck, and we walk on. "You screwed up, Son. There's no denying that. But that doesn't make *you* a screwup. It's time to be a man. Stop this wallowing and take charge of your life. I know you don't think so, but you have options, and you have Kiki to think about. That adorable little girl needs her daddy."

She's not the only one, I suddenly realize. I need mine too. I stop and fall into him and let him hold me while I get it all out. When the sobbing eases up, he sits down on the curb and pulls me down with him. Shep pushes his wet nose into my palm.

"You've had two weeks of your mom's coddling, Son. I've given you that. But that's over, okay? You and me, we're going to work through this. You need a job, and you need a plan. You're a bright young man. You can do anything you want to do."

"Except teach," I say, my voice cracking.

"Then you will turn your talents elsewhere. I'm not going to do it for you, Drew, but I will support you in whatever you decide."

I sniff and wipe my eyes on my sleeve. "Can I ask you something?"

"You can ask me anything."

"Are you disappointed in me?" I blink a few times, then turn my head to him.

"Oh, Drew." He stretches out his legs. "I've known you a long time, Son. At first, yeah, I was a little surprised, maybe even shocked. This Robert was your student and that is a sacred relationship. But I've never known you to be anything but completely honorable. Sometimes too honorable."

He smiles and scratches Shep's head, and I know he's thinking about my marriage to Maya.

"So," he continues, "I have to believe that he was someone pretty special to you." He pauses and fixes me with his eyes. "I just don't know what you were to him and whether or not he was really worth everything that it cost you."

I can feel the tears pricking at my eyes again.

"Look, Son, there's an opening at the kiosk in the mall. It's a decent job with some upward mobility. I'm not going to pave the way for you, but you're certainly qualified and it's a start."

Selling cell phones? Is that where all my education has led me?

Dad seems to understand my silence. He pats me on the back. "You can stay with us for a while, get caught up on your child support, pay down your attorney's fees some. And when you decide what you want to do with your life, you can move on."

Robert

I look away. This should have been one of the best days of my life. It's not, and I can't pretend any differently.

Mom lowers the camera and sighs. "It's just going to take time, baby."

Time is something I have way too much of.

"Give me the camera," I say, changing the subject. I hold out my hand.

She looks at me curiously. "Why?"

"I want to take a picture of you."

"I'm not graduating. Why would you want a picture of me?"

"Just because."

She hands the camera over with a curious smile, then strikes a diva pose. I snap a photo, then a few more because she will have photos.

"Enough," she says, laughing. "This is your big day."

"Yeah. Community college, here I come. Watch out world."

She picks up an envelope from the table and hands it to me.

"What's this?" I open the envelope. Inside is a large, a very large, check signed by Aunt Whitney. I look up at Mom.

"Whitney and I had a come-to-Jesus meeting. She was pretty upset that you aren't going to LSU. But, according to your grand-father's will, if you choose not to go and pursue a degree in medi-cine, the money he'd set aside was to be split evenly amongst all his grandchildren. It's not enough to get you through four years and veterinary school, but it's a good start. This is just a loan until the funds are released. It's her way of making peace." She grins. "And you're headed to Texas A and M, young man."

"I'm not going to A and M. I didn't make top ten percent."

"I know that," she says, touching my cheek. She's been doing a lot of that lately—hugging me, putting a comforting hand on me. "But this money means you won't have to work, and you won't have to depend on massive loans. You can focus on your classes and transfer in next year."

It takes only a split second to make my decision. "I don't want it." I stuff the check back in the envelope and hold it out to her. "I want to do it on my own, Mom. And I don't want Grandfather's money either. You can use it to pay down the house."

"It's not my money."

"Then I'll pay down the house with it. You've struggled enough."

"Robert—"

I shake my head, and when she won't take the envelope, I lay it back on the table.

Some state representative is giving the commencement speech today, but I'm not listening. I'm scanning the room. I don't expect him to be here, but I can't completely tamp down the hope spark-ing in my chest. I see Curtis sitting with Luke's mom and dad. They're the only faces that register with me as I fidget with the edges of my gown.

My row stands and I stand with them. We make our way to the stairs on the side of the stage. One by one, my classmates walk the stage.

"Blake Walker."

Mom waves from the audience. I smile back weakly.

"Johnathan West."

I climb the steps and take another good look at the families and friends who've come to celebrate this day. *Where are you?*

"Robert Westfall."

I imagine that the room is unnaturally quiet as I shake Mr. Redmon's hand—"I'm very proud of you, Robert"—and then the superintendent's—"Congratulations, Son."

And then I exit stage left.

It seems like everyone is in a hugging mood today, everyone but me, that is. Mom's never met a lot of my friends so I introduce them as we go. Even Nic stops me for a perfunctory hug in the parking lot as we make our way to my car.

"You sure you don't want to drop me at the house and go hang out with some of your friends?" Mom asks as I open the door for her.

"Robert."

My head snaps up, and my heart thuds in my chest. Luke is bounding between the cars lined up to leave, dragging Curtis with him. He drops Curtis's hand when he reaches the bumper and pulls me in for a big, swaying, back-slapping hug. "Congratulations, man," he says.

"Yeah. You too," I say when he releases me. "Hey, Curtis."

Curtis eyes me with that mixture of suspicion and warning I've long since gotten used to, but he reaches out to shake my hand anyway. Damn, he's possessive. But I know Luke is right when he says he's got Curtis wrapped around his little finger.

"We're not leaving for Galveston for another couple of hours," Luke says. "Still time to change your mind."

I turn away from Curtis and fix my eyes on Luke. "I thought he would be here."

Chapter 50

Robert

Early August. The summer has been long, hot, and exceptionally dry. Thousands of trees have succumbed to the drought, their brown leaves and needles in stark contrast to their luckier comrades with roots deep enough to weather the anomaly. I feel like one of those dying trees.

The bell over the door jangles as a woman enters with a towel-wrapped tabby in her arms. I check the appointment book. Ginger. Kidney failure. She was in two days ago for blood work. Dr. Nickels made the call himself yesterday morning.

"Ah, poor baby," Misty says, coming around the counter and taking the bundle from her owner's arms. "You don't look like you feel so good."

The owner, Ms. Sampson, hitches her purse back onto her shoulder. "She threw up again last night even though she hasn't eaten anything in two days," she says anxiously.

Misty runs her hand gently over the cat's head as I locate her file. "Let's get you weighed, girl." She takes the folder from me and leads the owner down the hallway.

I finish bagging up some flea and tick control for a toy Chihuahua, then print off the receipt and hand it and the bag over the counter to the young woman as the bell over the door jangles again.

It's been a busy Saturday morning already. We usually close at noon, but it's shaping up to be a late closing again today. That's okay. I like being here. I feel like I belong, and it's a way to keep my mind busy until classes start in a couple of weeks.

I smile as the woman scoops up her ridiculously tiny dog with a tiny bow clipped to the short hairs on top of its tiny head. She tosses me a thank you over her shoulder. I look around her to greet the next patient, but the greeting catches in my throat.

He's standing there, dressed in his *Math Geek* T-shirt—the one he wore the night we went dancing together—plaid shorts and flip-flops, holding Kiki with one hand. A round-bellied, spotted puppy is tucked into the crook of his other arm. He looks thinner. But he's every bit as beautiful as I remember him. He smiles at me. I look away for a moment and blink a few times to steady myself, then turn back to him. "It's been a long time."

He nods. "I don't have an appointment," he says.

No, you don't. I reach across the counter and take the puppy from him. "New doggie?" I say to Kiki, scratching the dog's spotted belly. He wiggles in my arms. "Let me guess his name. Um, Spot."

She screws up her face. "No."

"A puppy!" Misty says, coming back behind the counter and taking the dog from me. "Is this your puppy?" she asks Kiki.

"His name is Wobert," she says proudly.

I glance at Andrew. He shrugs. "She named him after a pony."

"His name is Robert too," Misty says, pointing to me. "Do you have an appointment?" she asks Andrew.

We say no at the same time.

"Yikes," she says, looking at the appointment book. "New-puppy visit?"

"Yeah," Andrew says.

"If you don't mind waiting, Dr. Nickels might be able to work you in."

"Great." Andrew takes the clipboard she hands him, and the puppy, then casts another unreadable look at me before taking a seat in the waiting room with the other pet owners.

I keep busy, but I can't help sneaking looks at him. I'd hoped one day I'd see him again, but I never anticipated this awkwardness. When he's finished filling out the paperwork, he leaves Kiki on the chair and brings the clipboard back to me. I take it from him without lifting my eyes. He loiters at the counter.

"Are you just here for the weekend?" I ask as I remove the papers and clip them into a file.

"No. I moved back."

My heart rises into my throat. I swallow and force it back down, then lift my eyes to his. "Wow. I guess you're surprised to run into me today."

"Robert—"

I turn my back on him and busy myself copying papers that don't need copying and shelving medicines that don't need shelving. I hold my breath until, finally, he leaves the counter and returns to his seat. I don't look at him again.

He hasn't tried to contact me. Not once. And how long has he been back? And now he shows up here with a new puppy. He must have been just as shocked to see me as I was to see him.

By the time Misty leads them to a room, the waiting area is empty. Only the man at the counter holding the leash of a Lab with a staph infection remains. Andrew hesitates as he passes the counter, but I'm busy checking out the Lab and spared the awkward moment. And when he returns to the counter twenty minutes later, I make sure I'm in an empty treatment room, sweeping up dog hair.

Andrew

He's angry. I don't blame him. But I saw something else in his eyes, too, something that's gotten me all goose bumpy and giddy.

I drop Kiki and Wobert back at Maya's. She blubbers when she sees the dog in my arms.

"It's just for a couple of hours," I tell her, quickly before she can say no. "He can stay with me. I just need to leave him here for a bit. Promise. Just a couple of hours."

She reluctantly takes the dog from me. I'm grinning like a nut, but I just can't help it.

"Did you see him?" she asks.

I nod.

Her eyes mist up, but she smiles. I plant a quick kiss on her cheek, then scoop up Kiki and swing her around in a circle and plop her back on the ground. "Gotta run!"

I crank up the stereo on my way to a quick stop at H-E-B. I don't care who sees me. I hope they see me. I hope everyone sees me. Then I beat a path back to the clinic and wait. It's ninety-eight degrees in the shade, but I'll wait all day if I have to.

At two o'clock he finally emerges from the clinic. He's still wearing the green scrubs. His eyes are downcast, so he doesn't see the whiteboard on his windshield until he's right on it. I watch from my post at the corner of the clinic as he takes it in his hands and reads the one word—*Glaze*. He squeezes his eyes shut and presses his fist to his mouth.

"I've missed you," I say, stepping out into the open.

He opens his eyes, fixes them on the whiteboard. "You're late," he says, his voice thick.

"I know," I say gently. "I was kind of tied up with this little legal matter, and . . . I just hope I'm not too late."

He stares at the whiteboard for another long moment, then erases it with the hem of his shirt. "Where's the puppy you scammed from the shelter?"

Scammed? "I left him with Maya. She's not too thrilled."

"So you moved back in," he says, matter-of-factly. He shakes his head.

"Actually, no." But I don't think he hears me. He looks up at me, his face stricken.

"You weren't even going to call me. And if you hadn't accidently run into me today . . ."

"It wasn't an accident, Robert."

Confusion pinches the features of his face.

"I just got back this morning. I drove all night. My first stop was your house. Your mom—and she's very sweet, by the way, and I think she likes me—" He doesn't react to my little joke. "She told me I just missed you, then she told me you work here. I picked up Kiki, we went to the shelter and found a dog—I may live to regret that one day." I laugh lightly. "And, well, you know the rest."

"No, I don't know the rest." That flash of anger again. He looks up at the sky and blinks a few times. Then he sniffs. "You never tried to see me. You never—"

"I did! But when you didn't meet me in the parking lot that night, I—"

"What night?"

"Your birthday. The note? The flowers?"

More confusion. "You never sent me—wait." I can see him scanning his memory. "Holy shit. *You* sent those flowers?"

"I wanted to—"

"I thought they were from Nic. I gave them back to him."

I exhale and close my eyes a moment, and then I laugh. My nose burns, and I laugh harder. *Holy shit* is right.

"What did the note say?"

I look at him, but I can't stop grinning. "You gave away my flowers?" I walk slowly toward him. "You think I'm just going to hand over that information now?" Hell yes, I am. "I was desperate to see you. I waited in the H-E-B parking lot for hours. But you didn't come." I shrug.

"I didn't know. I tried to call you, but she blocked my number."

I feel a white-hot flash in my chest. Maya. All this time, and she never told me. In fact, she'd worked hard to convince me that I'd thrown away my career over some fickle high school kid. She let me languish in Oklahoma for months until I just couldn't take it anymore. In the end, the need to see it for myself beat out my pride. I'd hardly allowed myself to hope for anything like the pain I see in his face now. I have to own up to the fact that Maya manipulated me to the bone, and I let her.

"I've really screwed up, baby," I say, walking toward him. "And I don't have anything to offer you anymore."

He looks at me now, really looks at me. His breath hitches and he blinks again to clear his own eyes. "You have flowers."

I'd almost forgotten about them. I look down at the flowers in my hand, the florist tissue damp from sweat. "Isn't that what a guy brings when he's courting his paramour?" I lift my eyes to his again.

"Yeah. I heard that somewhere."

"I should have been there for you."

"Yeah. You should have."

I nod. He's going to make me work for this. He should.

"So what happens now? Your ex-wife hates me. I doubt she'll be inviting me over for dinner anytime soon."

I realize he still doesn't know. "I'm not living with Maya, Robert. I got a job with a cell phone company. A few weeks ago, they agreed to transfer me here. I have an apartment, but no furniture. I haven't even picked up the keys yet." He's watching me as I draw closer, trying to make sense out of everything I'm telling him, still wary, I think. When I reach him, I get down on one knee and offer him the flowers, but the searing heat of the asphalt registers on my bare knee, and I get quickly back to my feet and brush at my reddened flesh. "Shit, that's hot."

He smiles. That's when I know we're going to be okay. "I'm not dancing on any damn futon," he says.

"I'll get a real bed. You can help me pick it out. We'll put it right smack in the middle of the living room. I'll even let you watch *Tosh.O* with your pants off if you want."

"Hmm," he responds, but his smile widens. He takes the flowers from me and studies them.

"I love you, Robert Westfall. I have loved you"—he throws his arms around me and I stagger back a few steps, then wrap mine around him—"since the moment you texted me that silly flasher joke," I finish.

It's a lie. I think I was lost long before that.

We cling to each other in the heavy heat like we've docked for recharging. And I think, *Yes, that's exactly what we're doing.*

"We have an awful lot to talk about," I say in his ear. "And I'm starved. Let me take you for a late lunch. I know a little deli around the corner."

He laughs. "I have a feeling there's a Subway sandwich in my future."

He knows me so well.

"Someone might see us together," he adds.

"I hope they do."

I really, really hope they do.

Where You Are

J. H. Trumble

About This Guide

The following discussion questions and playlist
are included to enhance your group's reading of
Where You Are.

Discussion Questions

1. The title of the novel comes from the belief that teachers should meet students where they are. Discuss the title as it pertains to Andrew's interaction with his students and, in particular, with Robert.

2. Why do you think Robert reaches out to Andrew as opposed to his own mother or Luke or Nic or any of his other friends? What do you think attracts Robert to Andrew? Andrew to Robert?

3. Discuss the role of social networking in the novel, especially as it pertains to Andrew's homosexuality. Do you believe that teachers should be held to a different standard than other adults, that they should be *above reproach* in their personal as well as their professional lives? And if so, to what extent? How does that apply to their sexual orientation?

4. At Sam Houston State University, Robert confesses to Andrew that he is anxious for his father's death: "I know he's my dad and all, but I feel like he's just this thing that sucks all the oxygen out of the room. Like the world has stopped spinning and it can't start again until he's gone." Robert is worried that he is a bad person because he feels nothing for his dad. Do you believe this is true? Is there anything that suggests otherwise? How do you explain Robert's feelings toward his dad?

5. The Texas law referenced in the novel imposes a penalty of up to twenty years in prison for a teacher convicted of having sex with a student, regardless of the student's age. The law is based on the belief that teachers have power over students, and that power undercuts the ability of students to

320 • *J. H. Trumble*

freely give consent. Discuss this "power differential" and your feelings about a law that makes criminals out of consenting adults.

6. Robert tells Andrew that in the Westfall family, if you're not a doctor, you're nothing. How does his belief play out in the Westfall family dynamics?

7. Robert frequently texts song lyrics to Andrew, and occasionally Andrew texts song lyrics back. A playlist, which includes some of those songs, is included on the following pages. What role do these lyrics play in their relationship?

8. There are a number of out gay students at Robert's school—Robert, Nic, Luke, the RW fan club. How realistic is this? In what ways does the school climate indicate that gay students are no big deal? Is this true for teachers as well? Explain. How does this compare to your own high school experience?

9. Robert's mom believes that her husband resented her because of his dependence on her after his cancer diagnosis. In what ways did this resentment play out? Do you believe his resentment is a function of his immaturity, or do you believe dependency breeds resentment?

10. Discuss Andrew's classroom management. Do you believe he is an effective classroom manager? Do you agree with his techniques? Do you believe he could have handled Stephen Newman better? If so, how?

11. When Andrew was in school, he had a crush on an English teacher—Mr. Jacobson. How did his memory of this crush affect his relationship with Robert? How did his experience with Kevin, the lab assistant in college, influence the way he treated Robert? Are there similarities, differences?

12. Discuss the consequences of Andrew's violation of the strict code of conduct regarding student-teacher relationships. Do you believe the consequences went too far or not far enough? Why?

13. At one point, Maya accuses Andrew of being selfish. Do you agree with her? Why or why not?

14. In J. H. Trumble's first novel, *Don't Let Me Go,* we get to see the characters ten years into the future. Where do you see Andrew and Robert in ten years?

THE *WHERE YOU ARE* PLAYLIST

This playlist is available on iTunes Ping: http://itun.es/isx6QR. Or visit iTunes Ping and search J. H. Trumble.

Music has a way of transporting you back to a time, a place, a moment. These are the songs that I imagine will always remind Andrew and Robert of the year they found each other. You'll recognize many of them from the story.

"Boys Don't Cry," Plumb
Robert struggles with his relationship with his father.

"Music Again," Adam Lambert
Texting with Robert makes Andrew feel alive.

"Alone," Heart
Falling in love.

"Cupid Shuffle," Cupid
Dancing in the band hall.

"Stereo Hearts," Gym Class Heroes (feat. Adam Levine)
Andrew shows his stuff in the parking lot.

"What About Love," Heart
Andrew puts on the brakes and devastates Robert.

"Dirty Little Secret," The All-American Rejects
Giving in to love.

"Down on Me," Jeremih & 50 Cent
Dancing in a club downtown.

"Low," Flo Rida (feat. T-Pain)
Robert dances dirty hip-hop on the bed.

"Redbone Hound," Idgy Vaughn
A real date.

"Edge of Glory," Lady Gaga
Sheer happiness before the fall.

"Not Afraid," Eminem
Facing the future together.